PARI
AND THE
GHOST WHISPERER

A Downtown Divas Romance

Dianna Dann

Wayward Cat Publishing

While inspired by wonderful Historic Downtown Melbourne, on Florida's sunny Space Coast, this book is a work of fiction and all the characters within it are products of the author's crazy imagination. Any similarities between characters in this book and actual people, living or dead, are purely coincidental.

ISBN 978-1-938999-36-9
Library of Congress Control Number: 2021917323

Wayward Cat Publishing
Palm Bay, Florida
www.waywardcatpublishing.com

Cover art © 2021 Wayward Cat Publishing
Illustration of girl © Heather McGrath via istockphoto (modified)
Illustrations of cats © sudowoodo via istockphoto
Illustration of ghosts and books © undefined undefined via istockphoto
(www.anastasiaskachko.com)

PARI

AND THE

GHOST WHISPERER

Chapter One

I don't believe in ghosts, it's true...but I do believe in signs. As a psychologist, I know the brain is always working whether we are consciously aware of its goings on or not. *And we're not.* But if we practice the skill of Positive Awareness, we can see and hear things we might have missed had we been too busy, say, slurping a smoothie or texting. This is why I like to keep my head up. You just never know when something will strike out at you as a clue. The Channel 5 News truck outside the Executive Suites office building was my clue. Something very big was about to happen and I really ought to have paid attention to it. Unfortunately, recognizing something as a clue is most often done in hindsight, no matter how diligently we practice Positive Awareness.

Who am I kidding? I was running late, missed breakfast, and had a black scrunchie on my wrist because my hair–way too long for its own good–was still damp. It was August in Central Florida and even at eight-thirty, the morning was a stifling, steamy, wretched monster. I wanted nothing more than to get into my office where it was always cold, because I was in no position to be positively aware of anything. Had I been in a better frame of mind, I could have paused for a review. Let's Review is a wonderful tool I've created to help my clients, and myself, practice Positive Awareness. When something unusual or important happens, stop to review. What did you miss? As it turned out, I'd missed quite a lot. I had no idea there was a Ghost Whisperer in town, and my office was his ground zero.

I walked across the courtyard, carrying my new plaque from the Downtown Strawbridge Professional Association and a thermos of lemon coriander soup, wondering if Marty Chapman had announced another run against Mayor Hawn, or perhaps Vicki Teslo had sued the county yet again over the potholes on her street. For a brief, ego driven moment, I wondered if the news truck was there for me. The Saturday before, I'd been given the DSPA's Bright Stars Award at a luncheon of local professionals. Maybe word had spread that there was a Bright Star in the building, and I was about to be ambushed by photographers and the press calling my name.

"Pari, Pari, over here. How do you feel being named a Bright Star in the professional world of Downtown Strawbridge?"

"Thrilled," I'd tell them. "I'd like to thank Mama and Daddy, er—my parents."

"What will you do with your major award, Dr. Logan?"

"Well," I'd say, smiling demurely, "I'm going to hang it on the wall in my office with all the other major awards I've received." I really ought to have pretended to be interviewed in the shower that morning to be better prepared.

Balancing thermos on plaque to free a hand, I pulled open the door to the Executive Suites lobby, felt the rush of cold air, and found a small crowd of people, their backs to me, being lectured by Lorena Elmore, the lobby secretary—she gets to shout at visitors to check in before they go up the stairs or into the elevator. It rarely works.

I heard her say, "Out of the question," before she noticed me. "Pari," she sang. "Wait."

I stood at the base of the curved grand staircase, my hand on the railing, watching her push between bodies. Impeccably suited in a pink tweed jacket and skirt—no fringe—she crossed the lobby on plunky heels while the men and women she'd left behind huddled together, whispering.

Smoothing her Margaret Thatcher hair against the sides of her head, Lorena pursed her lips and muttered, "Pari," as if she'd been waiting for me to arrive.

"What's going on?" I said. "Are all those people with Channel 5 News?"

"Channel 5, the Gazette, the Daily, you name it."

"What on earth for?"

"Pari," she said again.

Lorena Elmore had this way about her—I like to think of it as dramatic, as opposed to fear-based. Her preferred delaying tactic was to repeat your name several times. If you ask me, she had a distant, distracted mother, whose attention had to be begged for repeatedly and the poor thing continued this search for attention in everyone she met.

"Yes, Lorena," I said. "What is it?"

"It's the ghost. I'm afraid it's, well, they're up there."

"Who's up where?"

"Why, your hair is down. I can't recall ever seeing you with it down. It's so long."

"Yes, I know, Lorena. Who's—"

"That man. His people. Those people."

"What people?"

"He calls himself the Ghost Whisperer. He talks to them. To ghosts. And he says—"

"Ghost Whisperer?" I laughed and perhaps I shouldn't have. The Channel 5 group turned to look at me. "I really need to get to work," I told her. "I've got a nine o'clock."

"But that's the thing, Ms. Logan. He says she's on the third floor."

"Who's on the third floor?"

"Or, maybe it's a what?"

"Please, Lorena," I said. "Just tell me."

"He says the ghost is definitely on the third floor."

At that, the small mass of reporters and a Channel 5 cameraman hurled themselves at us. Amid the screeches of "Ms. Logan!" And, "Have you seen the ghost?" And,

"Is the third floor haunted?" I did the only thing that came to mind at the time–I ran upstairs, leaving Lorena, I'm sorry to say, to fight them off.

"Please," she was saying. "We must have order here."

So, we have a ghost in the building. I know that. *Everyone* knows that. The ghost of Historic Downtown Strawbridge is a legend. Nobody believes she's actually... *there*...haunting us. At least I assumed no one did. It's just a fun story we tell new tenants. We speculate over exactly whose window the poor lady threw herself out of. Obviously it was a third story window. You've got to get a good bit of height under you to do yourself in with a jump. Unless you, like Tildon Frakes of Frakes & Frakes Attorneys at Law, believe said distraught woman tied bed sheets together and hanged herself out the window, in which case, it could have been the second or third floor. But definitely not the first. Nobody on the first floor gets the privilege of speculation.

The story runs thusly: One bosomy wench named Aranthia or Athena, depending on whom you ask, way back in the glorious 1800s, lived at the old Strawbridge Hotel, or according to the Downtown Strawbridge Gazette, Ye Olde Strawbridge Hotel–as the Executive Suites building was known at the time. She was widowed and childless, and fell madly in love with a sea captain who came to visit her whenever he made port. Never mind that there wasn't a port in Strawbridge; but there is a lagoon. Anyway, he either dumped her, thus leading Aranthia to cast herself out the window in despair, or worse, he tried to return to her during a hurricane and died on the lagoon in his little dinghy and she, in even worse despair, tossed herself out the window. The prevailing view is that the sea captain was as boorish as they come and indeed broke dear Aranthia's heart over his love for the sea or a mermaid or some such nonsense.

I don't mean to make judgments about the woman, but I do hope our days of throwing ourselves out of windows because our sea captains perish or break our hearts have passed. Perhaps I'm too harsh; I'm told I am. And let's face it...women who live alone in hotels are not to be trusted. I picture Aranthia not so much as a morbid, depressed character deserving of pity, but likely a wealthy eccentric with many lovers, one of whom, no doubt feeling rather the cuckold, murdered her in her room at Ye Olde Strawbridge Hotel and tossed her body out the window for added effect. Either way, she died somewhere in the Executive Suites building–or outside it, as it were. Not that anyone has any proof of the matter. Like I said, we like to speculate.

I met Tildon on the landing between the second and third floors and was grateful for the chance to pause and catch my breath.

"Are they following?" I said.

He laughed. "There's supposed to be a news conference in the lobby as soon as the ghosting is finished." He walked with me up the last flight of stairs to the third floor and held the door open for me. "Lorena insists they stay there and wait."

Tildon was one of those men who was too tall. He'd look ridiculous riding a bicycle or wearing shorts, yet did both of those things regularly. One had to admire him. But in the office, he always wore a suit and bow tie. He reminded me of Bill Nye, the Science Guy. Younger. Deeper voice. But goofy in a way one imagines attorneys-at-law ought not be.

Our third-floor secretary, Abby, was leaning against the front of her desk instead of sitting behind it, chatting with the other tenants, and jumped when she saw me.

"They're going to want up here," Tildon told me as he walked backward down the hall. "The press is all over this. It's their community news story of the week."

"Pari," Abby said and all eyes turned toward me. Abby was shorter than everyone on the third floor and always had a pleading look on her face. If you ask me, she suffered from Imposter Syndrome and her hidden stash of Mallomars served to quell her anxiety at having to handle business professionals while feeling inferior. "He's waiting for you." She winced.

"It's all right, Abby." Patience and kindness were key with her. "Do you mean the ghost guy?"

"He said he needs to get into your office."

"Well," I said, stomping off down the hallway, "he can just forget it."

My office was on the north side of the building, a one-room space tucked between two much larger enterprises: Tildon's law offices and Harriet Hallibrent, architect. To get there each morning, I had to walk from the lobby at the center of the building down a long hallway where everyone with their doors open called hellos, turn right around the corner, and walk past Frakes & Frakes, Attorneys-at-Law, waving through their wall of glass. When I first opened shop, I often walked right past my office and found myself in front of the architect's door, so tiny and unimpressive was my own.

Today, the walk was different. As I headed down the hallway, everyone who wasn't in the third-floor lobby was at their doors cheering me on as I passed. I scowled—I've always been a good scowler—ready for battle. This was an office building, I was thinking, not a circus, and I was not about to let any sort of ghost talker come in here and disrupt our business. When I rounded the corner, I stopped, and the scowl fell off my face. In its place was more a look of...*wha*? I'm not proud of it, but there it was.

At my door, with potted Chinese palm on one side and small shelf table on the other—my solution to bypassing my office every morning—on his hands and knees was...well my first impression of Sam Preston was that he belonged in a college-buddy-hot-tub or road-trip movie. Our ghost expert was unshaven and a bit on the chubby side. Blond, in a dirty, messy, "I don't care enough about my appearance to comb my hair" sort of way. And his clothes! I could accept it if he was wearing a jumpsuit, like you'd expect of a Ghostbuster, but faded, ripped jeans and an over-sized, rumpled t-shirt with a ripped pocket? He glanced up at me, smiling through the palm stalks, and went back to what he was doing, which was trying to peek under my office door.

"Excuse me," I said, aware of every other third-floor tenant now cowering, and some snickering, behind me. "What exactly do you think you're doing?"

Chapter Two

The would-be frat boy looked up at me and, still on his hands and knees, said, "Hi, there."

I raised a brow.

He promptly jumped to standing. One fell swoop. One moment he's on all fours, the next, he's standing over me, wobbling a bit, breathing deeply from the exertion. I admit, it was rather...gymnastic.

"Are you–" he glanced at the placard on my office door, "Mrs. Logan?"

"Miss."

"Miss?"

"Miss Logan."

"What, not Ms? Not some kind of nonspecific, neither married nor single sort of title?"

"Doctor," I said and, still holding my silver thermos, put my index finger on the gold placard where there were clearly the letters D and R, with a period, before my name.

"Ah." Smiling, he backed up a few paces and seemed suddenly aware of our audience. He bowed slightly. "Sam Preston."

"If you'll excuse me." I set my plaque and thermos on the little wood table next to my door, got out my keys and turned the lock.

"Wait." He rushed forward and put his hand on the

door above my head. "May I come in?"

I glared at him. "Into my office."

"Yeah. I don't want to scare you or anything and you should know I think it's perfectly safe. But...I'm pretty positive your office is haunted."

"Pretty positive? Isn't that modifying an absolute? Isn't one positive or not?"

"Isn't one?" he said. "Do people still use that word. I mean, does one still use such language?"

"Mr. Preston." I dropped my keys into my purse and picked up my plaque, putting it between us.

"I was supposed to be there," he said, pointing at my award. "And call me Sam. If I'd known you were going to win the Bright Stars Award and be the *very* person I needed to see about Aranthia, I'd have shown up."

"You'd have had to wear a suit." I looked him up and down.

"Oh, you don't think I own a suit?"

"I have serious doubts, yes. I'm sorry, Mr. Preston, I don't have time for this ghost nonsense."

"It's not nonsense I assure you."

"It's unadulterated nonsense."

"You use such impressive words, Dr. Logan." He was mocking me; I was sure of it.

"And I've got clients to see."

Another glance at my door. "Don't you mean patients?"

"I'm a psychologist, Mr. Preston. Not an MD."

"So, I need to make an appointment?"

And before I could be *positively* aware of what I was saying, it slipped out. "Yes, Mr. Preston, I think you should."

I meant, of course, to say that any grown man who believed in ghosts and crawled around on his hands and knees in office buildings needed professional help. Instead, it seems I'd invited him to waste my time.

He chuckled. "Maybe I will. Really, though. I just need some time to investigate. I won't touch any of your..." His eyes fell briefly to my plaque. "Clients. Maybe after business hours?"

"Out of the question," I snapped and stood staring at him, waiting for him to take the not so obvious hint and leave.

His gaze ran leisurely over my office door, as if he were thinking of some way to make it disappear.

"If you'll excuse me," I said.

"Just a peek?"

"I'm not opening this door until you leave."

He threw his hands up and backed away. "Okay, no problem." He turned to our audience and shrugged. "The lady says no."

Unfortunately for me, an audible sigh rippled among them and I had the distinct feeling Sam Preston and his ghost hunting was going to be a problem. Inside my office, I leaned against the door, steadying my breathing. The space was meant to be a sanctuary for my clients. There's a walk-in closet to the right of my door and beyond that my desk sits cozy in the little nook the closet wall creates. While seated in my chair, I can see the sky outside my window, above the potted plants on the sill. I've arranged the therapeutic seating just so. Against the wall next to the window is a little couch; it could seat three small or two large persons—with tiny tables at each end, a tissue box atop each. Across from the couch sit two comfortable armchairs with a small round table between them where I keep yet another box of tissues.

The art on the walls is thoughtful. Cats, butterflies, flowers. Not too cheerful—don't want to overwhelm—but definitely not depressing. There are, of course, my diplomas, licenses, and awards: the Downtown Strawbridge Psychological Association's Psychologist of the Year Award which I received after my first year of practice—quite a feat; the Downtown Strawbridge Professional Woman of the Year Award after my second year; and now, the Downtown Strawbridge Professional Association's Bright Stars Award. After three years of practice, I heard whispers in my ear at the Saturday Award Luncheon that I was being considered for the Downtown Strawbridge Association of Professional Women's Standards of Excellence Award. I was, to put it mildly, on a trajectory of distinction.

And yet, despite the accolades on my wall and the soothing beauty of the room, I was uncharacteristically flustered from my altercation with the ghost talker. In the closet I pulled some ice cubes from my little refrigerator-freezer combo, dropped them into a tall glass, and poured a Diet Coke. While waiting for the fizz to fade, I checked myself in the large mirror behind the door. The light from the dangling bulb above me cast unflattering shadows on my face, but I could see well enough to run a brush through my hair and wrap it up in a black scrunchie. As I watched myself, I shuddered at the thought of Sam Preston looking me over. He had the eyes of a playboy. His tone was sarcastic. His demeanor unserious. His appearance was decidedly unprofessional. And he was annoying. I'd never been so perturbed by a man in so short a time and yet startled to find myself concerned about how I looked to him.

After sorting my hair and having a sip of fizzy soda, I sighed and gazed at myself as objectively as possible. What was it he saw and why did it make him smirk like that? I suppose if I were being described by a romance writer, it might read something like, "Long locks, black as night, with almond-shaped, thick-lashed eyes, and pouting lips." Because pouting lips sell books. No, I'd be better described by a humor writer. "Hair needs cutting, always damp, mildewed scrunchies tossed around the room. Her quasi-designer suits can't hide Pari's clumsiness as she trips over door frames and forgets she's wearing lipstick with a wipe of her hand." Was that why Sam Preston looked to be laughing at me? Nope. No lipstick smears...because I hadn't applied it yet.

I tapped a nail into the wall behind my desk, in the spot I'd purposefully left open for another award, and hung my Bright Stars plaque. Plopping into my comfy chair on wheels, my first instinct was to pull open the bottom desk drawer on the right, slide the file folders back, and lift my partial manuscript from its hiding spot. *Let's Review: A Guide to Positive Awareness: How You Can Take Charge of Your Life in Ten Easy Steps.*

"Seriously, Pari," I muttered. "*Two* colons in the title?" With a disgusted sigh, I shoved it back where it belonged. There wasn't time to think about failures now. A Ghost Whisperer was on the loose. I took my goals notebook from the top drawer and found the page on which I'd listed the awards I wanted to receive to feel validated, and drew a satisfying line through Bright Stars. I was a professional woman and damn good at my job, and no ghost hunter was going to ruin it for me. I tried not to care about him, his horridness and his ghosts, all day. And I could have forgotten the entire episode, had my clients not brought it up repeatedly.

"There's a ghost in this very room!" Mrs. Haggard sang. "Is it Aranthia herself do you suppose?"

"I'm sure it's nothing," I said, thinking I was soothing her. But my fury at the story getting out—and the blame resting squarely on Sam Preston—was no doubt creeping into my expressions.

"Oh, I hope not," she said. "I'd like very much to ask her about Kirkland. Do you suppose they've met in the afterlife?"

I swallowed. At least I tried to. Took a sip of water from the ever-present bottle on the table beside my chair. Smiled. "I doubt it. Tell me about your week. Were you able to get through the exercise we discussed?"

"Well, now that I know about this ghost thing, I'm glad I didn't get it done. Honestly, Dr. Logan, shouldn't I try a séance or something? What if dear Kirkland doesn't want me to rummage through his things? What if I should keep them a little longer?"

It had been three years. The poor thing. "Perhaps you're right. If you're not ready, you're not ready."

Each appointment went very much like this one. Lester Planck was convinced the ghost story was all concocted as a way for his ex-wife to make fun of him on social media. "There are cameras in here, I'm sure of it now." And so, we searched my office for cameras. It looked as if we would be back to meeting at impromptu locations around town once again.

I wished I could have told Wilson James that Mr.

Planck and I had done a thorough camera search, as he believed he was on camera all the time, but he'd given up on trying to find them. "This ghost thing is quite an interesting plot device for the show, right?" he said. Everything was part of the show for Mr. James.

I had lunch with the Downtown Divas at an adorable local place called Brunch. While we consider any Downtown Strawbridge business owner a part of the group, there are six original Divas: Me, Karen, Vanessa, Melissa, Kaya, and Sophie. They were all members of the Downtown Strawbridge Professional Association and had, except for Sophie, attended Saturday's luncheon with me. Sophie, aka Bookish Diva, had just returned from a vacation with her new sweetie Reese where she met his parents, and a quick Divas Lunch was called to get all the juicy details. So, while I did mention Sam Preston, it wasn't the right occasion to get advice on dealing with irritating ghost hunters from my friends.

By Wednesday, I thought things had settled down somewhat. There'd been no more sightings of the Ghost Whisperer and everyone was back to business as usual. But that morning, after seeing my nine o'clock to the door, Abby called telling me my ten o'clock had canceled, yet again. Before I could finish making a note in Tina Patterson's file, there was a knock on my door. I unwittingly opened it wide, ready to chat with Tilden—he was the usual culprit between clients, always offering to bring me a coffee from the kitchen. Instead, standing before me with that swarthy look on his face was Sam Preston. And once again, he'd attracted quite an audience of accountants, attorneys, agents, and real estate brokers.

"You're very popular, Mr. Preston," I said.

"Fans of the show, I'm sure."

"What show?"

"The Ghost Whisperer on WDTS."

"WDTS?" I smirked, doing my best to think up something silly that DTS could stand for. My brain failed me.

"Downtown Strawbridge Radio," he said. "You're not a listener?"

"Must be new."

"Oh, no," Abby chimed in. "It's been around for years. That's where you get the antique auctions and the Mr. Fix It show."

"That's right," Sam said.

"Shouldn't you be answering the phones?" I knew it was petty, and my tone sent Abby scurrying back to her desk. The others glared at me. But they did wander off, which was what I'd hoped for. "What do you want, Mr. Preston?"

"Please call me Sam."

I said nothing.

"I was in the building and just happened to hear your next appointment was canceled."

My mouth fell open and I shut it quickly.

"I thought maybe I could ask once more...I'd only be a minute."

"I'm not letting you in my office, Mr. Preston."

"Sam. And what's the harm?"

"I'll tell you what the harm is, *Sam*." At that, he smiled and it irritated me. "There are no such things as ghosts. They aren't in the building and they're certainly not in my office. I try to help people here and you're spreading rumors all over the place about ghosts and–" He was looking over my shoulder into my office as I was trying to scold him! "Do you mind?" I backed up and slammed the door shut.

"Sorry," he sang through the closed door. "Maybe another time."

I stood there, fuming, when suddenly another knock rattled the door. I swung it open, ready to pour my frustrations out on Tilden, but, again, it was Sam Preston.

"What do you want?" I seethed.

He held out a business card and smiled sheepishly. "In case you'd like to be on the show...or, something."

I snatched the card from his hand, slammed the door shut yet again, and stomped my feet. I wanted to scream. But that would be unseemly. Instead, I pulled a throw pillow off the client couch and beat the back wall with it. I knew better than to beat one of the side walls–the people in the offices next to mine could hear the soft *thwumps* and they'd come knocking on the door asking if I was all right. It had happened before. Who knew attorneys and architects had such fine-tuned hearing?

Chapter Three

MaryAshford has joined the chat.

MaryAhsford: What did I miss?

SamTheMan: She's going to be a problem.

LegitChris: Hey, Mary. Sam's in crisis mode. Hit a roadblock.

SamTheMan: More like an iceberg.

LegitChris: Snap!

MaryAshford: Don't say snap, Chris. Nobody says snap anymore, much less puts an exclamation point after it. And, Sam, don't call a woman an iceberg.

SamTheMan: So now we can't say iceberg?

MaryAshford: That's right. Grab your handy notebook on women and add it to the list.

SamTheMan: She's the only one in the building who's giving me trouble. Everyone else is fine with the plan.

MaryAshford: And what about that makes her cold?

SamTheMan: Unrelated. But her office is the one. We need access.

MaryAshford: Oh, that office. What's the problem? Is she a skeptic? Or did you do something?

SamTheMan: What's that supposed to mean?

MaryAshford: I know you. What happened?

SamTheMan: Nothing happened. She's just...

MaryAshford: Don't say it.

SamTheMan: You don't even know what I'm going to say.

MaryAshford: I know it's on the list. Try again.

SamTheMan: She doesn't want any part of the experience.

LegitChris: You need to exercise some of that Sam Preston charm.

MaryAshford: Where's my eyeroll emoji?

LegitChris: Talk about old people. My nephew says emojis are out.

SamTheMan: You can't accuse Mary of being old. We're the old people. She's the young gun.

LegitChris: Then what's with all the capital letters and punctuation? I thought kids these days didn't use those in texting.

MaryAshford: I can't believe you just said 'kids these days.' Anyway, my punctuation is a courtesy to you elderly folks. You'd never understand me otherwise.

SamTheMan: Can we get back in crisis mode, please? I already tried the charm.

MaryAshford: I knew it.

SamTheMan: She won't budge. She's...

MaryAshford: Don't say it.

SamTheMan: I really want to say it.

LegitChris: But is she cute?

MaryAshford: OMG. Eyeroll emoji!

LegitChris: Well, is she?

SamTheMan: No comment.

LegitChris: She is! Is she out of your league?

MaryAshford: You guys are supposed to be adults.

SamTheMan: No woman is out of my league.

MaryAshford: Where's the puke emoji. Can we get back on topic? We launch in a week. You can't promise people access to the room on our flyers without her permission.

LegitChris: First rule of business. Under promise and over deliver. Get her permission.

SamTheMan: It won't be easy. I'm telling you, she's a real...

MaryAshford: Don't say it!

SamTheMan: Maybe I was going to say professional. You don't know.

MaryAshford: How is it you two old guys are so immature?

LegitChris: Here comes the girls mature faster than boys lecture! Look out, Sam! Debris everywhere!

MaryAshford: Okay, new rule: one exclamation point per comment. I'm going to the printers. No promise on the room.

LegitChris: He'll get permission.

MaryAshford: Not if she sees that we've promised access before getting her okay.

LegitChris: True enough. Get back in there and turn on the charm, Sam.

SamTheMan: She's uncharmable. Seriously. Nobody could charm this one.

LegitChris: I'm disappointed in you.

MaryAshford: It's getting sappy in here.

MaryAshford has left the chat.

LegitChris: Okay she's gone. You can say all the words now.

SamTheMan: I think this one calls for some new words. I'll get back to you.

Chapter Four

Before you say anything about my childish behavior, let me say that I am a firm believer in stress relief. If it be stomping, pillow *thwumping*, or running–get it out. But of course, of those mentioned, running is the only acceptable behavior in public. After my stress relief, I marched myself down the hall to the third-floor lobby.

"Abby!"

I startled her badly and she nearly fell out of her rolling chair behind the desk.

"I'm sorry, Dr. Logan. You're right. I shouldn't have left my desk."

Oh, dear. The Dr. Logan treatment reminded me I'd been overbearing. "I'm sorry myself. I didn't mean to call you out. But you told Mr. Preston about my appointment cancellation."

"Oh, no. I'd never do that. That's privileged stuff."

"Then how...?" I looked around the lobby.

"He came down the hall while I was talking to you on the phone. I guess he overheard."

"Why was he here again?"

She shrugged. "He's talking to everyone. Planning some kind of ghostly sleepover, here in the building."

"You've got to be kidding me."

She shook her head. "Lorena told me to expect him

up here. I guess I should have warned you this morning but I didn't get the chance."

"That's okay." It wasn't her fault, after all.

Next up was Lorena. She was in charge of all the comings and goings in the Executive Suites building. But more than that, she was the building manager. I approached her where she sat behind the reception desk on the first floor and got absolutely nowhere with her.

"You're the only one to complain, Pari." Her steely eyes tried to look sympathetic but it only came off as irritated.

"But...people, strangers, sleeping in the building? It's absurd."

"Well, I'm not sure how much sleep anyone will get. They'll be hunting ghosts."

"Are they insane?"

She raised her brows at me with a sly smile. "Now, is that something a psychologist should say?"

While I felt duly chastened, I was livid. "This can't be good for business."

"That's the opposite of everyone's opinion. They think it's great. It'll bring in tourists—"

"Tourists in an office building?"

"Well, no, not exactly. I was thinking about Downtown Strawbridge. The shopping and dining."

"Then send him downtown."

"But most everyone in the building said they would be happy for people to visit."

"How could that be a good thing?"

"Don't you want people to know you're here?"

"No!"

She pursed her lips and shook her head condescendingly. "Of course you do, Pari. And think of the others. Accountants, real estate agents, attorneys, the nonprofits. They could use the exposure."

"So, you're just going to let people in off the streets? Let them wander around looking for a ghost?"

"I don't know what you mean by 'people off the streets' but it doesn't sound pleasant."

I sucked in a breath and tried to calm myself. "I mean

non-customers, Lorena. People who aren't here for the businesses in the building. Gawkers. Lookie-loos."

"Lookie-loos?" She chuckled and patted my arm. "These will be scheduled tours and events. After hours, perhaps. But Sam assures me they'll be organized."

She'd called him Sam, as if they were friends. "No way, Lorena. I'm calling Senator Richards."

"It'll do you no good," she said. "He's on board."

Already? How had all of this been going on right under my nose? "I can call him, can't I?"

"Suit yourself." She pulled a business card from her top desk drawer and handed it to me. "But you'd have better luck with Madaline."

"Madaline?"

"His wife. You know her."

Senator Richards was Madaline's husband? The real estate broker? "Why isn't her office in this building, then?" I'd mumbled the question, not expecting a reply.

"When she can be downtown, in the middle of everyone's business?" Lorena slapped ring-covered fingers over her mouth and through them loudly whispered, "Don't tell anyone I said that."

I couldn't help myself having a bit of a chuckle. It was true enough. Madaline Richards knew everyone and their business. But I'd imagined her husband as a meek sort–someone she could boss around. In fact, I always thought her husband was the other real estate agent in the downtown office...Ceril something. Oh, dear. I may have called him Mr. Richards once or twice.

The stories of Senator Richards, one-time mayor, one-time senator, playboy billionaire, riding free and easy off his wife's money and reputation were legendary. I was sure I'd seen his picture at some point in my life, at least, but I'd never met him. Could Madaline Richards be a wealthy socialite disguised as a busybody real estate agent? It's funny how little you can know about a person you see nearly every day.

"Very interesting," I mumbled as I made my way back upstairs. I had notes to write and a new client to see straight after my bag lunch.

Ida Nettlebaum was in her sixties. "I'm the quintessential cat lady," she said when I asked what brought her to see me.

In her preliminary interview, Ida had a lot to say. She was certain there was nothing wrong with her, but her son insisted she see a "shrink" as he called it. When I'd asked what concerned him, she'd only said it had to do with her cats.

"Tell me about the cats," I said as we both settled down in the comfy chairs across from the sofa.

"You should know straight off that they don't speak to me, not in English anyway. Of course not. I've tried telling Lenny that. Honestly, Dr. Logan, there's no shame in talking to one's cats and their talking back. Cats communicate as well as humans, even if it's just a meow or a *meooorl* or a *mewmewmew*. You see what I mean? Of course you do. So, I talk to them. I suppose the problem is that, well, if I have to be honest, it's sort of, you see, I'm nearly positive they're, now don't laugh, but...inhabited."

"Inhabited by what?"

"Oh, it's not a what. It's a whom. Several whoms if we get right down to it."

"I see."

"Do you? Do you really?"

"Who would you say is inhabiting them?"

"Well—" And here, Ida Nettlebaum pulled her heavy purse off the floor and pulled from it a small fat photo album. She opened it up and leaned over the little table between us to show me a picture of a black-and-white tuxedo. "This is Arnold. He used to be Whiskers, but I realized after my brother died that he'd come to visit through Whiskers every now and then. He liked it, apparently, because now he's there all the time."

"And what is it that makes you think Arnold has inhabited Whiskers?"

"The steak mostly. And the potatoes. It's no small thing, Dr. Logan. My brother Arnold ate steak and baked potato five days a week. I suppose at the end, it was less often. But he was mad for it. He said it was healthy because he always had a small salad or some asparagus on the plate. But he had a massive coronary last spring. Anyway, I was having myself a steak and baked potato not a week after Arnold died, as a memorial, if you will. I loved my brother and he loved a good medium rare steak with a potato drowned in butter–margarine to be precise–cheddar cheese, and sour cream. Oh, my mouth is watering just thinking about it. Anyway, you should have seen Whiskers, er, Arnold. I've never seen him so excited. He wouldn't let me eat it myself. I ended up giving him half the steak and letting him lick the butter and sour cream off the potato."

"Is it unusual for a cat to want steak?"

"It was for Whiskers. So, I was sure Arnold was with us. I decided to make chicken the next day, just to see, you know? And Whiskers didn't care at all. But then I made steak again and it was like night and day. Now all he wants is steak. All the time steak. And I told him, finally, I said, 'Arnold, you died of a massive coronary. I'm not going to feed you steak every day or you'll kill Whiskers the same way.' Because, you know, just because Whiskers is possessed doesn't mean he's not still in there."

"Of course," I said.

Chapter Five

The next day, I had plans to meet the Divas at Café Flamingo for lunch. The Divas, or at least some of us, meet up as often as we can–something like a women's business lunch where the last thing we want to discuss is business. Most of us had been getting together regularly anyway, before Sophie Childers, who works at Bookish across from Café Flamingo, called us Divas and suddenly a club of sorts was born. Every woman who owned or ran a business downtown was automatically inducted. But it was still the original six of us most of the time, meeting to talk about downtown and all its goings on. I'd already mentioned Sam Preston and his ghosting enterprise to my friends, and unfortunately they thought the whole idea was adorable. So I wasn't in the brightest frame of mind as I left the office to join them. In the parking lot, I got a call from the Downtown Strawbridge Gazette, of all places.

"Pari, hi, it's Toliver Weeks of the Gazette. We met a few months ago at a Chamber luncheon. I hear there's a ghost in your office."

"You what?" I dropped my keys in a grassy spot between parking rows.

"Not just any ghost, either. Aranthia, the legendary ghost of downtown–"

"I know who she is." Squatting–so glad I wore slacks today–trying to keep my Kate Spade purse from falling into the dirt. "Or was. Who told you she was in my office?"

"I heard it from one of our staffers and I guess she heard it from–"

"Never mind." Grabbing the keys. "I know exactly who you heard it from." Shaking them off.

"I'd love to meet you at your office to–"

"I'm sorry, Toliver, I've got to go." I dropped my phone into my bag and seethed. "I can't believe he told people!"

As I neared my little blue Civic, I turned toward the *ding ding* of child's bicycle bell and there was Eric Lawson, smiling at me, astride his very adult black Schwinn. A sudden rush of guilt swept through my gut and I tried to offer him a trembling smile.

"How've you been, Pari?" he said.

How to describe Eric Lawson...Imagine the most attractive human being on earth, cast a halo-like aura around him, and give him all the best qualities. Loves puppies? Check. Thoughtful, caring, observant? Check, check, check. Helps old ladies across the street? You get the idea. But on top of all that, add one tiny obnoxious thing you can't really complain about without seeming petty: Eric Lawson wants to save the planet. We hadn't seen each other for a few weeks, not since that Saturday he had the nerve to ask me how a person could own so many expensive pairs of shoes. Everything had started so innocently. He'd come to pick me up at my downtown apartment for dinner and I decided to change my shoes. I was in my bedroom, trying on various pairs and modeling in front of the mirror attached to the closet door when I heard him call out, "How long can it take to change shoes?"

"There are so many possibilities," I said, gleeful. We were going to a swanky new steakhouse beachside and I was wearing my shimmery turquoise dress. I had perhaps a dozen pairs that would look stunning, so okay, I was taking some time.

"How many pairs of shoes could you possibly have?" he said.

I suppose I should have noted the tone in his voice, but instead of practicing positive awareness, I was blissfully twisting this way and that in a pair of Louboutins I'd scored at an estate sale the week before. "Nearly one hundred fifty, I think." He didn't respond at all and I decided on a pair of Blahniks instead. Very sophisticated.

He was quiet all evening and I'm ashamed to say I didn't think much of it until we were in his car–an all-electric Chevy Bolt, naturally–on the way back to my place. And that's when he told me he couldn't imagine needing one hundred fifty pairs of shoes.

"It's not a matter of needing them," I said.

Then he lectured me, as if he'd been writing and editing the screed in his head during dinner, about child labor and plastics and leather and money...he was really shocked at the money. I confess, when he asked, I told him the retail price, not the price I actually paid, for my Blahniks. So, I got out of his car at my apartment, said something sarcastic about his driving us across the causeway instead of making us bike it, slammed the door and left him idling in front of the building.

"I'm well, Eric," I said. "On your way out to lunch?"

He nodded. "And you? Headed downtown?"

I was suddenly keenly aware of myself, standing at my car, keys in hand, preparing to drive the half mile, at best, to the other end of Historic Downtown to Melissa's café. In my defense, I'd forgotten to bring sneakers for a walk. Of course, had I walked the eighth of a mile from my apartment to work that morning, I'd have my sneakers, wouldn't I? And Eric knew that as well as I did. But frankly, it was too hot to walk to work, or downtown and back, without sweating profusely and I had more clients to see that afternoon. None of these excuses would impress Eric who kept a bar of soap and a set of towels in the men's bathroom on the first floor.

"That's right," I said.

"Well," he said. A few seconds of awkward silence hung between us and he glanced at my blush Garavani slingback pumps. "Maybe we can get together this weekend."

Let's Review:

1. Sam Preston was a slovenly ghost hunter. Unprofessional. Unshaven. Infuriatingly charming.

2. There are no such things as ghosts.

3. No way was I going to allow Sam Preston to sleep anywhere near my office.

4. Eric Lawson was always properly washed and dressed. But not what one would call charming.

5. I was certain, having known him for years, that Eric was as skeptical of the supernatural as I was.

6. And yet, there I stood, hesitating before finally saying,

"Sure."

And all I could come up with for a reason to see Eric again was, why not? He was, after all, the most beautiful man on earth. Charm is highly overrated.

Chapter Six

H istoric Downtown Strawbridge is a small stretch of
Strawbridge Avenue running east toward the Indian
River Lagoon. On the western end, where Strawbridge
branches off the main highway, an old-fashioned arch
tells visitors they're entering a wonderland of shops and
dining all housed in very old, some actually historic,
buildings. A few side streets crisscross here and there, and
on the east end, before you get to the railroad tracks
(Where the night club Tracks is. How very original, am I
right?) there's a catty-cornered street that creates a Times
Square sort of effect. On a much smaller scale, of course.
And then, east of Tracks is the Executive Suites office
building on the corner of Strawbridge and US 1. I can see
the lagoon from my office if I stand on a chair at the far
left of my only window and press my face against the
glass.

The point here is that Eric is right about driving the
distance necessary to get anywhere downtown. And the
truth of it is, the chances of my finding a spot in front of
Café Flamingo were slim to none. So, I'd end up parking
in a lot behind it on Woodplum Street and have to walk
anyway. Still, two hundred feet is so much better than a
thousand, don't you think? And in the heat of Central
Florida, even along the coast, the fewer steps outdoors

the better, if you ask me.

But I had another stop to make before lunch. Almost two hundred yards from the Executive Suites, I pulled up in front of Madaline's real estate office, tucked between Across the Pond, an all things British shop, and Ally's Formal Wear–Ally having built quite a reputation by hiring live models to walk the streets in wedding gowns prior to her annual sales. I'd called the number for Senator Richards that Lorena gave me and was unfortunate enough to have Madaline answer.

"Come on over to the office," she said. "He'll be here."

As soon as I saw Senator Richards, I realized I'd known him all along. Sitting at a desk in Madaline's storefront, leather booted feet crossed on top of a calendar, cowboy hat perched on his head, and cigar chomped between his teeth, was the man I only knew as, The Cowboy. He walked around downtown every second Friday night at Family Fun Fest with Leland Booker, owner of Stogies. They smoked their cigars and nodded at everyone like two old Texas oilmen. I'd assumed he was just Leland Booker's cigar buddy and never thought more of it. So this was Senator Richards, owner of Executive Suites, and probably a lot of other buildings downtown.

"Now, Dr. Logan." Still leaning back in the chair, he reached out and shook my hand.

I admit, I expected him to call me "little lady" and treat me like a child, but he was, after all, a politician. He knew how to gain trust.

Madaline's real estate office had one huge glass window and a glass door with a jingle bell that was still ringing in my ear. Senator Richards was at the first of six desks, three along each wall. Ceril Something was across from him at a smaller desk trying to look busy, wiping a hand over his balding head and chewing on a pencil.

At the bell, Madaline made her entrance from the back room where I imagined a kitchen and bunk beds for some reason. She leaned seductively against the door jamb and let her left hand roam down her hip as if smoothing her skin-tight skirt against her thighs. She flipped her highlighted brown hair and offered me a dazzling celebrity smile.

I glanced briefly at the front of the desk at which the senator was sitting, looking for a name plate. Was his first name Senator or was he a senator? Alas, it remained a mystery.

"I know why you're here," Senator said. "And I understand your concerns, but everyone I've talked to is excited about this ghost thing."

"You have to admit," Ceril Something broke in. "It's a lot of fun. Just in time for Halloween."

Senator Richards made a small snorting sound and mumbled, "Yes," before turning back to me. "It's good for business."

"Not my business. My clients want anonymity."

"Now, now." And the tiniest hint of condescension oozed out. "I'm only allowing it at night. None of your clients will be there."

"But that's worse. You're letting people into the building after hours."

"How can that possibly affect your clients?"

"Well, I...they..."

"You see?" Madaline said. "It'll be fine. And think of the exposure."

Exposure. I nearly harrumphed. "Don't you think it's a bad idea to get people all riled up about ghosts and such nonsense? It can't lead anywhere positive."

"It's not nonsense." He swung his feet to the floor and leaned forward on the desk. "That's the whole point. The ghost of Aranthia is very likely to show up. And then we'll be on the map for sure."

My mouth opened, but I couldn't seem to form words. I blinked a few times and shook my head.

"I saw her myself," he said.

"It's true," Madaline joined him, pulling herself up to sit on the edge of the big desk.

"You saw the ghost," I said, not kindly.

"And a more terrifying sight I'd never seen before. I was on the third floor. It was midnight or thereabouts and the big New Year's party was going on downstairs–"

"See," Madaline interrupted. "It's not like nothing

ever happens there after hours. Parties. Receptions."

Senator Richards glared at his wife and continued. "I can't say what drew me upstairs; it was as if I was called. And when I got off the elevator, I knew right away something was eerily different. The air was still, and it was so quiet it was like a *thund'*rous river in my ears." He'd obviously told this story many times. "I walked down the corridor, the one where your office is, and suddenly there she was, floating above the carpet. I stopped and stared and then she screamed at me."

"I get chills every time I hear him tell it," Madaline said rubbing her arms.

"Did she say anything?" Ceril asked.

"She called me Captain."

"No!" Ceril squeaked.

"Plain as day. 'Captain,' she said and screamed some more and rushed at me. I ran so fast. Didn't even bother with the elevator. I nearly fell down the stairs."

"It's true," Madaline said. "I thought he'd had a heart attack. But he wouldn't tell me what happened until the next day."

"I was traumatized. But you see what I'm saying? This town needs Aranthia. Business will boom."

"Senator Richards, we're both professionals–"

"Yes we are. And let me offer you my congratulations, again, on your Bright Stars Award. Madaline tells me you're up for the APW's Standards of Excellence Award later this year. Ain't that right, Maddie?"

Madaline smiled and nodded.

"Maddie here's the president of the APW, you know."

"Of course," I said. Senator Richards knew that I knew that his wife was the president of the APW–I'm a member of the association, after all. Was he threatening me?

"Now, Dr. Logan, as I was saying..." He stood, took me by the arm, and led me to the door. "This town needs ghost stories. We want ghost stories. It'll do us all good. Even you."

It looked like I would get nowhere with Senator Richards. He and Madaline followed me to my car and she told him to go out onto the street and make sure I could back out without any problem.

"It's a tough spot," she said. Then she turned to me. "Don't believe him." *Finally*, I thought. A rational person. But then she said, "He went up to the third floor because that's where the best bathroom is."

I smiled, really big–the kind of smile you give to someone you want to get away from. Senator Richards stood in the middle of the road blocking traffic so I could back out and make my way west toward the café. I waved a thank you, embarrassed, and fumed quite a bit. But the thought of lunch with the Divas settled me down.

Karen Morgan, aka Bella Diva–it's a long story and involves an umbrella–whose family owns Morgan's Office Supply is my best friend. I met her three years ago, while outfitting my office with Ticonderoga No. 1 pencils–the only place locally they can be found–pens, folders, office mats, etc., when I first set up practice. Karen is like a fresh breeze, a classic girl next door, in the strawberry blonde category. Shy, practical, smart, and loves pencils. She and I both respect order and sensibility. And yet...we do have our quirks. The Divas think I'm a fashion nut, hence my nickname: Fashion Diva. But I assure you, I merely want to promote a professional appearance for my clients. I do love shoes to excess, I suppose. And Karen is a romantic. All the world should be a fairy tale in her view. If you ask me, Karen and I simply seek perfection in our quirks, she in beautiful ideals, I in beautiful shoes. And there's nothing wrong with striving for perfection as long as we don't let it overwhelm us when we fail to reach it.

From the parking lot behind the café, I walked along Woodplum Street and saw Karen and Vanessa inside the restaurant at the big booth in the back. I knocked on the window and waved. Vanessa Torres, Glam Diva, totally gets Karen and me. While she couldn't care an ounce for orderliness or precision–she's as flighty and dreamy as they come–she loves beauty, whether in shoes or people. So we relate.

I have several clients who suffer from social anxiety and one of their worst fears is meeting new people, especially in large groups. And I imagine trying to remember all the Divas can be overwhelming, so here's Pari's Crash Course on the Divas—the main six of us, anyway.

Me, you already know. (Pari rhymes with barley, by the way.) I dress for success, typically pencil skirts and silk blouses. Long black hair, bound up in a ponytail or bun. Psychologist with a mild fixation on recognition in my field. I'd like to think I'm outgoing, but on that scale, I rate between a Karen and a Vanessa.

Karen is the girl next door. A green-eyed strawberry blonde and a bit shy, she's your floral print wrap dress and ballerina slippers type. Her family runs the office supply store and if she weren't there, she'd be a librarian or kindergarten teacher. Borderline inferiority complex. One of those women who has no idea how gorgeous she is. She's a good friend, sweet, and romantic.

Vanessa Torres is exactly what you'd expect from the owner of hair-and-nails salon Glam It Up! She's a walking promo for beauty with a carefree spirit in short, snug dresses that show a lot of cleavage, tons of dark brown curls, and dark laughing eyes. She's the *first* one in on the dare, and the one to take things too far. In fact, she's so obvious about not caring what everyone thinks of her, you might think that deep down she's terrified. One of those people who will make a fool of herself to keep you from doing it first.

Petite, blonde Melissa Stathem is all business on one side and all wild girl on the other. She's a jeans, t-shirt, and sneakers type most of the time, who won't hesitate to tell you exactly what you're doing wrong. But she's just as willing to give you a boost when you need one. She runs Café Flamingo, the hottest restaurant downtown and parties as hard as she works.

Sophie Childers is quiet and shy. Your basic bookstore owner—an introvert who'd love to spend all day reading, but willing to be pulled away for some fun once in a while. I'm afraid she has no real sense of style and is just as likely to show up in shorts and sandals as she is in slacks and a sport coat. She's got short, brown hair that curls up a bit at the tips when she's due for a cut.

Kaya Channing runs a vintage clothing store and you can tell just by looking at her. Dark, curly hair, dark somber eyes, Kaya is the calmest Diva I know. Reliable, rational, and kind. But her clothes scream fabulous! And once you get to know her, you realize *she* is, too.

The café was cold inside, gloriously cold, and I paused at the door letting the temperature envelop me along with the smells of grilled chicken and ripened fruit. Blenders hummed and griddles sizzled. I caught Melissa's eye and smiled. She was behind the counter with her bustling employees as they filled orders taken at the register and those brought up from the wait staff. Café Flamingo was a homey place, lots of seating, menu written in chalk on boards on the wall. Refrigerators filled with drinks you pick out yourself, bags of chips and baskets of cookies enticing you as you placed your order—one of the reasons I preferred to sit and be waited on. Who needs the temptation?

As I headed toward the back of the restaurant to join Karen and Vanessa, I thought I heard Sam Preston laughing. I turned to look, nearly knocked over a waiter, and stumbled forward again. I wish I could say it wasn't like me, but it was *so like me.*

"What is it?" Karen said as soon as I plopped myself into the booth next to Vanessa. "You look angry."

I did my best to smooth out the pinches in my face and felt my eyes go wide.

"Girl," Vanessa said. "Don't do that. You look like you're melting." A wide, silk, paisley scarf tied on Vanessa's head, the bow against her right cheek, held back her mass of dark curls. She looked as if she'd stepped out of a photo shoot. Dazzling eyes, black liner drawn upward at the outside corners, and earrings of gold strands brushing against her shoulders. She stirred a smoothie with sleek fingers tipped with long, manicured nails painted with sunflowers.

"Sorry," I said, trying to look normal. "You wouldn't believe what he did."

"Who?"

"That ghost talker. The crazy one."

"The one whose name you said to never mention?" Karen said.

"That's the one."

"I checked him out online. He's a professional photographer."

"That man is not a professional anything; I can assure you of that. It can't be him."

"Aren't you taking a photography class this fall?" Karen's face lit up like a child's on Christmas morning.

I shook my head, anxiety clutching my throat. "Don't even think it."

"Maybe he'll be a visiting expert or something?"

"No self-respecting teacher would allow that man in a classroom."

"Why not?"

"He's completely unprofessional."

"You don't expect a photographer to wear a suit and tie, do you?"

"He was on his hands and knees crawling around the third floor of Executive Suites showing off his intergluteal cleft."

Sophie from Bookish joined us. "His inter...what?" she said, taking a seat on my left making me scoot farther into the booth. She laid a short stack of books on the table as usual and ran her hands over her short, brown hair, fluffing it up a bit.

"His butt crack," I said, "to speak in the vernacular."

"What is this, *The Wizard of Oz*?" Vanessa said.

"What does *The Wizard of Oz* have to do with anything?" I asked.

She said, "The only time I've ever heard anyone use that word, it was in *The Wizard of Oz*."

"Who said butt crack in *The Wizard of Oz*?" Sophie said.

Karen piped up. "Technically, butt crack is a phrase, not a word."

"Nobody said butt crack in *The Wizard of Oz*," Vanessa said.

You should know, this is exactly how most Downtown Diva conversations go. Don't worry about keeping up. It's all nonsense. And so relaxing, you wouldn't believe.

"Vernacular," Vanessa said. "The word I'm talking about is vernacular."

Sophie: "Hold the phone!"

"Hold the phone?" Karen said. "What is that?"

Sophie: "You're telling me there's a scientific term for butt crack?"

Karen: "Again, intergluteal cleft–have I got it right, Pari?– is a phrase, not a term."

"I'm sure phrase and term are interchangeable," Vanessa said.

"I think it's more medical vernacular than scientific," I said.

"There it is again," Vanessa said. "Vernacular."

Sophie: "Who said vernacular in *The Wizard of Oz*? I can't see Dorothy saying it."

"Maybe it was Mrs. Gulch," Karen said.

I said, "What are you *talking about*?"

"Don't tell me you've never seen *The Wizard of Oz*," Sophie said.

Me: "I've heard of it."

"But who said vernacular?" Sophie asked Vanessa.

"The wizard."

Karen: "Not the wizard, the guy...the guy who she thinks is the wizard. Or dreams."

"Dear lord, someone explain," I said.

"That's it," Karen said. "I'm having a *Wizard of Oz* viewing party."

"But the point is," I said just as Susanne arrived to take our orders. "Sam Preston has been telling people the ghost of Aranthia is in my office. And worse, he told the Downtown Strawbridge Gazette." Audible gasps all around. Finally I was getting some respect. "Turkey on wheat, hold the mayo and an iced tea."

"You're sure it was him?" Sophie said. "Just a small salad today, ranch on the side. And one of those banana muffins. Diet Coke." And back to me, "Oh my god, we should have a sleepover. *In your office.* We've got books filled with ghost stories in the store. We can turn off all the lights and have a séance."

My mouth fell open. Thwarted again.

"He did cross a line," Susanne said. "Lemon in your tea?"

"No thanks," I said. "And thanks."

Sophie: "But it would be so much fun. I'll take a slice of lemon in my Diet Coke."

"He's a photographer," Karen said. "He *works* for the Gazette."

"That's different," Susanne said.

Karen: "Club sandwich on wheat. Side of chips. And a lemonade. How is it any different?"

"She's right," Vanessa said. "Paradise Smoothie and a bran muffin, thanks. If he works there, it's not like he was leaking to the press."

I felt a debate coming on. Emboldened, I dug the card he'd given me from the bottom of my purse and before I could talk myself out of it, called Sam Preston. By the time he answered, Melissa had joined us and as they were all watching me, perplexed, I put him on speaker.

"Dr. Logan," Sam said. He sounded as if he were at a loud party. "I'm surprised to hear from you so soon."

And before he could schmooze anymore, I laid into him. "How dare you? How could you? What were you thinking?" You get the drift. I didn't give him much time to say anything, but when I finally ran out of accusatory questions, for a moment I heard only loud noises and grinding.

"Can't talk now," he shouted over the din. "I'll be at MacAuley's tonight. Six?"

"Are you asking me on a date?" I shouted back. The Divas giggled and our drinks arrived.

"Do you want me to?"

"No—"

"Sorry. I'm having trouble hearing you. I'm out at the new interchange construction site."

"I said, no. I don't want to go on a date with you."

"Well, you could wait to be asked."

I nearly screamed at him. "Did you or did you not tell the Gazette there was a ghost in my office?"

"I can't hear you. Meet me at MacAuley's."

And then nothing.

"Aaargh!" That's right. I said 'aaargh.'

"So, it's a date," Vanessa cooed.

All the Divas laughed.

"No. Yes. I don't know. I don't like feeling manipulated."

"It sounded legit to me," Sophie said. "He was working."

"So he wasn't trying to get me on a date?" I said.

"Didn't sound like it."

"Are you going to go?" Karen asked.

"I've got to tell him to stop talking about a ghost being in my office. Can you imagine how this could affect my clients?"

"I suppose that's true," Vanessa said.

"And who knows," Karen said. "Maybe you'll find you like him after all."

"Not possible," I said. "He's awful."

"I heard he's kind of cute," Melissa said.

I gaped at her. She had this way of tossing her long blond curls over her shoulder and smiling at you as if to say, "I'm too sweet to be mad at." But don't be fooled. There's a tough, no-nonsense businesswoman in that delicate five-foot frame, and she'll let you have it if she thinks you deserve it.

"He is," Karen said. "I looked him up online."

At that, everyone had their phones out and they were Googling Sam Preston.

"Not cute," I said.

"Quick," Vanessa said. "What color are his eyes?"

"What does that matter?"

"Do you know or not?"

"Green. So what?"

She grinned. "You think he's cute."

"I don't know what you're talking about." A flush warmed my cheeks. "Anyway, I could never date someone who believes in ghosts."

"Hey," Melissa said. "I believe in ghosts."

"I'm not dating you."

"But...you think less of me? You don't take me seriously? What?"

I sighed. "I'm sorry. I don't mean to denigrate you...or

belief in ghosts."

"I should hope not," Vanessa said. "Some of your clients believe in the supernatural, I'm sure."

"But a relationship is different."

"It's just a date," Sophie said with a smile.

"It's not a date."

"I'll go with you," Vanessa said. "That way...it's definitely not a date."

"You just want to get a look at him," Melissa said.

"Don't we all?" Karen said.

"Ooh," Sophie said turning her phone to the table so we could all see. On it was Sam Preston's face grinning at us.

"If that's your Sam Preston, Ghost Whisperer, then he is a professional photographer," Karen said. She held up her phone to show us Sam's website profile.

"Hmph," I said.

There was something conspiratorial going on in the group and I didn't like it. But hadn't we all done the same thing when it was Sophie and her boyfriend Reese? We had certainly conspired and finagled and worked our magic to get those two together. This had to be nipped in the bud.

"Not this one, Divas," I said. "I'm not interested. At all."

"Why, whatever do you mean?" Melissa said with a sly smile.

"I'm serious. You'll see. Sam Preston is not a good guy."

"Whatever you say," Vanessa said. "Meet me at the salon this evening and we'll go give him hell."

Hopefully, Vanessa would see right through Sam Preston's phony charm and I'd have at least one ally.

"Where's Kaya?" I asked.

"Working," Melissa said. Our plates had arrived and she picked a French fry from Karen's and shoved it in her mouth. "I'm having lunch with her at her store in a bit."

"So you'll all come?" Karen said.

"To Kaya's store?" I said.

"I'll have get back to you on the date," she said.

We all stared at her.

Sophie: "What are you talking about?"

"*The Wizard of Oz*," she said. "You all have the attention spans of rabbits."

Chapter Seven

MaryAshford has joined the chat.

MaryAshford: I got the booking for the séance at Trudy's Treasures. It's the old antique shop. She's got this haunted attic upstairs that'll be perfect.

LegitChris: That's great, but we have an emergency.

MaryAshford: What did Sam do now?

SamTheMan: It wasn't my fault.

LegitChris: He's meeting the refrigerator lady tonight at the Irish place and she is pissed.

MaryAshford: You can't get around calling her an iceberg by saying refrigerator. Put refrigerator in your book, Sam.

SamTheMan: I want to lodge a formal protest. You can call people cold. You can call men cold. You can call women cold. There's even a song about it.

MaryAsford: It's no different than calling someone who doesn't agree with you a hater. She's not cold, Sam. She just doesn't like you.

SamTheMan: The feeling is mutual, believe me.

LegitChris: Cold as Ice by Foreigner.

MaryAshford: You Googled that, didn't you? Just tell me what's going on. <insert eyeroll emoji here>

SamTheMan: Why don't you use the emoji?

MaryAshford: Like you two would understand emoji speak.

LegitChris: You're so mature, Mary.

MaryAshford: I know.

SamTheMan: The Gazette called her about the ghost and she thinks I told them.

MaryAshford: Did you tell them?

SamTheMan: Not in the literal sense.

MaryAshford: What does that even mean?

SamTheMan: I wasn't interviewed. But I've talked about it with people there. I do their pictures, remember.

MaryAshford: So she's right to be angry.

SamTheMan: Everybody already knows. A bunch of people in her building were there when she was b–, when she was telling me to go away.

MaryAshford: Everybody already knows because you were there talking about it.

LegitChris: Whose side are you on?

MaryAshford: I'm trying to keep you guys straight. You'll get nowhere with her if you don't stop acting like she's the enemy.

SamTheMan: She is the enemy.

LegitChris: Mary's right. Remember the charm.

SamTheMan: I really don't think charm spells work on this one.

MaryAshford: Just be polite, please. Explain the proposition clearly. Do whatever you have to do. Promise she can be there the whole time.

LegitChris: Like she's going to go to every sleepover we host to supervise? I don't think so.

MaryAshford: Install a Dutch door. Then people can just look in.

LegitChris: A Dutch door?

SamTheMan: You think Senator Richards is going to let us install a Dutch door?

LegitChris: Oh, one of those double doors. Top could open, bottom stays closed. Good idea.

SamTheMan: It won't fly.

LegitChris: I'm starting to think we're asking for too much here. Maybe it'll be enough to just walk the hallways.

SamTheman: If I could just get in there myself. At least I could talk about what I experienced.

LegitChris: Charm, buddy. Lay on the charm.

MaryAshford: It's not like Aranthia is the only ghost in the building. You've got some other stories.

SamTheMan: Aranthia is the star.

LegitChris: I've got the equipment ready. Mary and I are going to try it out this weekend. You in?

SamTheMan: I don't do equipment.

MaryAshford: But people want to see it. You have to come along. We're a team, remember?

SamTheMan: <insert eye emoji here>

MaryAshford: Eye emoji?

SamTheMan: That's right. *Eye emoji.*

LegitChris: Look, Mary. Sam can use italics.

MaryAshford: Chris, has Sam ever admitted he was wrong about anything?

LegitChris: Only important stuff.

MaryAshford: I'll see you guys tomorrow night then. Late. Don't be drunk.

MaryAshford has left the chat.

LegitChris: So The Fort on Friday night?

SamTheMan: Insert eye here.

Chapter Eight

I waited for Vanessa outside Glam It Up!, staring westward down Strawbridge Avenue knowing full well I couldn't see MacAuley's from there. But a girl can hope. It sounds silly, I know, but I was concerned about arriving at the restaurant before Sam Preston. I didn't want it to look like I was eager to see him. I wanted to be able to march over to his table in the middle of the restaurant and let him have it in front of everybody. I wanted him to squirm and apologize and then I'd tell him to keep himself and his ghost nonsense away from me and my office. I'd dressed for the occasion, in a sensible skirt and blouse–dignified, but fashionable. And as I pictured the scene in my head, I heard myself telling him he was unprofessional. I rolled my eyes and caught a young woman glaring at me from the wrought iron bench in front of the empty storefront next door.

"Oh," I said. "Not you. I was thinking about a terrible person."

She smiled and nodded. "A man."

"Yes," I said. I felt empowered by solidarity.

And yet, the eye roll was actually for myself because in my revenge fantasy, I was behaving like a teenaged brat while accusing Sam Preston of acting childish. I was going to have to get hold of myself before I let this whole thing spiral out of control. I could do it—my whole philosophy of life meant I could absolutely keep my head through this experience.

Let's Review:

1. Sam Preston is not my type. He's a smarmy, scam artist. The Divas would see this and stop with the sly smiles and conspiratorial glances.

2. Eric Lawson is my type. A solid, decent person. Everyone who met him thought so.

3. Sure, Eric had that one big flaw: he was obsessed with his ecological footprint.

4. I should be more concerned about my own ecological footprint...but I'm not.

5. And I buy 99.99% of my designer shoes second-hand. Doesn't that count for something?

6. Eric asked me out again, so there's still some spark between us.

7. And finally, Sam Preston is not my type.

I felt much better, filled with new resolve. When the door to Vanessa's salon opened and she joined me, a whiff of perm solution and shampoo filled the air.

"Am I buxomy?" she said first thing.

"Hello to you, too." I nudged her with a smile and we headed toward the restaurant, weaving through and around small clusters of evening shoppers. The sun would set in about a half hour and the streetlamps were already flickering on.

"No, seriously," she said.

I looked her over. She was my height, except for the hair which always crowned her head in delightful up-dos. Curvy, yes. Vanessa was luscious to my trim, gorgeous to my pretty. "I suppose you could be described as buxomy," I said. "Why?"

"Is buxomy a good thing?"

"Buxomy means..."

"Fat. It means fat, right?"

"I thought it meant full-busted, in a sixteenth-century sort of way."

48

"Like a wench?"

"Wench. Buxomy. What are we talking about?"

She laughed. "Melissa said Karen told her Giselda was based on me."

"Her main character's rival?"

"And she calls Giselda a buxomy wench in the book."

Karen, as you may have guessed, is writing a book. It's a long story, but basically, Noah, the slight, sweet guy who owns Flower Power in Downtown's little air-conditioned mall, is actually Brianna Star, romance novelist, and Tucker Bronson, fantasy novelist. Once Noah's secret was exposed a few weeks ago, Karen admitted she too liked to dabble with ink and paper in a sexy manner and now the Divas are reading what she's written.

"She does not," I said. As Karen's best friend, not only do I get to read her drafts first, but I've committed them to memory, as any good friend would do.

"Okay, not the wench part. But don't you think buxomy means she's fat?"

"No. Full figured, maybe."

"Isn't that another word for fat?"

"Full figured means you've got a nice shape, Vanessa. Karen is probably trying to compliment you."

"Well, I don't think it's a good word. I don't like it."

"I agree it's not a good word, but only because it's anachronistic. You aren't feeling self-conscious about your figure are you?"

"I wasn't until Karen called me buxomy."

"You're fabulous and you know it."

She smiled. "I am. It's true. So why would Karen do that to me?"

"It's not you; it's a character."

"Well," she pulled the heavy door to MacAuley's open and a rush of cool air hit us. "I'm going to ask her to change it."

"Please, don't. She'd be horrified if she thought we were all looking for ourselves in her book. I'll tell her it's old fashioned and get her to change it to big boobed."

"Don't you dare!"

We stood inside at the door, waiting for our eyes to

adjust to the dim lighting, the smell of Irish stew intoxicating us. MacAuley Awley's Irish Pub and Restaurant was a dark place with thick wood floors and polished wood slat walls. Booths lined the sides of the front room. A long half-horseshoe bar with a kitchen behind it filled the back of the space and there was an enormous double door tucked into the left corner that led to another large dining room and beyond that, outdoor seating. Before I could make out any familiar faces, I heard him call my name.

"Dr. Logan," he said.

I was sure he was mocking me already. He was at a booth a few sets down from the door on the left. And he wasn't alone.

"See," Vanessa said. "It's definitely not a date."

Sam and his friend, a tall, well-built blond—not at all buxomy—scooted out of the booth and introductions were made. His friend was Christopher Reynolds and he motioned for Vanessa to slide in behind the table. Before I could take a spot beside her, he'd sat down leaving me to stare at Sam, waiting for him to sit.

"Ladies first," he said, motioning for me to slide into the booth opposite Vanessa. I gave in and found myself trapped against the wall. How could I possibly say what I had to say and make a dramatic, pointed getaway now?

"Where have I heard your name?" I said to Christopher.

"You're famous, Chris," Sam said. They each had a tall glass half filled with golden, foamy beer and Sam lifted his hand to catch the attention of one of the waiters. "He's a reporter for the Florida Daily."

"Not the Gazette?" I said.

"We both do some work for the locals, but I'm technically with the Daily."

"And you're a photographer," I said to Sam. "When you're not hunting ghosts."

"That's right."

"Tell us about the ghost," Vanessa said. "Is it really in Pari's office?"

"I think so."

"Why do you think that?" I said.

"He's probably got one of those electromagnetic ghost detectors, like on television," Vanessa said.

"I work strictly on feeling," he said.

"That's why they call him the Ghost Whisperer," Christopher said. There was a twinkle in his eye and a smirk on his lips.

"Is it all a joke?" I asked Sam.

"Not at all. I've investigated the stories of Aranthia and the layout of the building at the time. History says her room would have been nearly where your office is. And I feel she's there."

I did my best not to roll my eyes. "I appreciate your passion for the subject, Mr. Preston, but I don't like your telling people about it, especially the newspaper. I run a business—a personal, private business. My clients want discretion."

"Are you a madam or a psychologist?"

"What is wrong with you?" I said.

He held up a hand, "Just a little joke."

"My clients don't want to visit a psychologist with a tour group traipsing through the halls. Can you understand that?"

"I can."

"Then why would you tell the Gazette there's a ghost in my office?"

"I didn't have to."

A waiter carefully sat two foaming beers in the middle of the table and hurried away. I ignored mine but Vanessa's hand wrapped possessively around hers as she smiled at Christopher. This was feeling a bit like a date, if you asked me.

"Then how did they find out?" I said, trying to stick to the purpose of the evening. "You must have told someone."

"The entire third floor was standing there when I asked to get into your office."

That was true enough. "So you think one of my coworkers called the press?"

"The press was in the lobby."

I deflated. "If it wasn't you, why didn't you say so on

the phone?" I made a move to scoot out of the booth, but he didn't budge.

"I've been talking to the other tenants in your building. We've got big things planned."

"I'm aware. I can't believe anyone has agreed to it."

"Just on weekends. Off hours. And only late September through October every year."

"To start," Christopher said.

"Every year? How long does it take you to find a ghost?"

"This isn't about finding ghosts," Sam said. "It's a business venture."

"What sort of business?"

"Ghost Whisperer Events," Christopher said. "Ghost tours, cemetery walks, all-nighters in the most haunted buildings in town."

"That sounds amazing," Vanessa said.

I glared at her. "Ghost Whisperer Events? That's the best you could do?"

"I told you," Sam said with a shrug. "We need a better name."

"Ooh," Vanessa said. "Will you have a logo with a funny little ghost on it like the Ghostbusters?"

"I'll show you what we've been working on," Christopher said. "You got a pen?"

Vanessa dug one out of her purse and leaned into Christopher as he doodled on a napkin.

Sam turned to me. "I'd like permission to, at the very least, open the door to your office and let people look in."

"Are you out of your mind?"

"And at best, I'd like to let them inside, for a few minutes."

"Absolutely not."

"We'd take extra precautions. No one would touch anything."

"No. And I can't imagine anyone else in the building allowing such a thing."

"You'd be surprised. In fact, the guy in the office next to yours told me about strange thumps coming from inside the walls."

"He thinks Aranthia might be trapped between rooms," Christopher said, sliding the napkin in front of Vanessa.

"I like it," she cooed.

"*Thwumps*," I said.

"What?" Sam said.

"*Thwumps*. Not thumps. It's the difference between a pillow and a fist."

"You've heard the noise, too?"

"There are no such things as ghosts."

"But the thumps—"

"*Thwumps!*"

"The *thwumps*, then."

"It's me, okay? Sometimes I beat the walls with a pillow."

"You what?" Vanessa laughed and Christopher struggled to contain his amusement.

"It's a form of stress release. The point is, all of your supposed evidence of paranormal activity can be explained naturally. Ghosts don't exist, Mr. Preston."

"Are you a ghost whisperer, too?" Vanessa said to Christopher, oozing pheromones in his direction. I wasn't sure whether I appreciated her change of subject or not.

"Nah," he said. "Ghosts are really Sam's thing."

"You're not a believer, then?" I said.

Christopher shrugged with a smile. "Let's just say I'm skeptical. But I'm going to do my best to hunt them down. Sam and I are a team from way back."

"Chris is the writer," Sam said. "And I shoot the pictures."

"I'm not letting anyone into my office when I'm not there, Mr. Preston."

"You know, calling me Mr. Preston doesn't make this any less informal than it is."

"What is that supposed to mean?"

"It means you should relax."

"Let me out." I scooted and shoved until he nearly fell out of the booth.

"I think it sounds like fun, Pari," Vanessa was saying as Christopher stood to let her out.

"My office isn't a theme park. And there's no ghost in it. Do you know how I know that, Mr. Preston?"

"No rattling chains?"

I rolled my eyes. I'd literally given him the answer moments before. "*Ghosts don't exist.* They're a fantasy for people who can't make the real world exciting enough for them."

"Burned," Christopher mumbled.

Vanessa followed me out, leaving the two men gaping after us, and stood outside the restaurant looking at me. "That's not going to be good for business," she said.

"What do you mean?"

"Going around saying there are no ghosts."

"I don't care. In fact, if I can make this entire town ignore Sam Preston and his ridiculous ghost talking, I'll be happy."

"But you don't think a sleepover in a haunted building would be fun?"

"We're not sixteen, Vanessa."

Her eyes closed a bit and her mouth twisted into a pout. "We're not grandmas, either."

We were at a stalemate. "I'm going to go," I said.

She nodded. "I think I'll go finish my beer."

And with that, she pulled the door open and disappeared into the cold dark pub. I stalked away and was nearly at the door to Kaya Vintage Clothing on my way home when I heard Sam Preston calling after me.

Chapter Nine

D r. Logan. Pari..."
Reluctantly, I stopped and turned to watch Sam fight his way around shoppers in the evening light of Downtown Strawbridge. Something about Sam Preston didn't fit. He wasn't awkward, but he was far from graceful. He wasn't shabbily dressed...and yet, you wouldn't call him well put together. There was a casualness to him that bothered me. Even in his face. Friendly enough when he wasn't talking, he had the look of a jovial sort. If he weren't peddling nonsense, he'd be easily overlooked in my estimation. And I was determined to do so anyway.

"Sorry," he said to a group of teens he nearly shoved into the street. "Dr. Logan."

I said nothing. Tilted my head, raised my brow, waiting to hear what argument he'd try to make on his behalf. But Nothing he could say would change my mind. My office was not open for ghost whispering.

"I owe you an apology," he said. "I didn't intend to say you were uptight or...shrill."

"Is that so?" Okay, so the apology was unexpected and I struggled the tiniest bit to stay angry.

"I wanted you to see the fun in it. Ghosts. You know? Boo." Here he chuckled and I realized why he'd make a great photographer. He was so laid back, so carelessly calm, he put everyone around him at ease.

Except me. I wasn't going to fall for it. "So, it *is* a joke to you."

"No. Not at all."

"Then I'm confused."

"I'm seriously trying to find evidence of ghosts. But I realize it's a mystery. And while it's not a funny endeavor, there's joy in it—amusement. Even though it's deadly serious."

"Did you just make a pun?"

"Of course," he said. "I know all the death puns."

I smiled. Couldn't help it. "I accept your apology ...Sam." So, I tossed him a bone. A used one. Already chewed. The kind you find under the sofa years later.

"There you go." He was beaming.

"But it doesn't change anything. I still find it all ridiculous, even if it's fun for some. And I think it would be highly unprofessional for me to allow my office to be part of some kind of ghost tour, much less the epicenter or portal for the creature."

He stared at me, without emotion, for a few seconds. Then nodded—a tight, controlled movement. "Okay," he said. "I understand."

"I'm glad." What else could I say? Now to extricate myself. I made a motion with my hand, a sort of 'I was going this way' wave. Just before he turned to leave, he shot a glance over my shoulder and smiled. When I turned, I found Kaya Channing standing with the door to her shop propped open behind her.

"I see he found you," she said after Sam had walked back toward the pub.

"Why does it seem as if everybody knows something I don't?"

Kaya laughed. "It's no conspiracy, Pari. Come on in and visit with me. I've been stuck here all day."

"You want me to bring you some food or something?"

"I'm good."

Kaya's store was an artwork of colors, textures, and patterns and smelled of cloth, cedar, and vanilla. She had clothing from every modern decade, both original and reproduction. You never knew what you might find there and it was packed with blouses, skirts, dresses, pants and everything you might ever consider putting on your body, except for tattoos. No tattoos, not even the temporary kind, or as Kaya would say, especially not the temporary kind. Kaya was an all or nothing type, the complete opposite of what you'd find in a typical department store awash in sparsity and light; she liked the muted colors of earth and peace.

"Melissa brought me dinner earlier," she said. "But thanks for the offer."

"So tell me. What do you know?"

"Melissa said you were meeting the Ghost Whisperer —who calls himself that? Does he not have anyone in his life who cares about him and can warn him against embarrassing himself?"

"He was with this writer guy at MacAuley's. Christopher something. They're working together in the ghost business. So...no."

She laughed. "Melissa says everybody thinks he's cute, but even she doesn't think he's your type."

"Why would you guys be looking to set me up, anyway?"

"We had so much success with Sophie and Reese."

I shook my head. "We need to put a stop to it. They'll be after you next, you know."

"I wouldn't mind."

"Really?"

"Really, girl. You know of somebody decent and kind, you send him my way."

"Bad luck these days?"

"I could tell you stories."

"Now, you know I have to make you tell some next time we have a Divas Lunch."

"Me and my big mouth. Anyway, then I got a call from Vanessa. She said you were headed this way, but I was to stop you so Sam could apologize. I was all, 'Sam? Who's Sam?' And she says, 'The Ghost Whisperer! We're going to have ghost tours and a séance. Just you wait.'"

"Does that sound like fun to you?"

We both took seats on stools behind the counter in the tiny, cluttered space where Kaya spent most of her days. "Sure it does. There's no harm in it."

"Please tell me you don't believe in ghosts."

"Honestly, I haven't thought much about it, but I'd say no. Still, it might be nice if it were true."

"How's that?"

"Imagine if you'd lost someone and you had the chance to see them again, even if only briefly. You could apologize or make amends. I don't know."

"But a séance is just theater."

"Some people truly believe."

"That doesn't frustrate you? I mean...grifters scamming heartbroken people, telling them they're in touch with their loved ones. I don't see that as a good thing at all."

"If one of your clients believed in ghosts, would you tell them they were wrong for it?"

"Of course not."

"Damn straight, you wouldn't. You'd accept it and work with it. That's all you can do. People are going to believe what they want to believe. You can't fight it."

I sighed. "I spend my days accepting and trying to help. I guess outside the office, I've become a bit...brittle."

"Well, loosen up. It sounds like all of Downtown Strawbridge is hopping on the ghost train."

"Count me out." I got up. "I've got to get home."

The Gazette called only twice after that, and I told them there was no ghost in my office and they couldn't have a look either way. I got to my apartment to find a card from Sophie taped to the door. She lives right across the third-floor landing at Creek Overlook Apartments, the right amount of space between us for her to offer me a cat on a regular basis. Can you believe we both lived there for at least two years saying little more than 'hello' until that very summer?

On the front of the card, the furry face of a cat with enormous, weepy eyes tried to seduce me. And inside, Sophie had written that she'd found another stray and wanted to know if I was absolutely certain I didn't want to become a cat lady. Sweet Sophie. She not only had an apartment full of cats–well, three–but took care of I don't know how many at Reese's surf wear shop. He built them their own house out back. My first instinct was to knock on her door and take the cat. There were moments, after work or on a Saturday night, sitting ovn the sofa scrolling through the television guide, that I'd look around my apartment and wish for a cat or a little dog to be happy to see me. But I must remind myself often that I'm not home enough to give an animal the attention it deserves. I've told Sophie this several times. I think she's trying to wear me down. It's not working. Really. I mean it.

My apartment was the perfect combination of cozy privacy and being in the middle of everything. From my fellow tenants, and Sophie across the landing, to the whole of Downtown Strawbridge a short walk away–though walking in summer was not something I liked to do. Three rooms, basically, if you don't count the bathroom. A living room large enough to have a half dozen guests over–more if they didn't mind sitting on the floor. A kitchen in which I have room for a tiny two-person dining table. A bedroom large enough for a king-sized bed–which I make roomier by having only a twin. And one spacious balcony, accessed through both the kitchen and the bedroom, on the back of the building overlooking a small wood.

I poured myself an iced tea and sat at my little kitchen table to log onto my laptop. I was anxious to visit The Art Center website to make sure Sam Preston wasn't teaching the photography class I'd signed up for months before. What were the odds? I was relieved to find that my instructor was Ron Bernard. Good old Ron Bernard. I imagined him wearing a suit and tie, wire rimmed glasses on his nose, and perhaps a hat on his head.

I got a call from Eric late, close to nine. He apologized for taking so much time to get back to me about our date, but I didn't mind. I was expecting him to propose dinner, maybe on the beach, or even at Tracks.

"How about Saturday?" he said.

"Sounds wonderful." Saturday was Salsa Night, not

that Eric was a dancer, but the music is fabulous, if a bit loud, and the margaritas are half-price. But he had other ideas.

"Let's go out on the boat with my parents."

Not Saturday night? Not *the* night for romance? No dinner? No dancing? "You want me to meet your parents?"

"Well, it's not like *meeting my parents*. It's just going out on the boat."

"I don't know, Eric. I thought the first time I met them it would be a bit more..."

"On land?"

"Traditional."

"But like I said. It's not meeting my parents. It's just..."

"Going out on the boat."

"Exactly."

"Okay. Sorry."

I felt silly then, naturally. Meeting the parents is probably not the big deal it used to be. In my family it still is. If I brought Eric home, or even onto a boat, to meet Mama and Daddy, they'd assume we were engaged.

"Hey," he said. "I heard you talked to Senator Richards."

"There are no secrets in this town. Did you know he was the cowboy guy?"

"I thought everybody knew."

"How come I didn't?"

"I think you like a mystery, Pari."

"Why would you say that?"

"You don't ask very many questions."

"Is that good or bad?"

"You're the psychologist; you tell me." He chuckled, which was a good sign because I was feeling a bit peeved. "I heard he's claiming to have seen the ghost."

I sighed. "Yes. It looks like supernatural paranoia is going to overtake downtown. You don't believe in ghosts, do you? Please say you don't."

"I definitely don't believe in ghosts."

"You know this Ghost Whisperer guy wants to let people into our offices at night, right?"

"I heard he wanted to have overnight explorations or

something. But not inside our offices."

"He wants in mine."

"Because the ghost is in there."

"I won't allow it."

"I don't blame you."

"I don't like hysteria, you know?"

"Who does?"

"The hysterics crave it. I have a sinking feeling about this whole ghost thing. I'm afraid we're going to see a lot of insanity."

"We'll just have to stay above it."

"If we can."

It was refreshing to find him as annoyed by the idea as I was. That was the thing about Eric and me—we really understood each other...sometimes. After I hung up the phone, I shuddered a bit. There was a time when I was a child during which I was confronted by hysteria. That was probably what led me into psychology.

"Ghosts are not the same thing," I told myself. "It'll be okay." But I suddenly had the urge to call my mother.

Chapter Ten

Twila Harper was a wisp of a girl. Like a five-foot ballerina, her hair in a loose bun atop her head. At twenty-five, she was pale, her eyes dark and sunken, cheeks drawn and sallow. My first thought was anorexia, but one tries not to judge prematurely. She curled herself up on the thick padded chair, the small round table between us, hugging her knees. She wore an oversized fisherman's knit sweater and shivered a bit as she snuggled her chin into the collar. It was Friday, my last appointment for the day and I was still wondering if I was going to buy a cake on my way home and binge watch some show or take a cat from Sophie, since I had no better plans.

"What brings you here today, Twila?" I said. She'd been vague during our initial phone interview, only assuring me she was neither depressed nor suicidal.

She shrugged. "It'll sound crazy."

"That's what I'm here for." I smiled at her, hoping to put her at ease, but her brow pulled together and her lips twisted, as if she struggled to find words.

"I'm not sure I can explain it, really. I've always felt...small, you know? Like, the world is full of giants and they don't see me sometimes."

"Are we talking literally or figuratively?"

She brightened and sat up a bit. "Both. But in the last few months, there's something else. I'm starting to feel...This is really going to sound nuts."

"Go ahead; I don't mind."

She chuckled. "Well, the best way I can describe it is that I often feel as if I'm fading. Literally. Like I'm disappearing. Becoming...something not solid. Isn't that wacko?"

"I don't think so."

"You think it means something, right? Like, psychological. Have you ever had the feeling that part of you wasn't part of you?"

"No, but I'm familiar with the condition."

"There's a condition? Like, it's a real thing?"

I nodded.

"I used to feel like my teeth weren't mine and they weren't in my mouth just right. And then I'd feel like my right arm didn't belong to me. I thought it was bonkers, but what am I going to do, right? It goes away eventually. But this hasn't gone away. I didn't think too much of it until I was in class the other night and Lisa Turnow was talking about the ghosts in town."

"Turnow?"

"She's in my ballet class–a reporter, like... entertainment, I think. And she mentions the ghost in this building and downtown. And that's when it hit me." She stared at me, her eyes wide and round, startled.

"What hit you, Twila?"

"I think I'm becoming a ghost."

"Would this feeling include a sense of death?"

She shook her head. "No. Just that I'm fading away and I'll be a ghost soon. I walk around feeling thinner and thinner. And people act more and more like I'm not even there. Sometimes I think I'm *not* there."

"Would you agree that ghosts are associated with the dead?"

She nodded. "I know. I get it. It doesn't make a lot of sense. But what if..." she turned and stared at the window. "What if this is what it feels like before you die?"

"All right, Twila. Let's talk about your childhood."

Twila, in a solidly real sense, wanted to disappear, but she insisted everything in her life was perfect. I could tell it would take some time for her to see that it was almost certainly the stress of perfection at the root of her problem. As I drove home later, I puzzled over various techniques I could employ to help her see her life objectively. And when I walked in the door of my little apartment, I had a sudden, overwhelming desire to go back out. I called Karen; she was planning to settle in and watch movies all night, but she was up for something different.

"We're not really going out people, are we?" she said when she showed up an hour later at my door. "What will we do?"

"We could go downtown. The Fort, maybe? Or Tracks."

"I guess."

"You don't want to?"

"We'll look desperate."

"Maybe we are," I said.

"Let's call the others. Desperation is much less noticeable in a large group."

Eventually, we learned that Melissa and Vanessa were going to The Fort. Kaya said she'd go, too. But Sophie and Reese were on their own.

"How does five women at The Fort look?" I asked Karen as she drove us the short distance to a downtown parking lot behind the nightclub.

"I changed my mind. It's even more desperate."

I laughed. "We really need to stop caring what society says about women out on the town."

"I wasn't really worried. Were you?"

"Not at all." But I was. Just a little. Not so much about what society might think, but what my clients might think. What goes through a person's head when he sees his therapist at a bar drinking and getting loud with a bunch of other women? And what does he say, if anything, at his next appointment?

The Fort is an ordinary lounge with a small stage for music, a small floor for dancing, a bar that runs the entire west side, and a spacious upstairs loft overlooking downstairs.

There's a lot of outdoor seating and the whole thing is surrounded by a tall wooden fence that makes it look like an old fort. The five of us found two round tables downstairs and sat for two hours sipping drinks and shouting over the music about how bored we all were.

"I really need to find a man," Melissa said when we were nearly finished with our second round.

"We don't need men to be fulfilled," I shouted.

"Depends on the definition of fulfilled," Kaya said.

"And men," Vanessa said.

"I don't want to be fulfilled," Melissa said. Just then the band stopped for a break. "I want a man," she shouted. The entire bar laughed.

Karen said, "There's nothing wrong with wanting a relationship, Pari."

"Did I hear someone's looking for a man?" I looked up to find Sam Preston with his friend Christopher and two other men looming over us.

"Not me," I said.

"Pari doesn't need a man to be fulfilled," Karen said.

More chairs were gathered around our tables and Sam introduced Christopher and his other friends, Richard Warren and Michael Harding. I noted the way Christopher's arm draped over Vanessa's shoulders as he sat himself next to her. One night at MacAuley's and they were a couple. I felt a tiny pang of jealousy. But I was determined not to let it bother me. I didn't need a man...I told myself. And then I remembered I had a man.

I laughed and Karen nudged me. "What?"

"Nothing."

"Tell me," she whined.

"I just remembered I'm dating Eric."

"You and Eric again?" Melissa said.

"He's easy to forget," Karen said.

"Don't say that. He's great."

Melissa started singing "Reunited" by Peaches & Herb.

"*Dios Mio*, what an old song," Vanessa said, and sang with her.

Sam leaned in. "Who's great?"

"Not Pari's boyfriend," Kaya said.

"Is so."

"Is he a doctor, too?" Sam said.

"Yeah, what is he, anyway?" Karen said.

"Leave him alone."

"You're a photographer, right?" she asked him.

"That's right."

"Pari's taking a class this fall."

"Is that so?" He looked at me curiously. "Have I inspired you?"

"I signed up for it months ago." I hoped he couldn't hear the defensiveness in my voice.

"What's new with ghost hunting?" Kaya asked Sam. I could have kissed her for changing the subject.

"We've got a lot of stuff in the works. Ghost tours, that sort of thing."

"Sounds like fun," Melissa said. "Finally, we'll have something to do around here."

"You can't be serious," I said.

"You like bars, do you?" Sam said.

"No. But at least they're grounded in reality."

"I doubt that."

"Pari doesn't believe in ghosts," Melissa said.

"I'm aware."

"Are your friends also in the ghost hunting business?" I asked. I don't know why. I would rather have pretended not to be interested. But that's what rum will do.

"I have other interests," he said. Richard, he said, owned a landscaping company and Michael was a chef at a swanky restaurant over on the beach.

"I'm impressed," I said.

"About what?"

"You have an eclectic group of friends."

"Eclectic," he said. "That's a word."

I laughed. "Yes, it is." And suddenly I wondered if I'd used it properly. "I think I need another rum and coke." The waitress had appeared to take the guys' orders and Sam bought the entire table another round.

"Karen, are you driving?" Kaya asked.

She nodded.

"We can walk back to my place," I said. "And you can spend the night if you have to."

This was, as it turned out, a very bad idea. Once you establish that you can get drunk, it's more likely you will. We'd almost finished our third drinks when the band started playing again and everybody got up and headed to the dance floor as if it was a coordinated attack. Vanessa and Christopher made the first move. Somehow Richard, the landscaper, signaled silently to Karen and they were gone. Melissa accepted an invitation from someone she apparently knew well. That left Michael and Kaya to jump up and join them.

Sam turned to me and shrugged. "It looks like we have no choice."

"Succumbing to peer pressure?"

"Absolutely," he said. He took my hand and I let him lead me out onto the crowded little floor.

I love those scenes in movies when a group of friends gets out on a dance floor and acts ridiculous together. I was never what you'd call a popular kid; I never even had a group of unpopular friends to dance with. So, I admit, I let myself get sillier than I'd intended when the evening was planned. We all danced to a cover of The Motown Song, then to Call Me, which when sung by a man was odd to say the least. And then the band slowed down, because in those movies it always does and there's that awkward pause when all your friends pair off and you're left standing with the guy, wondering if you should sit down or just dance with him. Except in the movies, the girl wants to dance with the guy. I didn't have a chance to think about it.

Sam took me in his arms and looked down at me with a smile. "This is better," he said in my ear, letting his cheek rest on mine.

"Is it?"

"Mm hm. Couldn't you tell? I'm a terrible dancer."

I pulled away and laughed. "I was having too much fun to notice. How did I do?"

"Oh, you were worse. Much worse. But we were talking about me."

I couldn't help but laugh again. Back at the table, the guys ordered another round, and at some point, Sam leaned over and said, "I'm going outside for some fresh air. Join me."

We took our drinks and got up from the table. I knew the others were watching us leave, my hand in his, but I didn't care. Fresh air sounded wonderful, even necessary. We found a small table out front and even in the heat of the late August night, it was easier to breathe.

"It's late," he said. "I'm not usually one for bars and loud places."

"Me either. My ears are still clogged and ringing."

"Are we shouting?" He looked around at the others outside.

"What?" I said, joking.

"Are we shouting?" he yelled. And we laughed.

We sat quietly for a few minutes, trying not to look at each other, but failing, until a large group of people brushed by us and one of them stumbled and fell onto the table, knocking over my drink.

"Oh!" I said and stood too quickly, sending my wrought iron chair backwards, with me falling onto my bottom in front of it.

Sam had me up in a second and though I was laughing, he was concerned. "Are you all right?"

"I am," I said. "No, really. I'm fine."

He was standing so close, his hands on my upper arms, looking into my face like...like he loved me. And I remember thinking, in that moment before I, for some odd reason, kissed him, that I might never know that feeling again. His lips were eager for mine and he pulled me closer, his hands finding their way to my lower back.

"I'm sorry," I said, when I pulled away. "Florence Nightingale syndrome, I guess."

He chuckled. "Call me Flo."

In the end, I think it was the landscaper who drove us home, designated driver and all that. Sam rode with us and they both walked us up the stairs.

"I promise I'm not drunk," I said, perhaps too many times to make it believable.

"Better safe than face down on the sidewalk," Sam said.

"Okay, Flo. Whatever you say, Flo."

"Who's Flo?" Karen said.

I didn't answer. The next morning, I woke up tangled in my bedsheet and the first thing I remembered was the kiss. I groaned. "No."

"Me too," Karen said. She was lying next to me in her underwear, no sheet to cover her. "Water," she begged.

We nursed our dehydration headaches with protein and plenty of fluids before walking over to The Fort for her car. I knew I should tell her about kissing Sam Preston, but every time I thought about it, a wave of nausea swept through me. There was no way I'd get actual words out of my lips without puking all over her. I couldn't believe I'd kissed him. What was going through my mind? I wished I could blame it on the alcohol, and sure I was soused as a pickle, but even that wasn't enough to make me want to kiss Sam Preston. There was no explaining it. The long walk and fresh air, and yes, even the heat, did us good. My head was clearing. I was going to have to put the kiss out of my mind. I had to get the entire evening out of my system before Eric picked me up.

"Oh, no," I said as we reached the parking lot at The Fort.

"What's wrong?" She ran over and examined her cherry red Kia—not the *only* car left in the lot by a drunken patron the night before.

"Not the car," I said. "Eric. I'm going out on a boat with Eric and his parents this afternoon."

"You didn't plan this weekend well. Are you going to be all right? Maybe you should cancel."

"No, I'll be fine. We didn't get that drunk. How many drinks did we have?"

"I had three and you had four."

"I only had a few sips of the fourth one. Somebody knocked it over outside." *And I kissed Sam Preston.* Why would I do that? Alcohol is evil.

"We're not drinking people, Pari. Three was more

than enough. I feel like my eyeballs are being sucked out of their sockets. I don't know how Melissa does it."

"I think your body gets used to it."

"I don't want to get used to it."

"Agreed. So, I guess I need a high protein, high carb lunch. Early, so I have time to digest it before getting on a boat."

Yeah. It was a good plan. But it didn't work.

Chapter Eleven

MaryAshford has joined the chat.

MaryAshford: You two were grins. You promised not to be drunk.

LegitChris: We got the equipment tested, didn't we?

MaryAshford: That's not the pint. You try lauched the whine time.

LegitChris: Whoa, what's with the typos? Where's your autocorrect?

MaryAshford: I tune fast when I'm eyebrows. This IS AUTICORRECT!

SamTheMan: Stop shouting, I have a headache.

LegitChris: Slow down.

MaryAshford: Slowing down. You were drunk last night. I had to do all the work. You laughed the whole time.

LegitChris: We went to The Fort. She was there.

MaryAshford: The ice queen?

LegitChris: Hey, who said ice queen? I know that one's got to be in the book. Is that in the book, Sam?

SamTheMan: It is. Along with frigid, cold, and bitter.

MaryAshford: I'm not saying it. You guys kept saying ice queen last night.

LegitChris: Always our fault, Sam.

MaryAshford: I'm just trying to help. You'll never get women until you shed your college glory days.

LegitChris: You realize we're thirty, right?

MaryAshford: You're not doing yourself any favors, Chris. Yes, I realize how mature you should be.

SamTheMan: Maybe we're just not mature around our friends.

MaryAshford: Don't pull the she's just another one of our mates excuse. Just because we're friends doesn't mean you can disrespect women around me.

LegitChris: I don't see how calling a woman cold is disrespectful.

MaryAshford: I'm sighing annoyingly. Can you hear me sighing? If a woman is truly cold to you, I'll let it pass. But if a woman simply doesn't like you or doesn't swoon at the sight of you or buy into your

SamTheMan: You got her started Chris, do something

MaryAshford: ridiculous smarmy come-ons doesn't mean

LegitChris: She even put the hyphen in Sam.

MaryAshford: she's cold. You got it? And if you make a menstruation joke right now, this team is done.

LegitChris: I would never. I'm not that dumb.

MaryAshford: What were you going to say, Sam?

SamTheMan: It was worse.

MaryAshford: Say it.

SamTheMan: I don't want to.

MaryAshford: Did it have to do with my getting or not getting

SamTheMan: Please don't say it. And no, not that. I would never say that.

MaryAshford: You're still drunk, obviously. Look, I'm doing a lot of the work here on your big idea, Sam. So, I'm serious about the woman thing. It's not cute. It's not cute at fourteen. It's not cute at twenty-two and it's so much worse than not cute at thirty. So grow up or I'm out.

SamTheMan: Ok, sorry.

MaryAshford: So what happened when you met up with her on Thursday? I couldn't get anything out of you two last night.

LegitChris: He said a bad word again.

MaryAshford: What did he say?

LegitChris: He told her to relax.

MaryAshford: It's in the book, Sam.

SamTheMan: I can't believe I seriously can't tell a woman to relax.

MaryAshford: Well, you can't. Or to calm down.

SamTheMan: I apologized, ok? You happy?

MaryAshford: And...?

SamTheMan: No go. She's still the ice queen.

LegitChris: Except for the kiss.

MaryAshford: What kiss?

LegitChris: He kissed her.

SamTheMan: She kissed me. We were just drunk is all.

LegitChris: But you liked it.

SamTheMan: I didn't dislike it.

LegitChris: The point is, she must like you. So, just keep up the charm and you'll be in her office in no time.

SamTheMan: That's got innuendo all over it.

MaryAshford has left the chat.

LegitChris: That was abrupt.

SamTheMan: Well, we were doing it again. The woman thing. Your fault this time.

LegitChris: She has a point. Tell me the truth. Were you going to make a joke about her not getting laid?

SamTheMan: Absolutely not. I was going to joke about her not having a date.

LegitChris: Not as bad, but still not nice.

SamTheMan: I guess we've pushed her too hard.

LegitChris: It wasn't all that funny.

SamTheMan: It was at first.

LegitChris: Now she thinks we really are jerks.

SamTheMan: We're kind of jerks.

Chapter Twelve

It seems to me a date is something you do at night. It involves movies and dinner and maybe dancing. A walk along the river, perhaps. A play, or a party. Eric and I weren't at that point yet where boating with his parents was a thing to consider. But I suppose I have traditional expectations. I tried to look past it. Still, I was thinking, if the boat trip went well, he'd propose something else for that night. I tried to forget about kissing Sam Preston. It didn't mean anything. I was tipsy, that's all. But that look he gave me. I shuddered remembering it and the feeling of being loved. Why did I think I'd never find that? Of course I would. And maybe with Eric. I just needed to give the relationship a chance.

When he picked me up after noon, Eric looked like a character in a movie. Collared pullover, bermuda shorts, knee socks, deck shoes, and a captain's hat. I did *not* get the memo on uniform. But I was wearing shorts and tennis shoes instead of a bathing suit. I brought the suit in a bag along with sunscreen, a visor, and a bottle of antacid, just in case.

We met up with his parents at a little marina north of town on the lagoon. His mother was tall, ash blonde, and very thin, her face taut with a strained smile. I thought she was going to call me "pet." I don't know where I'd heard that before, but it was stuck in my head. "Hello, pet." It would drive me nuts until I figured it out. His father was taller, larger, and looked like the captain of a cruise ship. Sun worn and graying, he smiled more naturally, but barely looked at me.

"Let's get out on the water," he said, as if we'd been holding him back.

The Lawson's boat was as sleek as a sports car, with four seats, two in front with the steering wheel, if that's what you call it, and two behind. There was a diving platform at the back and something of a deck up front. I sat in the back and was surprised when Mrs. Lawson sat next to me. Eric and his father were up front and standing the whole time.

Why do people want to go out on the water? What is the point? You're trapped in a small craft, bouncing around, no bathroom in sight, the wind in your hair, sun on your skin, and did I mention no bathroom? Granted, the Lawson's boat wasn't tiny, but it wasn't large enough that we weren't being tossed about. Mrs. Lawson, Edith, insisted I eat her pastry-wrapped shrimp dipped in guac. (Who serves that? On a boat?) She had a cooler full of snacks and beer. I only vomited once. Everyone was duly concerned, even Mr. Lawson, aka Bud, for a moment or two. Then they went back to racing the boat back and forth on the lagoon, waving at other boaters doing the same thing.

"Eric tells us you're a psychiatrist," Edith shouted over the roar of the motor and splash of the water and the wind in my face. She pulled huge dark sunglasses on so I couldn't see her eyes anymore.

"Psychologist," I said. Bud whipped the boat around and I burped loudly when I hit the side and hung on, panicked.

"What's the difference?"

By that time Eric was on the front of the boat, lying back against the windshield. His slid this way and that occasionally but was otherwise undisturbed. Bud turned around (driving without watching where he was going!) and said, "A psychiatrist is a doctor."

"Oh," Edith yelled. "But I thought you were a doctor."

"I have a doctorate in psychology." My stomach rumbled. I held on tighter and attempted a weak smile.

"That's not a doctor," Bud said.

"Oh," Edith said, quieter this time. She pursed her lips and turned her head.

I looked to Eric for some help, but he might have been sleeping, his face turned up to the sun, drinking it in.

"Why don't you join him?" Edith yelled.

Sure. Why not? I mean, what's the worst that could happen? I stood up and wobbled as I took Mr. Lawson's hand. As the boat continued to speed along atop the water, he helped me step onto the seat next to his and then up onto the side of the boat. And when I was stepping onto the front, the boat went air born and so did I. It was like slow motion blow back; as if I'd been shot with a cannon ball–arms and legs spread eagle, I watched as the Lawson's sped away. I hit the water backward and sank for a while. I hadn't quite realized what had happened. My eyes were still open. That's probably what brought me back to reality. Even brackish water stings! I flailed, mostly because I imagined a boat running over me while I was just beneath the surface. Once my head was above water, I gulped, said, "Shit!" and bounced buoyantly for a bit while Mr. Lawson maneuvered the boat to a position in which Eric could haul me up. Unfortunately, I hadn't the sense of mind to pee while I was in the water. When we finally came ashore hours later, my legs wobbled like jelly and my stomach churned. But it was empty by then so no worries.

"Bathroom," I said, relieved to see one at the marina. Right off the pier, *like they knew.*

Eric drove me home, glancing furtively my way at odd moments. "Did you have a good time?" he asked as he followed me up the stairs to my apartment.

"It was great," I said.

"It was a perfect day for it."

"Sorry I puked in front of your parents."

"That's okay. People puke all the time on the boat."

"They do?" I found that hard to believe but at the same time, Eric wasn't one for lying to make people feel better. I unlocked my door and walked in, leaving it open behind me. The air conditioning!

"You have to get your sea legs, that's all."

"You mean my lagoon legs?"

He chuckled. "Yeah."

I plopped down on the couch and felt my stomach growl. "I'm going to have to eat something."

"Do you want me to make you some soup before I go?"

"No, thanks." *Hmph.*

"How about next weekend?"

"Could we stay on land?"

He smiled. "Sure. Maybe a movie."

"A movie sounds great."

He leaned over and kissed my cheek. I didn't expect him to kiss me on the mouth. There are no toothbrushes on a boat, after all. "I hope you feel better soon."

And that was that. I met the parents. I puked over the side of their boat. I flew off it, coming back on board looking like a drowned orphan lost at sea. And Eric still wanted to see me again. He really was a great guy.

"Oh, Pari," Karen said that evening on the phone. "Why do you put yourself through it?"

"Through what?"

"Eric is an outdoor kind of guy and you're an indoor kind of girl."

Karen and I were a pair. She was at home, watching a *Back to the Future* marathon, painting her toenails and I was curled up on the sofa watching my DVD of *Brooklyn* for the hundredth time.

"It was a date," I said.

"You realize you don't have to accept if you don't want to."

"He's my boyfriend. Ugh. I hate that word."

"We're not fifteen."

"So, he's my man friend. My..."

"Lover?"

"No. Not yet, anyway."

"So there's no chemistry at all."

"That's not fair. Things were definitely going well until the shoe thing."

"For which he has yet to apologize."

"Maybe he doesn't feel an apology is necessary."

"But how do you feel about it?"

"It's not worth my energy; that's how I feel about it."

"And so you're trying to be an outdoor girl for him?"

"I'm just dating him. He wanted to go out on the boat, so I went."

"And why no dinner tonight? Or a movie?"

"Well, I was pretty sick after."

"And is he taking care of you while you're sick? Where's the chicken noodle soup, Pari?"

"Our relationship isn't at that stage yet. Really, you're being too hard on him."

She sighed. "Maybe you're right. Maybe going out on a boat is a getting to know you kind of thing. Like a test."

"I failed, then."

"So, if he asks you to go on the boat again, will you go?"

"It's the least I can do. I mean, I should give it another try."

"But you don't like the water."

"There's nothing wrong with adapting to someone else's interests."

"If he's also willing to adapt to yours."

We sat silent for a while. I could hear her capping her polish bottle and setting it on her side table. Doc was shouting in the background. "Marty!"

"I don't think I have any interests." I worked. I sewed. I took art and craft classes at night. Those aren't sharing activities, exactly.

"There must be something you could make him do with you."

"Don't make it sound like a punishment."

"What about one of those pottery classes where you drink wine and make a bowl."

"That's not a bad idea. But can you really see Eric getting his hands dirty. He must pay a fortune for that manicure."

"You went on a boat, Pari."

"And puked over the side of it; what's your point?"

"You're impossible."

I promised I would invite Eric to a pottery class, or something like it. But the thought of it made me wince.

Let's Review:

1. Eric is gorgeous. He's physically fit and loves the outdoors. And we get along fairly well. I like him.

2. I'm not so bad myself, not that our appearances matter here. But if it doesn't matter, why do I always mention how gorgeous Eric is? I'm physically fit. I suppose. Practically speaking.

3. I'm willing to try things that Eric likes, such as boating. And, once, he mentioned biking over the causeway.

4. I should be enthusiastic about sharing my interests, scarce though they are, with him.

5. And yet, I'm hesitant. Why?

6. I will have to ponder this.

"Anyway," Karen said. "You and I are becoming dullards. We need to get out more."

"Not again."

"Not like that. We don't have to go to nightclubs and drink. But we could do the salsa and swing nights. Poetry night."

"I always do Poetry Night."

"Then I'll start going, too. I'm serious. I feel like I'm just sitting around here painting my nails so I can sell paper to everybody downtown. Let's do something more. Let's get lives."

Get lives. It was one of the things I helped my clients with. And it was never as easy as it seemed.

Chapter Thirteen

I felt much better the next day and met up with Karen for lunch. It was suffocatingly hot, but as locations go, Brunch was fairly close to my apartment, so I put on a white cotton sundress with lace edging, slathered myself in sunscreen, donned a pale blue, wide brimmed hat, slipped on some adorable blue sandals and *walked*. Karen was sitting at an outside table for two shaded a bit by a ripped, green umbrella that matched Brunch's store sign and decor. She'd brought a small ring-binder notebook and insisted we brainstorm ourselves a life.

Melanie, Brunch's owner, came out to chat with us for a minute or two after we ordered. Melanie and her employees wore a uniform—a green short-sleeved, button-up dress with a white cotton apron and white sensible shoes. It was because of this that Brunch always made me think of television shows like *Two Broke Girls*. And while it felt a bit odd for casual Downtown Strawbridge, it did lend it a certain amount of character. And the uniform certainly fit Melanie. She had thin, fly-away, blonde hair that she kept out of her face with a dozen or so bobby pins. Instead of worry showing up on her smooth forehead or around her wide, cheerful eyes, it was the rest of her face that dragged downward into a frown that let you know she was tired. But that morning, she smiled and told us Sam Preston had been all over town asking for ghost stories.

"He's cute as a baby's butt, isn't he?" she said. "I told him all about the ghost in the kitchen."

"You have a ghost in the kitchen?" Karen said.

"Since I bought the place. I never told anyone about it. I don't want people to think I'm a nut. My uncle up in Minnesota claims he saw Big Foot and I figure one crazy per family, am I right?" She glanced at me. "Sorry, Pari. I mean, sanity-challenged."

I smiled.

"Is it a scary ghost?"

I glared at Karen; she really shouldn't encourage Melanie.

"Not at all. She really likes it when we fry up bacon for the BLTs and clubs. You can see her sometimes, hovering over the stove, breathing it in."

After Melanie left, Karen was smiling slyly at me.

"What?"

"Oh, nothing much. It just sounds like your arch nemesis has the whole town talking."

Sophie stopped by our table on her way to Reese's surf shop and asked me about my boat trip.

"She puked," Karen said.

"I wish I could deny it."

"Oh, no," Sophie said. "I don't think you two have been dating long enough for that."

"He was very understanding," I said.

"Will you join us?" Karen said. "We're going to get our lives in order."

"Over brunch?" Sophie laughed.

"I've already started our lists." Karen opened her notebook and showed us what she'd done so far. It wasn't much. One page for each of us. Two items under her name: Take a class and write a novel. And under my name, she'd written: Finish book.

"Are you writing one, too?" Sophie asked.

"She's been working on a self-help book for over a year now."

I shook my head. "I gave it up. It wasn't working out."

"Why not?" Karen said. "You sounded so excited

about it."

"My first attempt was too academic. I tried to tone it down and make it more accessible, but then it sounded ridiculous. So I quit."

"But you wanted to share the whole 'Be Aware' thing with the world," Karen said. "It was a good idea."

I shrugged. "Not every dream comes to fruition. There are other things I can put on the list."

Karen looked defeated. "I suppose."

My phone started buzzing and I dug into my bag thinking Eric must be calling.

"I'll see you two later," Sophie said and was off.

I'd almost answered the phone without thinking when I saw it was Sam Preston's number. "Speak of the devil," I murmured.

"What?" Karen said.

"Nothing." I stared at the phone for a few seconds, not sure what to do. I remembered the feel of his lips on mine and blushed. I wanted to hang up—preferably in a way that he'd know he'd been hung up on. I'd tell my clients you can't run from difficult situations. Best to handle them head on. So I answered. "How did you get this number?"

He laughed. *Laughed!* "You called me to yell at me about something, remember? What was it you were mad about? You're angry at so many things."

"I am not angry." But I sounded pretty angry.

"So," he said, sounding oddly confused. "How are you?"

"I'm fine. Why do you ask?"

Karen whispered, "Is that Sam Preston?"

I held up a mind-your-own-business finger.

"I was calling because, well, I don't know the etiquette here. I mean, if we'd been on a date I'd have called you yesterday."

"A date?"

"But it was just a..."

"A kiss." I shuddered. Karen reached over and grabbed my other hand.

"Yeah. So, what's the etiquette here? How long do I

wait to call you after a kiss?"

"Technically, I kissed you." Karen nearly jumped out of her seat at that. "So I would be the one to call."

"I see." He paused. "When were you going to do that?"

"I wasn't."

"Ouch. After a kiss like that you weren't even going to call me?"

"It was just a kiss." And it was. No big deal. Nothing to write home about or obsess over. A stupid, impetuous act that I wished I could take back. And yet, hell, it was lovely. Karen smacked the table, pulling me back to the moment at hand. "Hold a moment, please," I said to Sam and hid the phone behind my back. "It was a drunken mistake," I whispered to Karen. "It didn't mean anything."

She opened her mouth to speak, but no words emerged.

"I'm back," I told Sam. "What were you saying?"

"You kiss guys like that often, then?"

"No. I mean, of course I kiss guys. You think you're the only man I've–" That little voice inside my head was screaming at me to shut up. "Never mind. I'm seeing someone." I rolled my eyes at my own inept kiss-discussion skills.

"Oh, right, right. The boyfriend. You cheated on him with me?" He was teasing.

"I guess I did. One last fling, perhaps."

"Aw, I'm so glad you made me a part of that. So, you're going exclusive with this guy?"

Our lunch arrived and I waved off a question about mustard. "What do you mean, *going*?"

"You said 'one last fling.'"

"I was joking."

"So, you're not exclusive?"

"Maybe. I'm not sure yet." Little voice again: *shut up, Pari.* "It's really none of your business."

"Okay, well, I'll check back later then."

When I'd hung up, Karen stared at me until I shoved a bite of sandwich in my mouth just to avoid the inevitable. "You kissed Sam Preston?" she said.

"It was nothing."

"And nothing just called."

I stuffed a potato chip in to chase the sandwich. "I was hoping to never have to speak of this."

"Oh, my god, Pari. What happened? Why didn't you tell me?" She was beaming.

"Please don't make a big deal about it. Honestly, I don't know what came over me. He's not my type at all."

"Maybe you don't know your type."

"It's not sarcastic, unprofessional cads, that's for certain."

"You're exaggerating his faults."

We chewed in relative silence for a few seconds as I tried to think of ways to impress upon her there was nothing between Sam Preston and me. "It was just a kiss," I mumbled.

"There's no such thing as just a kiss."

"Of course there is. I was relaxed. Drunk."

"Are you saying he took advantage?"

"I kissed *him*."

"You took advantage of *him*." She nearly choked on her sandwich, laughing. "And?"

"And what?" I was so embarrassed I sucked up iced tea like a dying man.

"How was it?"

"How should I know? I don't remember."

"You remember."

We were quiet for a few moments while she smiled at me, chewing.

"Okay. It was great. But it won't happen again."

"You don't think he's adorable?"

"I think he's nuts."

"Well, everybody else loves him. I think the whole town is about to go ghost crazy."

She was, unfortunately, right.

There were murmurs at first, nothing more. The Ghost Whisperer was setting up a walking layout of Downtown Strawbridge for a monthly ghost tour and the city was considering funding for brass markers at certain spots–they called them educational and my protest emails were responded to with a "thank you for your concerns" dodge. The cemetery had been contacted, according to Tildon Frakes, attorney-at-law, and had agreed to a regular tour of its most haunted and haunting residents. Worst of all, Trudy of Trudy's Treasures, whose antique shop was housed in an old 1930s house had apparently agreed to host the séances.

That last week of August, I felt like the world around me had gone fuzzy, like heat rising from tarmac. But I managed to stay above it all, steer my clients to their lives instead of the ghost in the building, and generally forget Sam Preston was meddling in a perfectly quaint downtown. Everything was settling down and I almost believed the whole scene would simply fade out from lack of interest until the psychic set up shop almost exactly across the street from Namasté.

Namasté is the wonkiest shop in town. And Pat Willard is its deceptively normal owner. Pat looks like a pixie–a smart, takes no crap from anyone, pixie. But at heart, she's a gypsy. While she wears sensible pantsuits, keeps her hair clipped short, and seems to own no jewelry at all, her soul is twirling about in yards and yards of gauzy skirt, bell-sleeved lace-up-in-the-front tops, hair down to her hips, and hoop earrings large enough for a parrot to perch on. Namasté is filled with charms, crystals, odd sitar CDs, and those very skirts and tops she never wears. And it reeks of incense. More than one person has held her breath and run past the always open door of Namasté. At least I hope I'm not the only one.

A few doors east of Pat's store on the same side of Strawbridge, is Begotten, Carolina Davies' very religious, very serious gift shop, and now between them both, on the opposite side, a glass shop window was being painted: 'Isabella's Insights. Psychic Readings.' It's a trifecta of whimsy. And when Isabella Bolton first left her under-renovation storefront it was noted by everyone that no one had seen her go in. She'd simply materialized there with her boxes of psychic paraphernalia. As Isabella, who was obviously the very soul of Pat Willard, hoop earrings and all, glided about town, wafting a certain muted incense of her own, she left in her wake a buzz so loud people swatted the air without thinking.

And what was first and foremost on everyone's mind? Would Isabella show up at Triple F, Downtown Strawbridge's monthly family festival, in a psychic booth ready to read our palms? We would have to wait and see. My introduction to Isabella Bolton was less than promising and I wish I could say the fault was hers. But I'm afraid it was all on me.

I made another effort to be active, probably at the thought of more boating with Eric. So on Wednesday, I dug out my fabulous butter cream Cucinelli sneakers and brought a change of clothes to work. I planned to walk all the way to the other end of downtown, a full half mile, to Melissa's Café Flamingo for a smoothie after my last client, and then back to my car. A mile round trip. I would walk a *mile*! I hung my suit in the large closet in my office and donned a sports bra, tank top, and yoga pants. I pulled my hair back into a scrunchie and slipped into my sneakers. I felt powerful. I dropped my suit and purse into the trunk of my car and I was off, fanny pack and all.

It was still suffocatingly hot and sunny at five-thirty. As soon as I left the Executive Suites building, I began to sweat. By the time I reached Madaline Richards' real estate office, about one third of the way, I'd melted. There, standing out front as usual, observing her domain, was Madaline. And with her was a woman in a gauzy maroon dress, its hem floating around her ankles, and a ripped, fraying scarf draped over her shoulders. She was full figured–dare I say buxomy?—with hair atop her head in a messy pile held together as if by magic. She was Isabella Bolton.

"Pari," Madaline grabbed my arm and I remembered how much I hated to sweat.

"I'm so sorry," I said. "I'm sweating like mad."

"It's hot to be out for a hike," Isabella said. Her voice was deep and throaty, like she'd smoked cigarettes all her life, but not unpleasant.

Madaline introduced us. "Pari is a psychologist. The one I was telling you about."

"You've got a ghost in your office."

"I assure you I do not."

"A skeptic." Isabella's brows flew up and she smiled as if she'd caught a tasty morsel in a fish net.

"There's no ghost in my office," I said. "That's all I know for sure."

"Perhaps you're not open to its existence. We sometimes need to allow a certain energy—"

"Prime ourselves to believe what we want to believe? No thanks."

Madaline gasped. "Now, Pari."

"I really have to go," I said. "I'm trying to get some exercise."

"I'll walk with you a bit," Isabella said. "My parlor is just down the block."

Her *parlor*? What could I do? I slowed my pace to let her walk with me.

"I admire your skepticism, you know. Too often I get people who believe so much that they don't really listen to what I have to say."

"Is that right?" I was trying to be polite.

"We're not all that different in what we do. We help people."

I let that hang out there between us for a while until we reached her storefront.

"This is my parlor," she said, holding up an arm as if she were in a showroom and this was a new invention. "Would you like to come in? No pressure."

"No thanks."

"Maybe another time."

"I don't think so. We're not really alike at all Ms. Bolton."

"Call me Isabella." At least she didn't want me to call her Madame Isabella. "How are we so different?"

I shrugged. "I have a doctorate, for one thing."

"So do I."

"You do?"

"I do."

"In what? Crystals?"

Isabella finally lost her smile and I felt terrible. I was being rude and I needed to stop.

90

"I was a professor of history for fifteen years. Retired recently. And now I do this." She smiled again. "So, what else makes us different?"

"I listen to my clients," I said. "You talk."

"That's true. Very true. But we both want to help."

I tried to smile. I really did. But honestly, I didn't believe what Isabella Bolton did helped anyone. "Please forgive me," I said. "I'm afraid I'm touchy about this whole ghost thing. And I'm sweaty. I hate sweating."

"I totally understand."

"Anyway, I'm sorry for being rude."

"Let's not hear another word about it, Dr. Logan."

"Pari," I said. I held out my hand for a polite shake but she pulled me in to a hug–a full-body, granny-squeeze, embrace–pinning my arms to my sides. "Oh," I said. "I'm so sweaty."

"No worries." She released me and held me at arms' length. "Sweat is perfectly natural."

"And it's all over your dress." And you know how that final word is hanging there in your head and your conscience warns you not to say it but sometimes it just slips out? Yeah, I said, "Gross."

"You don't get many hugs, do you?"

"I...uh."

"I should have asked first, but I had the sudden feeling you needed one."

And after a slight caress of my arms, she disappeared into her...parlor. What do you make of that?

Chapter Fourteen

We had a Divas Lunch at Brunch the next day. Brunch is not the best place for a Divas Lunch. There is very little seating and definitely not enough inside. The only reason we got a table was because Sophie, bless her, arrived ahead of time and snagged the only big one, draping the empty chairs with hats and shopping bags. It's a ruse, certainly, and we're not especially proud of it. We try not to do it too often and Melanie hasn't complained.

"I hope you didn't mind saving seats." I was late, but none of the others had arrived.

"A full hour of uninterrupted reading and people watching?" she said. "It was heaven." Sophie, like many of my Diva friends makes her own schedule. Retail has its perks.

Karen, my bestie and preferred office supplier, was next to show up. Then Kaya, all decked out as an advertisement for vintage clothing. Vanessa and Melissa staggered to the table last and dropped into their seats begging for cold drinks.

Downtown was hopping that morning. The shops had opened at ten, all the restaurants were piping out lunch aromas, the bakery was pumping sugar dust into the air, and the Divas were in various states of awake. Melissa spent the night before at Tracks with Vanessa.

They'd started up a Fifth Wednesday Game Night.

"How many months are you going to have a fifth Wednesday?" Kaya said.

"Something like five next year. Anyway, we played Pictionary with these huge white boards and dry erase markers. Ten teams. Our team was knocked out in the first round. It was Vanessa's fault."

"How was it my fault?"

"You just wanted to be on Christopher's team. He's a reporter, not an artist. And way too literal."

"Is literal bad in Pictionary?" Kaya asked.

"Absolutely. There are all sorts of ways to get someone to say the right word. Anyway, Sam Preston's team won."

"Sam Preston was there?" It just popped out of my mouth and my cheeks flushed. "He sure is ingratiating himself downtown." Fabulous recovery, if I do say so myself.

"That sounds like an insult," Sophie said.

"And I hear there's going to be a karaoke night coming soon," Melissa said. "But not on Wednesdays."

"We were out very late," Vanessa said.

"I'm the one who has to open a restaurant before dawn; I don't know what you're complaining about." She was teasing.

"Have you ever had to put in a perm when you're half asleep? I don't think so." Vanessa had a point.

"I guess the first thing we should discuss," Karen said, ready to start official Diva business. She pulled a strand of red behind one ear (she'd lately stopped wearing barrettes and I think she rather liked playing with her hair when it fell over her eyes). "...is what to call the new diva."

"What new diva?" I said.

"The psychic."

"Why not Psychic Diva?"

"That's not very creative," Melissa said.

"Divine Diva," Sophie said.

That was a hit.

"We should welcome her, somehow," Melissa said. "We should encourage her to set up a booth at Triple F.

Do you think she knows about it?"

"She's a psychic," Vanessa said. "Of course she knows."

"I'm sure she'll find out soon enough," Sophie said.

Melanie came to our table, breathless and with her apron strings dangling. "What'll it be, ladies?"

"Do you ever have a day off?" Kaya asked her.

"To do what?" she said. "Cry alone in my big empty house?" There were condolences all around, but she brushed them off. "Oh, it's not that bad. At least I'll get the house in the divorce. Working keeps my mind off it."

"Second on the list," Karen said after Melanie had hurried off, "is getting Melanie a date."

"Too soon," I said. Her husband had left her only a few months before and as much as she might pretend she liked to work to get over it, the truth was Melanie had always liked to work. "What she needs," I mused out loud, "is someone who works as much as she does."

"You said too soon." Karen gave me a playful elbow nudge.

"I have another project in mind," Melissa said.

"You sound excited." Sophie closed her book and shoved it in the bag next to her chair.

"Well," Melissa said. "With all this ghost stuff going on–"

"Oh, no." I'd had enough of ghosts already.

"I feel like some of you are...how can I say it...well, you think you're smarter than me."

"Why do you think that?" Sophie said.

"Because of my experience with a ghost. Karen!"

"What?"

"You just rolled your eyes at me."

Karen dutifully frowned. "I'm sorry. I thought I was being funny."

"It doesn't feel funny to me."

"What ghost?" Sophie said.

The five of us, without Sophie, had been a loose set for a couple of years until a few months before. It was Sophie who brought us together, made us an actual gaggle of friends. But she'd missed quite a lot and I can't say she's the worse for it. We'd heard Melissa's ghost story several times, especially right after it happened last year. And now we got to hear it once more as we watched the skepticism emerge on Sophie's face.

It went something like this: It was late and Melissa was alone in her office at Café Flamingo. While going over a complicated catering order she suddenly heard faint music, so she left her office and went into the darkened dining room. It seemed as if everywhere she turned, the origin of the music changed. Chills ran up and down her body, so she said. And then, just as she'd decided it must be coming from outside, a figure appeared at one of the tables along the south-facing window of her restaurant. A woman, she said. Eating soup. Melissa ran to flip the main light switch and when the room was filled with light, the woman disappeared.

"You thought you saw something," Vanessa said gently. "But it disappeared when you turned on the lights."

"Not in an instant," she said. "She just...faded away."

"Oooh," Kaya said. "I just got all tingly."

I did my best not to roll my eyes. "The mind makes patterns."

"You're saying my mind created a woman in a little pillbox hat eating soup at a table for two?"

"Honestly, Melissa." Kaya pulled her thick dark curls into a headband away from her face. "There's got to be more evidence than something you experienced alone. In the dark. And after you were already a little freaked out."

"I know what I saw."

Sophie said, "We don't dispute what you saw...just what it actually *was* that you saw."

"Ever since I told you all about it, except for you Sophie, you've made little comments here and there. Jokes at my expense."

"We didn't realize..." Kaya said.

"Here's my project." Melissa held up a hand to forestall any further discussion on the matter. "None of you believe in ghosts." And before we could all speak again, she slapped her hand on the table. "Not like me. So, I propose a series of activities."

"What sorts of activities?" I was not happy.

"You're the worst offender," Melissa said.

"How's that?"

"You act as if it's already a proven fact that ghosts don't exist. You're not open minded."

"I have a very open mind," I said. "Just not so open my brains fall out."

"Oh, ha ha," she mocked.

"Okay," Kaya said, a little too eager for my liking. "What do you want us to do?"

"I will plan activities for the group and if by...let's say Halloween night, you still don't believe in ghosts, fine. At least you gave it some thought. And maybe at the end of it, you won't think I'm crazy."

"Nobody said you were crazy," I said. "Did they?" I looked around at the Divas. "Who said she was crazy?"

They shook their heads, innocence bouncing all over their faces—except for Vanessa.

"Okay," Vanessa said. "It was me. I confess. But I didn't mean *crazy* crazy."

Melissa smiled. "I know you didn't. But just the same."

"And I said *loco*."

"Like there's a difference?" Melissa said.

"Will these activities have anything to do with Sam Preston?" I didn't really want to know the answer.

"He's the Ghost Whisperer, Pari," Melissa said. "How could they not involve him?"

"Yeah, Pari," Karen said with a wink at me. "You'll have to spend time with Sam Preston."

I glared at her, daring her on pain of death to tell the others what had happened between Sam and me. "The last thing Sam Preston needs," I said, "is more people joining him in his delusion." I was overruled.

So, Let's Review:

1. The Downtown Divas (some of them):
Sophie Childers. Bookish. Introvert. Book and cat lover. Boyfriend Reese. Does not believe in ghosts.

Karen Morgan. Morgan's Office Supply. On the shy side. Loves a great pencil. Does not believe in ghosts.

Kaya Channing. Kaya Vintage Clothing. Ready for love, apparently. Does not believe in ghosts...but it would be nice.

Vanessa Torres. Glam It Up! Extrovert. Maybe believes in ghosts.

Melissa Stathem. Café Flamingo. Enthusiastically extroverted. Absolutely believes in ghosts.

2. The Downtown Divos:

Eric Lawson. Consultant. Sweet, but a little too perfect. Does not believe in ghosts.

Reese Fuller. Owner of Summer Sun Surf and Beachwear. Reluctant lover of cats. Stance regarding ghosts unknown.

Noah Holland. Novelist. Secret identity: flower shop owner. Ghost opinions unknown.

Sam Preston. Photog. Obnoxious. Believes in ghosts.

I only included Reese and Noah because I didn't want it to look like I was preoccupied with Sam Preston. I think it worked nicely. Even with the unknowns, I felt certain non-ghost believers outnumbered ghost believers and if we worked together, we could tamp this whole nonsense down into some sort of manageable size.

I'm afraid the ghosts had other ideas.

Chapter Fifteen

Friday night Eric took me to a play in a little community theater across town. There's a larger playhouse right here in Downtown Strawbridge and I asked him why we didn't go see *Hello Dolly* there.

"The Garage puts on plays written by locals," he said. "It's like Indie music. You like Indie bands, right?"

I had no answer for that. Located in an old plaza at barely fifty-percent occupancy with stores selling futons, mattresses and used exercise equipment, the theater was tiny, only five rows of metal chairs and a stage big enough for a ventriloquist act and nothing more. But the ten members of the cast made it work. The play was about Little Mamsy, mother of four, whose oldest son Robbie brought his girlfriend home for dinner who turned out to be Mrs. Gambolini, Mamsy's high school gym teacher who she'd thought was a lesbian. Halfway through, when Mamsy, Robbie, Mrs. Gambolini, along with the rest of Mamsy's family is having dessert after a tense meal–the entire play took place around an invisible dinner table– Mrs. Gambolini perked up and said, "Oh, now I remember you, Mamsy. You were the girl who failed volleyball."

I burst out laughing. It was *funny*. But no one else thought so. Especially Mamsy who went on with a soliloquy about her fear of balls. I laughed again and Eric shushed me. He *shushed* me! I spent the remainder of the evening trying to keep from snorting.

"I'm so sorry," I told him once we were outside. "I just thought it was funny."

We made our way across the now dark parking lot where Eric had parked his car under a flickering light on a cracked concrete post.

"That's okay," he said. "It *was* funny."

"But you weren't laughing."

"No one else was. I figured it was supposed to be serious."

"Eric," I said stopping to face him as he opened the passenger side door for me. "A would-be lesbian gym teacher. Fear of balls. It had to be satire."

Mamsy's Fears was reviewed in the Gazette and it appeared our resident theater critic, Lionel Beardsley, couldn't tell if the play was meant to be farce or not, either. Eric was vindicated, but I never mentioned it to him. When he saw me to my door that night, he asked if I'd like to go fishing with him the next morning. After the initial shock, my first concern was getting on another boat.

"No boat," he said. "Just me and you down at the inlet."

"On land?"

"On land."

Look, I'm not the outdoorsy sort and there's nothing wrong with that. We don't have to be all things, to count ourselves strong independent women. So I will not tolerate snide remarks over what I am about to disclose. Millions of women love the water. Millions love fishing. I imagine millions love hunting as well. I'm just not one of them. I eat fish; they're delicious. But I've never felt the need to prove my worth by catching one. Still, I admit the shudder I have to quell at the thought of touching a fish does our gender no favors. So, I will be strong. How bad could it be?

Eric picked me up at seven in the morning and drove us out to Sebastian inlet, north side. We paid a fee and he showed his fishing permit and purchased one for me. I am now the proud owner of a completely useless fishing license. We parked under the A1A overpass and from the back of his Bolt, Eric pulled a collapsible wagon and loaded it up with gear. A tackle box; two coolers, one with sodas, water, and snacks, and the other for, I assumed, dead fish; a bag of sun screen and repellents of all sorts; and two folding chairs. He brought five fishing poles.

"Who else is coming?" I asked.

"Just us," he said, not at all bothered by the fact that we had four available hands between us–and I'd need two for one pole–and five poles. What do I know about fishing? Nothing. "Did you bring a hat?"

"I did." I dug my straw sun hat from my oversized bag and plopped it on my head. I was ready this time. Capris and tennis shoes–the old ugly ones I used for potting plants–gloves in case I had to touch a worm or a fish, and the stained tee I wore once when helping my mother paint her house. I was prepared to get dirty.

"Where do we buy the worms?" I asked him.

He *laughed*. He laughed the way he should have laughed when Mamsy said she'd never get over getting hit with that fly ball when she was seven. "This is salt water. We're using shrimp and mullet."

Now I know for a fact you can use worms in saltwater fishing because I'd Googled it that morning, bleary-eyed, when I studied how to bait a hook with the pesky wigglers. Shrimp can't be much different from worms when it came to getting them on a hook, right? *Hah.*

The park was scattered with people. On the west side, opposite the beach, swimmers, sunbathers, and picnickers enjoyed a cove of moss-green water.

I volunteered to pull the wagon and left the management of the fishing poles and their hooks to Eric. We weaved among cars toward the inlet where a catwalk, dotted with fishermen, was tucked beneath the enormous bridge. From there we walked along the water on a sea wall before finally reaching the sturdy, concrete pier stretching beyond the beach. I followed Eric, switching hands occasionally to keep a good grasp on the wagon handle, until he found what he declared was the perfect spot, nearly to the endpoint. I'm sure we'd walked a quarter of a mile by then. I leaned against the thick metal railing and looked down into the teal water below. Across the bridge, on the south side of the inlet, a jetty jutted briefly toward the sea, on which people fished while risking their lines on the rocks. On our side, a spattering of surfers floated atop the waves, yards from shore. It was only eight o'clock by then, sunny with a warm salty breeze, and the pier was filled with poles. A few radios competed for attention, gulls screeched occasionally, the varying smells of fresh and decaying fish hit my nose, and I spotted the dorsal fins of a pod of dolphins arching over the surface of the ocean.

"Do you want me to bait your hook for you?" Eric said.

"I can bait a hook." Damn it, I thought. *I can bait a hook.*

He opened the other cooler and pulled out what looked like paper-wrapped deli meat. It was the mullet, cut in chunks. Beneath it was a slotted tray and when he lifted it, I saw that the cooler was filled with saltwater and shrimp.

"They're alive!"

He laughed again. "Of course they're alive."

"Okay," I mumbled. And once more with confidence, "*Okay.*" I reached in and after a few tries, grabbed one. "They still have their shells on!"

More laughter. "It's an exoskeleton."

"Sorry," I said. "I've never fished before." Of course they have their exoskeletons on. *Of course, Pari. What were you thinking?*

"Never?" He was truly astonished. "Your dad never took you?"

I shook my head. "It wasn't my thing. He and my brother went out all the time. My mom and I did our thing."

"Shopping?"

"No." I was perturbed. "We took art classes and went to museums and shows."

"So," he looked at the shrimp I'd held up, squeezed between my thumb and fingers. "You sure you don't want help?"

I grabbed the pole he'd set out for me and leaned it against the railing a few feet away from him. "Sorry little dude," I mumbled, taking the hook and shoving it into the shrimp, right through the shell, out the other side and back in again. *There. That wasn't so hard.* Now I just had to cast the line. Eric gave me a quick tutorial. Click and hold. Cast and let go. My first try went about twenty feet. But I reeled it in and did it again and again until I got the hang of it. And I only went through three shrimp doing it. We sat in plastic woven beach chairs, our poles resting on the railing, for three hours catching absolutely nothing. Eric didn't seem to mind at all, though every time someone else pulled a fish out of the water he dragged me over to look at it.

"Shouldn't we have caught something by now?"

He shrugged. "Some days you get nothing."

"My dad always caught something."

"Was any of it frozen?" He chuckled. "If I don't catch anything, I stop by Publix and get a filet."

Suddenly I felt a quick pull on my pole. I stood from the chair and waited, trembling with fear and anticipation. I felt it again and jerked the pole backward. I had definitely caught something. I let Eric talk me through it, reeling and resting and reeling and resting until we could see a fish just beneath the water.

"Holy cow," he said. "You got a big one."

"What is it? What is it?"

Fishermen (and women...fisherpeople?), kids too, were gathering around me, encouraging me, *oohing* and *aahing*.

"It's a snook," Eric yelled.

"Must be a ten pounder," someone said.

"I can't get it," I wailed.

Eric stood behind me and helped me reel it in and once we had it above water, a woman in a hook-filled fishing hat, gray hair falling down her back, leaned way over the railing, held steady by a huge man in a fishing vest, and scooped it up in a long-handled net.

103

"You did it," Eric said. As soon as the net was settled on the pier, he wrestled with it, pulled the enormous silver fish out by the gills and shoved it toward me.

I screamed and trampled three kids behind me trying to get away from it.

"Go on, honey," the old woman said. "You've got to get your picture took with it."

Timidly, I approached the monster. "Sorry, fish," I said. I slid my gardening gloves on and grabbed its tail with both hands as Eric let go of the head. It twitched and I held it away from me, a queasy smile on my face.

The picture Eric sent me from his phone shows me, terrified, trying to hold a slimy squirming fish as high as I could. I didn't look happy. But I still sent it to Daddy and Rav. Eric slapped the fish on a table littered with scales and guts, right there at the pier. First he measured it to make sure it was a keeper. Twenty-nine inches. He taught me how to scale it and I only got three of the little buggers in my mouth. I let *him* do the fileting.

The best part of our day was eating the fish. We took it to the little restaurant by the pier and they fried it for us. We bought coleslaw and hush puppies to go with it and sat out on the deck under a big umbrella watching people jerking their poles and reeling in nothing. A few beach goers passed us on their way to the surf.

"We should do this every weekend," Eric said.

I looked at him and frowned. It was fun. But not every weekend fun.

Chapter Sixteen

I was home by two that afternoon and Eric was off to see his parents. I suspected they were going out on the boat again, so I didn't even pretend to want to spend the rest of the day with him. Still, I thought we might do something that night. It was Saturday, after all. But he didn't mention it, and neither did I. After a glorious shower and a shedding of salt and fish guts, I took an iced tea onto my balcony to relax. I sat in a lounge chair, propped my feet up on one of the wood planks of the railing and played with the leaves of the areca palm next to me. It was a good day, even if it was fishing. I'd had fun with Eric, but I couldn't get rid of the feeling I was missing something. And while I did think for a moment that a cat cuddled up on my lap just then would be a comfort...that wasn't it. Karen's call was a welcome distraction.

"So?" she said. "How was *Hello Dolly?*"

With a loud sigh, I pulled at my scrunchie, letting my wet hair down to dry in the natural heat. "We didn't see it. We went to a little theater in a strip mall."

I swear I could hear her smirking. "Seriously?"

"It wasn't so bad. The play was hilarious, but I was the only one who laughed." I told her the basic plot of *Mamsy's Fears*, including all mentions of balls. "Did you see the review this morning?"

"I didn't know they reviewed that sort of thing. I'll have to look for it. Where is he taking you tonight?"

"We went fishing this morning."

There was a long pause. "Fishing? Like...with bait and a hook."

"I'm afraid so."

She laughed so hard I thought I heard a snort. "I can*not* imagine you fishing."

"I'll send you the picture."

"Only if you want it plastered all over social media."

"You wouldn't."

"Pari," she said. "You went fishing. That's big news. Did you catch anything? A shoe, maybe? A message in a bottle at least."

"I'll have you know I caught the biggest fish on the pier."

"A real fish? Or a blowfish?"

"It was a snook. And we ate it, too."

"Raw?"

"Don't be daft."

"Well, that's lunch. I suppose that counts as a date. Even if you had to catch your own food. But what about tonight?"

I sipped my tea. "I admit, I expected we'd do something later. But now that I think about it–"

"He didn't ask you out for Saturday night *again*?"

"I don't think we're at that place yet."

"What place? The not letting a beautiful girl sit at home on a Saturday night place? Because I'm in that place, Pari. Without the beautiful–"

"Stop."

"Whatever. It's not the worst thing in the world, but I'd really rather be out. On a date. With a man."

"I hear you."

"I don't get it."

"We're just dating. We're not a couple yet."

"I bet Sam Preston is available on Saturday nights."

"Don't go there. I mean it."

"Fine. Well, I've got a brand new pair of roller

skates..."

"Sometimes I think you're high."

"Pari, you need a real cultural education," she said with a laugh. "Let's go out."

"I'm not roller skating."

She started singing a song about roller skates and keys before the line went silent. Karen picked me up after dark and we sat in her car with the air conditioner running, considering all the places we could go downtown. Tracks, where there would probably be a jazz band. Pub's Sports Bar where there would be, obviously, sports on the televisions. Maybe even MacAuley Awley's for a late-night snack and some improv. But we knew the whole time we would end up at The Fort.

"We should walk," she said. "We can't hold our liquor. Let's plan to walk it off and I'll sleep at your place again."

"It's hot. We'll be sweaty by the time we get there."

"We'll cool off."

"We'll stink."

"We'll be in a bar, everybody will smell."

"It's September. In Florida. We could *die*."

She laughed. "One. It's not that far. You walked to Brunch in the middle of the day and didn't whine about it."

"I wasn't wearing Kenneth Coles."

"And two. It's in the mid-eighties. We won't die."

So, I went back up to my apartment and grabbed a pair of sneakers while Karen dug some flops from her trunk and we carried our heels to The Fort where we changed back before going in. A quick stop in the ladies' room for a cool wet towel-off and a spritz of Karen's Jo Malone Orange Blossom Cologne–travel size and always tucked in her purse–and we were ready for the evening. The Fort was always packed on Saturday nights, but for some odd reason, most people around here prefer to stand, so it was easy enough for us to find a little table upstairs overlooking the bar and dance floor. When a waitress showed up, Karen suggested margaritas.

"But I'd like a limit, please. Just two."

The waitress winked at me.

"Three at the most," I found myself saying.

"Sure thing," she said. As she headed down the stairs, Vanessa came up in a shimmering sapphire tube dress and a gorgeous pair of ocean green four-inch-heeled sandals. Sling backs with a gauze bow tied at the ankle. As soon as she saw us, she squealed.

"Divas," she said.

"Are those Jimmy Choos?" I said.

She laughed. "You think I'd pay a thousand bucks for some simple shoes, Cariño? I put the bows on myself. You like them?"

"I love them."

"May we join you?"

And suddenly there was Sam Preston–*of course*–and his friend Christopher, who sidled up to Vanessa draping an arm across her shoulders. They pulled chairs around our table and sat down, Sam beside me. It looked as if he'd put on a newer t-shirt, but the rest of him remained carelessly casual.

He turned to me and leaned over. "Dateless again, I see."

"As are you."

"But I don't have a girlfriend."

Hmph.

"I thought you two would never go out again after last Friday," Vanessa said.

"What happened last Friday?" Sam winked at me. "I thought we all had a great time."

Vanessa spilled, "These two got so drunk Pari vomited all over Eric's boat the next day."

"Vanessa!"

"The boy owns a boat," Sam said.

"It was his parents' boat," I said. "And it wasn't all over it. Just once. Over the side."

"Well," Sam said with a sly smile. "Maybe it was the sea and not the spirits."

"Could we please not talk about it? How do you even know that?"

"There are no secrets among Divas." Vanessa turned to Sam. "Karen and Pari hardly ever go out."

"We go out," Karen said. "Just not to bars."

"And yet," Sam said, "here you are...again."

Karen, in what I can only assume was an attempt at salvaging my reputation said, "Pari and Eric already had a date today." And then she ruined it by adding, "They went fishing."

"What?" Vanessa said. "I would never."

"Not with those nails," Christopher said.

"I could do it," she said. "Even with the nails. I simply choose not to. It's boring."

"That's true," I said. "And hot."

"So you'll never fish again?" Sam said.

"I didn't say that. I might do it again. Yes, I think I would. I caught a big one."

He smirked. "Prepare for the fish tale, folks."

"It's true." I pulled my phone from my purse and showed them all the picture.

"Nice snook," Sam said.

"Do you fish?"

"We live on the coast; of course I fish."

"Well, it was my first time."

"That's how they get you," he said. "The fish. They let you have one the first time and then for the next six years you sit for hours with nary a nibble."

"I guess that explains all the beer on the pier."

"Let's do it, then," Christopher said. "The five of us. Maybe next weekend."

"No thanks," Karen said. "I'm not against fishing, but I'm not going to be the odd girl out."

"We'll invite a bunch of people," Sam said.

"Next weekend's too soon," I said. "I can't see fishing more than twice a year, personally."

Luckily, the band started up and all talk of fishing was replaced with shouting about music and, for some odd reason, shoveling. The music was...interesting. And loud. If I read the name on the bass drum correctly, they were Bar Maids From Hell. There was shrieking. I was on my second drink and tipsy when the Bar Maids took a break and the DJ attempted to apologize with some smooth R&B.

Karen said, "Okay, it's a date."

"What's a date?" I said.

"Next weekend."

"I don't want to fish again."

"Where have you been?" Sam said. "We're going birding."

"What was all that about shoveling?" I said.

They looked around at one another and then laughed.

"Shoveler," Sam said. I looked at him blankly. "The northern shovelers are here."

"Christopher has an SUV," Vanessa said. "We're going on a wildlife drive. You have to come."

"How early do I have to get up?"

"You work for a living," Sam said. "I'm sure you can manage."

"Unlike you," I said.

"The birds are noisier in the morning," Christopher said. "Easier to find."

"We have to go to Sandy Point," Vanessa said. "We should get an early start."

Sam looked at me. "Is that okay with you?"

"I haven't agreed to go."

"Please, Pari," Karen said. "Let's do it. Get a life, remember?"

Sam chuckled and I glared at him. "Why do you want to go so badly?" I asked her.

"Maybe she likes to try new things," Sam said. "It's fun. You know what fun is, don't you?"

"Fine," I said. "I'll go for you, Karen. But you owe me."

We sat through another set of Bar Maids in which they brought a man out of the audience and sang to him as two of them tied him up. He enjoyed it immensely by my calculations, until they forced him to hop off the stage, still entangled in ropes and chains. Karen and I were ready to go. I wasn't tipsy anymore and she'd had only one drink all evening, but Sam insisted on walking us home, for protection. Vanessa and Christopher planned to drive to my place to pick him up and take him back to his car.

"We can drive you home," Christopher offered.

I looked pleadingly at her, but Karen insisted on walking. I told Sam he didn't have to escort us, but it was after midnight, so I let it play out. Outside, we changed back into our sneakers and walked behind the nightclub and along Manatee Road. I took Karen's arm and moved her forward a bit, leaving Sam trailing behind us.

"Why are we going birding?" I asked Karen.

"I told you; it sounds like fun."

"You'll love it," Sam said.

I glanced back at him, wishing he'd at least *pretend* he couldn't hear us. "Seriously, Karen."

Once we arrived at my apartment complex, the three of us stood under a streetlight swatting at bugs while waiting for Christopher to pick Sam up.

Karen started toward her car. "You two don't need me."

I grabbed her arm and nearly tore it off. "But you were going to..."

"No need," she said, peeling my fingers from her wrist. "I'm perfectly sober. I'll call you later."

I stood and watched as she got into her Kia, revved the engine, and left me with Sam Preston. I turned to grimace awkwardly at him, but he was grinning, as if he knew Karen had left us alone together on purpose. I swatted bugs again.

"You could walk back to The Fort," I said. "I'll go on up."

"I'd better wait here for Chris. Don't want any trouble."

"Sure, I guess." I glanced longingly up to my apartment. "I can keep you company until he gets here."

"I appreciate it. Let's get out of the bug zone." He took my arm and we moved away from the light. "This is your car, right?"

We leaned against the trunk of my little Honda and I scooted away from him a bit. There was a buzzing in my ears, not exactly like mosquitos, and I felt electric, as if I'd get a shock if he touched me. Maybe I was still tipsy.

"So..." I felt like I had to say something. "Do you just look at the birds or take pictures?"

"I take pictures of everything."

"Except ghosts."

"Funny."

"I'm a regular comic."

He stood away from the car and faced me. I could still see his face in the light we'd just left.

"You're photogenic," he said.

"How can you tell?"

"It's what I do for a living."

"How does a person make a living taking pictures? It seems like it'd be difficult."

"I make a lot doing events. I teach classes and take people on tours."

I flinched at the mention of photography classes and just kept repeating 'Ron Bernard' in my head. How embarrassing would it have been to wind up taking a class from Sam Preston? Especially after kissing him? And there I was, in the dark, tipsy again, with the kissee in question. *What was I thinking?* Despite my alcoholic state, I deftly moved the subject away from classes. "What's a photography tour?"

"I've done walking tours of Boston and San Francisco. I'd like to do something in South America."

"I'm impressed."

He smiled. "And I do some portrait work. So, if you ever need a picture..."

"I'll keep you in mind."

For some reason, I was standing. I don't recall how it happened. But before I knew it, he'd stepped closer to me. He put his hand on my back and pulled me to him and we stood, our lips inches apart, looking at each other.

"This one's on me," he said and kissed me.

I can't for the life of me figure out why I didn't step back. But I didn't. Instead, I put my arms around his neck and let myself melt into him. But as soon as I heard a car approaching, I jumped backwards, hit the trunk of my car, and started to slide off. In trying to stand I lurched forward and stumbled. So there we were, silhouetted in the headlights of Christopher's SUV, me halfway to the ground and Sam holding me up, as if in the middle of the stupidest dance move ever. I could hear Vanessa shouting, "You go, girl," over Christopher's laughter. Sam and I managed to right ourselves, brush ourselves off, and shake hands like platonic acquaintances. But I knew this would be blown way out of proportion on the Diva network.

As soon as I was inside my apartment, I called Karen.

"You left me stranded with Sam Preston!"

"Did you kiss him again?"

"No."

She was silent, as if she knew more was coming.

"He kissed me this time."

"He likes you."

"He does not."

"You've smooched twice. You can't tell me there isn't something there. And whenever I see you together, there's sexual tension all over the place."

"The first kiss was a fluke. Just a...blunder. And this one was like, his revenge."

"Revenge kissing? I'll have to put that in a book."

"Don't. It sounds creepy."

"You said it."

"I didn't mean it like that. Anyway, it'll never happen again."

"Uh, huh. Sure."

"Really, we don't like each other."

"He talked to you all night."

"Nobody could talk over the Bar Maids. And we spent what little quiet time there was arguing. He likes beer; I like liquor. He likes sports; I like romcoms. He likes dogs; I don't like pets."

"He was trying to get to know you."

"He told me he couldn't trust a person who hated dogs."

"But you don't hate them. You've never had one."

"I had a dog when I was eight. His name was Ruff. Or Boxy. I can't remember."

"You can't remember the name of your dog?"

"It was Ruff. Definitely Ruff. Boxy was the cat."

"That's just sad."

"Own it, Karen. You're trying to fix me up with Sam."

"I am not. This is about Richard."

"Wait. What?"

"Sam's bringing Richard. You remember him from last week. He was cute, right?"

"You're fixing me up with Richard?"

"No. Richard's mine. I need you to occupy Sam."

"Why can't Vanessa and Chris occupy him?"

"You can't be serious."

"But I don't want to occupy Sam Preston."

"Please, Pari. You said you'd go. You need to be my emotional support...friend."

"You almost said 'dog' didn't you?"

She laughed. "It did come to mind."

And so I agreed to go birding. For an indoor sort of girl, I was spending quite a bit of time outdoors.

Chapter Seventeen

MaryAshford has joined the chat.

MaryAshford: What do you guys talk about before I get here?

SamTheMan: You.

LegitChris: You don't want to know. So are we all set for the interview?

MaryAshford: Flyers are up and out. Advertisement done. I'll check in with the restaurant again tomorrow.

LegitChris: The ghost tour is ready, too. Maps are at the printer.

MaryAshford: Are you ready Sam?

SamTheMan: I could do it with my eyes closed.

MaryAshford: Any more on the Gazette story?

LegitChris: It's a go.

MaryAshford: Is your psychologist friend going to have a problem with it, Sam?

LegitChris: I don't think I'll approach her for an interview. No need to ruffle feathers.

SamTheMan: She'll be surprised though. We should tell her about it.

LegitChris: Her friends will tell her.

MaryAshford: Why don't you tell her, Sam?

SamTheMan: If I can bring it up naturally.

MaryAshford: Any more on the kiss thing?

LegitChris: Funny you should mention it.

SamTheMan: It's nothing.

LegitChris: They did it again.

MaryAshford: You know, charm's one thing. But this is going too far.

SamTheMan: You think I'm just trying to get into her... office?

LegitChris: Can't. Make. Joke.

MaryAshford: Isn't that what you're doing?

...

...

LegitChris: Which one of us are you talking to?

MaryAshford: Either one.

LegitChris: Yes, I was making a joke.

SamTheMan: I'm not kissing the woman to get into her office. I don't think.

MaryAshford: Very unprofessional, Sam. I think we should forget the office and just do the sleepover as a general haunted building. Forget the ice queen. Nothing but trouble down that road.

LegitChris: Unless he likes her.

SamTheMan: You can't call her ice queen if we can't.

MaryAshford: You can't let your relationship problems interfere with the business.

LegitChris: What makes you think they'll have relationship problems?

MaryAshford: History, I guess.

LegitChris: That's hardly fair.

MaryAshford: Sam spent the first week trying to come up with synonyms for frigid, so I think it's an accurate assumption. The woman doesn't believe in ghosts, anyway. You really think a psychologist is going to go for a ghost hunter?

LegitChris: I think it'd be cute.

SamTheMan: Cute?

LegitChris: Sorry. Vanessa's rubbing off on me.

MaryAshford: Can we just stick to business for a while? Sam, keep your paws off the psychologist.

SamTheMan: Here's where I roll my eyes and say something about being an adult, right?

MaryAshford: Can you give me a ride on Wednesday night?

SamTheMan: Sure thing.

MaryAshford: See you then.

MaryAshford has left the chat.

LegitChris: For a college student, she sure sounds like my mom a lot.

SamTheMan: She is doing a lot of the leg work for us. We should let up on her.

LegitChris: We keep saying that. But we still irritate her.

SamTheMan: I guess we're just irritating guys.

LegitChris: Speak for yourself. I think I'll ask Dr. Logan for an interview. At least she'll be prepared for the story.

SamTheMan: Maybe she'll say yes. If she does, can I be there?

LegitChris: Sparks would fly.

SamTheMan: It'd make a great story.

LegitChris: But not for her.

SamTheMan: You ruin all the fun. So, should I call her?

LegitChris: Oh my god, Mary's right. We're fourteen-year-olds. You're on your own, buddy.

SamTheMan: Gee, thanks. No, okay. I can do this.

LegitChris: Can you?

SamTheMan: I'm a grown up.

LegitChris: You keep telling yourself that. I'm going to go see how the mustache is coming in. Puberty is hell.

SamTheMan: I really don't know what Mary's problem is. We're amazing.

Chapter Eighteen

The next morning, I slept in. Not that I actually *slept.* But watching the sunrise slowly lighting up the window behind the curtains in my bedroom counts. As I snuggled deeper into my pillows, the thought of a feline hopping gracefully onto the bed, sniffing at my nose and meowing for breakfast tugged at my heart.

"Sophie," I muttered. "What have you done to me?" I was thinking of Boxy. She wasn't my cat, but my mom's —followed her around the house all day and cried at the door whenever she left. Those few times a week Boxy deigned to curl up on my lap or against my head at night were special memories of a wonderful childhood. But that was just what they were: memories of a blissful time when I had no obligations and deadlines. "I will resist," I said and eventually dozed off.

My phone woke me a few minutes later. I grudgingly grabbed it from the bedside table and saw it was Sam Preston.

"What?" I said.

"Well, you're charming in the morning."

"I didn't sleep well." I sat up abruptly and wondered why I was telling Sam Preston about my sleeping habits. "I mean, what do you want?"

"How soon they forget," he said, laughing. "I kissed

you last night, remember? So, I'm the one who is supposed to call."

"It's really not necessary."

"I see your point, Dr. Logan. This is getting to be a thing with us."

"No, there's no thing with us."

"Okay, let's say two kisses isn't a thing. Three and it will definitely be a thing. A big thing that we should talk about."

"Agreed, Mr. Preston. If there is a third kiss, we'll talk. But I can guarantee you, we will never kiss again."

"Oh, ouch. Well, nonetheless, I kissed you last night so I'm calling. It's obligatory."

"*There's* a word."

"Mm hm. So, how are you, did you sleep well, can I see you again? All the usual questions a suitor should ask."

"Suitor?"

"It's old-fashioned word Sunday, didn't you know?"

"I did not."

"So...?"

"So, what?"

"How are you?"

"This is really unnecessary."

"Did you sleep well?"

"I've already told you I didn't."

"Can I see you again?"

I paused. Why did I pause? "I'm still seeing Eric."

"But you haven't decided on exclusivity yet, have you?"

"I must have. If I didn't want it to be exclusive..." I couldn't finish that sentence. Why did I even start it?

"You'd see me again?"

"No. I mean. I wouldn't have kissed you. Wait." That made absolutely no sense.

"Uh, huh. I get it." I could almost hear him grinning.

"I'm not awake yet, that's all."

"I'll let you get back to it then."

After we said our goodbyes, I dropped back into the bed and shouted. Nothing in particular, just an *arrrgh*. I had to admit to an attraction–like a gravitational pull toward disaster. Luckily, we don't have to act on every drive we experience, especially when a distinct repulsion exists along with it. Yet, at that moment, I couldn't remember any of my anti-gravity reasons for pulling away, and could only remember kissing Sam Preston. *Arrrgh*. This was just the sort of moment a girl could use a cat to distract her. But as I had no cat, I decided to putter about my apartment. I had a sewing project to finish–a purse modeled after a Prada I'd seen in Orlando, but mine was all cloth, including the straps. I sat on the balcony imagining a cat sitting beside me. Took a walk to Manatee Park and along the tiny little boardwalk there. And then watched an afternoon *Lord of the Rings* movie marathon on television. Not a bad Sunday.

I got a text from Melissa the next Tuesday night. The first challenge was set. On Wednesday evening, WDTS was hosting a reception for Sam Preston and his ghost team at MacAuley Awley's Irish Pub. "There'll be an interview followed by questions. And then we can mingle and meet his team of ghost hunters. I'll see you at 7:00."

I wanted to text her back with, "But I can't see Sam Preston again because we've kissed twice and it will be very awkward considering I swore never to kiss him again." I realized that would make it sound as if the two of us couldn't keep our lips off each other so I decided against it. Not that I was *actually* going to text that. The best thing to do would be to see Sam Preston and get it over with. I'd be professional, and aloof, and he'd know I meant it when I said there would be no more kissing.

Nelson Gardner was wiry thin, pale with a frothy bit of white hair atop his head. His large, round, green eyes always looked at me with longing. He desperately wanted someone to fix him and struggled with the necessary lessons he would need to help himself through his deepening depression. Every Wednesday afternoon at two o'clock, he sat on the little sofa against the wall next to the window in my office, knees together, the toes of his shoes touching and told me sad stories.

"And three good things?" I said. "Has that been any

help at all?"

"I like lizards," he said with a shrug. "I ran over one in the driveway by accident. I can't think of lizards anymore without tearing up."

I nodded. "And have you spoken with your brother recently?"

"I hear there's a psychic opening up next week."

"So soon?" I blurted out.

"Have you ever been to one? I never have. Do you think they really know the future?"

"What do you think?"

He thought about it for a moment and said, "Yes and no. I mean, they tell you the future. But then you know what's going to happen and you'll probably do something to change it. I think I'd like to know just the same."

"Would it change how you feel today?"

"Maybe," he said quietly.

"What would you want to know from a psychic?"

"If I'll ever meet a girl and get married. If I'll ever see my mother again. If I'll be happy."

"You can feel happiness now, Nelson."

"But I'll never be truly happy. Not all-the-time happy."

"No one can be happy all the time."

"If they knew the future..."

My appointment with Ida Nettlebaum didn't go much better, though it started out promising.

"I heard about the psychic. Did you? A psychic; can you believe that? I don't need a psychic."

I breathed a sigh a relief.

But then she said, "My cats on the other hand. That's what this town needs. A pet psychic. Although, if Arnold is inhabiting Whiskers' body, and Aunt Rachel is inside Fluffy, and Scuttlebutt is possessed by Mother. Oh dear. Maybe a people psychic is the thing. What do you think, Dr. Logan? What does your psychological expertise say about such things? Have you seen that Jackson Galaxy? He's...what? Oh, a cat whisperer. Did you hear about the Ghost Whisperer? Did we talk about him last week? I can't remember. I wonder if he whispers to cats possessed by—that's it! That's the very thing, Dr. Logan. My cats are, after all, inhabited by ghosts. I don't suppose you have this Ghost Whisperer's number?"

"Tell me about your mother, Ida."

"Let's just say she chose the right cat to possess."

MacAuley Awley's was packed with people that evening. The back dining room had been cleared of tables, leaving just the booths along the walls. A small stage was set up next to the door to the outside dining area, on which they'd placed stuffed leather chairs for the interview. I squeezed my way through the throng of bodies looking for any Diva I could find. I heard Kaya call my name. She was jumping up and down a few yards away.

"Thank goodness," I said. "I need someone as a witness that I was actually here."

Thankfully, the interview didn't last long. But even at about forty minutes, a lot of people had found their way outside or gone completely. It's a long time to stand and listen to people talk about ghosts. Sam Preston had dressed for the occasion...the same way he dressed every time I'd seen him. Dumpy jeans, a t-shirt, and worn-out sneakers. His reporter friend Christopher Reynolds sat next to him, much less dumpy. And a woman was at the end of the stage. Shoulder length hair, the color of chocolate; wire rimmed glasses she kept pushing up on her nose. Her name was Mary Ashford, she said, and she was a student of paranormal studies at WBU Paranormal Institute. I nearly laughed out loud while she was speaking, but Kaya was there to nudge me into behaving.

Sam was asked about the ghosts downtown, the stories of Aranthia especially. "Brevard County is one of the most haunted places in Florida, surprisingly."

"Is it really a surprise?" I whispered to Kaya.

"Isn't it?"

"It's not very cosmopolitan."

"There aren't as many ghosts in big cities?"

"Too many rational people for the stories to get traction, I'd think."

Somebody hushed us. At that point we could see the

rest of the Divas at a booth on the right-side wall and we made our way over. Sam was asked about how he got involved in ghost hunting.

"I've always had a fascination with the spirit world," he said.

Christopher blurted out, "*Ghostbusters*! It was *Ghostbusters*, for me."

That brought out a lot of laughs and the talk digressed into ghost films and ghosts in literature. Finally the question and answer period arrived and most people wanted to know about equipment, spectrometers, if that's even a thing, what do ghosts want, can they cross over, etc. When Melissa raised her hand, I wanted to climb under the table.

"Would you say," she said, her voice squeakier when she tried to yell over the crowd, "your plans for tours and stuff would help people who don't believe in ghosts to believe?"

I looked at Sam and I swear he was staring right at me with that smirk on his lips.

"Maybe," he said. "But for most skeptics, it would take an actual sighting or paranormal experience to change their minds."

"Wouldn't you say, though," I found myself shouting and shoving Kaya out of the booth to stand next to Melissa, "most skeptics are rationalists and would recognize the mind creates patterns and interprets biological reactions to align with our beliefs and therefore would naturally question their own senses if they saw something for which the only existing evidence is individual experience?"

Sam nodded and the room went silent. "And those same skeptics would claim a group sighting is nothing more than mass hysteria."

"Mass hysteria is a proven psychological phenomenon." I heard grumbles and a few low boos. "We know, for example, the Salem Witch Trials did not actually uncover any witches. Or are you going to claim otherwise?"

Sam shifted in his chair and looked uncomfortable, not an easy thing for someone in jeans with a hole in one knee. "I don't deal with witches," he said.

"Because they'd be visible?"

"Okay," the emcee interrupted. "Why don't we move on to the sharing portion of our evening."

I watched Sam and he watched me while people lined up to get on stage and tell their ghost stories, until he had to turn his attention to the first hopeful.

"Do we have to stay for this part?" I asked Melissa.

"Yes," she said. I sat down next to Kaya and watched as Melissa joined the eager hauntees.

"We'll have to stay at least until she tells her story," Sophie said.

"She's like, fifteenth in line," I protested.

The sharing went on for two hours, but the upside was that we got a table order of beer cheese with Guinness pretzel bites and potato gratin stacks. I wouldn't recommend stress eating, and I'm not sure that was what was going on, but I do know I ate more than my fair share. I'd planned to leave before the evening was over, mostly to avoid Sam Preston, but before we were finished scarfing down pub food, he showed up at our booth.

"Thanks for coming," he said to the table. "Maybe we'll see you at one of our events."

"You can bet on it," Melissa said.

"No witches," he said to me with a wink. "I promise."

Before I could say something snarky–because I couldn't think of anything, and I had a mouthful of potato–he was walking back to the stage.

"That man is infuriating," I said when I could manage it.

"Well, you did practically accuse him of being a phony," Vanessa said.

"I did no such thing."

As we all counted out singles for a big tip, Karen leaned over and whispered, "I guess I was wrong." She nodded toward the back of the room. Sam Preston was there with his colleague Mary Ashford. She was beaming up at him as she took his arm and they left the restaurant together.

"That's odd," I said. He'd flirted with me. The man

practically asked me to go out with him. What a cad. But he was hung up on exclusivity, so maybe his relationship with Mary Ashford wasn't a big deal. Not that I would consider dating him.

"Jealous?" Karen said.

"Don't be silly. It just seems like he'd have mentioned it."

"Why?"

I hadn't shared all the little details of my dealings with Sam Preston. That was bad bestie karma. "I'll tell you all about it later, I promise."

Chapter Nineteen

Twila Harper was in the chair again that Friday looking less drawn, eager to talk. "It's still happening," she started.

I was surprised by that. While her childhood was clearly one of determination toward perfection, she laid none of the blame on anyone but herself. Her parents were, in her estimation, loving and supportive, and often questioned whether she was enjoying her activities. She was a busy kid, but claimed to have loved it, never tiring from dance classes, theater, or academics. And yet, there she was, almost certainly under pressure to meet harsh expectations, whether of her own making or from some external source she had yet to recognize. So, while I fully expected her to still feel the sensation of disappearing, I was surprised she appeared to be excited by it, rather than perturbed.

"People are starting to not see me. They come into the restaurant and stand looking around. I have to call to them. 'Hello, how many, table or booth?' and all that. And they act surprised, as if they hadn't seen me. But I'm standing right there. And I was in the bookstore the other day and I knew I was fading out. I tried to reach for a book, but it didn't feel solid. It was there all right. It just didn't feel like it was an actual book."

"The book was fading as well?"

She shook her head. "Not exactly. It was more like my hand couldn't quite touch it fully." She was watching me, her face filled with wonder, until suddenly a darkness fell over her and she fell back into the chair. "It's not possible. I know that. I'm losing my mind."

"It's good to be skeptical. And it is an odd thing you felt. But I wouldn't say you're losing your mind."

"What should I do?"

"When you started the story," I said. "You were excited to tell me." She nodded. "Why?"

She looked at the floor for a long moment and I thought she might cry. "I guess I like that it's happening to me."

I nodded. "What other things are you excited about, Twila? In your life."

She sighed. "Nothing, really. I used to do a lot of stuff. But not anymore."

"Why is that?"

She shrugged. "I don't know. I got to the point where I was bored, I guess. Dancing was fun, but I feel too old for that now. I haven't been to class lately. I thought maybe I could try out for a professional cheerleading team, but I doubt I will."

"Why not?"

"I don't think I'd like it. It was my mom's idea, anyway."

"What else did you used to do?"

She listed all of the activities she'd done as a child that she'd left behind. A picture of her was coming into focus.

"When you were a kid," I said, "how did the idea of playing soccer come to you?"

"I think that was my dad's idea."

"And piano lessons?"

"My mom, for sure."

"Which activities were *your* idea? Which ones did you ask to do?"

None. Not a one. Twila had never known what she liked or wanted. She'd never been given the chance.

Eric had invited me to go with him to Poetry Night at

Mr. Booker's cigar shop, Stogies. He'd never shown much interest in Poetry Night, only going a few times before, and I thought it proof that he was willing to do things I liked. Poetry readings are definitely not his thing. Eric is into trash cleanups, walks on the beach to pick up trash, picnics in parks during which he picks up trash; and to that list I could now add boating and fishing. I liked Poetry Night, not just for the poetry and the chance to read some of my favorites, but for the camaraderie of local poetry lovers. The group wasn't what many would expect–highbrow, librarian types with buns (men and women), wine glasses tinkling. It was held at a cigar shop, for one thing. Bikers loved it. College and high school students showed up, and not all of them dressed in black. Shop owners, surfers, salespeople, and yes, a few authors and playwrights too. When I told Eric I wouldn't be reading that night, he surprised me by stepping up to the mic and reciting Rosetti's *An End*. He knew Rosetti was one of my favorite poets. He'd read a few out of my treasured collection the first time he came to my apartment and asked me why I should like such depressing topics. I don't think I handled that argument very well. He read nicely, if a tad wooden, but I wondered if he understood the poem's meaning. *Does he realize it is love that has died?* I suspect he read the poem only to please me. But then I wondered if he was trying to tell me something. Maybe I hadn't been enthusiastic enough about boating and fishing. But what was I supposed to do? Pretend? Maybe.

Let's Review:

1. I am a firm believer in staying true to oneself in relationships.

2. But I also recognize the beauty and charity in giving one's partner's hobbies a chance.

3. That being said, we should only, in my opinion, adopt a partner's hobbies if we truly want to.

4. And despite knowing and trusting in that, I wondered if I'd really given Eric's enough of a chance.

I'd have to think more on it. In the meantime, Eric seemed completely unaware the poem had any deeper meaning than a lovely sentiment and while that perturbed me from a literary standpoint, I was relieved to not have to think too hard on it.

"How about tomorrow?" Eric said at my door that night.

"Dinner?"

"I was thinking morning. A bike ride maybe."

"Oh, I forgot," I said. "I promised Karen I'd go birding with her and Vanessa."

"Birding? Sounds like fun."

"I'd invite you along, but it's sort of a group thing. Vanessa's boyfriend is driving."

"Ah. No room for me."

"I could call her and ask."

He politely declined. "But next Saturday," he said.

"I promise."

I'm not going to lie. I really enjoyed birding with Vanessa and Karen, even though I still felt I'd been set up with Sam. Now that Karen and I knew he was at least dating someone, she'd dropped the attitude and seemed almost apologetic at having dragged me into it.

Christopher's large SUV had three rows of seats and Karen claimed the cozy double in the very back of the car, inviting Richard the landscaper along. Richard was, to put it mildly, adorable. Tanned and strong and all too willing to talk about birds and shrubberies all day. More than once I heard them both shout out, "Bring me a shrubbery!" Each time, I'd look over at Sam, with whom I was sharing the roomier middle seat, with a confused look on my face and he'd laugh. Finally, he said, "Monty Python. Look it up."

Christopher drove, with Vanessa in the front passenger seat, up the Interstate to Sandy Point, about forty miles north, and west to the Merritt Island National Wildlife Refuge where we rode along a one-way, no getting out until the end, road, winding between large and small bodies of water or beside ditches. By that time Richard was telling Karen all about the plants she'd need in her little garden to attract bees and butterflies.

"But it's the bees that count," he was saying. "We've got to save the bees."

I turned slightly to Sam and he was smiling. He looked at me and winked. "Buzz," he whispered.

We stopped along the road often and Sam and Christopher pointed out various birds. He and Sam were mostly interested in the shovelers, one of Sam's favorites–a cute duck-like bird with a large funny bill. But they thrilled at all sorts of birds.

"Over there," Sam would shout and point across one of the brackish lakes. He'd name a bird I'd never heard of. "An avocet," he said once, and Christopher nearly threw us into the seat in front of us stopping so quickly. We all piled out of the van and Sam leant me his binoculars while he took pictures.

"Which one?" I said.

"Here," he said and before I knew it, he was behind me, his face next to mine, hands on mine, aiming the binoculars to just the right spot. "See them? Long, thin bill with the upward curve. Graceful bird with black on its wing."

I had trouble concentrating with him so close to me. I tried to breath smoothly, as if it meant nothing. "Yes," I murmured before actually seeing the bird. And when I did see it, I realized how gorgeous it was. "I see it," I said. "I see it now."

"Beautiful, isn't it?" But he didn't move away from me.

I lowered the binoculars. "Yes."

Finally, he stood aside and took more photos. Karen caught my eye and smirked. I was blushing. *Damn it.*

"I didn't realize," I said when we were nearing the end of the trail, where the water had given way to a canal and pine woods and we were lucky enough to see a pair of bald eagles, "this place was here."

"We're just at the edge of the migration season," Christopher said from behind the wheel. "It can be pretty barren during the summer months. But from now until February or March, I could come out here every weekend."

"Me, too," Vanessa said.

Richard was now giving Karen advice on bird feeders. "You'll never find one that's squirrel proof. I've spent my adult life trying to ward off the little thieves."

"I love squirrels," Karen said.

Sam leaned over and whispered, "She won't get far with that attitude."

"Or maybe he won't get far with his."

"Touché."

"Well," Karen said on the phone that evening. "What's the deal? Does he have a girlfriend or not?"

"I didn't ask him."

"He was still flirting with you. Either he's not seeing that Mary girl and I can go back to insisting you two are into each other or he's a playboy, in which case I'm going to have to start keeping you two apart."

"No problem there."

"And yet, you two keep acting like you're falling for each other."

"It was you and Richard who were doing the falling."

"Richard wasn't getting all next to me, helping me spot those little whatchamacallits in the binoculars. So romantic."

"So awkward." But she was right. Something magnetic sizzled between Sam and me. But I didn't like him. There was no point in considering it. Whether he had a girlfriend or not. "I like Eric," I told her. "I want a man who's rational. A skeptic. Like me."

She sighed. "I guess. Lust isn't everything. I mean, it could be something. But you do sort of have a man already."

"Yes," I said. "Exactly. Definitely."

I swear I could hear her smirking. "Okay, Pari. I'm convinced."

Chapter Twenty

Triple F was the Family Fun Festival hosted monthly by the Historic Downtown Strawbridge Business Owners Management Board–HDS BOMB. Most of the businesses are involved in some way, along with crafters, food trucks, a farmers market, featured musical groups and the like. Eric and I were wandering in the crowd the week after our Poetry Night date. It was seven o'clock, still daylight, and we stood in front of Ally's Formal Wear, eating ice cream from waffle cones, watching dark storm clouds creeping in. I suddenly caught a whiff of rain.

"I love it when this happens," I said.

"You love storms?" His voice hinted at surprise.

"I do, actually. I love rain pounding against the roof of my apartment, when I can sit outside on the balcony, my toes wet with raindrops. I even like lightning and thunder."

"But it's not so great to get caught outside in it."

I stifled a laugh. "I don't mind. There's nothing like racing to your car with your arms full of groceries."

"And then having to make three trips to your apartment with them? I never shop when the chance of rain is above fifty-percent."

"First of all." I took a huge slurp off my cone of chocolate ice cream. "We live in Central Florida. It's always above fifty-percent chance of rain. And secondly, why would you need three trips to carry your groceries? Are you feeding everyone in your building?"

"Maybe I exaggerated a little."

"And thirdly, I meant I love it when the sky darkens with storm clouds and then night takes over and you're never sure how much is night and how much is storm."

His face pinched up and his head shook almost imperceptibly. "Wouldn't you feel better assuming it's a storm and heading for shelter?"

"You don't want to leave, do you?"

He looked up at the sky, turning this way and that. "I think we've got a little time before we have to go."

I was about to protest the thought when Melissa and Vanessa came up the street.

"Have you seen it?" Melissa said dragging me back the way she and Vanessa had come. "It's awesome."

"She has a booth?" I said.

"What she?"

"The psychic."

"No, not her."

A few yards down the street, Sam Preston had set up a booth—a ghostly haunted house, complete with a soundtrack of rattling chains, shrieks, and boos. Isabella would have a hard time competing with it.

"It's a go!" Vanessa said as we approached Sam's setup. "You can sign up for the ghost tour, a cemetery walk, a séance. The works."

Before I knew what was happening, Eric had led me right up to the front table and I stood in front of Sam Preston. I reached out and took Eric's arm possessively—or dependently, or worse...as a statement to Sam. *You see? I told you I was dating someone.* He smiled halfway, almost a smirk, as if to say, *don't pretend you aren't attracted to me.* I was infuriated over this completely imaginary conversation. Get a *grip!* I told myself.

"Do we have to sign up ahead of time?" Melissa asked Sam.

"You have to register in advance, but there are forms on the website if you need to check your calendar."

"Great," she said. "We're doing it."

"Which one?" I said.

"All of them. Don't make that face, Pari. You promised."

I glanced at Sam and saw a distinct look of satisfaction on his face. "Okay, whatever," I said. "Just let me know when. Come on, Eric." I pulled him along down the street.

"What was that all about?" he said.

"Melissa challenged us. She's planning activities to open our minds."

"To what?"

"Ghosts. The supernatural."

"That's right, she saw the ghost last year."

I was pleased he remembered. Sometimes it seemed as if Eric wasn't really listening when I talked. He was always so preoccupied. "I guess we've made a bit of fun at her expense. So, now I'm stuck with the full paranormal experience package."

"If you take part in the guy's delusions, will he expect you to let him into your office?"

"I won't give in on that. No way. But I promised Melissa I'd do her challenge."

"Maybe it won't be so bad. Think of it as psychological research. It could even be fun."

And he was right, of course. It wasn't as if we would actually see a ghost. But learning about the history of supposed ghost sightings downtown ought to be fun. We wandered past several more booths, heading toward the stage where a band was setting up and then crossed over to the other side of the street to check out the north facing booths. Isabella had set up a tent in front of her shop. We stopped and peered in. She sat facing us at a velvet draped table, a crystal ball in the center. There was a line down the street waiting to get in.

"I guess you're right," Eric said as we continued our stroll. "The town's gone nuts."

When we headed back to my apartment, the threat of rain still in the breeze, I thought Eric was going to finally ask me out for Saturday night. At my door, he took my hands in his—still a bit sticky from the ice cream—looked into my eyes, a smile at his lips, and said, "Can I see you tomorrow?"

"I'd love that."

"You still owe me a bike ride across the causeway?"

I think my eyes glazed over and the hopeful smile froze on my face. "The bike ride," I said.

"Bright and early. We can be at the bridge's peak as the sun comes up."

"Romantic," I muttered.

"I'll be here at five-thirty."

"In the morning?"

He chuckled, planted a brotherly kiss on my forehead and said, "You're so cute. See you tomorrow." And off he went to his car.

Five-thirty in the morning. On a Saturday. It was ridiculous. Why hadn't I said no? Well, it was done and there was nothing to do about it except spend hours that night figuring out what on earth I could wear on a bike ride in mid-September. The causeway bridge connected the mainland and Indialantic–beachside as we called it. At least there would be a good breeze; but even at dawn, a Florida morning would be warm and muggy. I dreaded it. I'd have to take a shower before and after. And Eric would almost certainly want to stop somewhere over the bridge for a bite of breakfast. The thought of entering a cold restaurant after having biked across an enormous bridge in the sweltering heat. The sweat. The outfit. The shoes! I barely slept at all.

But there I was in the early morning darkness, outside my apartment complex, watching a ghostly silhouette of Eric approach, with the two bikes he'd walked all the way from his place on the river–almost a mile and a half. He didn't say a word about my outfit. But it was probably too dark to see. I'd managed some faded denim capris with embroidered hems, a ripped black tank over a blue Fabletics sports bra, and a wide-brimmed hat that tied ingloriously under my chin–a cross between Scarlett O'Hara and Ellie May Clampett. (And Karen says I'm culturally illiterate!) Add a pair of black Pumas with blue trim I found in the back of the closet, and I looked the part. Let me just admit right here and now that I was exhausted by the journey before we even got to the causeway. And by the time we got to the top of the bridge...excuse me, I mean, by the time I got to the top, a good twenty minutes after Eric had arrived there, I was ready to be carried back down. The sun rose at six-forty-nine and by god I was there to see it. A giant orange ball rising above the ocean eastward. It was glorious. A crowd of people stood all over the south side of the bridge–the only side walking was allowed–and cheered.

"Does this happen every morning?"

Eric turned to me. He looked wide awake and ready to run a marathon. "Every day, yes."

"I mean the crowd, Eric."

"Oh, sure. Every Saturday and Sunday. I don't know about the rest of the week."

"Did you really think I was asking if the sun rose every morning?"

His face pinched up and his eyebrows rose. He *had* thought it! "Not the fact of the sun rising." He blushed and I must admit I was glad he felt some shame over it. "But the...reality of it. If that makes sense."

I laughed. What else could I do? The truth was...when had I seen the sun rise before? Had I *ever?* I turned to walk the bike back down the bridge.

"Aren't we going all the way over?" he said.

"I'd never make it back up again." He was obviously disappointed. "Maybe I'll get in better shape," I said. "If we do it more often."

"Good point."

"But does it have to be before dawn?"

Eric was kind enough to walk with me for a while but soon he encouraged me to get back on the bike. It was downhill after all. How hard could it be? And I have to say, the first thirty seconds or so were fabulous. The warm lagoon breeze against my face, and in my armpits. A glimpse of dolphins breaking the surface of the water on my left. Cars rushing past on the other side of the barrier on my right. Exciting stuff. But then I realized I was going faster and faster and I tried to slow down without throwing myself off the bike as I weaved around the pedestrians walking up the bridge.

"Slow down," Eric called from behind me.

Duh. "I'm trying," I screamed.

And as I reached the bottom of the bridge where the sidewalk ran up against a small grassy bit of land along the lagoon, I careened off the concrete, into the dirt. The front wheel twisted. I pulled hard on the breaks and lurched off the bike into the grass and weeds. I lay there for a moment, looking up at the pale blue sky, thankful the sun was still near the eastern horizon, deciding I hated bicycles and frankly didn't see their point. At all.

Eric rode up and sat on his bike looking down at me. "You okay?"

"Just lying here, relaxing."

"You took a tumble."

"To put it mildly."

"Need help getting up?"

No. No I did not. Once on my feet, I picked up the bike and rolled it over to Eric. "You can walk the bikes back to your place. I'm going home."

"I'll call you later, okay?"

I waved. "You owe me dinner," I yelled to no one in particular.

"It's the least I can do," he said.

I mumbled to myself, "You've got that right."

Chapter Twenty-one

M elissa had, as I'd been warned, signed us all up for the very first ghost tour. This was all in, as far as I was concerned. I'd be *seen*. By *people*. On a ghost tour all over downtown. I had barely a week before the outing and little time to rehearse my reasons for engaging in such a nonsensical activity. To anyone, clients especially, who tried to claim I was a ghost enthusiast, I was prepared to say that this, and future silly dates Melissa had planned for us, was nothing more than social entertainment. For anyone who believed in ghosts themselves, especially Mrs. Haggard who frequently suggests the ghost of Mr. Haggard still tries to weed his garden, I would simply say it's one thing to imagine the possibilities of ghosts, but quite another to let the idea consume the living.

As it turned out, I had completely misplaced the concern. Ghost tours were the least of my problems. I should have been more concerned about psychics. Isabella Bolton, specifically. The Wednesday after Triple F and my biking...er...excursion, Nelson Gardner spent most of his appointment talking about crystal balls, tarot cards, and incense.

"The insights could be helpful, don't you think?" he said.

"You still feel that's an avenue you'd like to explore?"

"If I knew what the future was, you know, even far off…if I knew everything was going to be okay eventually, I could, maybe, get through today."

"What if things are okay right now? And you simply need to work yourself around to seeing the good that's already here?"

But Nelson had a hard time finding good. I tried to help him understand there was good in the future, and good now, and skills he could practice to help him find that good and hold on to it. He wanted comfort. The next morning, he left a message with Abby saying he went to Isabella for her "insights" and wouldn't be coming back to see me. I was saddened, naturally, and hoped Nelson could find something useful in the experience. But I was also peeved. I did my best to put it out of my mind. That night was my first photography class at The Art Center. I'd purchased a camera with a zoom lens back in April when I'd signed up for the course and was eager to learn to use it. I'd tried drawing, painting, weaving, and paper crafting in the past couple of years and failed at all of them, in my opinion.

"You don't want to create," Mama had told me over the phone last spring, after I threatened to burn my origami swan. "You want to observe."

"Then why do I feel like I need a creative outlet?"

"Sewing isn't enough for you, then?"

"It feels…utilitarian. It has its creative aspects but…no, I guess it's not enough. For me."

"You have too much time on your hands. Get married, Pari. Have babies."

"Mama." I dared an eye roll knowing she couldn't see me. "As soon as I find a good man, I promise. But until then…"

She sighed and tsked like she usually did before offering up a wise opinion. "I have it, then," she said. "Photography. The art is already there. You simply have to interpret it."

That was why I loved my mama so much. She was truly the wisest woman I'd ever known. So I bought a camera and signed up for the class. Unfortunately, that was four months ago and all I'd managed were some blurry pictures taken around the little park down the road.

I was nervous as I pulled into a parking spot in front of the building. The main level at The Art Center housed classrooms, and upstairs was a museum where local artists' work was shown. In the basement they did pottery–I'd yet to take that class. After watching *Ghost* one too many times, I couldn't think of a pottery wheel without being aroused. Yes, that class would have to wait many, many years. As I walked through the front lobby and paused to enjoy the textile art on display, I calmed my breathing and let myself focus only on the imagination of the artists. A few more students entered, and the echo of chatter floated out from the back rooms where the class was gathering. I was feeling better until I heard his voice.

"No," I mumbled. "Just. No."

It couldn't be Sam Preston! Why would he be there? Part of me wanted to slink back to my car and go home. Instead, I stomped down the hallway into classroom four where I found him standing at the front of the class, his name scribbled on the white board.

"What are you doing here?" I said.

"Good evening, Dr. Logan. If you'll have a seat, we'll get started."

"Where's Ron Bernard?"

"Out of commission, I'm sorry to say. I'll be teaching this class for him. The Center is giving everyone fifty percent off their next class for the trouble." The half dozen others in the room were very pleased by this news. "But I'm sure they'll give you a refund if you insist on it."

I stood at the door–somebody nudged me out of the way a bit to get in–and fumed. Was he stalking me?

"In or out, Dr. Logan. It's time to get started. Unpack those cameras and let's see what you've brought."

What could I do? Like a middle school kid faced with detention I slunk to the table in the back of the room and fell pitifully into a seat. Classroom four was like all the others on the first floor with a few six-foot tables and hard metal chairs. On one side, clothes lines strung between the front and back walls held student work, pinned up to dry. A warehouse of equipment packed against the opposite wall: easels, stacks of art pads, oddities to be used as subjects like vases and ceramic faces. Every room had a nook, like a heaving hoarder's lair, piled high with aprons and whatnot. At the front of the room, a padded stool for the instructor and a white board on the wall. Sam spent most of the class at the tables, examining our cameras and lecturing on how to use them. But when he was on the stool, he'd spin around as he talked like a fourth grader telling his parents about school that day.

"I spent the entire class refusing to look at him or engage in any way," I told Karen at lunch on Friday. We were at Brunch, at a little corner table inside where it was cool. The September heat was nearly unbearable, and we were lucky to get an inside spot. "I feel like I should drop the class."

"I hear a 'but' in there," she said with a smile.

"But then he's won, of course. I know, I know." The look on her face was priceless. "I'm not even pretending to be mature about it."

"Was he a good teacher?"

I sighed. "Unfortunately, yes. I learned a lot. He does know his cameras. Luckily, another woman had the same Nikon as me, so he used hers to demonstrate for both of us. I didn't have to interact with him too much."

"You're going to let this ruin the experience, aren't you?"

"When class was over, I asked him what happened to Mr. Bernard and when he would be back. He said the man was out on a shoot and fell, broke his something or other."

"And you suspect foul play?"

"Yes!" Then I laughed. "Karen, it's awful. I can't get away from the man."

"If only you hadn't kissed him."

I dropped my forehead to the table in front of my iced tea. "Ugh." I might have sat there like that for an hour had Melanie not brought our sandwiches. "Enough about him," I said, popping a potato chip into my mouth.

But I found myself telling her I was worried about my practice. I couldn't talk in specifics, of course, but in general terms. "And my being mixed up in all of it. It's not professional. Why did I promise Melissa I'd do it?"

"You're worried about the Standards of Excellence Award."

"Yes. Am I being petty? Don't answer that."

"I really don't think the committee is going to pass you over because you went on some ghost tours."

"But honestly, it's not *just* about professionalism. I'm seriously concerned all this ghost nonsense will make things worse for my clients."

"Of course you want what's best for them. But if ghosts and psychics can help them deal with life's downsides, that's a good thing, right?"

"I suppose." And she was right. I had to be sure I wasn't letting my ego get in the way. I took a bite of ham and Swiss on rye and tried to forget the whole thing.

"Let me tell you what the real problem is." Karen leaned across the little table and whispered, "I've heard a lot of people aren't happy with the psychic or the ghost guy. But mostly the psychic."

"Why? What's she done?"

"She opened up shop. I'm hearing that someone is planning to protest the place."

"You mean, go to the city council?"

"No, I mean posters and marching and chanting."

"Downtown?" The idea was absurd. Downtown was one of those diversity places, where everybody was weird and nobody cared. "Who would do that?"

"The only name I've heard associated with it is Carolina Davies."

"Of Begotten?"

"Yes, but don't spread that around."

"I wouldn't."

"If you ask me, the only reason her name is attached to the rumor is because no one could imagine who else would be against a psychic in town."

"That's not fair, is it?"

"But what do we really know about Carolina? I mean,

she comes into Morgan's, but she never shops anywhere else downtown. She's not the friendliest person."

"Who's to say she's the one being unfriendly? When was the last time any of us went into her store to visit?"

"That's true."

"It's probably just more people like Sam Preston. Outsiders, coming here to stir up trouble."

Karen chuckled. "You're so cute when you try to be tribal."

"Yeah, it felt weird."

"Promise me you'll try to have fun with the challenges. What's the worst that could happen?"

I held up a hand. "I don't even want to think about it."

"If we do see a ghost on the tour, all of downtown will go crazy."

"If we see a ghost," I said, "it'll mean Sam Preston is a fraud."

"How do you figure that?"

"There are no such things as ghosts, Karen. If we see one, it must be a trick, thereby proving the Ghost Whisperer is a phony. And I'll be sure to let everyone know it."

Suddenly I was enthusiastic about Melissa's challenge. Why hadn't I thought of it that way before?

"I see that look," Karen said. "What is it they say about pride and the fall?"

"Fine. I'll be humble when I expose Sam Preston and he's run out of town." I was already celebrating my triumph as I finished lunch.

Chapter Twenty-two

MaryAshford has joined the chat.

MaryAshford: Today's the day! Are you guys ready for the ghost tour?

LegitChris: But did you kiss her again?

MaryAshford: What did I walk into here?

LegitChris: She's in his Wednesday photography class.

MaryAshford: You told me your class was on Monday.

SamTheMan: This is another class. I'm taking over for somebody.

MaryAshford: And you kissed her? During class?

SamTheMan: We're not animals. And no, I didn't kiss her.

MaryAshford: Did you ask her about the office?

SamTheMan: No. Let's see what happens tonight.

MaryAshford: What difference does tonight make?

LegitChris: She's supposed to be there.

MaryAshford: Wait. What? Why?

SamTheMan: All I know is she's on the list.

MaryAshford: Spying on you?

LegitChris: Melissa challenged them.

MaryAshford: You know these people, Chris?

SamTheMan: He's dating one of them. So, what's the challenge?

LegitChris: Do ghost stuff.

SamTheMan: But why?

LegitChris: Melissa had a sighting. She spoke at our interview a couple of weeks ago, remember?

SamTheMan: I still don't see why.

LegitChris: So they'll stop making fun of her, I guess.

MaryAshford: They sound like really nice people.

LegitChris: It's not like that.

MaryAshford: It's a good thing I'll be there tonight. I'm going to have to keep you from kissing everybody.

SamTheMan: It was just a kiss. Two kisses. Whatever. She made it very clear it won't happen again.

MaryAshford: Good. See you tonight. Don't be drunk!

MaryAshford has left the chat.

SamTheMan: I almost kissed her again.

LegitChris: What happened?

SamTheMan: She's standing in front of me, angry, wanting to know why I'm teaching the class. I swear she thinks I broke Ron's leg just to piss her off.

LegitChris: And that made you want to kiss her? That's just weird.

SamTheMan: It's sick, I know. But you should see her when she's mad.

LegitChris: I bet that's easy enough to arrange. I gotta go. See you tonight, weirdo.

Chapter Twenty-three

Not surprisingly, when the Divas gathered at the old Crisper House next to MacAuley Awley's at nine o'clock that Saturday night for the start of the first official Downtown Ghost Tour, every one of the us had heard of the approaching protests. At least one hundred people were expected, if you believed what Sophie had heard around her grandad's bookstore. People were buying up poster board and markers from Morgan's Office Supply and there were rumors of wild poster making parties.

"How wild could they be?" Melissa said. "They're a bunch of stick in the muds."

"Shouldn't that be 'sticks in the mud?'" Sophie said.

"Who says 'sticks in the mud' anymore?" Karen said.

"Nobody says 'sticks in the mud.'" Kaya said. "It's always 'stick in the mud,' singular."

Sophie: "You're saying you can never have a group of sticks in mud?"

"That's exactly what I'm saying. They're loners. That's why we call them sticks—wait."

Sophie: "See. You can't talk about them without making it plural."

"Can we get back on topic?" Karen said. "The point is, I never saw a group of stick...sticks...muddy people buying up poster board. I just know stock is way down."

We were huddled together whispering about the crazy accusations when I caught, out of the corner of my eye, a glimmer of purple, green, and orange silk glistening in the glow of the streetlamp and the distinct aroma of spiritual rose perfume hit my nose. There, right next to our little group, within earshot, was Isabella Bolton, decked out in a caftan, her wild curls pulled atop her head and left dangling, bouncing when she turned away from me. Before I could make a move to introduce the Divas, Lord Ghost Whisperer himself showed up. Christopher Reynolds and Mary Ashford were with him.

Christopher waved to Vanessa. He wore a thick, stuffed backpack and I wondered what sorts of spectral equipment he might have stashed in it. Mary was scanning the group of ghost hopefuls, as if looking for the most gullible among us—but I could be letting my skeptical bias cloud my assessment. Sam Preston was dressed in his usual ripped jeans and faded t-shirt, a thin pack of index cards stuffed in the front pocket. A Canon with an enormous lens was strapped across his chest.

An excited hum swept through the small group of ghost enthusiasts, and I let out a groan. "Here we go."

Melissa nudged me. "Be nice."

Though the shops had just closed, the restaurants and night clubs kept the main street busy. Sam raised his voice and managed to command the two dozen in the group. After he introduced himself and his team—he called them the Ghost Corp and I rolled my eyes where Melissa couldn't see—he swept an arm out toward the old house in front of us and said, "The Crisper House, the third most haunted spot downtown. Keep your eyes on the upstairs window at the end there. You might see the ghost of an unidentified woman. Many believe she is one of the victims of a serial killer who owned the house and lured his victims to it where he murdered them by choking them with a bull whip."

The crowd hung on his every word, their eyes wide and attentive, as he weaved for us the entire history of the Crisper House, at least, he said, as much as we know. It was all factual, nothing scary, but he'd started so well, his audience patiently waited for the gory details. To my surprise, there were none.

"Eliza Crisper, daughter of William, was the last resident of the house and died in that upstairs bedroom of old age. Many claim the room was actually a sitting room and she looks out the window at times waiting for the man who left her at the altar."

"Oh, for–"

"Hush," Melissa said.

"But there is no corroboration for that story. Letters and diaries suggest Ms. Crisper had no desire to marry and was never engaged."

"But what about the serial killer?" a young woman asked.

Sam smiled kindly at her and shook his head. "There's nothing in any newspaper or history of this area to suggest that story is at all true, I'm afraid. So, if there is a ghost in that room–" He dramatically peered upward to the window and paused. "It's probably not a murder victim."

"But it could be anybody," someone else said.

Sam nodded. "That's right. I guess we'll never know."

I let out a loud sigh. I couldn't help myself.

Sam had the group quiet down and watch the window for several minutes. I was ready for a ghostly appearance and fully prepared to accuse him of fraud. Someone was in that house, ready to play the specter for his enthusiastic fans. But it didn't happen. No ghost. No specter. Nothing hovering above the floor. Sam shrugged and told us we'd have to do our own investigating in the future.

"Next stop," he said, "the Moaning Door."

As everyone followed Christopher and Mary across the street, Sam hung back and joined the Divas. "You found Ms. Crisper's story unsettling?" he said to me.

"Hardly."

"But something about it bothered you."

"Why do all the women ghosts pine for lost love? It's so cliché."

"I said that's probably not true."

"Everybody believes it, though."

"I just repeat the stories," he said. "I don't make them up."

"I seriously doubt women back in the 1800s and earlier, when all your ghosts seem to have lived and died, were as fragile and boy crazy as we'd like to make them. They had hard lives and much better things to do."

He raised a brow and smirked. "I guess people love a tragic romance."

We'd approached the spot where the rest of the group was waiting for us, and Mary Ashford cleared her throat.

"Do you mind?" She was looking at me.

I put on my it-wasn't-me face and pointed at Sam.

"Sorry to keep you waiting, folks," he said, joining Mary and Chris.

Mary glared at me.

"He started it," I whispered to Vanessa next to me.

"Yes, he did," she said with a grin.

"You think Mary's the boss?" Sophie said.

"Once again," Karen sang, "Pari is the teacher's pet."

"Teacher? Pet? What did I miss?" Melissa said.

Suddenly we realized the tour group was staring at us.

"Sorry," Kaya said. "We'll shut up now."

"Yeah," Karen said. "Tell us about the doors."

"Oooh," I said. "Doors."

And then the Divas broke out in giggles and Mary Ashford's face fell into a pale shade of fury.

Chapter Twenty-four

I'd never noticed the doors—wait. That's not exactly true. They've always been there; they're interesting; I've seen them. I'd just never thought much about them. Three doors, as Sam Preston pointed out, all made of wood and dating back to sometime in the early Nineteenth Century. Each door had a different carving on it, much of it worn away by time and abuse. The knobs, he said, were almost certainly brass at first, but had since been stolen and replaced several times over. One of the doors, the Moaning Door, was held shut with a bit of rope. The others had old metal knobs.

All the doors—and Sam said there had been more in the past—were on the south side of Strawbridge and opened onto narrow alleys, closed at the other end by similar doors all of which were now missing. So historic were these doors, the city had agreed to place markers at each one and allow only certain people to open them.

Hmph. They were nice enough, I suppose. But they were just doors. The Moaning Door, across from the Crisper House...well, it apparently moaned. Usually at night, after downtown had emptied and only the few residents who lived in small apartments above some of the stores heard it.

"It's said to sound like someone slowly opening and

then closing the door," Sam said. "And there are those who claim to see the ghost of Eliza Crisper appear each time the door moans."

"Shouldn't it be the 'creaking' door?" I asked. I thought I was being sarcastic.

"Good point," Sam said with a smile. "But those who hear it say there is a distinct moan to the sound...as if the door is...unwilling."

This brought out *oohs* and *aahs* from the group.

"Couldn't we open it and have a listen?" someone said.

"I've been given permission to do it. But it doesn't sound like anything when a person opens it." He undid the rope, telling us that along with the historic marker, the city planned to get replica brass knobs for all the doors. Gently, he pushed the door inward toward the alley. "You see? Nothing."

"Creepy," Melissa said.

"How is that creepy?" I turned to her.

"It only moans in the middle of the night."

"How do we know that? You just believe everything you hear?"

Most of the group was now glaring at me, most notably Isabella, the psychic. It seemed I'd broken a spell. But not Sam; he was smiling.

"Everyone will have an opportunity to hear the door in the middle of the night in the safety of a group setting," he said. "In a few weeks Ghost Whisperer Events will be hosting its first sleepover in the Executive Suites building and participants will have the opportunity to tour the haunted spots of downtown at two in the morning."

Audible *oohing* and *aahing* echoed around me.

"The bewitching hour," Isabella sang.

I rolled my eyes at Karen. "Like that's really a thing."

"Oh, hush," she said.

Sam pulled the old wooden door closed and as he knotted the rope someone gasped and the group, like a flock of birds, turned around to look at the Crisper House. There, in the window on the second floor, for the briefest moment, I caught a glimpse of...a figure.

"Eliza!" someone shouted. "I saw her."

It was all Sam could do to get in front of the group before people started darting across the street. While traffic was certainly light after hours downtown, there were still rules to be obeyed. He stretched out his arms and calmed everyone. But the electricity raging through the gathering was palpable.

"That was fabulous," Sam said.

I wanted to believe he'd planned it, but the look on his face said he was as surprised as everyone else.

"I didn't expect to have an actual sighting on the tour," he said. "Just imagine what we might see during the sleepover." And he was back to advertising.

"We are definitely doing the sleepover," Karen said.

"Not you, too."

"Oh, come on, Pari. You can't tell me that wasn't fun."

I glared at the window as the rest of the group moved along.

"You think he did it?" Karen asked me, draping an arm over my shoulder and leading me to follow the impassioned ghost hunters.

"No," I mumbled. "He'd have done something more obvious. Something indisputable. That was just shadows."

"Unless he's an evil genius."

I stopped and turned to her, shaking my head. "As his nemesis, I'd say you could be right. He'd want to pur-posefully show us something fuzzy so everybody could fill in what he left out. That's diabolical. But as a psy-chologist, no. He may be unprofessional and boorish–"

"Ouch."

"–but he's not evil."

"Not evil. Why Pari, that's the nicest thing you've said about him since you met him."

"What was that?" Suddenly we were in front of Sam, the group mingling around us, on the sidewalk at our next stop–the empty building between Namasté and Begotten.

"Nothing," I muttered.

"She said you're not evil," Karen said, nudging me.

Sam looked at me, his eyes wide. "Thank you?"

"It's hardly a compliment," I said.

"You saw her, though. In the window."

"I don't know what I saw."

"This is going to drive people to the sleepover in your building."

I rolled my eyes. "Don't even ask. You're not getting in my office."

Luckily, he had to get back to his tour and I didn't have to argue with him. There were no more spirit sightings, but plenty of spider webs, hooting owls, voices from afar, creaking sounds, and the odd suspicious clank from the buildings we passed. Enough to send goose bump plagues throughout the attendees and ensure they'd spread stories of ghosts and things going bump in the night. The Divas were thrilled. But I was going to have to side with all the sticks out there, stuck in their mud puddles. The more excited Downtown Strawbridge got about ghosts and hauntings, the more pressure I would be under to let people into my office. And that was out of the question. If only I had confidence the Divas would stand with me against the haunting tide.

Chapter Twenty-five

F irst of all," I said, "it's not the 'bewitching hour.' It's the Witching Hour. Also called the Devil's Hour. And it's not two o'clock in the morning, it's three."

"Someone's been looking into the supernatural," Melissa cooed, very pleased with herself.

It was Sunday afternoon, and the Divas were gathered outside Melissa's Café Flamingo where we would be led into our next ghostly challenge. All of downtown was electric that morning, abuzz with the news of Eliza Crisper's ghost appearing after a years-long absence. Ghost Whisperer Events was a raging success. Sophie and I had already been stopped on the walk from our apartment complex by Madaline Richards, town crier *slash* realtor.

"Tell me everything," she said. "What did Eliza's ghost look like? Was she crying? Was it real? Do you think it was that Ghost Whisperer? Did he set it all up?"

"I couldn't even tell if it was a person," Sophie said. "It could just as easily have been a reflection."

"But they say she moved. Disappeared. Or faded away. Did she fade away?"

"She moved," I said. And there, I'd done it. I said 'she.'

"What was she wearing? What did she look like?"

"I didn't really see anything much either, Madaline."

"Well, Chrissie was there—she's Chelsea's daughter, one of my realtors, have you met Chelsea? Anyway, she was there with her boyfriend, and she said it was definitely Eliza Crisper. She was wearing a long dress with a lace collar and her hair was done up in a bun. She was at a velvet curtain, one hand pulling it back to reveal her face and when you all turned to see her, she let the curtain drop to hide herself."

"I didn't see anything like that," Sophie said.

We managed to get away from Madaline only because someone entered her real estate office. Business is business, after all. Sophie and I laughed all the way to Morgan's Office Supply where we met up with Karen. We picked up Kaya at her store and as we walked in front of the Crisper House, we slowed our pace and stared at the window upstairs. Several people were taking pictures and talking about the ghost.

"It's ridiculous," I said as we moved on.

"Who are you trying to convince?" Karen said with a chuckle.

"Don't turn on me now, bestie. Did any of you see anything like a ghost last night? Really?"

Kaya and Karen shrugged.

"Not really," Karen said.

"I admit it," Kaya said. "I didn't see anything. But only because I wasn't sure where everybody was even looking. By the time I figured it out, the whole thing was over."

"There wasn't much to see," Sophie said. "A shadow, maybe."

"A shadow in a dark window?" Kaya said.

"The glass of the window was lit somehow, if I recall. By the moonlight. Or the streetlights."

"And there was a vertical shadow on the right side that moved," I said. " At least, I think it did. It happened so fast. There's no way for any of us to know what we saw. Right now, we're inventing details after the fact so our memory will make some sense to us."

Melissa and Vanessa were waiting for us on the corner outside the café.

"Did you sleep at all?" Melissa asked us once we'd crossed Woodplum Street to join them.

"I didn't," Vanessa said. "Not a wink. I can't wait for the sleepover. We're all signed up for the first one."

"Not me," I said.

"It's part of the challenge."

"We've already seen your ghostly evidence," I said. "Can't we say now whether we've changed our minds on the ghost question?"

"No way," Melissa said. "You agreed to do all of my challenges until Halloween."

"But how can I do the sleepover and still keep Sam Preston out of my office?"

"We'll be there," Kaya said. "We'll protect the sanctity of your domain."

They all nodded.

"Promise?"

"What do you think is going to happen, Pari?" Kaya said. "Sam Preston knocking down your office door?"

"I don't know." There was a detectable whine in my voice. "I just feel like everybody in town is going to want into my office. People are getting...fanatical. You hear it all over town. Ghosts, ghosts, ghosts."

Sophie patted my arm, sympathy on her face. "It's not that bad."

"It's harmless fun," Vanessa said.

"Okay, okay. We can do the sleepover." I had to give in. It was part of the friendship code. But I still felt dread seeping in. Past trauma, no matter how much you believe you've overcome it, can startle you when it grabs hold of you once again. But this was different, I told myself. For one thing, I wasn't ten years old anymore.

"And the Divas will protect you," Melissa said.

And I had friends now. I held onto that thought.

"We need a Diva handshake for times like this," Karen said.

"We'll work on it," I said.

"So, what's going on today?" Sophie asked Melissa.

"You guys are going to be so freaked out."

"Just tell us." I couldn't tell if Karen was excited or

scared.

"Divas," Melissa said. "Walk this way."

As soon as she headed east, we knew what she had planned for us.

"You're not serious," I said.

"This could get weird," Kaya said.

"I don't want to," Sophie said.

"I am. It will. And I don't care," Melissa said as she marched us down Strawbridge Avenue to Isabella's Insights.

Isabella's front window was covered with draped velvet in shades of dark green and blue. The glass door was covered with horizontal blinds. I expected it to be dark and gloomy inside, but when Melissa opened the door and ushered us in, one by one, we found ourselves in a tiny well-lit room. The back wall was covered in more dark velvet. Shelves for trinkets lined a side wall. Earrings, necklaces, and bracelets with crystal ball pendants. Tiny crystal ball paper weights. Books on psychic phenomena. Packs of tarot cards. The price tags were all blank cut-outs in the shape of a crystal ball on a stand–a small cashwrap area sat on the opposite side of the room. And against the front window was a futon with fat, warped cushions behind a beat-up natural wood coffee table.

The space was quiet, muted, and as Isabella was nowhere to be seen, we gradually stopped chatting until none of us made a sound. I think we'd all stopped breathing when the loud bang rang out. We jumped and somebody shouted, I'm not sure who. Karen was almost out the door when Isabella appeared from one end of the velvet wall, her hair a curly mess atop her head and wearing a gauzy purple caftan.

"Ladies, I knew you'd come!"

"Well," Melissa said hesitantly. "We have an appointment."

Chapter Twenty-six

B ehind the curtain, we found the source of the bang, a gong the size of a kiddie pool. Very clever, I thought. The room was dim. One wall was lined with shelving piled with books, globes in all colors, well-worn decks of tarot cards, crystals, and scarves. But the table in the center of the room was empty, covered with a maroon cloth. The reading started off badly when, after we all sat around the table in what Isabella called her 'sanctuary,' Melissa said, "We want to know about romance."

"I thought you wanted us to learn about ghosts," I said.

"This is a psychic reading," Melissa said. "We want romance. And our futures."

"I'm not sure I want to know any of that," Karen said.

"Not to worry," Isabella said. Her accent was hard to place. There were hints of Minnesota, with a breathy Great Lakes to New York to Paris to Florida quality to it. Like your great aunt who likes to think she's descended from Louis the Fourteenth and does local theater in the high school auditorium. She waved her arms in front of her, as if trying to breathe in our collective odors, then clasped her hands together, kissed them, and laid her palms flat on table. Closing her eyes, she drew in a long, deep breath and held it for an eternity while we all glanced at one another uneasily. Except for Melissa. She was right there with Isabella, eyes closed, chin up, smiling–ready for psychic elucidation.

"You," Isabella said, now glaring at Vanessa who sat to her right. "You run the hair salon, right?"

Vanessa nodded. "And nails. Threading, waxing."

"And I can walk in, or do I need an appointment?"

Vanessa glanced at me before answering. "Either one."

"You will be a model. Local, I think. Yes. But successful."

Shaking her head, Vanessa said, "I don't want to–"

"Doesn't matter. I see your picture in a glossy magazine. Not news. No. You're modeling something."

"But romance," Melissa said. "Who will she marry?"

Isabella seemed to think for a moment, staring at a point in the center of our group. "It's not clear. You'll have to come alone sometime. I'll do a better reading. You!" She pointed right at me, and I nearly jumped out of my chair. "It's nice to see you again. The psychologist."

"I only take appointments. No walk-ins."

"You're very skeptical."

"As I told you."

"This will serve you well in the future."

She was speaking as if she'd been inhabited by a different person. She was much less New York now, and a lot more European—a tickle of Bulgaria lisped about on every other word. This was not the same casual woman I'd met and insulted on the street some weeks ago. And she must have known she sounded like someone else, but she gave off no hint that she knew that I knew.

"No doubt." I rolled my eyes, but she'd already turned to Karen who was sitting beside Vanessa.

"The office supply store," she said. Karen merely nodded. Her eyes were round, and it looked like she was terrified to blink. "I'm always jittery in the office supply store. Why is that?"

"I..." Karen let out a nervous laugh. "I'm not sure."

Melissa said, "I had an uncle who was allergic to

160

paper."

Isabella closed her eyes and shook her head slightly. "No, that's not it. I see tragedy in your future."

"What?" Karen said, her voice like a mouse.

"But you will survive it. You will endure."

"What are her other options?" I whispered and Isabella shushed me. Seriously. She held her hand up to me and said, "Shush."

Then she went on with Karen. "I see an artist...a brilliant talent."

"I can't even draw," Karen said.

"A man. Quiet. Reserved."

"Right," I said.

"Shush."

"You don't see a...landscaper, maybe?" Karen squeaked.

"Artist," Isabella said. "Be patient with him. Very shy. You must bring him out of his shell. Encourage him."

"I can do that," Karen said to me.

"You're an introvert. You need an extrovert to bring *you* out of *your* shell."

"Maybe it's the opposite," Sophie said. "Someone even more introverted could help her be a little bit extroverted."

"That's not the opposite," Melissa said.

"Whatever," Sophie said.

"Like you would know, Sophie," Vanessa said.

"Shush!" Isabella glared at us.

"What's that supposed to mean?" Sophie said.

"You're an introvert and Reese is an extrovert."

"What does that have to do with anything?"

"You wouldn't know about introverts being able to bring even more introverted people out of their shells."

"What?" Melissa said. "That doesn't make any sense at all."

"*Hello*," Sophie said. "As an introvert, I think I'd know what an introvert is capable of."

"Thank you," Karen said. "I think."

"Ladies," Isabella said. She had her head bowed and was rubbing her temples and I didn't know if she was receiving word from the spiritual realm on the subject of introverts or just ticked off. "As I said, Karen...artist. Take care with him, okay?"

"Sure, okay."

"Do me," Melissa said.

Meanwhile, Kaya had been sitting next to me quiet as the dead, not moving at all, as if she was hoping Isabella wouldn't see her.

"Yes, the café owner. You will have continued success in business. I see that."

"And romance?"

Isabella tilted her head, "Eh."

"Eh?" Melissa said. "What is *eh*? What kind of psychic says, 'eh?'"

"I see you out with groups, always groups. Friends, lovers, none of it serious. But wait–" She raised her hand, palm out, to Melissa just as she'd done to me, but somehow this palm was friendlier than the one I got. "I see a man, yes."

"Oooh," Melissa cooed.

"He is distant, though. Watching you. Waiting."

"Like that's not creepy," I said.

Suddenly, Kaya slapped her hand on the table and her forehead hit it. She shrieked and just as I was thinking she was having some kind of psychic-induced possession reaction, she lifted her head and laughed so hard her whole body shook. This, naturally, set us all laughing. And I must say, to her credit, Isabella laughed too.

When we all finally calmed down, wiping tears from our faces, Isabella said, "No, not like a stalker. He is your soul mate. I don't see him literally watching you. He is here already, though. You know him."

"Still creepy," I said.

"You." She pointed to me.

"You already did me."

"You resist the man who is right for you because you don't trust your true self."

"What does that mean?"

Isabella frowned, as if coming out of a trance. She shook her head. "I'm not sure. I think it means you have this idea about who you are and what sort of man you should love. But you're wrong."

"I'm wrong about who I am?"

"Yes."

"I'm a psychologist."

"As you say."

"And I don't know myself?"

"You believe yourself to be immune to the things that plague the rest of us?"

"I didn't mean that." I looked around the table and they were all looking back, pretty much telling me Isabella was right.

"Just think about it," Isabella said. Then she turned her eyes to Kaya, and I could almost feel her shrinking under Isabella's gaze. "Do you have children?"

"What? No," Kaya said.

"You will meet a man with children. He's the one."

"I...I don't like children."

"Hah! Like that means anything," Isabella said.

"Okay," Sophie said. "What about me?"

Isabella smiled at Sophie, sitting across from her. "You will surround yourself always with books, but you won't be lost in them. I see a December wedding."

"Whoah."

"I didn't say this year."

"Okay, I have to ask," I said. Isabella looked only a tiny bit perturbed. "How can you see a December wedding? I mean, we live in Central Florida. December looks like every other month of the year."

"I don't see literally," she said. "I see it in my spirit eye. I see Sophie in a white veil. That tells me wedding. I feel a chill. I hear the music. It's Christmas. It's a December wedding." She threw her hands up as if to say, 'what do you want me to do?'

"Anything else?" Melissa said.

"I would need to see you each alone for more detail," she said.

"So that's it?" I said. "Love and romance. Men. This session doesn't pass the Bechtel Test."

"What is this Bechtel Test?" Isabella said.

"It's about movies," Karen said.

"And books," Sophie said.

"If the film doesn't have any scenes where women are talking about stuff other than men and romance, it fails the test," I said.

"I only did what I was asked."

"But you said I was going to have a tragedy," Karen said. "I really don't like the sound of that. And it didn't have anything to do with romance. Did it?"

"But aren't we all going to experience tragedy?" Sophie said. Melissa gasped, but I could see where Sophie was going with it. "My grandfather isn't going to live forever. You've all got older parents, right? They're going to die someday, maybe sooner than later. That will be a tragedy."

"No," Isabella said. "This tragedy is different."

"That's not nice," I said. "Why would you tell her that?"

"I see it. What am I supposed to do?"

"Keep it to yourself."

"Is that why you came here?"

"We came here," Karen said, "because of Melissa."

"Don't blame me," Melissa said. "I didn't know you were going to have a tragedy."

"Maybe tragedy is a strong word," Isabella said.

"Oh, really?" Sophie said. "You want to take it back?"

"I do. There will be sadness. Deep sadness. But you will be okay. You have your friends to guide you through it."

Karen looked upset so I figured it wasn't a good idea to note that Isabella hadn't said anything about her parents helping her through it. Not that I believed any of her nonsense.

"Okay," I said. "I think that's enough for today."

Melissa paid–a reduced rate, so she said. Introductory or party rate. Whatever. The worst thing about the entire episode was that as we left Isabella's shop, I ran right into Eric–literally.

Chapter Twenty-seven

E ric looked at Isabella's window with the draped velvet backdrop, the fancy gold letters on the glass, and the cheesy 'open hours' sign stuck in the corner shaped like a witch's hat, then at me.

"Did you have your palm read?" he said.

Melissa piped up, "Isabella doesn't do palms. I don't think."

I turned to the Divas. "I'll catch up with you later."

"Is he the right one?" Vanessa said. "Or the wrong one?"

"Shush," I told her.

I could hear their excited chatter even over the Sunday crowds as I turned back to Eric. "What brings you downtown?"

"What, you can't tell?"

I looked him over. "Hair cut?"

"And I had my brows done."

"Of course you did."

Eric wasn't overly petty about appearance, but he did enjoy a good grooming. That Sunday, he was wearing his drawstring, safari pants so I knew he had his bike shorts on underneath and had pedaled his way downtown from his condo on the river. Biking a mile and a half on a Central Florida afternoon would leave me wilted and wet, but there he stood beautiful as ever. If he had any sweat on him, it came off as sunlit sparkle.

"I was heading down to the café for a smoothie," he said. "Care to join me?"

"I'd love to."

"So, seriously. What were you doing at the psychic? I'm not judging. Just really curious."

"I bet you are."

"I'll buy your smoothie if you tell me all about it."

Who could resist that? We navigated the busy sidewalk as best we could and paused in front of the Crisper house.

"You'll have to tell me all about the ghost sighting, too."

"Has everyone in town heard about it?"

"I heard it from Alphonse. Well, technically it was Rowena, foiling some highlights in the next chair. She was telling Alphonse all about it, as she heard it from Vanessa."

"What did Vanessa say?"

"Just that she saw a ghost. Literally. Rowena said Vanessa said 'literally.' So, she figured it must have really happened. Alphonse was skeptical."

"You too, I imagine."

"And you."

I said nothing.

"And you?" he persisted.

"Yes," I said. "Of course."

"Oh, my god, Pari. You're not falling for the ghost huckster, are you?"

That was an odd way to put it. "You think he staged it?"

"Of course he did."

"I don't think so. I saw the look on his face. He was surprised and...amazed. As if he'd never actually seen a ghost before."

"That's all he does."

"He talks about them and searches for them. But has he actually seen one?"

"I guess I don't know. I don't listen to his show or

read his blog."

"He has a blog?"

"How do I know more about this guy than you do?"

By the time we crossed Woodplum Street to Café Flamingo, the Divas were nowhere to be seen. We got strawberry banana smoothies and found a table for two by the front window. The air conditioning and those first few sips of icy fruit slush sent a chill through me, and I rubbed my arms.

"So, tell me," Eric said.

I rolled my eyes. "It was part of Melissa's challenge."

"I thought that was only ghostly stuff."

"Me too. Trust me, I wasn't thrilled."

"I have to know," he smiled. "If I hadn't run into you, would you have told me about it?"

"I'm not even going to tell my mother. So, no. Absolutely not. In fact, I'd like to get through all of Melissa's nonsense without having to talk to anyone about it."

He laughed and we were silent, slurping our smoothies for a few minutes.

"I should apologize." He glanced around as if trying to come up with the right words. "About the shoe thing." Well, this was interesting. "I...well, I own sixty-four pairs of bicycle shorts."

I gasped and nearly spit smoothie all over him. "Sixty-four!"

"I counted. I told my mom about our fight, and she said I should take a look in the mirror. She's right. I get my hair trimmed every five weeks. I buy a new pair of walking shoes every eight weeks. I own every spice available at the health food market and Publix combined and throw them out the day they expire. I'm a hypocrite."

"I think most of us are in some way or another."

"Anyway, I thought you should know I'm sorry about it. I hope we've moved past it."

"All is forgiven," I said. And yet... I couldn't put my finger quite on it. I knew I had wanted Eric to come to just such a realization, not because I loved shoes so much and thought he shouldn't care about what was on my feet, but because I wanted him to relax a bit. Maybe this was enough. And maybe not. "I got the impression your mother didn't like me very much."

"Why would you think that?"

I shrugged. "I'm not sure. Just the feeling I got. That's it!" I plunked my smoothie on the table a bit too forcefully and strawberry mush popped out of the straw.

"What?" I think I scared him.

"That movie. The one with the twins. What's it called? Lindsay Lohan."

"*The Parent Trap?*"

"That's the one."

"Are you okay?"

"It was your mother. She reminded me of Cruella's mother in that movie."

"Cruella was in the dalmatian movie."

"But they called her Cruella, remember? And when one of them, I don't remember which one, met Cruella's mom, she said 'hello, pet.'"

"And that reminded you of my mother?"

I suddenly realized it wasn't a compliment. "Yeah, I guess. Sorry."

"No. I can see it. She might have a bit of a condescending vibe. But she liked you; I'm sure of it."

"Hello, pet," I said, hoping to ease the tension.

"Okay," he said. "Tell me the gory details. Are you going to meet a tall, dark stranger?"

"I'm afraid it *was* centered mostly around love. But not *that* cliché. I was surprised she said some specific things."

"Like what?"

"She said Vanessa would be a model. Locally, not necessarily as a career. And Kaya would meet a man with children. She did say Karen would experience a tragedy, but she didn't give any details."

"Vanessa owns a business, so maybe she'll have her picture somewhere. That's nothing. And Kaya probably meets men with children regularly. Unless Isabella said she'd marry one."

"She said Sophie would have a December wedding."

"It's Central Florida. Of course she'd have a December wedding. And if she doesn't, Isabella could claim her telling Sophie about it made Sophie change her mind, whether she was aware of it or not."

"You're right," I said. "It's so easy to get sucked in."

"But what about you?"

"What about me?"

"What did she say about you?" He twisted his mouth into a goofy grin, as if he knew I was stalling.

I didn't want to tell him, but if I didn't, he'd think I was hiding something, and he'd assume it was about him. "She said the man I think is wrong for me, is really right for me."

"You think she was talking about me? That brings up all sorts of questions, Pari. Do you think I'm wrong for you? Or is there some other guy you've decided is wrong for you, but he's the right one? Just how many guys are you considering?" He was laughing.

"Eric," I punched him gently on the arm. "We don't believe in that stuff, remember?"

"Of course we don't."

We spent the next few minutes slurping.

"So," he said, stirring his smoothie with the straw and gazing intently into the cup. "Friday night?"

"I'd love to. How about dinner?"

"I was thinking we could try a double date."

And before he could mention his parents, I said the names of the first couple that popped into my head. "How about Sophie and Reese?"

To my relief, Eric thought that was a great idea. Now I just had to convince Sophie or come up with an alternative couple. I was *not* ready for dinner with the folks. "Sounds like a plan," I said. "I didn't think you were the double date type, to be honest."

"Maybe I'm not."

"Why do you want to go on one, then? You don't want to be alone with me?" I gave him a teasing smile.

He slurped up the last of his smoothie. "Maybe I want to get to know your friends a little better."

"And what about your friends?"

"I don't have any friends."

I gave him a curious look and nodded. "None at all?"

"I work hard," he said. "I have colleagues. I belong to a bike club, and a yacht club, and a fitness club. I think of those people as acquaintances. Friendship is different."

"Is that a problem for you?"

"Not at all. But friendship is clearly important to you."

I nearly melted, right there in the frigid café with one last slurp of fruit smoothie. "That's sweet," I said.

This, of course, made Isabella's reading all the more problematic, because at that moment, Eric felt more like the right guy than he ever had before, which, if we're going to trust her psychic abilities, made him the wrong guy. Luckily for me, and for Eric, I considered Isabella to be about as psychic as a moth hugging a streetlight and thinking it had found the moon. I reached out and took Eric's hand across the table, giving it a squeeze.

"Right or wrong, Eric. You're a great guy."

Chapter Twenty-eight

MaryAshford has joined the chat.

LegitChris: The story comes out this week.

MaryAshford: Hey guys. Ready for the cemetery?

LegitChris: We're all set. But the girl Sam keeps kissing doesn't know about the newspaper story yet.

SamTheMan: I'll try to work it into conversation the next time I see her.

MaryAshford: You mean if you can keep your lips off her? <insert pissed emoji here>

LegitChris: We wanted him to charm her, remember?

MaryAshford: You wanted him to charm her. I just wanted him to be nice.

SamTheMan: You're saying kissing isn't nice?

MaryAshford: Forget it.

SamTheMan: Does Vanessa know about the article?

LegitChris: I mentioned it in general. Not that minor detail.

MaryAshford: Why don't I call them both?

SamTheMan: Absolutely not. Let's just let it play out.

LegitChris: She's not going to be happy.

SamTheMan: There's nothing we can do about it now.

MaryAshford: She should be warned. I'd want to know if it were me.

SamTheMan: I told you I'd try to say something when I see her.

MaryAshford: Do you have a date or something?

SamTheMan: No.

MaryAshford: Good. It's bad enough you're kissing her. Getting mixed up with her is bad for business.

SamTheMan: That's a bit alarmist.

LegitChris: We know where she'll be on Tuesday. We'll just happen to be there at the same time.

MaryAshford: Clever. <Insert eyeroll emoji> You should call her, Sam. She'd think of it as a courtesy and maybe let up on the skepticism. Maybe let us into her office.

SamTheMan: I'll think about it.

LegitChris: He's afraid of her.

SamTheMan: Am not.

LegitChris: Are too.

MaryAshford: omg. I'll see you at the cemetery.

MaryAshford has left the chat.

LegitChris: Are too.

SamTheMan: Maybe a little.

Chapter Twenty-nine

To my surprise, when I showed up at Café Flamingo for the next Diva lunch the following Tuesday, there sat Isabella in a large inside booth with Melissa, Karen, and Kaya. She was dressed in purple again and her hair, as usual, a jumble atop her head, held together by unseen, ghostly mechanisms. A thick purple band held the flyaways and tendrils from her face and large gold and navy earrings dangled from her ears. As I sat down beside her, taking in a whiff of an unearthly scent, I saw they were comets, hanging by their tales from her lobes.

"You like them?" She smiled and shook her head so they jostled against her neck.

"They suit you," I said.

"Hmm." She frowned at me. "That could mean a lot of different things."

I smiled, trying to be friendly. "They're mystical…in a scientific way. So, yes; I like them."

"But you would never wear them."

"I wouldn't." It was the truth, after all. But unfortunately, the truth can cause all sorts of problems.

"Just a few short weeks ago," Sophie said, apparently overhearing, as she sat down next to me, forcing me to scoot closer to Isabella. "Pari wore sequined sneakers."

"That's true enough," I said.

"Why don't you wear them anymore?" Melissa said. By the sly smile on her lips, I imagined she knew very well why I hadn't worn the sneakers.

"It was a phase," I said. "But I still have them."

"I should hope so," Karen said. "You'd spark a riot at the Goodwill if you were to donate them."

"I hope you mean from all the ladies trying to buy them."

"Of course. What else could I mean?"

"I thought you might be saying they're hideous."

"Are they?" Isabella asked.

"They are not hideous," Karen said. "They're adorable. But Pari is usually dressed conservatively."

Suddenly I felt self-conscious in my black skirt, silk blouse, and heels. At least I hadn't worn the jacket. It was ninety-two degrees outside so the jacket stayed home.

"She's a professional." Isabella came to my defense. "We each wear the costumes of our outer selves."

"Well, your costume is much more fun," Kaya said.

"But you get to wear all that retro stuff," Melissa said to her. "That's fun. More fun than an apron over jeans."

"Not as fun as a purple whatever-that-is." Kaya waved at Isabella.

"I think the Florida word is muumuu."

At that we all laughed. There was little on our agenda that day and I could tell we were being very careful not to talk about our psychic reading with Isabella. One rule of Diva's Lunch was that we did not talk business unless the person involved brought it up first. And Isabella seemed to live buy a psychics' code that must be similar the psychologists' code: what's said over the crystal ball, stays over the crystal ball.

We each ordered some version of a salad and I asked after Vanessa and was told she was working through lunch for the Downtown Strawbridge Ladies' Club who were having their monthly dinner that evening.

"All up-dos," Melissa said. "With different sorts of purple hats and ribbons."

"A Purple Hat club?" Isabella asked.

"You mean the Red Hat Society," Karen said. "The

Ladies' Club appropriated the idea...with purple."

"But the poem," Sophie said. "It was about purple, wasn't it?"

"Red hats," Karen said. "Purple clothes."

"I'm confused," Isabella said.

"Get used to it," I said. Diva meetings were nothing if not chaotic.

"The Red Hat Society clubs wear red hats and purple clothing, from the poem," Karen explained.

"What poem?" Melissa said.

"You're just trying to make things more confusing," I told her. It was true. I bet.

"The Ladies' Club wanted to have hats too," Karen continued. "But they couldn't use red."

"Why not?" Isabella asked. It was a legitimate question.

"Because the Red Hat Society was doing it."

"They can't have two Red Hat Societies in town?"

"That would be copying the Red Hat ladies," Sophie said.

"I see."

"But what poem?"

"And the Ladies' Club," Karen said with a smirk, "had to make sure their dinners–not lunches, mind you–were official club functions. They can't allow any non-club members to join their activities, after all."

"I sense an inside joke," Isabella said.

"Indeed," Melissa said. "The Red Hat Society is not friendly with the Ladies Club."

"Cat fight," Karen said.

"Or maybe," Sophie said, "it's the other way around."

"What does that mean?" Melissa said.

"Hiss," Karen said.

"I'm just saying..." Sophie smiled as a salad was placed in front of her. She stuck a fork in it. "Maybe it's the Ladies' Club that has the problem with the Red Hat Society."

"What poem?" Melissa said again, a bit louder.

"Can you believe September is almost over?" Sophie seemed to want to change the subject, which was fine by me. We had enough to worry about with ghosts, psychics, and rumors of protests without having to bring the Elderly Ladies' Social Conflict into it.

So we spent several minutes on the weather, lamenting the sweaters folded and neatly stored under beds or on top closet shelves—sweaters our mothers claimed a person could actually wear in Florida way back in their day, but that we rarely bothered to dig out of moth balls.

After we'd finished our salads, Melissa cooed, "Pari, one of your men is here."

She was looking behind me and I turned to see Sam Preston and his friend Christopher. Unfortunately, he caught me staring and waved. I offered him a half-hearted, stupid smile—not on purpose—and a slight raise of my hand.

"Not bad," Isabella said. "How many men do you currently have?"

"None," I said, my face flush. "He's not my man. I have no men."

"She's still sort of dating Eric Lawson," Melissa told her. "He's a...what is he?"

"A mimbo," Karen said, laughing.

"He's not a mimbo."

"What's a mimbo?" Isabella asked.

"A beautiful but silly guy," I said. "A male bimbo. Karen's been watching reruns of *Seinfeld* again."

Melissa said, "Eric's anything but silly...or dumb."

"Bimbo is sexist," Kaya said.

"How can it be sexist when there's also a mimbo?"

"Just because you invent a term for men doesn't make the original any less sexist."

"Anyway," Melissa said. "I meant what does he do... for work?"

"Human resources consultant."

"You mispronounced 'boring,'" Kaya said with a smirk.

"I thought you all liked him," I said.

There were denials all around. Of course they liked him. But he was too perfect, dull, unfriendly. I had no idea

176

what they were talking about, and as they hadn't spent much time at all with him, I didn't think their opinions mattered so much. But then it occurred to me their opinions may have been formed by things I'd said about him.

"I hope I haven't complained about him unfairly," I said. "If I have, it wasn't meant to speak as if his faults define him. He's really a wonderful man."

"Such praise," Isabella said.

"No, really. Which reminds me, Sophie–"

"Hello, ladies." Sam Preston interrupted me. Christopher was taking a seat at a small table across from us. He nodded and scanned the group. I almost told him about Vanessa having to work but stopped myself.

"Ladies?" Kaya said.

"Hello women? Hey guys. What's up my dudes?"

The Divas laughed, except for me.

"We're Divas," Melissa said.

"No," I said. "Do not call us Divas."

"I would never," Sam said with a huge grin. "I don't mean to interrupt but, Pari, I'd really like to talk to you about the other night."

"Oooh," Melissa said.

"The ghost tour," I said. "Right?"

"Exactly."

"Why would you want to talk about that?"

"I want to know what you thought. What you saw, or think you saw."

"What makes you think we saw anything?"

"We all saw it," Melissa said.

"We saw something," I said. "Not an 'it.' Maybe a shadow or reflection. But not a ghost. It seems Melissa is the only one who saw anything and not surprisingly, she's the only one of us who believes in ghosts."

"What about Vanessa?" Melissa said.

I looked up to Sam. "If you want to know about the supposed sighting, it's Melissa and Vanessa you should talk to."

He nodded. "Okay, then. Thanks anyway."

"You don't want to talk to Melissa?" I said.

"I already have. I'm sorry to have interrupted your lunch."

He stood there for a moment, as if he had more to say, but finally turned away. When he sat down across from Christopher, the two engaged in what I can only describe as a whisper fight. At one point, Christopher hitched his thumb our way. I looked at the Divas, wondering what that was all about. But they were occupied with other thoughts. I could tell Melissa wanted to say something to me, but I glared at her. Sam and Christopher would hear every word. We sat in silence for a few minutes, sipping our drinks.

"It's just," Melissa said quietly across the table to me. "On our way from the Moaning Door, I heard you say it was a 'figure' you saw. Like a person."

I had said that. I shook my head. "It was all so fast. And it was dark. Everyone was excited. I can't be sure now what I saw. None of us can."

"Well," Melissa said a bit louder. "There will be more chances."

"I'm ready," Kaya said. "I thought the ghost tour was hilarious. Did you see the sign in Trudy's window?"

Trudy owned Trudy's Treasures, one of the three antique stores in Downtown Strawbridge. She had the advantage of housing her collection in an ancient house. She'd been sitting on the front porch in a rocker waiting for Sam's tour group to arrive and happily led us quietly through her dimly lit store. Imagine a hoarder of antiques–not in a piles-of-stuff-everywhere way, but an every-surface-covered way. And the house is so old the floorboards creaked with every step we took so it sounded as if the spirits were criticizing our very presence as we walked through, breathless, everyone but me (apparently) hoping to have another ghostly encounter. "Aranthia is here," she'd told us. "She's always been here."

"She's advertising the séances," I said.

"No, it's more than that," Kaya said. "She wants everybody to know Aranthia is in her store."

"We didn't see anything when we were there," Melissa said, disappointment in her voice.

We'd heard plenty of spooky noises. A few people gasped and jumped, startled at their own reflections in one of the dozens of antique mirrors. But no floating figures or moaning vapors.

"Doesn't matter," Kaya said. "She painted her front window. 'Aranthia Shops Here! Aranthia's Favorite Haunting Spot!'"

"Oh, no," Sophie said. "Mr. Cornell isn't going to like that."

Let's Review:

1. Mr. Billy Cornell. Owner of Old Geezer's Antiques. West end, south side, next to Bookish. Has the best antiques in town.

2. Ms. Trudy Spencer. Owner of Trudy's Treasures. East end, south side, before the railroad tracks. Has the best antiques in town.

3. Mr. Swanson. First name unknown. Owner of Venerable Trinkets. Smack dab in the middle, north side. Actually voted as having the best antiques in town.

4. Mr. Cornell and Ms. Spencer fight and Mr. Swanson always seems to win.

"So, what's next?" Kaya asked Melissa.

"I'll give you a hint. Where is the place we're most likely to meet up with a ghost?"

A slight chill ran up my spine and I caught sight of Sam Preston looking at me. I turned toward him. He winked. Dear Lord, not the cemetery tour.

"*Warning*," Sophie said.

"It's not that scary," Melissa said.

"No," Sophie said. "The poem is called *Warning*, by Jenny Joseph." She held up her phone to show us she'd been Googling. "'When I am an old woman, I shall wear purple, with a red hat that doesn't go.'"

"Doesn't go where?" Isabella asked with a laugh.

"With the purple," Karen said, too serious.

"It is hideous, isn't it?" They all looked at me in horror. "Well, it is."

"You are forthwith not invited to the eventual Divas'

179

Red and Purple Hat functions," Karen said.

"Eventual?"

"We're not old women yet," Melissa said. "Which is a good thing. Can't have any clutching of pearls or fainting on the cemetery walk."

I shuddered.

Chapter Thirty

The next morning, Sophie knocked on my door and when I pulled it open, she shoved the front page of the Strawbridge Gazette at me. In huge block letters it read: Ghost Haunts Downtown Strawbridge.

"Oh, no," I said.

Sophie handed me the paper. "The main story is in the Downtown insert. It's got quotes from nearly everybody."

"Not me, I hope." I read the tag line–Christopher Reynolds has the story. "I bet he does," I muttered. "You don't think he printed anything I said, do you?"

"I didn't see any quotes from you. But Vanessa and Melissa are in there."

"That sneaky man!"

"And lots of people in your office building. Keep it," she said. "I've got to get to the store."

"Wait, I wanted to ask you something." Suddenly I felt awkward, like I was asking my crush to the prom. "Eric and I were wondering if you and Reese wanted to have dinner with us on Friday."

Suddenly I wished I could take it back, but Sophie seemed pleasantly surprised, and the date was set. I realized then this was a test, and not a small one. It's not quite a meet-the-parents nail-biter but bringing your boyfriend–for lack of a better word–into your circle of friends is only slightly less important.

After Sophie left, I stood on the landing reading the article until I heard a door slam on the floor below jolting me out of the world of hauntings and Aranthia, the forlorn ghost of Downtown Strawbridge. I couldn't read it all as I had to get to work but I brought it with me. Everyone in the Executive Suites building was talking about it, sharing it, reading it again. I hurried to my office, closed the door behind me, and quickly finished the article before my first appointment.

Sam Preston and Christopher Reynolds certainly made a great team. Christopher's writing was crisp and laced with humor, even as he seriously evaluated the ghostly evidence, while Sam's photos of supposedly haunted spots downtown were prominent on every page. Christopher pieced together Aranthia's story from the various accounts floating around and included quotes from all sorts of downtown business owners and residents. Suddenly dozens of people were claiming to have seen the ghost. "Preston is certain the ghost of Aranthia is connected to the Executive Suites building and believes she originated in the office currently occupied by a psychologist. He has yet to gain permission to enter the office for further study."

"He didn't!" Sure, Christopher didn't mention my name, but I was the only psychologist with an office in the Executive Suites building. But worse, just as Sophie said, many of the people in the building, even on my floor, claimed they felt the ghost's presence near my office.

So...Let's Review: I was livid!

I forced myself to breathe deeply for ten seconds; I touched my toes and rolled my spine back up five times; then I beat the back wall with the sofa pillow five times before I felt calm enough to see my first client. And things only got worse from that point.

Mrs. Rosen was so excited about the ghost in my office, she chattered on about her week absentmindedly as she peered about–at the painting of cats opposite my desk, at the corners where I kept potted plants, at the ceiling and the slowly turning fan and all around at the dancing shadows it created. "Do you think she's here?" she finally said. "Is she listening?"

"I haven't seen any evidence of a ghost in this office," I said.

"But that man says she's here."

"He thinks she may have lived here when she was alive. But that doesn't mean her ghost is here."

This seemed to calm her down somewhat, but it was obvious she was disappointed. "Well, you should let him come in here and do his tests."

"Does it matter?"

"Oh, yes. Don't you think? I mean, I'd want to know if there was a ghost in my house."

The rest of the day was no better, and worse, I had three calls from people wanting appointments and I had the eerie feeling it was only because of the ghost. Still, I wasn't about to refuse anyone counseling, even if it turned out they just wanted to see my office. And then came the call from Sam Preston himself. When Abby buzzed me, telling me he wished to speak to me, at first I wanted to refuse. But that would have been petty.

"I'm sorry about the article," he said first thing. "I should have told you before it came out. I argued for not including information about your office at all. But Christopher wanted it in, and the editor was okay with it."

"Why?"

"The idea of a psychologist doing business out of a haunted office was too much irony for them."

"They must realize I'm the only psychologist in the building."

"Yeah, but everyone Chris talked to already knew I thought the ghost was in your office. They knew your name."

"Well, now everybody else in Strawbridge knows, too."

"So, I guess asking for an appointment is futile at this point."

"I don't make ghost hunting appointments."

"What if I gave you half the time...you know...to

actual counseling?"

"What are you proposing?"

"Half the hour, I spill my guts and you counsel me. And the other half I get to do my ghost thing."

"And I would be present for the ghosting?"

"Absolutely."

"What will you be spilling your guts about?"

"I can't spill them right now."

"Standard procedure, Mr. Preston. I also have to ask if you are, or have been, considering hurting yourself."

"Hurting myself? No. I don't have to want to hurt myself for counseling, do I?"

"Of course not. If you were planning to do yourself harm, I'd be getting you into a hospital. Do you need a hospital, Mr. Preston?"

"No."

"Well, then. What is the problem? What is it you would like counseling about?"

"Can't I tell you when I get there?"

"It's not usual that my client doesn't at least know what's bugging him. Why don't I put you down for delusional thinking?"

I could almost hear his brain ticking over the phone. "Whatever it takes. So, how about it?"

"I'll give it some thought."

He was much too happy at that, if you ask me. I'd barely promised anything.

"We can talk more about it tomorrow after class," he said.

I'd forgotten all about my next photography class. Obviously, a case of avoidance.

"You're still in the class, aren't you? You haven't dropped it."

"You don't scare me, Mr. Preston. I'll see you then."

I'm sure he was stifling a laugh as he said goodbye.

Having spent a fair bit of time with him completely sober, I'd say Sam Preston was a man who desperately wanted to be believed. Not just about ghosts, but probably about a great many things in his life. He wanted to be taken seriously.

One of the strangest quotes in Christopher's story was from Isabella Bolton. "There's definitely a ghost in this little downtown district," she said in a caption beneath a picture of her standing outside her parlor. "You feel the presence of despair and confusion everywhere you go here. I'll attempt to contact the ghost of Aranthia and any other spirits lurking about."

This did not sit very well with some of our more conservative residents, and from the gossip traveling store to store and finally to me through Abby, the protest against the supernatural evil in our midst was set for Friday night. So much for a relaxing double date with Sophie and Reese.

Chapter Thirty-one

As busy as my life was–and I'm not complaining–I managed to do two photo shoots for my homework. The first, as instructed, on auto mode, and the second on aperture. I walked east on Manatee Road, crossed over the railroad tracks and under the US1 overpass to Strawbridge Harbor, where boats bobbed in the water, tethered to posts along a boardwalk in a little marina. Picnic tables, gazebos, and flowering plants– plenty of subjects to photograph–dotted the grassy area beside road. Auto was a piece of cake. Just aim and snap. All my pictures turned out fairly well. But aperture mode was less clear. I had to select the eye-width of the camera, if you will, telling it how much light to let in. If I didn't let in enough, the shutter speed opened and closed like a yawning baby and all I got was blur. Our homework included emailing Sam one picture from each setting, and I felt as if I were back in high school, both hopeful to be chosen as an example, and horrified at the thought. But, as our final class count stood at eight, it looked like we would all be up on the big screen, cringing at the exposure –pun intended.

That Thursday night, Sam went through our pictures, splashing them up on the screen he unrolled from its tube attached to the ceiling against the far wall, zooming in on each subject, basically showing us we were terrible photographers. My auto mode picture captured the butt of a bee as it buried itself into a flower. The original shot looked great. But when enlarged, it was clear, my bee butt was blurry.

"Take dozens of shots," he told us. "Zoom in on your best and I think you'll find at least one that works." He promised us that over time, our pictures would get better.

We spent the rest of the class taking pictures in the dim light of The Art Center, playing with the various tools that would give the lens extra light. Once our time was up and everyone was filing out of the room, their cameras tucked back into bags and backpacks, Sam called my name. I stayed back, waiting to defend my position on ghosts in the office. He put away the big screen–it slurped back up with a snap–and pulled himself onto his teacher stool.

"Are you enjoying the class?" he asked, spinning this way and that.

Surprised, I said, "Yes."

"What made you want to take a class on photography?" All the way around this time.

"It wasn't you," I said. "I swear."

He clutched his chest but smiled. "I'm heartbroken."

"I've taken all sorts of artsy classes. Just looking for a creative outlet that suits me."

"Why didn't you tell me?"

I shook my head. "Why would I?"

"When we were at your apartment, after The Fort. Remember? You asked me about photography. I told you I teach classes. I was just wondering why you didn't mention you were taking one."

"Maybe I didn't want you to know."

"Didn't want us to have anything in common, huh?"

"I'd hardly call taking a class and being a professional having something in common. Besides, I'm clearly going to suck at this as much as I did the other classes. My bee butt was really blurry."

He laughed. "How many pictures did you take of the bee."

I stared at him. "I'm embarrassed to say."

He raised his hands and spun around again. "No judgement."

I sighed. "Maybe one hundred."

He whistled.

"You said no judgement." But I was smiling. Even I was sure one hundred pictures of a bee was excessive.

"Why did you choose that particular picture for class?"

"It was the cutest one. He was all over the place. I even got one of him flying, which was cool. But I loved his blurry bee butt."

He stopped spinning and looked at me for a few seconds, long enough to make me uncomfortable, long enough for me to think about kissing him again. Just when I was about to slap myself into consciousness, he stood up and gathered his things.

"I don't think you're going to suck at this class. Come on, I'll walk you to your car. There's danger afoot on the dark streets of Strawbridge."

He turned off lights behind us as we made our way out of the center and bolted the door. We'd both parked in front of the building a few empty spots between our cars. I looked back and forth a few times between my little blue Civic and his hulking silver Range Rover.

"I carry a lot of equipment around," he said with a sly grin. "And I get out in the wild now and then."

"I didn't say anything." Not with my mouth anyway.

"You looked a little scared of it."

"Not scared...exactly. My car just looks so tiny now."

"Big car envy." He winked.

"Weren't you going to ask me again about getting into my office?" I said as I dug my keys out of my purse.

"You make it sound so dirty."

I smiled and shook my head. "You're hard to dislike, Mr. Preston."

"Ah, but you'll keep at it. No, I think I'll cut you some slack tonight. You've got a lot of bee butt on your mind. Go back and look at your photos again. Start asking yourself what you like about them, what you'd like to do better next time."

"Yes, sir." I smiled.

Sam stood on the walkway in front of the center and waved as I drove off. As I made my way home, I couldn't help but feel there were two Sam Prestons. One was more real than the other, and he was fighting hard to keep that one in check around me.

The next afternoon, Friday, Twila Harper curled up in the chair opposite mine in my office and said, "I'm definitely becoming a ghost. Like dead."

"Why do you say that?"

"It's obvious. I'm spending more and more time in a ghost like state. I spent all day Wednesday at work watching the way people look at me. Even once I've gotten their attention, they look confused. How confusing could it be? I'm a hostess. It's not a weird thing to be greeted and seated by a hostess. But I'm not sure it's such a bad thing. I mean, I admit, I was scared at first. That's why I'm here. But the more I think about it, the more I like the idea of just...fading away. Haven't you ever wanted to fade away?"

I smiled. "I imagine a lot of people feel that way once in a while. Tell me, how is your list coming along?"

She pulled a folded, crumpled piece of paper from her little purse and spread it out on her lap and sighed. "I came up with a few things. I like music. But I could only think of being a roadie and that would be more like a hobby."

I laughed. "We'll work on that. What else?"

"I thought more about dancing. I'm not interested in ballet and such anymore, but I thought I could try swing or salsa. They have special nights over at Tracks for those and I could take lessons."

"Those are good options. But have you thought about something completely different from anything your parents ever encouraged?"

"I did, actually. Don't laugh."

"I wouldn't dare."

"Cake decorating." She looked triumphant. "I even thought about working at the bakery in Publix and one day, I could have my own cake shop."

"That's wonderful. Maybe you could start with some classes."

Twila was off to a great start. My hope was once she found interests of her own, outside what her parents had nudged her toward, she'd feel a bit more solid. Pun intended.

Chapter Thirty-two

Getting ready for a night out with Sophie and Reese later that evening, I thought about Twila and that feeling of wanting to fade away. I hadn't felt that way in a long time, unless you counted moments of embarrassment. If those counted, it happened a lot.

I told Sophie I'd promised Eric we'd walk to the restaurant downtown, which meant I had to wear comfortable shoes. To *dinner*. At Tracks. I made a wild and crazy decision to go with sneakers. I wasn't exactly happy about it, but I was determined not to let the sneakers tell me how to dress. I had a most adorable skirt I'd patched together using a cut-up natural silk evening gown with added bits of denim lace, all in the most glorious shade of aster blue. My sneakers were a paler shade of denim and I topped it all off with white three-quarter sleeve crop. It was definitely more casual than I was accustomed to. But I felt...free. And if I was going to have to wear sneakers to dinner, the least I could do was look great while suffering through it.

"Oh, my god, I love it!" Sophie squealed as we met up on the landing outside our apartments. She pulled at the skirt, and I twirled for her. "That must have cost a fortune."

"Not really that much."

"Now I feel under dressed."

"Don't be silly. You look great."

Eric was already coming up the stairs and we met him halfway down. He was sporting a collared, long sleeve shirt, and slacks with dress shoes. He might as well have been wearing a tie.

"We're going to look like two couples who met on the street," Sophie said. "And you guys took pity on us and are buying us dinner."

"Should I change clothes?" We were down the stairs and already heading over to Reese's surf and beachwear store.

"Why would you do that?" Eric asked.

"She's right, Eric. We're overdressed."

We argued for a bit until we realized Sophie had started walking again. "Come on Fashion Divas," she called. "You guys can't help it if you're fancy."

Our building was just across Manatee Road from downtown, where it sat on Crane Creek—not that we could see the water from our apartments. From there, it was a few hundred feet to Mangrove Street where Summer Sun was located, somewhat on the outskirts of the main shopping corridor. Reese left his manager in charge and was, as Sophie warned, decked out in jeans and tie-died tee. He looked confused when Sophie laughed.

"Great skirt, Pari," Reese said. "Looks almost casual enough for our shop."

"Who designed it?" Sophie asked. "Maybe you could get some, or some like it."

"I don't know, actually," I said.

"How can you not know?"

"Do you know who designed your jeans?"

"Lee," she said. "Duh. I thought you were into designer clothing."

"Not everything I buy has to be a designer label."

I must have sounded peeved, because Sophie said, "Of course. Sorry." But she glanced at Eric who'd had little to say since we left our apartment building. When we started to cross Strawbridge Avenue to Tracks, we heard the commotion. Before we crossed the railroad tracks, we peered westward. Even from that distance, we could see the road had been blocked by a large crowd of people.

"It's the protest," I said.

"We should check it out," Reese said and before I knew it, he and Sophie were heading down the street.

"We have a reservation," Eric said.

Eric was not an impromptu sort of person. I frowned and watched Reese and Sophie rush headlong toward the excitement. She turned back and waved an invitation to join them.

"It won't take long to check it out."

He wasn't happy about it, but we managed to catch up to Reese and Sophie and together we made our way into the heavy crowd. The mass of bodies was so thick in front of Isabella's I lost Eric as Sophie and I followed Reese through the throng. And there, pacing back and forth carrying signs made from poster board, were three teenagers–two boys and a girl. They were smiling, laughing even. And Isabella was at the door to her shop yelling at them.

"You haven't got the sense God gave a chicken," she was saying. "I'm not a witch, I tell you. And even if I was, there's no law against it."

That's when I got a good look at their signs. "Witch Go Home!" "Just Say No to Witchcraft!" And the third one, poor girl, said "Don't Turn Me Into a Newt!" They were neatly made, at least, like the kids had spent quite a bit of time on design and lettering. A few artsy touches here and there: a lizard that was supposed to be a newt, I assumed; a witch's hat; a broomstick.

Above the honking car horns, I heard Officer Palmer's whistle. (Officer Palmer is our dedicated downtown protector of the peace.) He shouted, "Come on, folks. Let's disperse. You're blocking traffic."

There didn't seem to be any movement to lessen the mass of bodies and I could certainly understand why. This was priceless.

"She's right," Pat Willard said, pushing her way through the crowd to face the teens. "She's no witch. I'm the witch."

Everybody laughed and I wasn't sure if it was because there stood Pat Willard in her navy suit, conservative white blouse buttoned almost to the neck, her dark hair cropped to her scalp. I mean, witch? Hardly. Or they might have laughed because the teens stopped their pacing and gaped at her, as if no one would ever dare to proclaim oneself a witch. And then it went straight out of control from there.

"I'm a witch, too," Melissa shouted. I caught her smiling face peeking out from between two much taller people across the protest—such as it was.

"Me, too!" At this revelation by Mr. Cornell, owner of Geezer's Stuff Antiques, everyone declared his preference for coven-hood.

Sophie looked at me, her eyes dancing, and called out to the crowd, "We're all witches here. What are you going to do about it?"

Over the laughter rose the most operatic screech you could imagine. "William Rochester Davies!"

The crowd, stunned into silence, split like the Red Sea as Carolina Davies, owner of Begotten, came forward. Tall and trim, she wore pink, plaid, polyester pants, and a three-quarter sleeved rose tunic. Over that, her muslin Begotten apron, with its picture of praying hands against a sunrise, hugged her chest. And she was pissed.

"Mom!"

Little gasps and twitters spread around as we realized we'd been teasing the child of one of our own.

"And Lisa Pattinson," Carolina said. "I'll be having a word with you mother." Lisa didn't take it well. "What in Heaven's glorious name are you doing here?" she said to her son, but not without a stern glance at the other young man.

William Rochester Davies was a puddle of goo in the face of his mother, and everyone hushed to hear: "Blaine dared me," he mumbled.

"Did not!" The other one was, apparently, Blaine.

"Did too."

"This was your idea, man," Blaine said. "Tell her,

Lisa."

Lisa's eyes went wider than I thought possible, and she took a few steps back.

"Okay, it was my idea," William Rochester Davies groveled. "But I was joking. Then you dared me to do it. And you're doing it too."

"I had to," Blaine said. "You made me."

"I will deal with you in a minute," Carolina said, holding up a threatening finger to poor Blaine. "Where would you get such an idea?"

"You said she was a witch." Oh, he did it now. The entire crowd gasped.

"I said no such thing."

"You said...something. Psychic something."

"Oh, dear." Carolina turned to the crowd. "Now, I did say something over dinner," she admitted. "I said I didn't believe in psychics any more than I believed in witches. How on earth does that lead you to...to..." Carolina had lapsed into speechlessness.

Her son shrugged. "I thought it would be fun. And anyway, they said they're all witches."

"I'll witch you in a minute. Come on, let's go." But instead of marching the kids through the crowd and presumably home, she pushed them toward Isabella. "These kids would like to learn more about what you do," she said. "May we have a psychic reading?"

Isabella, glowing in a purple and gold caftan allowed them into her store. With a smile, she waved goodbye to the crowd, and we all stood gaping at the sudden end of our entertainment.

"Well, that was odd."

I turned to the speaker to find, as I knew I would, Sam Preston behind me. He had his camera at his chest.

"Did you get pictures?"

"Of the back of the crowd, yes," he said. "And a few close ups on the signs."

"Not the kids? Not Carolina?"

"The kids are minors," he said. "And I'm not here to embarrass anybody."

"Sure," I said. "You can tell Christopher that despite

what he might think he heard, I did not proclaim myself a witch with the rest of the crowd."

"Not much of a team player, are you?"

"How can I get you to understand I have a professional reputation to maintain?"

"Seems kind of rough to let your profession control your entire life."

"And if my profession is my entire life?"

As soon as I said it, I wished I could take it back. This is what happens when you don't practice positive awareness–a habit that is at its best when used to think *before* we speak. I have to give Sam Preston credit, though. He didn't take the opportunity to look down on me with pity and do that *tsk tsk* thing my mama always does when I've proven myself silly.

"If that's the case," he said instead. "You can't use it as an excuse. You can't say you didn't join in the with confessions because you were thinking of your professional reputation. You didn't join in because that's just not you."

"Fine," I said.

"But that means, unfortunately, Dr. Logan, you are no fun." He looked at Eric now standing at my side and held out his hand. "Sam Preston."

"The Ghost Whisperer," Eric said, accepting the handshake with a nod.

Sam's face lit up. "That's right. Are you a fan of the show?"

"Never listen to it."

We three stood in the dispersing crowd in awkward silence, Sophie and Reese looking at us from a distance.

"Well, we'd better get to dinner," Eric said and led me away.

"Try to have some fun, Dr. Logan," Sam said.

Luckily, he couldn't see my face as it burned–from embarrassment or anger or probably a little bit of both.

Chapter Thirty-three

Sophie and Reese carried dinner—figuratively speaking. We were seated in one of the quiet back rooms at Tracks. Its front room is dominated by a long bar and some dinner seating to one's left and an enormous dance floor and stage on the right. Three back rooms and a terrace on the roof, overlooking the Executive Suites Building and the river beyond, offered quiet dining for those not wanting to dance. Tracks hosted Swing Night, Disco Night, and Line Dancing Night, as well as general dancing every weekend evening. That Friday we could hear the muted tones of a local band playing R&B from our table in the back corner of the Bird Room. The rooms were Florida themed and this one had paintings, photographs, and other artwork celebrating Florida birds, including an enormous iron statue of two sandhill cranes with their two colts in the middle of a water fountain in the center of the room. Very fancy stuff for Downtown Strawbridge.

Their awkwardness at having to keep a conversation going with minimal participation from me and Eric was hardly noticeable. For my part, I couldn't get Sam Preston's accusation out of my head. Was I no fun? Had I become that person in every group who couldn't let everyone else enjoy something simple? Something like ghost stories or psychic readings? Was my skepticism a downer? And there I sat, letting my worry about being no fun consume me to the point I was actually not being any fun.

I cast a few glances at Eric, remembering what the Divas said–about him being boring. Maybe he was boring, and it had nothing at all to do with the way I presented him to them. And yet, there was something else going on. He wasn't simply lacking in social skills this evening. From the way he kept his eyes on his plate most of the time, and the short smiles he offered when he did respond to Reese and Sophie, I got the distinct impression he was...angry.

And that's when Sophie said, "How's photography class going? It's started by now, hasn't it?"

Somewhat stunned, I said, "Great, really great."

"Was Karen right about Sam Preston? Is he going to be a guest lecturer?"

"What are we talking about?" Eric said as if suddenly awakened from slumber.

"I'm taking a photography class at The Art Center. I'm sure I told you about it."

"I don't think you did. And what about Preston?"

"As it turns out, he's teaching it."

Sophie gasped out a laugh. "Does Karen know?"

I nodded. "He's not a bad instructor, actually. So, it'll be okay."

"Your nemesis is now your teacher," Reese said with a smile.

It felt odd, realizing Sophie had apparently told Reese about my awkward but too obvious bickering with Sam Preston. But I couldn't fault her for it.

As Eric had barely looked at me all through dinner, by the time the bill was argued over, split, and paid, and we were walking away from our generous tip on the table, I realized he must be angry with *me*.

I'd never let my clients get away with such presumption, so, as we walked behind Sophie and Reese toward downtown for some ice cream, I put my hand in his and asked him.

"You seem edgy." Okay, so I didn't ask him outright. Speaking up is easier said than done, am I right?

"I feel off."

"Why?"

He squeezed my hand and smiled. "You'll laugh."

"I'd never."

Raising his brows at me, he said, "You like to think you wouldn't."

"So, what is it?"

"I'm not sure I can put it into words."

When he didn't continue right away, I put my psychologist hat on and said, "Just do your best."

"Okay," he said and sighed. "When you let Sophie and Reese drag us to the protest, I was...disturbed. I didn't want to go. I held back when you guys moved forward."

"I thought we'd lost you."

"I felt more like I'd lost you. And when Sam Preston said you were no fun..."

This surprised me. "What about it?" I hoped my unease didn't come through in my voice.

"I just stood there. Like I was on the outside again. I should have said something."

"What would you have said?"

"I should have defended you."

"I didn't need defending."

"You could have used solidarity, don't you think? If Sophie had been near enough to hear him, would she have said something?"

"Maybe. Yes. I suppose she would have."

"What would she have said?"

"She'd have pointed at my feet and said, 'Look at those shoes! Those are the shoes of a fun person!'"

He laughed and it felt as if we both relaxed finally.

"You are fun, Pari," he said. "Don't let that jerk tell you any different."

"I promise," I said. But I still wondered if Sam was right. "So, you think he's a jerk?"

"Absolutely. Why would you take his class?"

"I signed up last spring, before I knew him; and he wasn't supposed to teach it. The other guy broke his leg."

"How inopportune."

"I'll say."

Reese was holding the door for us at the mall, and we all stopped for a moment or two to gab with Octavia Washington and Noah Holland. They both worked in the little air-conditioned corridor on the north side of Strawbridge, he in his flower shop, Flower Power, and she in her second-hand clothing and accessories booth, Octavia's Closet. Octavia sang, "Look who's out on the town on a Friday night!" Octavia sang everything. Eric stood a bit behind us, but I took his hand to make sure we didn't lose him again. Not that Octavia was equal to a teen angst *slash* experimental protest. But I realized finally that Eric was uncomfortable where I was relaxed: with my friends. And he was going to need a leash.

We moved on to Moo's, a tiny little ice cream shop, no bigger than the booths Noah and Octavia worked in. I ordered a mint chocolate chip cone. Reese and Sophie shared a waffle cone. And Eric ordered a child sized cup of vanilla. I saw the look on Sophie's face when she saw it. It was a "who orders a child-sized cup of vanilla?" look.

"So," Sophie, bless her, turned to Eric. "You work in Pari's building?"

"Perry, Sax, and Sax," he said, perking up. "Human resources consulting."

"What is that, exactly?"

Ah, Sophie. She knew how to bring people out. Eric finally showed up—the Eric I knew. Animated, smiling, even humble, making jokes about going into huge corporations to help them fire hundreds of people and then helping those people find new jobs at other huge companies. Only Eric could make that interesting.

Once he'd wound down, there was a noticeable pause in conversation and he said, "What's next on the Ghost Challenge?" See? Eric was as friendly and sociable as the next person.

"Cemetery, I'm afraid," I said.

Eric shuddered. "No thanks."

Well, I hadn't asked.

202

Chapter Thirty-four

It's an unfortunate thing about people that they like to copy one another. Certainly, mimicry is a great evolutionary advantage for any species, but one ought to be careful what one emulates. As it happened, the protest we witnessed on Friday night was mere child's play. Nobody knows if the kids had got their idea from the general buzz about protesting and Carolina Davies' comments to her son, William Rochester, led him and his friends to pull off their stunt, or if it was the other way around. But the Saturday protest didn't look as if it had come together overnight.

I spent my Saturday morning sewing and then went to lunch with Karen at Brunch where we went over the latest chapters of her romance novel over salads and cold, sweet tea. We'd waited forty minutes for a table inside against the front window and watched people pass by laden with summer shopping bags.

"It's too hot to shop," I muttered and turned my attention back to Karen. "Have you come up with a title, yet?"

"About a dozen." She sounded despondent. "Nothing fits. I need to figure out what it's about, first."

"It's about romance. And sex. Lots of sex."

"Too much sex?"

"Who am I to judge?"

"But would you read it?"

"I am reading it."

"If I hadn't written it?"

"No. But that doesn't mean anything."

"You read such sad stuff."

"I suppose. But sometimes there are happy endings."

"My book will definitely have a happy ending and yes, lots and lots of sex." She giggled and speared several leaves of Ranch-covered romaine with her fork.

"The books I read don't have sex in them."

"How is that even possible?"

"What's the point?" Karen and I had already had this sex-versus-no-sex-in-books discussion several times.

"People have sex." Her *duh* was implied.

At just that moment Tildon Frakes was at our table, his mouth open ready to say hello, but thwarted by, I assume, the mention of sex. Small talk ensued with Karen and I pretending no one had said the word sex at all. I waited until he was all the way out the door and onto the sidewalk before I stuck a forkful of cuke and tomato in my mouth and said, "But if sex isn't part of the story, what's the point?"

"It is part of the story."

"Of your story, yes. It's a romance. Though not all romance stories have sex. Oh, never mind. The sex isn't the point. Just because it's not my kind of book means nothing."

"So, you think it's good?"

"Definitely. Except..."

"What? Tell me? It's terrible, isn't it?"

"I think maybe you shouldn't use the word 'buxom' so much."

"How many times have I used it?"

"A dozen at least."

"Agreed. Too many times. All this will work out in editing, don't you think?"

I smiled. "Absolutely."

"I could help you with your book."

I smiled. "I promise you, if I decide to finish it–"

"You really should."

"–you'll be the first one to read it."

We munched our greens for a few minutes, and I knew Karen was waiting for right moment to ask. "So," she finally said. "A double date, huh?"

I chuckled. "It was odd of Eric to propose such a thing. At first I thought he wanted us to double with his parents."

"He wouldn't. *Would* he?"

"I wouldn't put it past him."

"It's sweet he wants to get to know your friends."

"It is, isn't it?" I sipped my tea and watched the cars on the street stop and go.

"You don't sound convinced."

"I admit, when he suggested it, all sorts of crazy ideas ran through my head."

"Because it was so unlike him."

"Exactly. My first thought was, yes, his parents. I was worried he was one of those adults who can't fly the nest, right? But then I thought maybe he needed a kidney and was going to see if any of you were a match."

Karen laughed. "You're nuts sometimes."

"And then I thought maybe he wanted to sell us all time-shares or involve us in some multi-level marketing scheme."

"Anything but want to get to know us?"

"You're right. I'm nuts. But yes. The idea that Eric would want to hang out with my friends–it just didn't fit."

"What are you saying?"

"Nothing. *So what* if he's not a group sort of guy."

"I know that tone of voice," she said. "You have doubts."

"I have no idea what you're talking about." I sipped tea again, feeling trapped.

"You can't fool me."

"What is there to doubt? Eric and I are just dating. We're not serious yet."

"No grand, lusty beginnings for you."

"Nothing's wrong with slow and steady."

"You mispronounced boring."

"You're being mean."

"I'm sorry. Really I am." She looked contrite. "You know who you remind me of? In *Pride and Prejudice*. Elizabeth Bennett's friend."

"Charlotte Lucas? Plain and unmarried at twenty-seven? And I'm older than she is. Oh, no! I *am* Charlotte Lucas."

"You're hardly plain, Pari. I was talking about when she says, 'I'm not romantic, you know.'" Karen did her best in a terrible imitation of Lucy Scott as Charlotte Lucas in the BBC miniseries.

"You think I'm not romantic?"

Karen grimaced. "Well..."

I did my best to convince Karen I wasn't grievously insulted at the comparison and left her at Morgan's Office Supply after lunch. Back home, before I had the chance to cool off in my apartment, Sophie showed up with a craving for something sweet and back downtown I went. We stood on the sidewalk front of ChocShop, me shoving fudge into my mouth, and questioned how long we'd been in the candy store, because something had gone drastically wrong in Downtown Strawbridge while we'd been salivating over chocolate.

By then it was two in the afternoon and people were rushing past us toward the center of town. Shouting echoed against the buildings; chants against witchcraft rang out, filled with rage; and five storefronts away, in front of Isabella's Insights, poster-board signs danced above the crowd. Police sirens played their screeching melodies nearby. Apparently, it's against the law to block the street without a permit. Sophie and I never got close enough to see much of anything, despite trying to wiggle our way through the gawkers. Rumor had it there were only about thirty psychic haters involved and it was all over within a few hours, mostly because of the late afternoon downpour. You can imagine two hundred people suddenly running for cover under storefront canopies.

All in all, by about five o'clock, Downtown Strawbridge

took a tentative sigh of relief...before it prepared for battle. The first clue that nobody, and I mean *nobody*, messes with Historic Downtown Strawbridge was the signs showing up in store windows early that Saturday evening. Karen had used her store's copy machines to print them on bright pink and purple card stock and walked all over town offering them to willing business owners. "We support Isabella's Insights!" and "Psychics welcome!" On the sign in the window of Namasté, someone had inserted "and witches" before "welcome." But the genius was awarded to Trudy Spencer.

On Sunday afternoon–a drizzly, cloudy, muggy enterprise–Sophie and I stood in front Trudy's Treasures in awe of her newly painted window. "Aranthia Loves Psychics!" it screamed in bright yellow letters. "Come On In And Ask Her Yourself." Her store was filled with lovers of ghosts and psychics buying up trinkets having nothing to do with either.

"Mr. Cornell isn't going to like this," Sophie said.

We'd been shopping downtown, Sophie for some new foods to try from Across the Pond and me for pencils at Morgan's. And yes, I did spend forty minutes browsing office supplies, much to Sophie's amusement. But she bought Marmite and planned to trick Reese into trying it, so we were both a bit odd. We were on our way home—well, I was going home, and Sophie was off to spend the afternoon at Reese's store, when we thought we'd stop by to check on Trudy. The bell over the door tinkled in the muted, dust-sprinkled air as we entered, and the smell of old stuff enveloped us. Trudy came through the cluster of shoppers in her packed space, wiping her hands on her apron as if she'd been cooking dinner. She was a plump woman with graying blonde hair wispy about her face.

"Sophie," she said. "So happy to see you." Sophie turned to me, a smirk at her lips. She and I both knew Trudy was hoping Sophie would tell Mr. Cornell how crowded her store was. "And Pari. What brings you two into the bowels of antique-dom today?"

Trudy was a woman who loved her job. And second to that, she loved to torment Mr. Cornell of Geezer's

Stuff Antiques.

Let's Review:

1. Trudy Spencer's store looks like your standard wealthy ninety-year-old widow's house—if she were a hoarder of old stuff.

2. Billy Cornell's store looks like an upscale department store, except with really old stuff. And yet, Trudy calls her store Treasures and Mr. Cornell's is Old Geezer's. Go figure.

3. When they met, Trudy, or as Mr. Cornell calls her, That Godforsaken Woman Selling Cheap Knockoffs (a scandalous accusation), commented rudely on the Old Geezer's manner of store decor and from that moment they were mortal enemies. Everyone in Downtown Strawbridge knows it was Mr. Cornell, or as Trudy calls him, Billy Bob Jangles, who started the incendiary rumor that there were bodies buried beneath Trudy's Treasures. No one in Downtown Strawbridge—and certainly not Mr. Cornell—expected the slander would actually be a boon to her business.

4. What followed was a back-and-forth graffiti war on their respective store windows. Sophie knows more about that than I do.

5. We'd just managed to overcome the latest in the Downtown Strawbridge Antiques War when, after declaring their own stores had the best antiques in town, and insisting on a downtown vote, Mr. Swanson's store, Venerable Trinkets, won in a landslide.

"Oh, she's definitely haunting the place," Trudy told us as she rang up purchases behind her cluttered cash wrap. "She's easier to catch at night, of course, when things are quiet."

"You've seen her?" a customer asked, excited.

"You bet I have. It's just, I didn't realize who she was until this Ghost Whisperer came around. And now it all makes sense. The As everywhere."

"As?" Sophie asked her.

"As!" For a moment, until she started talking again,

the store was quiet, all eyes on Trudy. "Nearly every day, after opening the store, I'd catch sight of something cloudy swirling about in the corner before vanishing. And then I'd find some of my displays had been rearranged. Into the letter A."

Her customer gasped, her bag and receipt clutched in her hands. Trudy had to look past her, to encourage the next shopper to nudge her aside. No one wanted to leave.

"A," she said, shaking her head. "Aranthia. It's Aranthia. She's practically living here. Right here in Trudy's Treasures. Imagine that!"

Sophie and I took a short tour around the store and as we left, I said, "I suppose you're going to tell Mr. Cornell."

"It's my duty to keep him apprised of the competition?"

"You're an instigator, Sophie Childers."

She laughed. "I admit I'm fully invested in getting those two together, finally and for good."

"You don't think there's too much animosity between them? And it's only getting worse."

"It's all passion, Pari. You know what they say. There's a fine line between love and hate."

As we parted, her for Reese's store and me for home, we agreed to meet up outside our apartments at five-thirty for the cemetery walk.

"Are you excited?" she said.

"Hardly. I'm not a fan of cemeteries."

"Not that." Her grin was irrepressible. "You'll get to see Sam Preston again. Get a chance to test my theory of love and hate."

"You Divas are such buttinskies."

"Payback is hell," she sang as she wandered down the sidewalk, leaving me walk home alone. Truth was truth. But what we Divas did with Sophie and Reese was different. They wanted to be together; they just didn't know it until the Divas helped them along. My situation with Sam Preston wasn't the same at all. I could hear Sophie's laughter in my head as I readied for the dreaded cemetery walk.

Chapter Thirty-five

There was another rain shower, with a touch of thunder, while I had an early dinner, but it cleared up by five-fifteen and I wasn't exactly glad about it. I no longer had an excuse not to go on the tour. The thought of the Divas trying to finagle a relationship between Sam and me made me queasy. I wanted to convince them it was useless, but they knew I'd kissed him. Twice. It wasn't that big of a deal. It's not like I haven't kissed plenty of men. Well, okay, I could count them on one hand, but that didn't make me an innocent or a *nun*. I was, perhaps, sheltered, is all. The whole thing would have to play out, along with the ghost mania. Everything would get back to normal at some point and my life would be ordinary again...with Eric. Or at least with someone more my type.

"What is type?" Mama said on the phone.

She'd called tell me my brother had proposed to his longtime girlfriend, which naturally led to a borderline interrogation regarding my prospects.

"It's like art," I said. "I'll know it when I see it."

"I don't mean what is your type, Pari. What is type at all? Can you really point to a man on the street and turn away from him based on some ideal you've created in your head? It's the heart that loves."

"You know I don't agree, Mama. Love is all in the

head."

"But love doesn't care what you think is your type. There's no such thing as your type. There's who you fall in love with. That's all."

"You want to tell me the story of you and Daddy again, but I don't have time."

"Go on your cemetery tour," she said. "But you remember what I've told you."

Her story is that she was a strait-laced, conventional woman whose heart bound her to a hippie with wanderlust. And a nerd at that. The heart wants what it wants, she always said. Well, my heart wanted a man who wore button-ups at least on occasion and that was the type of man I was going to find. If I hadn't found him already.

A walk in a cemetery after a hard summer rain called for jeans and hiking boots that could grip the slick grass. And, wouldn't you know it, I happened to have an adorable pair of Gucci black leather boots I'd found at a consignment shop for only two-hundred dollars. They were worn and haggard enough to make me look like an experienced outdoorswoman. I had some wide yellow laces that would match my long-sleeved tee–too warm for summer, but necessary to help ward off mosquitos. And so, at five-thirty, Sophie and I met outside our apartments and sprayed each other liberally with insect repellent. It was other than lovely. But Central Florida, even on the first weekend in October...at night? Lay it on thick.

Coughing and laughing we took Sophie's new Elantra–dark gray to match the evening's event–over to the old Strawbridge Cemetery, north of downtown, across the street from the civic center and library. The biggest burial ground in town, it covered several acres along the main highway. The parking lot along the front fence was small and I felt irrationally sad looking at it. If ghosts were real, and the dead lived lives after this one, how might they feel about being left in their tombs with no visitors? I shook off the feeling as Sophie pulled her car into a spot. Melissa was waiting for us, bouncing up and down with glee.

212

"I need an answer now," she said.

"Then, no," I said. But I smiled as she completely ignored me.

"Listen up," she whispered. "Quinn Norris called me earlier."

"Who's Quinn Norris?" Sophie asked.

"He owns Tracks. You've seen him."

"If I saw him, I didn't know."

"Anyway, he's having a big costume party on Halloween night and the theme is The Ghosts of Downtown Strawbridge." She squealed and stomped her feet, but as soon as she saw others gathering, waiting for the cemetery walk to start, she pulled us to the back of the car. "He said he was calling some of the business owners early, to give us first shot at tickets. I told him we'd all want to go, but I have to pay up before he goes public. Are you in?"

"How much are we talking here?" I said.

"One-twenty per person."

"Holy Moly," Sophie said.

"That's pricey."

"It's actually a special rate. Early bird, he said."

"Are drinks on the house?" Sophie wondered aloud.

"Two drink tickets plus free *hors d'oeuvres* all night. Come on. I want it to be part of the ghost challenge. The final night."

"Can we add Reese?" Sophie pleaded.

"Sure," Melissa said. "Quinn told me to just let him know how many."

"We'll do it," Sophie said.

"Okay," I nodded. "I'm in."

"Do you want me to include Eric?"

My mouth fell open and I hesitated. "I...uh..."

"I'll take that as a no," Melissa said.

We made our way to the cemetery entrance, a wrought iron archway covered in vines. I wondered why I didn't say yes about Eric right away. And why I didn't correct Melissa. I reasoned that Eric wouldn't want me to make plans without discussing it with him first. Especially one-hundred-twenty-dollar plans. And that was almost certainly true. But there was more. I knew I wasn't even going to mention it to him. This confused me. I liked Eric. A lot. I wanted to date him. But he was definitely not a party person. Still, if he was my–*ugh*–boyfriend, I should invite him despite my assumptions and let him decide. So why didn't I want to? I knew the answer; I just hated to admit it to myself: When Eric isn't having fun, I don't have fun. Sometimes Eric was, to put a fine point on it, a drag. But if he was going to be my drag, I'd have to find a way to live with it. We all make compromises for love–or in this case, like. Strong like. Fairly strong. Okay, somewhat strong like.

The cemetery at dusk was a creepy sight. Surrounded in wrought iron fencing, dotted with ancient moss-draped oaks, it was speckled with tombstones. The section at the front was more modern, to be sure, with shiny new marble, flat or somewhat slanted, slabs on the ground. But as we headed farther into the silence of the sanctuary, the stone markers rose higher, and grew older, chipped, cracked, and leaning.

Sam had checked our names off his reservation sheet–a total of twenty-four curious ghost hunters–and handed us each a flashlight emblazoned with a Ghost Whisperer logo in fluorescent yellow. All the Divas were there. Karen had a notebook, open, pen poised. "I've got a great idea for another romance," she said. Kaya was decked out in a vintage 1920s gangster outfit. High wasted pants, striped button up, tie, and suspenders, topped off with a fedora. Sometimes I wished I could be Kaya. Vanessa was picture-perfect as always, her hair done up in a riot of curls. There were some vaguely familiar faces in the crowd, but no one else we knew, other than Christopher who waved at Vanessa but remained professionally aloof, and Mary Ashford who, if I'm not completely out of my mind, glared at me several times.

As Sam and his team led us along the main road among the graves, and then onto a dirt path toward the back and away from the busy highway, he told us the history of Strawbridge Cemetery. It had once been the burial grounds for a tiny church, the building he was now guiding us to. A stone structure, its steeple broken off, now served as a meeting place for those seeking a quiet moment while visiting their loved ones.

"There's no electricity," Sam said. "But you're welcome to go in for a minute."

In the dim twilight, we all formed a line and snaked our way through the little chapel. When I walked in, the hairs on the back of my neck stood up and I got a chill.

"You can almost imagine," Sam was saying outside, "the ghosts of the dead comforting those who enter this place."

"Comforting?" I said. "More like haunting."

"It's all in how you respond to it," he said.

In the ancient section, where for some reason ghosts are more likely to roam, Sam and his team had set up citronella candles and torches which only made the place eerier.

"There are three ghosts that haunt this cemetery more than any others," he said as we all gathered around a group of tombstones sequestered within a two-foot-high iron fence.

Karen, beside me, whispered, "Is it ghosts *that* or ghosts *who*?"

I laughed, bringing Sam to pause his speech and look at me for a few seconds making me blush.

"As I was saying," he continued. "This is the family plot for the Beardsberrys. I'm not kidding." We'd all chuckled. "The Beardsberrys were early settlers in Old Strawbridge, when the town was called Crane Creek. And it's said the ghost of Theodora Wilcox can often be seen here, her anguished body draped over the headstone of Arthur Beardsberry." How poetic. "But if you look at the plot," he continued, "you'll see Theodora Wilcox is not buried with the Beardsberry family."

"Is she buried here at all?" a young woman asked.

A sly grin spread across Sam's face. "She is. Way back over here in this corner." He led us around the graves to a cluster of dangerously uprooted plots, set among the exposed roots of an old oak. "Here lies Theodora

Wilcox. Born 1886. Died 1907. And yet, Theodora supposedly cries over the grave of a man born in 1857 and died shortly after settling here, in 1881."

"Maybe she isn't mourning him," Sophie said.

"But, why that grave?" Sam said. "She's always seen there, crying for Arthur Beardsberry." We all stood in the growing darkness wondering why ghosts were so stupid. Well, I was wondering that. "Unless," Sam said, "Arthur Beardsberry isn't buried in that plot."

"So..." an older woman, shining her flashlight up at her face—scary—said. "Why would they uproot Arthur and bury somebody else there?"

"The theory is..." Sam started leading us along a path behind Theodora's grave. "Theodora's lover was murdered by her father and brothers for dishonoring her. And to cover up their crime, they dug the grave up in the dark of night and dumped the body into the casket with Beardsberry."

I laughed. Loud. Everybody glared at me. "Oh, come on."

"I researched Theodora as much as possible," Sam said. "And the only thing I found out was that she was...how can I put this...dumb as a rock." Vindication is mine! We were all laughing now. "Seriously," he continued. "I shouldn't be so cruel. She was put into an asylum up north for not being of sound mind, and as one item put it, with the maturity of a child of three. So, maybe it's not a crime story or a funny story, after all. Maybe Theodora is lost and confused and is crying over, as you can see now—" his swept his arm wide over the back section of the cemetery in front of us—"the tallest headstone around."

"Aww..." someone behind me said. I think I heard sniffling.

"Isn't there something we can do?" another woman asked. I turned to see her, but her face was indistinct in the new darkness suddenly enveloping us.

"That's where the Ghost Whisperer comes in," Sam said. "I'll be trying to make contact."

"But," I said, "if you help the ghosts settle their issues,

won't they...cross over?"

"That's the hope," he said. "I don't actually know if it works."

Because he's never actually seen a ghost, no doubt. "Won't that put you out of a job?"

He smiled at me. Here I was, trying to be snarky, and the guy offers us a kind, almost self-help-guru smile. "Does that matter?"

A few of us waved bugs away from our faces, while most of the women cast adoring glances at Sam, soaking it all in.

"Another regular visitor," Sam said, breaking the sacred silence, "is said to be George Peterson." He led us around to another group of headstones in the open, under bright moonlight. "He's been somewhat identified because he wears the uniform of a Confederate soldier and he's the only one buried here who died at the right age—around fifty, people say. He's often seen wandering around the grounds stumbling and shouting."

"Still fighting the war?" a deep voice from the back asked.

"I don't think so," Sam said, still walking. "Town drunk."

"Oh, my god," I said.

Sam stopped suddenly and I ran into his back. I bounced off, stumbled, and turning into my fall, took a few angular steps only to trip over a small rock, landing on my face, sprawled out over somebody's grave. Yes, there were some gasps and shouts. But there was also laughter. I *definitely* heard laughter. I'm pretty sure it was Melissa.

"Are you okay?" Sam Preston was pulling me up by my armpits. He dropped me on my feet and pushed the hair out of my face.

"I'm fine. I think."

"You could have hit the tombstone," he said.

"With your face," the older flashlight face lady said.

"With your face," Sam repeated looking at me, concerned. His hands were on the sides of my head, and we stood like that for a few seconds too long.

Awkward. "I tripped." Stating the obvious. "What the

hell?" I took a step back. As it turned out, Erin O'Connely's grave had not only a headstone, but a foot stone as well. The rock that had led to my tumble. "Well," I looked at the group, moonlight highlighting their half-faces. "I've made contact."

Sam laughed. "You sure did."

"As I was saying–" Dodging the sly smiles of the Divas, I stepped carefully off Erin's grave and headed back the way Sam had been leading us. "–If George died drunk and is spending the afterlife in that condition, it doesn't bode well for us. Does it? I mean, what if a woman died in childbirth? Or what if I die with a migraine?"

"Or eaten by a shark," a guy shouted.

"Smashed by a steam roller," Melissa said. Where does her brain come up with these things?

"Exactly," I said.

"That does present a very interesting idea," Sam said.

"Damn straight," I muttered.

"You're going to love the next ghost," Sam said with a wink at me. "This way." He led the group back toward the start of the older section, to a set of graves seemingly buried at random. "Harry Lemons," he said. "Reports have him standing on his grave, hands up, pressed against an invisible barrier."

"He died in jail?" someone asked.

"Nope."

"Trapped in a mine?"

"Close."

"Inside a shark?"

We all laughed.

"You'll never guess," Sam said. "My research discovered that Harry Lemons was a performer. Specifically...a mime."

A cringing groan erupted in us all.

"That means," I said, "the first few people to report his ghost had to have known he was a mime."

"Why do you say that?" Sam said.

"Oh, come on." I rolled my eyes and appealed to the group. "Seriously. You don't actually believe the ghost of Harry Lemons haunts the cemetery as a mime...do you?"

I looked to Karen, then Sophie, my only hope for support. They shrugged. *Cowards.*

Just before he turned to lead us along the path toward the front of the cemetery, Sam shook his head at me, as if I'd ruined his fun. The group split up, encouraged to scout out the cemetery on our own. Sam taught us how to "whisper" for ghosts. It's like this: Stand quietly, eyes closed, listen carefully, then whisper whatever words come to your mind. Listen, listen (seriously, he said it twice) and if you hear a reply, open your eyes. I was walking around with Karen, our flashlights shining on tombstones so we could read who died when, and at what age. Even in the modern section, there were too many babies and children. What had been fun was turning into something morose.

"Pari," Melissa whispered loudly. "Sophie, Kaya. Everybody over here."

Melissa was standing on a narrow path at a group of modern marble stones. When we approached, she pointed to the one in front of her.

"Melissa," I said. "You've found a ghost."

Chapter Thirty-six

The granite headstone read: Walter James Preston. Born June 8, 1985. Died August 23, 1997.

"Do you think he's related?" Melissa said.

"The bigger stone, there," Sophie said, pointing to a double headstone with names and birth dates carved into it. "The parents are still alive."

"There's no stone for Sam," I said. "If it is his family's plot."

"So, this would have been his brother?" Vanessa said. "That's so sad."

"He died when he was only twelve," Kaya said.

"That's awful," Karen said.

As we stood silent for a few moments, the evening wind whispered through the nearby oaks. I could hear traffic from the highway, and then Sam's voice telling stories about ghosts and spirits and the dead. Each of us turned, one by one, to watch him talking to the rest of the group, animated, having fun. Flashlights flitted about, making them look like a search party mob as they moved along the path away from us.

"No," Melissa said. "I don't think it's his brother. How could he come here?"

"It was a long time ago," I said. "And he would have been a kid when it happened."

"So, maybe," Karen said.

At that moment, Sam looked back at us. He paused and let the group pass him. I couldn't see his face in the dark, but I was certain, somehow, he knew exactly what we'd seen. Sam Preston had a brother who died young.

"Well, that would explain a lot," I said. "Come on, let's see what else Sam wants to show us."

The cemetery walk, I have to admit, was a lot of fun. Sam seemed to know the history of nearly every family buried there and he had plenty of ghost stories to regale us with at the spookiest, darkest spots of the burial ground. When the Divas had gathered outside the fence preparing to leave, they all stared at me, sly smiles on their faces.

"What?"

Then they all turned to look at Sam, approaching our group.

"Dr. Logan," he said.

I was, dare I say it, *positively aware* that every set of eyes was on me. "Thanks for the walk," I told him. "It was much better than I expected."

He tilted his head with a smirk. "I'm not sure how to take that."

"I meant it as a compliment. Really."

He smiled. "I wanted to check on you. Make sure you're okay, after your tumble."

"I'm fine."

He took my hands in his and turned them palms up toward the light from a streetlamp. "No scrapes? No bruises?"

I blushed. "Really, I'm not hurt."

"Okay," he said. He stood looking at me, still holding my hands.

He's going to kiss me, I thought. Embarrassed, I pulled my hands from his and took a small step back.

"Insurance," he said. "Can't have any injuries on my watch."

"Of course."

"Maybe," Melissa cooed, "you should make everyone sign consent forms before each tour. Who knows what other dangers lurk among the tombstones?"

He nodded. "Good point. Good. Good point."

And with that he saluted–I kid you not–and was gone.

"Insurance," Kaya said with a chuckle. "You make him nervous, Pari."

"You think he was lying?" I said.

"You're the psychologist," Sophie said. "You tell us."

"He's caring...about people. Nothing wrong with that."

"He sure is," Karen said and nudged Vanessa.

"*Pienso que le gustas,*" Vanessa crooned.

"What does that mean?" I said, feeling rather dumb. Everybody else laughed. "Oh, sure, like you know what she said."

"One day, we will all begin Spanish lessons," Vanessa scolded. "So, Melissa. What's next on the challenge? If you ask me, your victims are softening up to the paranormal possibilities."

"Well, don't harden," Melissa said as we all split up at our cars. "You've got until next Saturday night."

"But that's Swing Night," Sophie said.

"I think you'll have time afterwards."

"After what?" I said, not at all liking the devious look on Melissa's face.

"The séance."

"Oh, no. Is Sam Preston leading it?"

"It's part of his ghost thing. But he's not doing it. He's got some psychic lady."

"Isabella?" Kaya said.

"No, somebody named Fiona, or something like that."

"As in, Fiona Phony?" I said.

"Open mind, Pari," Melissa sang as she closed the door of her Jetta with Kaya, Karen, and Vanessa inside.

"I'm not looking forward to a séance," I muttered once seated in Sophie's car. "It's not that I believe any of it is real. But the idea is disturbing."

"I'll be embarrassed," Sophie said as she pulled her car onto the highway.

"Why should you be? It's Fiona who should be

embarrassed."

"Exactly. Don't you feel, like...residual embarrassment for people."

"Like sympathy pains?"

"Maybe that's a better word. Sympathy embarrassment. Except the person who should be embarrassed doesn't know they should be."

"That's empathy for you."

"Can a person have too much empathy?"

"Of course. If you're too involved in feeling for others, you may lose sight of your own needs."

"So, you're saying I should picture Fiona naked."

I laughed so hard I nearly choked. "Whatever works for you, Soph."

Her name, as it turned out, and as I learned from the flyers posted around town, was Felicia and from the look of the picture, she was about fifty years old with weirdly green eyes–like tree-frog green. I had a week to imagine every sort of disaster awaiting us on Saturday night at, of all places, Trudy's. Word on the street said Mr. Cornell was really, really not happy.

That Monday, I had my first new appointment since the ghost in my office made the papers and was pleasantly surprised and perplexed. A Mr. August Langdon, about sixty, wearing a denim blue untucked supposed-to-be-tucked silk shirt, with the top buttons open as if they simply couldn't contain the enormous bounty of curly gray chest hair beneath. His cuffs were folded to three-quarter length and he carried a brown tweed jacket, with brown elbow patches, over one arm, draping it over the back of the little couch before hiking up his beige twill pants and having a seat.

"I appreciate your taking time to see me," he said straightaway.

"I'm happy to do it."

Mr. Langdon, an English teacher at the local high school, said in his initial phone interview that he was suffering from anxiety and depression–something new to him–and he spent the entire hour explaining to me why. For the first twenty minutes I expected him to break off into his true purpose–Aranthia. But he never did. He kept his eyes on me, only glancing about the room when trying to put words to feelings, and never once approached the subject.

"I can't tell you," he said when our time was nearly up, "how much better saying these things aloud makes me feel. And not just to myself in the mirror, or to the cat. To a person, such as yourself, who listens. And understands."

I nodded. "Absolutely. Would you consider some homework?"

His smile was wide and genuine. "About time someone else did the assigning."

"I can understand your hesitation to confide in colleagues or your elderly parents. And I'm more than happy to be a sounding board for you. But I'd like to suggest you at least consider seeking out some relationships not related to your work."

"Are you suggesting...dating?"

"Not necessarily. Friendships."

"I used to have friends, but it seems as if that sort of thing is for young people."

I smiled. "It's not; I assure you."

"At my age? How would I begin?"

"What about Poetry Night?"

He looked confused.

"Once a month at Stogies, a shop here in the downtown area. There's quite a crowd."

"Poetry, you say?"

"Sometimes there's a theme, sometimes not. You can look Stogies up online for info or stop by the shop. Mr. Booker will be happy to tell you all about it."

"That does sound right up my alley."

I was pleased to make a second appointment for Mr. Langdon and then, out of the blue, I heard myself say, "Where did you hear about me, if you don't mind my asking. Did you look up local psychologists?"

"Oh, no. Do you know I hadn't even considered seeing someone until I read about the ghost in the Gazette. I must admit the idea of a ghost haunting a psychologist's office was hilarious. But suddenly it hit me.

I've struggled now for a few years, since...you know, the election–"

"Yes..."

"And I thought, I should try that. And since you were the only psychologist listed at Executive Suites, I called. And I'm so glad I did."

This was not going to help my reasoning against Sam Preston and his crazy sleepover plans for my office. But there were still two more new appointments to get through. I wasn't ready to discount my eggs before they started to stink.

Chapter Thirty-seven

My first thought upon finding Karen's invitation in the mail that evening after work was, isn't that adorable? Dinner and a Movie; Saturday after next. I mean, sending an invitation to the Divas for a get together. So sweet. Then I started to worry. It was an actual printed invitation. Karen's family owned the stationery store, so maybe it wasn't a big deal. She'd threatened a viewing of *The Wizard of Oz* so it shouldn't have been a surprise. When I pulled the card out of the envelope, tiny bits of confetti—the color and shape of ruby slippers, of course—fell out all over my kitchen table. Okay, I thought. A little overdone. But fun, right? *Be prepared to click your heels together for heavy hors d'oeuvres and a movie!* Egad. *Just follow the yellow brick road!* And at the bottom, it said: *Casual dress. Be prepared to curl up on the floor with a big pillow.* That's what really got me. How many people were invited to this thing? And that Karen hadn't told me about it beforehand ...I had a very bad feeling about the whole thing.

I called her right away. "How many people are you expecting?"

"About twenty-five," she said, as if it was no big deal.

"Twenty-five people!"

"Oh, come on, Pari. It'll be fun."

"Who all did you invite? I mean...is it just..."

"Just what?"

I couldn't think of a good way to say what I wanted to say. "Girls?"

She laughed. "No, Pari. This isn't a girls' night out. There will be boys. Do you want me to tell someone you like him?"

"Who, Karen?"

"You know who."

"You *didn't* invite Sam Preston."

Ah, but she did. After giving it a few minutes, I realized it wouldn't be that bad. I could bring Eric, for one thing, though she said she didn't send him his own invite– "I thought I'd leave it up to you"–and twenty-some-odd people in Karen's condo would be a crowd large enough to easily avoid Sam Preston. Eric would hate it and I would therefore have a rather bad time. But better to be miserable than dateless at a party with the so-called Ghost Whisperer. Imagine it. I'm out on Karen's balcony, overlooking the moonlit ocean, a salty breeze on my face and suddenly Sam is there with his sarcasm and teasing and then he's kissing me and why am I kissing him back?

"I'm bringing Eric," I blurted out like a talisman, and the image of Sam and me locked in a passionate embrace popped right out of my head.

"Does Eric know he's supposed to keep you and Sam off each other?"

"I have no idea what you're talking about." But she knew I knew.

"Sure, Pari, sure. Oh, I forgot. I talked to Kaya today and we were wondering about the Halloween party at Tracks."

"What about it?"

"It's a costume party. We thought we'd get the Divas together and shop for costumes at the Halloween store that pops up every year at the mall."

"Absolutely not," I said. And before I could stop myself, "We'll make costumes."

"Make them? Are you out of your mind?"

"We can't show up in costumes sold by the bag."

"We could rent some."

228

"Nope. We're sewing."

"I can't sew."

"Don't be silly, Karen. Of course you can sew."

"I don't think making a Barbie skirt when I was ten counts. Oh, wait..."

"Uh-huh. You sew." Sewing is one of those skills we lately try to pretend we didn't acquire.

"A few things. But...a costume?"

"Nothing to it. It's time for Group Diva!"

She did not sound happy. But she'd manage. We'd all manage. I texted Group Diva: Meet me at JoAnn Fabrics NOW! And surprisingly enough, I ran into Sophie on my way out, and when we arrived at JoAnn Fabrics across from the mall, the rest of the Divas stood waiting out front wanting to know what was going on. Reactions were mixed, to say the least. First, nobody would admit to knowing how to sew, but when pressed, all confessed to having at least tried. A pair of pants on which the crotch hit the knees. A button-up shirt on which the buttons didn't line up properly. A tee with a neckline that looked as if it were a coiled snake. We'd all failed but apparently, I was the only one to stick with it until I found success. Admittedly, it took quite a lot of time and practice. And nobody even thought about sewing anymore. Sewing was something our *grandmothers* did, that they taught us to do, and that we conveniently forgot about.

"I don't have a sewing machine," Vanessa said as they followed me into the store and to the pattern book tables.

"Neither do I," Melissa said. "What is this place, anyway? What's that smell?"

"Fabric," Kaya said.

"It's glue," Karen said.

"That is creativity," I said. "Breathe it in, Divas."

We all stood around the enormous rectangular table laden with chunky pattern books, and they stared at me as if they didn't know me, and I had three legs, and what could I possibly wish to accomplish in this bizarre repository of parts and pieces. Jazzy, adult-ish music played throughout the store and I suddenly felt as if I were in a horror film. This is where we drag our victims and sew lace trims and zippers all over their–I plastered a supportive smile on my face.

"Pari," Melissa said soothingly. "You can't *really* think you can make a Halloween costume. I mean...wouldn't you prefer to buy one?" She looked me up and down as if I was supposed to know what she was talking about.

"Look through the costume sections. You can pick the same pattern if you like, but you'll use different fabric."

"But what kind of pattern?"

"The easiest profile to make," I said, "is a shift or A line. So, let's go with the Roaring Twenties."

They liked that idea, though they remained skeptical. I found a pattern in one of the costume books set out for Halloween and there were enough variations that we would look like a typical group of Flappers out on the town.

"And we'll make hats!" Kaya said.

"We can get one pattern," I said, "and trace it for each of us. Or we can each get our own pattern and cut out our size." Judging by the looks on their faces, I was speaking an alien language. And I suppose that was true, in a way. I held up the pattern envelope and pointed to the size. "See. This covers every possible size."

"How is that even possible?" Kaya said.

"What do you mean trace?" Vanessa said.

"You use a tracing wheel and tracing paper and draw out the pattern onto your fabric. It's easy. But pattern paper is super thin and can't take much tracing, so let's get two copies, just in case."

"What is she talking about?" Sophie said.

"Like you know how to sew," Melissa said to me.

"Actually," Karen said.

"Never mind," I said, interrupting her. "Off to the fabric section."

We barely made it out of the store before they locked the door on us. I had the Divas pile all their stuff into Sophie's car and told them to meet me at my apartment on Wednesday night for our first sewing adventure.

On the way home, Sophie said, "We forgot one very

important purchase."

"What's that?"

"Sewing machines."

"I think we'll manage."

I had a secret. A secret I'd kept from most everyone. I only confessed to Karen about a year before. And now I was about to share it with the Divas. Not that I'm ashamed of it...exactly. It's just that I'd sort of been acting as if I wear only certain types of clothing. It happened so naturally I simply never corrected anyone of the notion. A few occasional designer pieces, found mostly at estate sales and even when retail, never at full price, and people get the impression everything you own is a Versace or a Chanel. The truth is...I sew. Not only do I sew...I...No. I can't bear to say it.

Chapter Thirty-eight

Our first night sewing in my apartment was a riot... almost literally. Tissue patterns everywhere, lost pieces, wine-stained pieces, ripped pieces. Pieces spotted with chocolate. But we managed to get everyone fit and cutting out fabric. Sophie lent her coffee and kitchen tables, and the Divas went back and forth between my apartment and hers all evening. I helped with all of it.

"I'm starting to think I can actually do this," Melissa said. "You could teach sewing."

"How long have you been sewing, Pari?" Kaya asked.

"All my life."

"But I've never seen you wear anything homemade," Sophie said on her way out my apartment door over to hers.

"You've seen me wear my own clothes almost every day," I said.

"No way," Vanessa said.

"It's true," Karen said, tossing a large piece of faux silk onto the cutting table. "Pari sews most of her clothes."

This brought Sophie and Melissa back into my apartment where I was forced to confess.

"Okay," I said. "There's something you don't know about me."

They stared...waiting. Vanessa grabbed another brownie and Karen followed suit with a devious smile. This was going to be spectacular.

"I knock off designer clothing. There, I said it. Now everybody knows."

"What does that even mean?" Sophie said.

"I can't afford designer clothes. So...I copy various design specs on various pieces of clothing. Like this divine Versace jacket I saw. It was almost fifteen hundred dollars. I can't spend that. But I have a basic jacket pattern. It was just the adorable lapel and collar treatment I wanted. Or I might see a top with a particular yoke, or a sleeve I adore that is ridiculously overpriced."

"You steal it?" Sophie said. "How?"

"No. It's not stealing. Not really. I don't literally remake the designer piece. I take the parts I like, the parts that look fresh and interesting, or classic and technically difficult...and I clone them into my own patterns. So I get my jacket, with a designer collar. I could figure it out just by looking at it, I suppose. But there's a particular thrill involved in getting on your hands and knees on the floor the Versace dressing room at the Mall at Millennia and ever so quietly ripping off pieces of wax paper from the roll you smuggled in inside your second-hand designer purse."

"Wait," Vanessa said. "What?"

"There's a Versace store at the Mall at Millennia?" Vanessa said.

"Do I even know what a Versace is?" Melissa said.

"What is a Mall at Millennia?" Sophie said.

"It's in Orlando somewhere."

"But how do you do it?" Vanessa said.

"How do you spell millennia?" Sophie said. She was on her phone Googling already.

"It's not that difficult. I lay the garment on the floor—"

"You put a fifteen-hundred-dollar Versace jacket on the floor?" Kaya said.

I winced. "Just for a bit. You arrange it so the piece you want to copy is in position, then lay the wax paper atop it and use a fingernail to trace the design."

"You have got to show us this trick," Kaya said.

"I'm not getting caught in the Versace store ripping off designs," Vanessa said.

"What are they going to do?" Kaya said. "Kick us out? Like we'd ever be able to shop there, anyway."

"Would it be less offensive if I just did it by looking at the piece?" I said.

"Maybe," Sophie said.

"I don't see anything wrong with it," Melissa said. "Fifteen hundred dollars for a jacket is ridiculous."

We took a break in which I was forced to model a few of my rip-offs and was accused of making the shoes too. I didn't tell them it was possible to cover shoes with new fabric and add other details. They didn't need to know everything at once.

"I can't believe all this time I thought psychologists were rich," Melissa said.

"If you wrote a book, you could be," Karen said with a wink in my direction.

I changed the subject to her romance novel and, as we worked on our costumes, we listened to Karen detail her search for various ways to describe heaving bosoms and throbbing loins. The Divas couldn't help offering their own suggestions, none of which would ever make it into a romance novel. At one point, I was helping Melissa with a yoke facing when Sophie shouted from her apartment, "Pulsating bayonet!" and all work stopped for twenty minutes.

Everyone left exhausted, some with pin pricks, and at least one of us had to return to JoAnn Fabrics the next day for extra material after a disastrous cutting error. I won't say who. (It was Melissa.) We all agreed to meet up that Friday night for Friday Fest and as I'd already told Eric I'd go with him, I pulled Karen aside before she went downstairs to her car.

"Do me a favor, will you?"

"Don't make me slip you a roll of wax paper under a dressing room door."

"Very funny. Could you, maybe, not mention your party to Eric?"

She looked at me, confused, but I got the feeling it was just a show. "You're not going to invite him?" Her sly smile let on.

"No, I am. I just haven't yet."

"You don't have to bring him. I won't have a date, either."

"I want to bring him. You don't mind, do you?"

"Of course I don't mind. I'm just saying...you don't have to."

I sighed. "I know you think things aren't great with Eric. But I do like him. He's so..."

She raised a brow when I didn't come up with anything. "You let me know when you come up with a decent adjective." She winked and left.

The next morning was the first day of October. I jumped out of bed, raced to open the sliding glass door in my bedroom and rushed out onto the balcony only to be disappointed that it was still summer in Central Florida.

"Just you wait," I told the trees. "Before Halloween, there will be a somewhat cool, at the very least *not hot*, breeze."

I worked through lunch, meeting up with Tildon Frakes in the snack room while grabbing a cup of iced tea before heading back to do paperwork over my veggie and hummus pita.

"Looks like the sleepover is a go," he said.

"You're not letting them into your office, are you?"

He shook his head and sipped his coffee. "No, but our walls are mostly windows. If they see any ghosts, they'll have to be happy with contact through the glass."

I felt like I'd climbed mount contrary and stood alone at the peak trying get everyone else to join me, but they all just looked up at me and shrugged.

"It'll be okay, Pari," Tildon said, turning to head back to his office. "The fuss won't last."

But there was major fuss at the moment, and I felt powerless against it. I was *surrounded* by fuss. Ghost fuss and Sam Preston fuss and...well, okay, that was all the fuss. It felt like more than it was, and I knew the best thing for me to do was practice what I preached. Positive Awareness would prepare me for those moments I dreaded, and a good Let's Review now and then would keep me rational. Why is good advice easier to come up with than to practice?

That night's photography class, at least, was a lot of fun. Sam screened our pictures from the week before, taken around The Art Center; I'd like to say we'd all improved, but no signs of brilliance yet. After class, he asked me to stay again. A few of my fellow students cast sidelong glances at us as they left. I was riding on a bit of a proud moment for having spent the last two hours in the same room with him without once feeling concerned about ghosts and my office or the rampant delusions around town.

But then he said, "I was wondering if you'd made up your mind about letting me have an appointment." He was sitting on the teacher's stool, twisting this way and that.

"After everything...I have to reiterate that it's not a good idea."

"What everything?"

"You know what I'm talking about."

"Kissing. You're talking about kissing, aren't you?" He smiled, his brow raised, daring me to admit it.

"It would be highly unprofessional of me—"

"Let me stop you right there. I'm not asking to be a client, right? I'm not really seeking counseling. So no professional line will be crossed. I'm just willing to spill my guts for your professional curiosity. You're intrigued by the whole ghost thing. That's why you've been going on the Ghost Whisperer tours. It's not like you actually believe in ghosts."

"Very clever." Sam Preston had all the answers it seemed, and he was offering me the perfect alibi. "All right." I experienced a terrible relief at having given in when I still felt I shouldn't, and a joyful apprehension at what story Sam would tell. "I'll let you spill your guts in exchange for a ghost session."

"How about next Wednesday? We can do it after

hours to make it even more legit." He spun himself the full three-hundred-sixty degrees with a childlike grin. "How about seven?"

"Out of the question. We can do it before I leave the office unless it has to be dark for your ghosts to come out."

"Five or five-thirty would do."

"Let me check my schedule and get back to you."

He stopped spinning. "You're trying to get out of it already."

"I'm not, really."

"I noticed you and your friends are signed up for the first Overnight with Ghosts event. Does that mean you've decided to let the tour group have a peek in your office?"

"That wasn't part of the spill your guts deal."

"I know. No pressure. But you'll be there anyway."

I mumbled a curse.

"What was that?"

"You know I'm only doing your tours with the Divas because Melissa challenged us. It's like a dare."

"I distinctly recall you telling me I could not refer to you all as Divas."

"That still stands, Mr. Preston."

"Oh, I see how it is. Double standards." And he was back to spinning.

"That's right," I said.

"So, Melissa's trying to get you to believe in ghosts?"

"Something like that. Aren't you getting dizzy?"

"Yes, but it's good for the brain. I don't think believing in ghosts is something that can be forced. You either believe or you don't."

"And you believe? I mean, you seriously, really and truly, believe in ghosts?"

There was a pause as he let the chair slow on its own, stopping with him facing the far wall where the same student artwork that was hung during our first class waited to be claimed. "We'll talk on Wednesday."

I sighed. "Fine. Make it five o'clock."

"Will do. And I guess I'll see you next Saturday night

for sure." He stood and started to collect his equipment.

"You mean *this* Saturday, for the séance."

"Then, too."

"What's next Saturday? A haunted house? I don't think scaring me half to death is going to work in Melissa's favor."

He chuckled. "Karen's movie party." He motioned for me to take the lead out of the classroom so he could turn out the light behind us. "I haven't seen *The Wizard of Oz* since I was a kid."

Karen's party. I'd almost forgotten.

"I suppose you'll be bringing your boyfriend," he said.

"He's not my boyfriend." I let out the tiniest gasp. I couldn't believe I'd just said that. "I mean. We're dating."

"So, the exclusivity is still in question."

"No. I mean, yes. What difference does it make?"

"None whatsoever," he said.

I headed straight to my car while he bolted the front door to The Art Center, not waiting for any more conversation. I'd had enough.

"See you tomorrow night," he called after me.

I stopped, key poised in lock. "Tomorrow? What's tomorrow?"

"Poetry Night. You're going, aren't you? We're seeing an awful lot of each other these days."

"I guess so."

We said a final goodbye and I drove home with the radio off, exhausted. Why did I always feel as if I'd run a marathon after talking to Sam Preston?

"Why won't he just go away?" I asked my empty car.

No response. Traitor.

Chapter Thirty-nine

When Eric came to my apartment to walk with me over to Stogies the next evening, I was reminded of how much easier he was to talk to than Sam Preston. There was never any sparring; I never felt thrown off balance. Miffed sometimes, sure. Eric didn't mean to be critical. He couldn't help it. And he wasn't only critical of me. He treated everyone and everything that way. And what's so wrong with that? What's wrong with voicing your opinion and your disappointment with people? Litterers, for example. Maybe they ought to be shamed. Even if they are five. I suppose that wasn't a good example. The little boy didn't cry, but his mother was not happy.

"I appreciate your letting me know," she'd said as she helped her child pick up the candy wrappers he'd inadvertently spilled from his pants pocket. "But you didn't need to scold my child."

"He has to learn," Eric was saying as I dragged him away.

Yes. Eric certainly had his issues.

As we walked along the sidewalk downtown, I reached for his hand and gave it a squeeze. He turned to look at me with a smile. We entered the crowded cigar shop, the smell of sweet tobacco enveloping us like incense. Leland Booker, Stogies' owner and cigar enthusiast, stood at the front of the room, sitting atop the glass case at his cash wrap. Mr. Booker was a large man, in the commanding-a-room sense. He had wavy, but smooth, blond hair that fell slightly past his shoulders; a graying, short but unevenly trimmed beard and mustache; and a face that could easily play villain or hero. His voice too, neither deep or squeaky, could woo and charm as well as instill a sense of dread. And he put all his neither-this-nor-that personality into every poem he read.

"Welcome all," he said with a wide smile. "If you read your monthly Poetry Night at Stogies email, you'll have come prepared with your favorite ghostly poems. First up, Octavia."

"Even Poetry Night," I mumbled to Eric as we nestled ourselves in the back of the room. All the tables and chairs were taken, but we knew this crowd was fluid and there would be seating available at some point. Often, Mr. Booker would toss heavy pillows to the SRO crowd, anyway. But I thought I'd better stand. I looped my arm in Eric's and leaned into him. "Can we not escape the ghosts even here?"

"Shh," he whispered. "I like this poem."

Octavia Washington was performing a stellar reading of *The Raven* by Edgar Allen Poe. Octavia sang most everything she said, and this was no different.

"She does lend a new interpretation," I said. But Eric was entranced with Octavia.

I looked around the room, not because I wasn't enthralled with her performance myself–which, okay I admit, I wasn't–but because I was perturbed–both at the seeming constant barrage of ghostliness I felt under, and at myself for being bothered by it. Noah Holland was standing by the front window, smiling at Octavia. His lips were moving along with her recital, as if he'd been coaching her all month. Why didn't that make me happy...in that 'aw, they're so cute' way?

Sophie stood behind Mr. Cornell of Old Geezer's who was at a table against the opposite wall with her grandfather, Mr. Childers. Funny, now that I saw them together, I realized Mr. Cornell actually looked like an old geezer–in a complimentary way, of course–and Mr. Childers looked like a respected literary author...of the ladies-swooning sort. Now, see...that was fun. That was a *fun* observation.

I was getting angry with myself, and Sam Preston. It was his fault. And not his fault at all. Why did I care? If I wasn't a fun person there wasn't much I could do about it, was there? It's not as if we can change the fundamentals of who we are. Isabella said I didn't know myself. Did that mean I was fun or I wasn't?

"I'm so confused," I whispered.

"It's his imagination," Eric said. "The raven probably isn't really saying 'nevermore.'"

I, naturally, burst out laughing. One loud sort of sneeze-ish guffaw, followed by snickers with my hand over my mouth. I turned to the wall, hoping Octavia wouldn't see or hear me. But she was loud, so I was thinking she didn't. Glancing up, of course I found Sam Preston just a few feet away, leaning against the wall, smiling at me. He'd heard Eric; I was sure of it. I quickly turned around and punched Eric, not very hard, I swear; but I could tell by the look on his face he had no idea he'd made me laugh. He really thought I was confused about Edgar Allen Poe's *The Raven*? Maybe it was Eric who wasn't any fun.

The evening was wonderful, despite, or even because of the theme, Sam Preston's presence notwithstanding. We heard *The Apparition* by John Donne, no small feat of a poem and read fairly competently by Harry Trenthem, owner of Across the Pond, an all-things England shop. (Or would that be...shoppe?) Mrs. Trenthem read *Ghost* by Paul Mariani and got the reaction she'd obviously hoped for–a general 'What the bloody hell?' of gasps around the room. Lori Walker, owner of ChocShop, my favorite go-to for candy, read *Ghosts That Need Reminding* by Dana Levin. I never understand any of the poetry Lori reads.

We found Sophie and Reese outside in the mingling crowd after the readings were finished and the four of us walked back to Crane Creek apartments, up the stairs to the second-floor landing where Eric and I said goodnight to Reese and Sophie who disappeared, smiling like the newly in love, into her apartment. Inside mine, I got a couple of iced teas and Eric and I sat on the sofa talking.

"I'm not sure I understand poetry," he said.

I tried not to agree. "It's not all obscure, you know. It's not all figurative, even."

"There's always Dr. Suess." He chuckled.

"Exactly. I'm willing to bet there's a poet out there for everybody."

"And Dr. Suess is for me?"

I smiled as tenderly as I could manage. "There's nothing wrong with an adult reading Dr. Suess. Stogies had a kids' poetry night. We had a great time."

"For kids or for adults reading kids' poetry."

"The latter. Stogies isn't really a great place for children."

"Did anyone read Dr. Suess?"

"No. Too long."

"I enjoy Poetry Night, though. Even if I don't understand what a poem's about; they all had a melody to them. I'm surprised Sam Preston was there."

"The theme was ghosts. I figured he'd want to be a part of it. It's as if, lately, he's everywhere."

"You've noticed, too," he said. "I'm not sure he belongs here."

"Why not?" I hated being put in the position of defending the man, but still.

"He doesn't work downtown."

"He does now, apparently."

"That's what I mean. It's like he's exploiting us."

I hadn't thought of it in that way before, but now that Eric said it out loud, I realized maybe that's what had been needling me. "You know, you're right. He lives in Strawbridge, sure. But he's coming here and taking over...putting everything downtown under his ghost talking enterprise. The Executive Suites, the Crisper House, now Trudy's Treasures. The entire downtown area, actually, with his ghost tour."

"He's a rouser," Eric said. "A rabble rouser."

"Well, now...that sort of makes us out as rabble."

He laughed. "Don't look at me. You're the one going on the tours."

"True enough. But I was hijacked into it."

"Tell me you're not doing the séance tomorrow night."

I winced. "I promised Melissa."

He shook his head. "What sort of friend has you doing crazy nonsense like that? You don't have to do all this stuff just because Melissa wants you to."

"I know. It's actually kind of fun."

"You're not twelve, Pari." He looked at me as if I had spaghetti on my face. "You don't have to prove to anyone you're fun, either, if that's what this is about."

"And you don't have to psychoanalyze me, Eric."

For a few seconds I could feel the tension, like electricity, threatening to spark. Finally, he said, "You're right. I'm sorry. Maybe I feel left out."

"Really?"

He looked at me, his face soft and questioning. "I'd like to get to know you and your friends better. But I guess I'm wishing they did things I like to do. Things I think are fun."

"I get that." I scooted closer to him on the couch, and he put his arm around me. "This whole ghost thing will be over soon, by Halloween, in fact. And then we can find some things we can all enjoy together."

"I'd like that," he said.

We sat looking at each other for a moment, and when Eric leaned in to kiss me, I almost pulled back—I moved the tiniest bit and luckily, he didn't notice. As his kiss grew deeper, I was...surprised. Eric and I had never kissed like that before and I now understood that all this time, I'd been wondering if he was really into me. Now it was clear. He *was*. One of his hands was behind my head, tangling itself in my scrunchie—I think he was trying to pull it out but failed. His other hand squeezed between the couch and me and pulled me closer, to the point I was practically on his lap. Awkward. Both my arms were stuck over his shoulders, and I had hold of his head with one elbow and tried to grasp his back with my other hand, which only resulted in it scuttling about like a spider. Eventually, his lips left mine and he tongued his way down my neck. I let out a muffled groan–part ecstasy, part reluctance. He groaned back and suddenly, as if an alarm had gone off, I pushed him away and flung myself off the couch, tripped my feet up in the legs of my coffee table and stumbled backward.

Holding out a hand to steady myself that could plainly be taken as a motion to stop everything, I said, breathlessly, "I'm sorry."

"It's okay." He stood too and we stared at each other for a moment. "I guess I've been holding that in for a while."

I nodded. "Yes."

"I didn't mean to startle you." He reached out and took my hands in his. "We can take a step back, go a bit slower."

I started to protest. Did I want to go slower? At the moment, I had no idea what I wanted, so I said nothing.

"I should get going," he said.

At the door we kissed again, our bodies pressed together like lovers. This was the Eric I had always dreamed of. Where had he been all this time? And why did I stop him?

Chapter Forty

MaryAshford has joined the chat.

MaryAshford: Hey.

SamTheMan: Hey, Mary. We're waiting on Chris.

MaryAshford: Is he going to the séance?

SamTheMan: No, are you?

MaryAshford: Do you want me to?

SamTheMan: You don't have to.

MaryAshford: But do you want me to?

LegitChris has joined the chat.

LegitChris: Hey guys. So what's the deal with the séance?

SamTheMan: We were just talking about it.

LegitChris: Are we still arguing about it?

SamTheMan: Nobody's arguing. Are you arguing, Mary?

MaryAshford: They're not technically ghosts if they're being channeled through a medium.

SamTheMan: So we are still arguing.

LegitChris: It doesn't matter anymore. séances are part of our events lineup.

SamTheMan: Mary doesn't want to go.

MaryAshford: I didn't say that.

SamTheMan: If you're not going to be into it, don't go.

MaryAshford: Fine. I won't go.

LegitChris: I can't go. It'll just be you, Sam.

SamTheMan: No problem.

LegitChris: Is she going to be there?

MaryAshford: Who?

SamTheMan: She's on the list.

LegitChris: Any More kissing?

MaryAshford: Oh, her.

SamTheMan: No more kissing.

LegitChris: She's in his photog class, did he tell you?

MaryAshford: He did not.

SamTheMan: There's nothing going on. I'm telling you. But I did get an appointment.

LegitChris: There it is. The Sam Preston charm does it again.

MaryAshford: When do we go?

SamTheMan: Not we. Just me.

MaryAshford: That's not how this is supposed to work.

SamTheMan: Sorry. Her terms.

LegitChris: Sure, Sam. Whatever you say.

SamTheMan: What's that supposed to mean?

LegitChris: You keep saying there's nothing there.

SamTheMan: This is strictly business.

MaryAshford: If that were true, Chris and I would be going too.

SamTheMan: I'm not going to argue about it. It's just me and her.

MaryAshford: Fine.

SamTheMan: But listen, the guy with the other antique shop. Old Geezer's. He wants an event too. He's in some kind of competition with Trudy. Wants it the next day.

MaryAshford: Too soon.

LegitChris: What kind of event?

SamTheMan: I told him we could do a conjuring Sunday night. Who knows, we might get a ghost.

MaryAshford: Should we be throwing events into the mix without any planning?

SamTheMan: He's driving it. Inviting everybody. Advertising.

LegitChris: Could be another avenue for us. Are you charging him?

SamTheMan: No, but in the future, we might.

MaryAshford: I'll see you Sunday then.

MaryAshford has left the chat.

LegitChris: Does she seem pissed off to you?

SamTheMan: Always.

Chapter Forty-one

I woke the next morning knowing exactly why I'd jumped off the couch mid-smooch with Eric. The signals were mixed. Hand holding and a few light kisses then–Bam!–I'm on a boat meeting the folks. Back to friendly chatter and a hug then–Pow!–a meet-the-friends double date. We're back to casual, getting to know you stuff, then–Holy Ravish Me!–we're all over each other. No wonder I was confused. I could only assume Eric was as baffled by our so-called relationship as I was. But I had no time to sit around and ponder the possibilities. The dreaded Séance Saturday had arrived. After lunch, Melissa and Vanessa came to my apartment for help with their costumes and neither mentioned it until they were at the door ready to leave at three o'clock.

"So, I guess we'll see you tonight at Trudy's." A sly grin crept over Melissa's face.

"Can't wait," I said.

"Oh, it'll be fun," Vanessa sang.

"Well, at least there won't be many people there," I said.

"What do you mean?" Melissa said. "I thought there would be a dozen at least."

"Where would they sit?"

She laughed, and I detected an evil twang to it. "The

séance is upstairs in the attic."

"Attic!"

"Don't worry," Vanessa said. "We'll protect you from the ghosts you don't believe in."

And sure enough, when Sophie and I walked over to Trudy's Treasures, there was a sign on the door that read, *Ghost Whisperer Event: Around back, upstairs.* It was already getting dark, and I can't say I wasn't spooked a bit, walking around Trudy's old store. A light, warm breeze teased the air and I imagined the wind whispering spooky warnings.

"I never noticed these stairs before," Sophie said.

I certainly hadn't either. "Are they safe, do you think?"

"I hear people up there—" The windows upstairs were open and lighthearted chatter wafted down to us. "—so they must be okay."

We delicately made our way slowly up the rickety steps and stood on a small deck at the old, paint-worn door.

"Are we going to knock?" Sophie said. "Or just go in?"

I couldn't help but laugh. "What are we so afraid of?"

"This is just what they want," she said. "Get us all hopped up on suspense and creepiness, so we'll start seeing and hearing things."

"Exactly. Let's vow to keep our heads."

The attic smelled of mold and old things. The walls slanted upward to the top of the roof in the middle of the room, but there was enough space for us to stand around a large table. Melissa had been right; I counted a dozen chairs. A yellowed lace runner was stiffly draped along the middle of the table with six candles spanning the length atop it. And to our right as we walked in, under the angled roof there was a table filled with snacks.

"Come in, come in," Trudy called to us and worked her way among her other guests. "Sophie, Pari, I want to introduce you to the medium. You will love her. Felicia! Felicia, dear."

A tiny woman, no more than five foot tall, with large round eyes and wild, untamed hair held out a delicate, tiny-boned hand to me.

"This is Pari, and Sophie, our skeptics."

"Oh, I wouldn't...that is..." I stammered.

"It's no worry," Felicia said with a slight haunting smile. "I get unbelievers all the time." Then she shoved half a donut into her mouth and chomped on it while giving us the once over.

She was wearing what looked like a chiffon poncho, pink and purple, and seemed to have no body beneath it. She floated away from us toward the large table.

"Isn't she wonderful?" Trudy said.

Felicia started speaking and it was a few moments before anyone heard her and quieted down. She was seating us and I grabbed hold of Sophie's hand. "No matter what she says, we're sitting together."

Melissa was already at the table with Vanessa and across from them were Karen and Kaya.

"I think," Felicia said to me, laying a hand on my arm so lightly I couldn't feel it, "you would like to sit here." And she put me next to Karen.

She began to lead Sophie away and I startled. "We'd like to sit together."

"No, no. You will sit across from each other. That way you can make faces at each other when you hear things that make you want to...doubt."

Well, I had to admit that would be fun. And anyway, I had Karen on my left. "How did she know I'd want to sit with you?"

"She's a medium," Karen said. "Duh."

I gave her a gentle nudge. "Seriously."

"Don't look so worried," Karen said with a smirk. "I'm sure Melissa told her we're besties."

"I'm not worried."

"You look like the entire foundation of your life's philosophy is about to be challenged. In other words, scared to death."

"Do I? I suppose I am antsy. The cemetery had a charm to it, if a bit creepy. The ghost tour was fun and there was history. But this? On the one hand, this woman is going to pretend to talk to dead people. It's going to be awkward."

"And on the other hand?"

I looked around the table. Sam Preston was sitting at the opposite end from Felicia. He smiled at me. On one side of the table Trudy sat next to Sam. Beside her a young couple who looked to be married–maybe in their thirties–leaned together nervously. And next to them were Sophie, Vanessa, and Melissa. On my side of the table, next to Felicia, was a young man in his twenties then Kaya, Karen, me, and two older women, I'd guess in their fifties. It was quite a varied group.

"On the other hand," I said, "a lot of these people are going to believe her."

Everything started out smoothly. Felicia had us close our eyes as she chanted in some strange language– probably one she made up herself. She left the table and moved around the room. I peeked to see what was going on and nudged Karen again.

"Ouch," she whispered.

"She's lighting more candles."

"So?"

"It's not safe."

"Shh."

Finally, Felicia disappeared from my view and I didn't dare turn my head and let her know I was spying on her. When the lights went out, I jumped and opened my eyes. Felicia lit a lamp and draped a lightweight scarf over it. The room was dim and spooky. When she'd returned to the table, Felicia called on us to open our eyes. "Those of you who had them closed anyway." She smiled at me.

The room was haunting. Shadows flickered rhythmically over the walls and the slanted ceiling until an outside breeze wafted in and stirred them into a brief frenzy. Karen's hand slipped into mine and I gave it a reassuring squeeze.

Felicia closed her eyes and laid her palms flat on the table in front of her. She began to moan, if you will. Though you could say it was a song of sorts. Finally, words formed.

"Spirits of the dead, I call upon you. Reach into the hearts of those present, help them find their kin."

Skeptically speaking, this was a brilliant move. One does wonder how the ghosts of dead relatives know we're about to have a party. When does the invitation go out?

Felicia swayed side to side chanting, "Come to us, spirits." Then she opened one eye and smiled at me. "This may take some time. Please bear with us."

It was enchanting, if you must know the truth. Everyone started swaying. It was like the wave at an outdoor sporting event. A person feels compelled to participate. I glanced to the other side of the table and caught Sam Preston smiling and swaying. I was about to smile myself when he winked at me. There was definitely something frustratingly deceptive about him. He could be so kind and sincere one day and cavalier the next.

"They are here," Felicia whispered and everyone stopped swaying, excitedly looking around the room. "Who is it?" she asked the darkened spaces. "Who do you wish to contact?"

We all looked at one another wondering whose dead relative would show up. And what would they say? Would my father's mother, my Dadi Gayatri, show up and want to know why I was wearing makeup? Or would Dada Oliver, my father's dad, try to steal my nose like he used to? This could be embarrassing. I chuckled and Karen nudged me.

"Sorry," I whispered.

"Jeremy and Elaine," Felicia said. The married couple next to Sam leaned forward, excited for a visitation. I only hoped they wouldn't be disappointed.

"Mother says..." Felicia opened her eyes so wide it had to hurt. "Onyx is here with me." The man burst into tears and buried his head in his wife's shoulder. It was, I have to say, quite astonishing.

"Onyx?" I whispered to Karen.

"How could she have known?"

Felicia droned on about Onyx for some time–her favorite park, favorite toys, favorite places to nap–and I wanted to comfort her parents until I realized Onyx was a French poodle.

"I was going to recommend a colleague," I said to

Karen.

"Grief is grief."

And that was true enough.

Felicia was less specific about Melissa's aunt, but, of course, who doesn't have a dead aunt whose name starts with an E or a B. It was Edith. Old Aunt Edith. And Vanessa had a great grandfather, from the Old Country. To which Vanessa said, "Brazil?" And wouldn't you know, Brazil it was.

Once Jeremy had stopped sobbing, I started noticing the sounds. Ticks, at first. A clock, maybe. Then something sliding. A ping of some kind. Each sound seemed to herald a spirit or a message. By that time I had hold of Kaya's hand across Karen's lap, and the three of us were as tense as kids in a monster inhabited swamp. Felicia was speaking to one of the middle-aged women about a husband and a dog named Pete—one of them was Pete, anyway—when a loud bang rang out—the lamp falling off its table—followed by the candles snuffing out. There was screaming, chairs groaned and scraped away from the table, the old door creaked open like a shriek and slammed shut again. The woman next to me knocked me in the head with her elbow as she scrambled out of her chair. I scooted away from the table as Karen stood up unsteadily; she fell onto me, lying across my lap laughing and shouting, "The spirits are revolting!"

When the main lights were back on, Onyx's living relative had fled with his wife, and I could hear her crying as they tumbled down the rickety staircase. Trudy was huffing down after them yelling, "It's okay now. It's over." The middle-aged women were huddled under the slanted roof behind their chairs crying, and the man in his twenties was over at the food table eating chips and salsa, a delighted grin on his face.

Best séance ever.

Chapter Forty-two

F elicia was talking to them about the dog before you two showed up," Kaya said at lunch the next day. "It was totally faked."

"Just because she knew the dog's name beforehand," Melissa said, "doesn't mean she wasn't in contact with it."

The whole of downtown was abuzz about the séance. Of course, most of the stories going around were wildly inaccurate. We were, by most reports, definitely visited by spirits and one of them was very angry to have been disturbed, tossing things across the room, blowing out the candles, and slamming the door. But the silliest claim, in my opinion, was that it was actually Billy Cornell, owner of Old Geezer's Stuff Antiques, who'd caused the chaos. Billy Cornell was all over town confusing the matter by neither confirming nor denying any interloping séance antics. But he made sure to invite everyone over to his store that night for an event of his very own.

The Divas were at Melissa's Café Flamingo, which just happens to be across the street from Sophie's store, Bookish, which is next door to Old Geezer's Stuff Antiques. We were at a large wrought iron table out front and when Melissa saw the old geezer's front window, emblazoned with "Séance Tonight!" she turned to all of us, beaming.

"No," I said. "We just did one."

"But look," she whined. We all turned dutifully to watch Billy Cornell up on a stepladder, painting crystal balls in gold on the glass. "He guarantees Aranthia will be there."

"That's the one from your building, isn't it?" Kaya gave me a smirk. She pulled her thick dark hair behind her head and wrapped it with a scrunchie.

"She killed herself in your office," Karen said.

"She did not."

"Anyway," Sophie said. "I don't think it's going to be a séance. The way Billy describes it, it'll be more like an exorcism."

"With a priest?" Vanessa said. She'd just arrived from her salon, and I could still smell the hairspray, a sweet grape scent, on her bouncing curls.

"I think Mr. Cornell will do the exorcising," Melissa said. "Come on. It'll be fun."

"I'm in," Karen said.

Everyone else agreed, so what was I supposed to do? That night, I drove downtown and had to park behind Melissa's café because the lot behind Mr. Cornell's store was full. Old Geezer's Stuff Antiques was packed with people. Ghostly music and sound effects echoed off the walls and crowds milled around like wiggling sardines trapped in a tin, sipping cocktails, snatching *hors d'oeuvres* off the several buffet tables lining the walls. He'd cleared out a lot of space by piling his antiques in the back half of the store and in his elevated cash wrap area, he'd set up a microphone and speaker. I made my way through the bodies looking for the Divas—any Diva would do—silently cursing and threatening their lives if it should turn out I was the only one to show up. But there they were, in a back corner against a velvet rope protecting Old Geezer's stuff from ghostly vandals: Vanessa, her huge hoop earrings dancing on her shoulders; Melissa, short and sweet, still in her work clothes sans apron; Sophie, on Reese's arm, her dark eyes gazing up at him as she laughed at whatever he'd just said; Karen with an arm draped over Kaya's shoulders, their heads resting against each other, like best buds. As I made my way to them, I realized they surrounded none other than Sam Preston.

"It's about time," Melissa scolded. "The–" she turned to looked up at Sam, "–what did you call it? The coursing or cursing?"

He laughed. "Conjuring."

"The conjuring's about to start," Melissa finished.

"Like that's an actual thing." I nearly rolled my eyes.

"It is," Sam said.

"How is it any different from a séance?"

A sarcastic smile spread across his lips. "Well," he said, as if he really had an explanation. "In a séance, you have a medium calling on spirits to show up for the people in attendance. A conjuring is more like a get together at the location of a known ghost where the attendees ask the spirit to join them."

"Very scientific," I said.

"If you say so."

A perceptible tension rippled through the group, and I was already defensive. The room was too crowded, making me antsy. I wanted to move closer to the door, but Mr. Cornell was tapping on his microphone and saying "testing" again and again.

"Never underestimate the power of stupid people in large groups," I muttered.

"Did you just call us stupid?" Sam said.

"It's a George Carlin quote," I snapped. "I was thinking about group dynamics and the how easy it is to manipulate people who are desperate to experience the intangible."

"It's all in good fun."

"It starts out that way, sure. But large groups of influenced people can turn...mean."

"It's just a ghost, Dr. Logan. There's nothing to be afraid of."

I turned my back to Sam and decided I simply didn't like him. I suppose I could see the attraction for everyone else. He was attractive, in a Chris Pratt sort of way–goofy, but cute, and able to cast a vulnerable face when needed. Sometimes he was kind and attentive to those around him. He was your basic good and decent guy. But he clearly enjoyed antagonizing me. He was irritating.

"Welcome, welcome," Mr. Cornell said. I got the feeling he was tipsy already. His long gray hair, often tied in a ponytail high up on his head, was down now, pouring like a river split in two by his round, friendly face. His mustache was long enough to look as if it joined in the flow. Pudgy, I suppose, wearing a leather vest, he always gave me the impression he took himself much less seriously than his face suggested. He pulled wire-rimmed glasses off his nose, wiped his forehead with a plaid sleeve and replaced them. "Aranthia is here. I know it. She's haunted my store for years. Let me tell you a few stories."

And he launched into them with abandon. Sound effects, dialogue, shrieking at the appropriate times.

"And I said to him, this is Walt, mind you, Sophie's granddad. Hi Sophie." He waved in our direction. "Anyway, I say, 'Walt you got to stop with the banging on the wall.' And, of course, he said he never banged on the wall in his life. It was her." Gasps. "Finally, after the moaning and singing and all the antiques and whatnot being moved around, I heard about Sam Preston. Sam, come on up here."

The crowd applauded him like he was famous. I turned to Karen. "He thinks he's some kind of celebrity."

"He kind of is."

"Is not."

"He's got a radio show and a website and everything."

"That doesn't make him famous."

"Are you jealous, Pari?"

"What?" My cheeks burned.

Sam was thanking everybody and there was more clapping.

"If you want to be a star, write that book of yours."

"I'm not jealous. And even so, writing a book is more—"

Sam invited Mary Ashford up to the mic with him and now she was talking, her voice quavering.

"More what?"

"Never mind."

Karen smiled and gave me a brief hug. "This is Sam's thing. He's good at it. And people like him."

"You like him?"

"Sure I do. Not *like* him like him. But you know what I mean. It's not like you to be threatened by someone else's success."

"I'm not."

"Not usually."

Mary Ashford was talking about her own ghost experiences and how she met Sam.

"I'm not threatened by Sam Preston."

Suddenly the room was fairly quiet. Sam, Mary, and Billy Cornell were looking at me. I stammered out something of an apology and elbowed Karen.

"Sorry," she whispered.

"All right, everybody," Sam said. "Let's get started. We all need to think about Aranthia. Dim the lights. That's right. Perfect. I'll tell you a little bit about what we know, and we'll all be on the alert for anything that might signal she's with us."

I shook my head. "This is just theater," I said to Karen. I don't think she heard me.

We didn't, as it turned out, know very much about her. They hadn't found any historical person to match her. But it was assumed Aranthia could have been a nickname, or more likely, a mistake. "I continue to search through records for anyone that could be her. And I'm looking for more information on the captain who supposedly broke her heart."

"What do you mean, supposedly?" Trudy Spencer moved through the crowd toward the counter and confronted Sam.

"We're not sure of all the details. That's one reason we want to contact her."

"But the stories..."

"Maybe," I called across the room, "they're just *that*...stories."

This led to quite a bit of, well, not booing and hissing exactly, but let's just say I wasn't making any new friends.

Trudy said, "These stories have been passed down for generations. Why would they be repeated and cherished if they weren't true? Maybe Aranthia wasn't even from here and only staying at the hotel. That's why you can't find her."

"We're looking everywhere," Sam said.

"If we could continue," Mr. Cornell said with a glare at Trudy.

"I'm not stopping you," she said. "I'd just like us to all be clear that—"

"Did I come to your séance?" Mr. Cornell said. "Did I crash your party? Why are you even here?"

"There's a huge invitation on your window, Billy."

"It's the principle of the thing."

"No need to shout," Trudy said. "I'm leaving. I'm going back to my store where Aranthia actually does hang out."

"She's here, I tell you." Mr. Cornell's face was turning beet red.

After some grumbling under their breaths, Trudy left, and Mr. Cornell relinquished the floor once again to Sam Preston. The entire room was on edge by that point.

"Let's stay focused on why we're here," Sam said. "If we want the ghosts to show themselves, we need to be open to them, calm, and quiet. Close your eyes." The lights were dimmed, but there was enough light to spot a ghost if one dared to show up and once Sam had everyone under control and we were standing about with our eyes closed, he spoke to us in a soothing tone, telling us to relax. "Listen," he whispered into the microphone. "Wait for a sign. You'll know when to open your eyes again."

And at that moment, a strange sort of humming arose and a pringle of electricity ignited everyone. Karen took my hand, and I heard a tiny gasp from Sophie behind me. As soon as I opened my eyes, the lights went out. A woman screamed. A man shouted, "Holy hell!" and then the lights were on again. After a few seconds of silence, all of us looking at one another, voices erupted.

"A ghost."

"It wasn't a woman," someone yelled.

"Hovering in the corner."

"The captain! It was the captain!"

I searched the cash wrap stage for Sam Preston, but only Mr. Cornell was there, a smile spreading slowly on his face.

Chapter Forty-three

The Divas met outside Old Geezer's, huddling together amid the crowd of spectators. Melissa swore she saw the captain; Vanessa certainly saw something ghostly; and the rest of us claimed ignorance.

"So, you're still a skeptic?" Melissa said.

"I'll always be a skeptic."

"Isn't that the same as being closed minded?"

I frowned. "Look, the thing about ghosts is even if you see something–"

"I know, I know. You're still in on the challenge, though, right?"

I sighed. "A promise is a promise."

"Darn right," she said. "So, here's the plan. Next Friday we're doing the haunted house at the civic center."

"How is that supposed to convince us to believe in ghosts?"

"Who cares?" Sophie said. "I'm in."

"But that's Triple F," Karen said.

"We can do both." Melissa was determined.

"I don't know," I said. "I don't like being scared, people jumping out at me."

"It won't be that bad," Kaya said. "They let kids go in."

"Okay," I said. Maybe Kaya was right. And anyway, I

could invite Eric and hide behind him the whole way through it.

"And the weekend after that is the sleepover at Pari's office building," Melissa said. Before I could say anything, she glared at me. "You promised."

"I said I would do it. But I'm not letting people in my office."

Vanessa said, "Chris says they just want you to let people look inside. They don't have to go all the way in."

"And you'll be there the whole time," Kaya said.

They were all looking at me hopefully. "Fine," I said. I'd given in. Completely, it would seem. "But I'm there the whole time. And they stand at the door. That's it."

Melissa put a finger to her lips and took my arm, turning me around. A few yards along the sidewalk, Sam and Mary Ashford were standing close together, both talking at once, obviously angry.

"What do you suppose that's about?" Karen said.

"Shh," Kaya said.

I could just make out Sam saying, "Can we not do this here?" before they walked around the corner, apparently headed to the parking lot.

"We should follow them," Karen said.

"Absolutely not," I said. "That would be a breach of their privacy."

"My car is in the lot and it's time to go," she said with a conspiratorial smile. "Would you like a ride home?"

I shook my head. "I've got my car," I said. "And I don't want to hear any gossip."

"Yes you do."

And with that, the Divas dispersed.

On Monday I had lunch with Karen at Vagabonds, across Strawbridge Avenue from the Executive Suites. One of the pricier restaurants in downtown, it was quiet and dark. Karen and I had a table for two tucked in a corner. A candle lit up our faces as we ordered salads.

"Well, you won," she said, placing a five-dollar bill on the table after we ordered. I'd bet her that Melissa would claim to have seen a ghost at Mr. Cornell's conjuring party the night before. "She said she saw him plain as day."

"Wouldn't plain as day mean she saw a person, not a ghost?"

Karen chuckled. "You'll never convince her with an argument like that. Anyway, she said a lot of people saw the ghost. Sam's going to have them call into his radio show this week to talk about it."

I rolled my eyes. "The longer this nonsense goes on, the more repulsive I find Sam Preston."

"That's a strong word."

"I don't understand why everyone likes him so much."

"By everyone, you mean...you?"

"I do not like him."

"I think you spend a lot of time trying to convince yourself and everyone else that you don't."

"Because I don't. What's there to like?"

She sighed, and when our iced teas were put in front of us, took her time adding artificial sweetener to her glass and stirring. "He's cute," she finally said. "He's funny. He's not an axe murderer."

"You don't know that."

"Come on, Pari. It's obvious why you don't want to like him."

"It's not obvious to me."

"He's not serious."

"About what?"

"About anything. Life. His job. Tell me you don't think photography isn't a serious occupation."

"Of course it's a serious occupation."

"Mm hm." She offered me a sly smile and sipped her tea. "Ghost hunting."

"Now that is not serious. But what does that have to do with me?"

"You like serious people."

"You're saying I'm not any fun. Why does it seem like lately everyone is saying I'm no fun?"

"You're fun, Pari. But you like to have fun with serious people."

"That doesn't make any sense."

"You think he's cavalier."

"Yes," I said. "He's cavalier."

"And you don't like that."

"Why would anybody like that?"

"We don't all think he's cavalier, Pari. Just you."

"Well, what do you call it, if it's not cavalier?"

"I think we call it relaxed, jovial, loving what he does. Sarcastic, sure. But you see it as being un-serious."

"I must have some un-serious friends."

"Nope."

"Vanessa."

"Owns a salon, businesswoman. No nonsense. And just happens to be the life of every party. But she's a serious woman. Especially about her career. Same for Kaya, joyful and always ready with a joke, but owns her own store and styles the rich and famous of Strawbridge. Melissa, wacky, silly, party girl, *runs a restaurant.*"

"And Sophie..."

"She's more serious than all of us."

"And you."

"Office supplies. Serious and boring."

"You're not boring. But you're right, I suppose. I see you all as serious people."

"But not Sam Preston. I wonder why?"

"You're going to tell me why, aren't you?"

"It's because he's having too much fun."

"He does seem to have more than his share."

"Do you think it has anything to do with your chosen career path? You help people who aren't having fun. So, maybe you see him as..."

"As what?"

She shrugged. "Not in need of you."

"Oh, no. Don't put any of that on me. I'm not looking to mother anyone. Or even Nightingale someone. Look at Eric. He's serious, and he doesn't need me."

She cocked her head briefly to one side. "Maybe. You know, it occurs to me this is why you haven't finished your book."

"What does that have to do with any of this?"

"When you told me about it, it sounded like a lot of fun."

"I was trying not to be academic."

"Exactly. It started to feel un-serious, so you stopped."

"Have you always been this insightful?"

She smiled. "It's why you love me so much."

For a while we chatted about work–Karen's mostly. You know I can't blab about my clients. And she told me Trudy, of Trudy's Treasures, had put out word she'd be having a conjuring of her own where Aranthia was sure to show up.

"She says that séance woman–"

"Felicia."

"Do you think that's her real name?"

"Unlikely. But what about her?"

"She's going to call on Aranthia and ask her about the captain, specifically, whether or not he's hanging out at Old Geezer's."

"Sophie still thinks those two should get together."

"They had dinner once," Karen said. "That was years ago, wasn't it? I think antiques came between them. Too much competition. Anyway, Melissa wants us to go to Trudy's. It's the night before the sleepover."

"Ugh." I literally said, 'ugh.' "I'm trying not to think about the sleepover. Sam's coming to see me on Wednesday."

"What for?"

"He wants to check out my office for ghosts."

"I can't believe you're letting him do it."

I glared at her.

"I'm glad you are," she said. "Just surprised."

"We made a deal. He tells me about his life, and I let him hunt the ghost."

"So, you're curious."

"Maybe. A little. But we're clear it's not professional. Because...you know."

"Because you kissed the man twice within the first two weeks of meeting him?"

I felt my cheeks grow hot. "Another thing I'm trying not to think about. But no. It would be disrespectful to my profession if I counseled him. So, it's more like he's telling me about himself for insight into the whole ghost thing."

"How convenient. Which one of you will do the kissing this time?" She winked at me.

"You think I should cancel?"

She slapped the table. "Don't you dare." We both laughed.

When we finished lunch and were outside the restaurant, cars on US 1 rushing by, occasional honks blaring, she said, "You're really not going to ask me about it, are you?"

"About what?"

"Last night. Sam and Mary."

I shook my head. "It's none of my business."

She stared at me with a smirk.

"Okay, fine. Did you hear anything else?"

"No. They were already in his car by the time I got to the lot."

I slapped her playfully. "I can't believe you got me to ask."

"But you did. Maybe you can ask him all about it in your session this week."

"I don't care, remember?"

She took my arm as we crossed Strawbridge Avenue to my office building and, once we were at her little red Kia, we hugged our goodbyes. She took my hands in hers and looked gravely into my eyes.

"All you need," she said, "is Post-it notes placed strategically around the office."

"What for?"

"To keep you from kissing Sam."

"I thought you were a serious person," I said, laughing. "What would they say anyway? 'No kissing?'"

"No, silly. They must be coded so Sam doesn't understand them. So, for What Would Karen Say, it'd be WWKS."

"But the KS would look like 'Kiss Sam' and then I'll be kissing him."

She climbed into the front seat of her car. "You're hopeless, Pari. Give in and kiss the man."

Over the roar of her engine, I shouted, "I promise there will be no more kissing."

I watched her drive away and turned toward the building only to find Eric waiting for me. I stammered a hello and let him hold the door to the lobby for me.

"Good lunch?" he asked.

"Mm hmm." What could I do? I couldn't explain what I'd said to Karen about no more kissing. If I told him I wasn't talking about him, he'd know I was kissing someone else. Maybe he hadn't heard me at all. But what if he had and thought I didn't want to kiss him again? "Oh, bother," I mumbled. "I wasn't talking about you...if you heard what I said."

"Something about kissing?"

"Yeah. It was just one of those crazy conversations I have with Karen."

"So, you didn't promise her you wouldn't kiss me again?"

"Absolutely not."

He nodded, his eyes looking about the lobby making sure we weren't being overheard. "Okay, then. Good to know. I'll call you later."

And with that, he headed toward his office on the first floor, and I started up the stairs, shaking my head. Wham!–Eric was back to being aloof.

Chapter Forty-four

B efore we get started," Sam Preston said that Wednesday evening as he sat down on the little sofa in my office, "I want to make it clear that I don't consider this an actual appointment. I mean, there's no client *slash* doctor confidentiality you need to worry about. We're friends."

"Agreed." I sat in my comfy high-backed chair across from him. "I'm not your doctor."

"Exactly. We could still date after this...if we wanted to. I mean, you wouldn't be breaking any rules. That's all I'm saying."

I blushed. "I...don't know what to say to that."

"Just as a theoretical."

"Understood." I couldn't help smiling. "So, no equipment?"

"What equipment?"

"Ghost-o-meters, spectral enhancers?"

He laughed. "That's Christopher's thing, remember? It's not how I work."

"How do you work?"

"I listen mostly. It's a lot like what you do."

"I doubt that. So, which is first? Spill your guts or whisper to my ghosts?"

"If you don't mind," he said. "If you trust me, I'd like to do the ghost thing first."

"What does trusting you have to do with it?"

"You never considered I might make contact with Aranthia or some other apparition and then bail before the promised gut-spilling?"

"Never crossed my mind." Though it might have. I was having trouble remembering right at that moment. "So, what can I do to help?"

"Seriously?"

"Seriously."

"Well, if you don't mind, un-cross your legs and sit up straight, but stay relaxed."

I did as told. "You're not going to try to hypnotize me, are you?"

"I'm not into that. Close your eyes–" My brows shot up. "–you said you trusted me." Fair enough. "Breathe normally and just listen. And if I say something, try not to laugh or react."

"What might you say?"

"I might say her name. Or ask for a name. And there might be some conversation."

"One-sided, I presume."

"You'll let me know if you hear any voice other than mine, right?"

"I promise." I did my best not to look skeptical. I'm actually quite good at it. It's part of my job to keep a calm and accepting expression on my face. "Will your eyes be closed, too?"

"Yes. But if I start talking to Aranthia, or anyone who might show up, we can open our eyes."

"You first," I said.

He closed his eyes, so I closed mine and we sat there for the longest time just breathing. I noticed how lovely my office is. The air conditioning hummed softly, and the sounds of the offices next door were muted. Traffic from the main road came through as if wind rushed by at regular intervals. It wasn't bad for meditating.

I'd begun to think nothing was going to happen when I heard Sam whisper, "Is there anyone here with us?"

I found myself tense up, my ears straining to hear something, anything.

"Aranthia?" he said.

And then, though I'm sure it was my imagination, I had the sudden sense of something else being in the room. A spot of density, a presence. And it...moved. My eyes shot open and I gasped. But there was nothing there.

Sam was searching my face. "You felt it?"

"It was nothing."

"I think it was something."

I sighed. "Sam..."

"Go ahead with the lecture."

"But it's true. When we go looking for mystery, when we prime ourselves for it, we tend to find it."

He seemed to think about that for a few moments, looking around the walls of my office.

"My brother died when I was nine," he said, looking back to me.

"I know."

"I thought so. At the cemetery."

I nodded.

"It was sudden. He was hit by a car while riding his bike. There were a few really tough days. Especially at first, when I didn't understand what had happened. It was hard to accept it was real. My mother made me look at him in the casket. I'm not saying that was a bad thing. It was just really hard to do. But she said if I didn't see him there, I'd always wonder if he'd really died. I don't know why she thought that." He shrugged. "Anyway, the night of the funeral, I woke up and he was sitting on my bed watching me. We talked a little bit. He told me he was okay but he missed Mom and Dad. He was crying because he could feel how much pain they were in. I promised him I'd take care of them. I'd make them happy." He stopped talking then and met my eyes only briefly before looking away.

"That's a lot of weight for a nine-year-old to shoulder."

He nodded. "But I did my best. And my parents did manage to find some happiness after several years."

"How would you say you did your best?"

"What do you mean?"

"What did you do, as a child, to make your parents

happy?"

He looked at me, an odd expression on his face, like he'd never thought about it before. He drew his brows together and said, "I wanted them to smile, at first. I think it was three or four months after, I said something funny. I don't remember now what it was, but I remember their faces." Sam relaxed and deflated into the chair with a sigh.

"You remember how it felt."

He nodded. "I guess I started making them smile and laugh whenever I could."

"Did you see your brother's ghost again?"

"No. But I've been looking for him ever since. And I know you'd say it was my imagination." Again, he paused, waiting for me to respond.

"As a psychologist, I wouldn't. I would let you decide for yourself what was real and what wasn't."

"But...?"

"As your friend, I'd say yes, it was your imagination. Or a vivid dream."

"And I'd agree that's a possibility."

"Have you made contact with any other ghosts, Sam? I mean...honestly?"

"Honestly? No. But I enjoy the hope that one day I might. So, now that I've spilled my guts on the floor. Can I ask you a question?"

"Sure."

"Why are you so dead set against ghosts?"

"I see what you did there."

"Purely accidental," he said.

"Accidental as in, falling off a ladder?"

"Of course. And haunting the construction site afterward."

I laughed. "I can't picture you as the haunting type."

"Thank you, I think. Still, I want to know. Why are you so adamant about it?"

"Well, mostly it's the professional thing. I feel that for people to trust me, to spill their guts as you say, I need to remain a bland sort of sponge. People don't want to tell their secrets to someone they think is..."

"Human?"

"You know that's not what I mean."

"But is that fair?"

"Fair?" I was on the defensive again.

"To you or to them?"

"What are you talking about?"

"Don't they want to know who they're trusting?" He ran his hands through his hair and slapped them back to his legs. "Sure, there might be some who hear about you going on ghost tours and falling face down on graves at the cemetery, or maybe you sing karaoke and you suck at it, and those people will be like, 'I'm not telling her anything.' But there will be other people who see that and say, 'That's her! That's the person I can talk to about this stuff.'"

"You make an interesting point."

"Your vibe attracts your tribe. Isn't that what it says on the Dove wrappers?"

"Dark or milk?"

"Both."

"At the same time?" I must have sounded aghast because he sat back against the sofa as if I'd hit him.

"If possible."

"You're an odd sort, aren't you?"

He smiled and nodded. "So, what's the other reason?"

"For what?"

"You said it's *mostly* professional. What else is there?"

I shrugged. "It's connected. There are people out there barely hanging on and people like you are offering them hope."

"What do you mean, people like me? You make it sound sinister. And what's wrong with hope?"

"I mean people who tell them there's more than what's going on right here. Vulnerable people will grab hold of anything they can work with and risk turning it into something dark and obsessive. They fail to grow, to move on."

"Do you think I haven't grown or moved on?"

"No, I don't. You've tempered your enthusiasm with reality, and humor, and a sense you could be wrong. But other people are so easily manipulated into focusing on an afterlife, they lose sight of the one they're living. There are even some who are all too willing to join their loved ones who've passed."

He winced. "And you think I'm responsible?"

"Not at all. I believe the people who listen to you and follow you are responsible for their own growth. It's just that...I wish people like you would be aware that there are vulnerable people out there who want so desperately to believe what you're saying. Just be aware and have empathy for them."

"That's a lot to think about."

"I hope you *will* think about it. Anyway, that's enough of that. Is there any more ghost whispering you'd like to do?"

"Not today." He got up and looked around my office. "Maybe another time?"

"You mean the sleepover."

He winced slightly. "I'd be lying if I said I didn't want your office to be part of the event."

"Would it be enough if my door was open, but entry was blocked? Your guests could look in, at least."

"That would be plenty."

"Okay," I said. His face broke into a smile. "But only because everyone I know–except Eric, naturally–wants me to allow it."

"Dr. Logan! You? Succumbing to peer pressure? What will people think?"

"Don't tell anyone."

"You'll be here then, for the night? You can stay in your office, making sure no one desecrates it."

"You do talk funny, Mr. Preston."

And with that, we shook hands, for a tad longer than is typical, I think. And I tried to tell myself any sort of spark I felt was my imagination.

Chapter Forty-five

L ilian Vanderhoff breezed into my office on a whiff of gardenia, pulled an ivory silk scarf from her head and wrapped it around her shoulders; she twirled about in the space between my desk, chairs, and small couch. Then she went to the window and peered out. All before saying so much as "Hello."

"You've no doubt why I'm here, surely," she said finally. "I read all about you in the Gazette. Well not you, exactly, but there's no other psychologist in the building, now is there?"

I took my usual seat in the chair nearest my desk. I always left the spots closest to the wall for any clients who liked the sense of protection a large slab of drywall gave them.

"On the phone you said you were struggling with feelings of aggression."

She turned to me, her brow furrowed, her lips in a frown. "I said that?"

"You said you wanted to strangle some people."

"Oh, yes. That." With another glance out the window, she entered the seating space, looked around and chose the chair next to me. "I want to see the ghost. Aranthia. I told my husband it would be okay. To make the appointment, I mean. I said to him, 'I'm paying her, aren't I?' But he said it wasn't right. So, I told him I'd agree to talk to you about a certain problem I'm having as long as I got to sit here and, you know..."

I shook my head, a question on my face.

"Commune," she said. "With the ghost. Look, she and I have a lot in common. Not that I've thrown myself out a window, but I'd sure like to, sometimes."

"Tell me about it," I said.

And she did. Lilian Vanderhoff wanted to strangle her mother-in-law, son, son-in-law, husband, dog, cat, the neighbor's dog, the neighbor on her right, the neighbor on her left, the woman who lived across the street, and a particular bag boy at the grocery store. And after spending all day not strangling anyone, she sometimes felt like throwing herself out a window.

"Not literally, of course," she said. "Metaphorically."

"Why don't you ask your neighbor to stop letting his dog poop on your lawn?"

"Bruce won't allow it. He wants nothing but goodwill in the neighborhood. And the family."

"And the grocery store."

"Exactly. He says if I complain about the young man who bags my groceries, he may lose his job and we'll never be able to go to the store again."

"And what is it the clerk is doing?"

"Singing!"

"I see."

"All the time singing!"

Mrs. Vanderhoff spent the rest of her time going into meticulous detail about her complaints against the people in her life and when her appointment was at end, she stood up, smiled grandly and said, "This has been marvelous. I feel so much better already."

"Would you like to do it again next week?"

She would. I had an idea Mrs. Vanderhoff just needed someone to truly hear her. And I was happy to be that person.

"And Aranthia," she said at the door. "I completely forgot to watch for her."

"Oh, I think we'd both know if she popped in."

"Maybe next week." She winked and was gone.

280

That made two new clients who'd found me after reading the Gazette article and none so far who only wanted to see a ghost. Mrs. Vanderhoff was close, but as she didn't mention Aranthia once she got going, I was going to have to put her on the side of good results. I had one new client left to see. I honestly couldn't decide if I wanted him to be a gawker, just trying to get into my office for the ghost, or to be in real need of my services. The desire to be right is intoxicating. The only negative impact on my practice recently was Nelson Gardner defecting to Isabella for her psychic insights. That certainly wasn't Sam Preston's fault. Thus far, his ghosting presence hadn't interfered with my practice and was likely not to. But taking part in the tours and events still sometimes felt degrading—to my professional reputation. But once again, Sam wasn't to blame. That was on me.

As I got ready to leave for the day, I gazed at the wall where my degrees and awards were displayed. Then I took my goals notebook from my top desk drawer and flipped through the pages to where I'd listed the accolades I wanted to receive. Psychologist of the Year Award. Crossed off. Professional Woman of the Year Award. Crossed off. Bright Stars Award. Crossed off. There was one other local award I coveted: The Association of Professional Women's Standards of Excellence Award. I was being considered before ghost panic descended on Downtown Strawbridge. I had no idea where I stood with the awards committee now.

Sam was subdued during class that evening. Fewer jokes, less sarcasm than usual. A bit on the technical side of things, as far as lectures go, so maybe that's all it was. But I remembered the fight with Mary and wondered if they really had been dating. Maybe she found out about the kissing. How do you tell your girlfriend you've kissed another woman and it meant absolutely nothing? If anything, kissing her was just another way for you to antagonize her. Somehow, I didn't think that would go over well. When class was over, I stayed behind, uninvited.

"Is everything okay?" I said.

He looked up and nodded. "Yeah. Everything's good."

"Oh, I see how it is." I tried for levity. "Now that I'm letting you in my office, the friendship is over."

He smiled as if filled with relief. "My evil plans have been exposed."

"It's okay. We lasted a day. We can go back to being enemies if you want."

"I wouldn't say we were enemies, would you? I thought we were in something of a truce mode."

"Truce mode it is, then."

"No way. You said we were friends, so we're friends."

"And you're all right?"

"Just a bad mood." And to prove to me he was fine, he spun around on his stool.

We left the building together and he told me about a photography workshop he was hosting in November. "We'll be meeting up at the beach and two parks over a weekend. It's for intermediate photographers. You should join us. But it's a bit pricey."

"Am I intermediate?"

"You will be when this class is done."

"What if I fail?"

He laughed. "There's no failing in photography."

We stood in front of the building in the spotty lighting above the walkway. It had rained during class, turning the evening muggy. Cars passed on the slick road, making that swishy wet sound that always reminded me of childhood afternoons walking home from school.

"I'll check it out at your website," I said.

He nodded and we stood there with an awkward silence between us.

"Are you sure you're okay?" I said. "Do you feel awkward because of our session? We can make it professional if you want. You don't have to stick to that whole 'friends' thing."

"That's not it."

But he looked at me as if he'd lost something.

"Well, I'm glad we've got a truce or friends, or..." I said. "I'll see you later." I walked out to my car knowing he was watching me.

"I'll be at the haunted house on Friday," he called as I put the key in the lock. "Maybe I'll see you there."

I smiled. "It's a date. I mean. Not a date. A friend thing?"

Laughing, he said, "I got it." He waved and went to his car, leaving me feeling strange, as if I'd just brought home a puppy and had no idea what to do with it.

Chapter Forty-six

MaryAshford has joined the chat.

MaryAshford: The haunted house isn't part of our events.

LegitChris: Hi to you too, Mary. So what about it?

MaryAshford: It's listed on the website.

SamTheMan: It's a Halloween thing. And spooky. I didn't see anything wrong with advertising it.

LegitChris: The zombie walk is on there too.

SamTheMan: And we put a disclaimer saying it's not one of our events.

MaryAshford: I don't think it should be on the website at all.

LegitChris: We'll be there, though.

MaryAshford: I wasn't told about it. Or invited.

LegitChris: Well that was an oversight. Sorry.

MaryAshford: ...

LegitChris: Are you going to be there then?

MaryAshford: Is it okay with you, Sam?

SamTheMan: Sure. Why wouldn't it be?

MaryAshford: insert eyeroll emoji here.

MaryAshford has left the chat.

LegitChris: You want to tell me what's going on?

SamTheMan: Not really.

LegitChris: She's obviously not happy. Is she quitting?

SamTheMan: Mary and I went out a few times. I should have told you before.

LegitChris: Great. Now I need an eyeroll emoji.

SamTheMan: What's the big deal?

LegitChris: She's pissed off.

SamTheMan: She's always pissed off.

LegitChris: And now I know why. What happened and when?

SamTheMan: The last time we went out was two weeks before the interview at MacAuley's. I think she's too young for me.

LegitChris: Then why did you go out with her?

SamTheMan: I liked her. And she liked me.

LegitChris: You really do need to grow up, man.

SamTheMan: She's twenty-three. It's not like I'm a pervert.

LegitChris: So, you broke it off and she can't handle it, or what?

SamTheMan: Not exactly.

LegitChris: So tell me already.

SamTheMan: I never actually broke it off. I didn't think there was anything there to break.

LegitChris: So you strung her along?

SamTheMan: No. I just didn't call her anymore.

LegitChris: But you brought her to the interview. And the conjuring.

SamTheMan: She asked for a ride. What was I supposed to do?

LegitChris: Did you make it clear it wasn't a date?

SamTheMan: How am I supposed to do that? Oh, by the way, this isn't a date?

LegitChris: You're right, that would be weird.

SamTheMan: I think she thought they were dates, though. She got mad at the conjuring and accused me of wanting to be with Pari.

LegitChris: And we've been talking about her. You kissed her twice.

SamTheMan: I told her it was none of her business.

LegitChris: How'd she take that?

SamTheMan: Scary silence.

LegitChris: I hate those kinds of silences.

SamTheMan: I handled it like a jerk.

LegitChris: Yeah. You did.

SamTheMan: Thanks.

LegitChris: Anytime. Mary's done a lot of work for us. You need to make it right somehow.

SamTheMan: Okay, okay. I'll figure it out.

LegitChris: You're going to have to do it without sarcasm. It'll be hard.

SamTheMan: I'm eyeroll emoji-ing you right now.

Chapter Forty-seven

Twila Harper rattled on excitedly about her cake decorating class and a painting class she'd decided to take. She was my last client that Friday afternoon.

"But I'm still fading away," she said. "I'm thinking, maybe it isn't psychological after all."

She seemed solid enough to me. "What could it be?"

"Either I'm pre-dying, which is what I think it is, or I'm not really even here. I'm a figment of everyone's imagination."

"How would that work, exactly?"

"I have no idea. But it makes me wonder how many other people throughout history have been figments and just faded away."

"Wouldn't the rest of us realize you were gone?"

"No. Once I'm gone, you won't remember my ever being here, because I'm not really here."

I let that linger between us for a while. I wasn't sure what I should say at that point, beyond what I did: "But you are here, Twila."

"Am I?"

"Yes," I said. "You're here."

She looked at me funny and said, "Maybe. Anyway, I think I know what to do about it. I think I should talk to that Ghost Whisperer guy."

"How would that help?" It had come out a bit jarring and she looked startled. "I mean, he hunts ghosts, and you're not a ghost."

"Not yet. It can't hurt."

I wasn't so sure about that.

"I'm working the haunted house tonight," she said, seemingly wanting to change the subject. "In the hell room."

"The hell room?" I shivered.

She shrugged. "Typical fire and damnation stuff. I'll be screaming. We won't have to do it more than once per weekend. So maybe tomorrow night I'll get to be a corpse in the cemetery scene."

"It sounds like...fun?"

She laughed. "Yeah, it is. This is my second year doing it."

"Is it really scary?"

"It's mostly for adults, I guess. We have rules about the kids. We go easy on them."

"Well, I'd appreciate your going easy on me."

"If you don't want to be scared, why go?"

That was a very good question. "I promised a friend." That seemed to be enough reason for Twila.

The haunted house was put on by the Halloween Team, a group of actors from the Strawbridge Theater who hosted the annual Zombie Walk as well. The Strawbridge Theater was housed in the old Strawbridge High School, circa 1920. While it had been renovated extensively for the theater's use, it was still something of a creepy old place, especially the back half, which was used for dressing rooms and storage. As a teen, I'd performed in ballet and tap recitals there and more than once got lost in the maze of rooms. I shuddered at the thought of going back in, this time to be terrorized by a stream of volunteers trying gleefully to make me scream. I hoped Melissa understood what I was willing to go through for our friendship.

As it was Friday night, Eric and I had a date, but he said he'd rather have his eyeballs scraped than walk around in a decrepit, old building with people shouting and flashing lights in his face. I got the feeling he'd done it before.

"You're going to pass up being my protector and having me hang onto you in a panic as we fight for survival from a group of scary kids?"

"We're not fifteen," he said.

Well, okay then. Eric agreed to pick me up after I succumbed to the house of horrors and we'd do Triple F together, where he promised to buy me another ice cream cone. Sophie and I met up outside our apartments and walked westward on Manatee Road. It was hot, but a warm breeze drifted off the lagoon. The Strawbridge Theater sat behind Burgers between Palmetto and Woodplum roads. It had its own street called School Road, but for the past thirty odd years various groups tried to get it changed. Suggested names were Hurricane, Playhouse, Alligator, and lately, Roady McRoad Face.

The back parking lot abutted Manatee and that was where the entrance to the haunted house was.

"It's not technically a haunted house, is it?" Kaya said as we joined the rest of the Divas in line.

Spooky music stuttered with screams blasted from speakers mounted outside the building.

"It's worse," I said. "Four floors and it's like a maze. We may never make it out."

At that moment, Sam Preston showed up with Chris and Richard the landscaper. "I'll protect you," he said with a wink at me.

"And I've got mad orienting skills," Christopher said. He put his arms around Vanessa. "Don't be scared."

"Don't you be scared," she teased. "I'll protect you."

"Thank you." And at that, they started smooching.

I sighed. Richard took Karen's hand and Reese showed up beside Sophie. Melissa moved to stand with Kaya and said, "Looks like it's you and me, babe."

"What about me?" I said.

Melissa glanced at Sam and said, "You've got your scare buddy."

Sam grinned at me. "The boss has spoken."

The first thing that hit us when we walked through the

door was a blast of cold wind, heavy with the scent of rotten apples. Deep toned, thumping heart beats vibrated around us, and I instinctively wrapped my arm around Sam's. I didn't care what he thought about it. This did not bode well, and I was going to hang on. The ceiling was strung everywhere with wispy bits of who knows what—some slimy, some wet, some like straw. Everywhere the smell of dead fruit hit my nose, and occasionally the sound of buzzing flies flew past. We were directed into the first room by a volunteer dressed as a dead butler, his tuxedo slashed open and his organs pouring out slick and gooey.

"Oh, no." I heard Sophie in front of us. I reached out and touched her back, hoping to soothe her but she jumped and screamed.

"Sorry," I said.

Inside the first dungeon, couples danced but each contained one dead person—a life-sized doll but very real looking—being dragged by the other.

When we filed out the other door, I turned to Sam and said, "That wasn't so bad."

He winked.

In the second room we were chased out by a masked man with a chain saw. A real, live, roaring chain saw.

"That was dangerous!" I insisted.

But Sam said it couldn't have been real. "Insurance," he muttered.

Okay, I thought. He's right. I needed to get hold of myself. There couldn't be anything in the place that would actually hurt anybody. Right? Right. But before I could completely calm down, we were suddenly assaulted by a group of young people rushing at us from the wrong direction spraying everyone with something wet. Sam pushed me against the wall and held his body against mine until they passed and when he let up a bit, there in the darkness, I could see the outline of the right side of his face, my heart pounding, his breath heavy and fearful.

And you know, it was inevitable. I reached out and pulled his lips to mine and kissed the man. Like teenagers, we made out in the haunted house paying no mind to the screaming, laughter, and rattling chains all around us.

Finally, I pulled away slightly and he leaned in so that his lips were against my ear and said, "That's three. You definitely like me, Dr. Logan."

Chapter Forty-eight

I laughed. We were in the dark, haunted screams and buzzing all around us, our friends long gone, huddled against the wall.

"You definitely like me," he said.

"Not necessarily," I told him. We parted and he took my hand as we continued along the haunted path our butlers, all having been killed in strange ways–the next lady had an alligator head stuck on her own–forced us to follow.

In the swamp room where the victims were being eaten alive by alligators–*so* Florida–I told Sam, "Strong emotions often elicit passionate behaviors. But it doesn't mean we're compatible."

"True enough," he said, stopping briefly to call out to one poor player trying to extricate herself from the obviously fake gator jaws. "Can I offer you a hand?" She ignored him. A true professional. "You're not my type either."

I was a bit stunned and I'm afraid, even in the dim light of our torture chamber, he saw it.

"Oh, I see how it is." We moved on with the crowd to the next room, the obligatory electric chair scene in which the condemned has managed to get the jailor in the seat and has his hand on the switch. When the screaming started, Sam gently pushed me along. "Nothing to see here."

"What do you mean, 'how it is?'"

"You get to say I'm not your type, but I can't say the same."

"I didn't say that."

"But you think I like you, don't you?"

"I never said that, either." And after a pause. "What is your type?"

"My last girlfriend was an artist."

I nodded, letting myself be ushered into a dining room where everything on the table had a talking head. "This is just silly," I said. "So, what happened?"

"She moved to California to start a jewelry design business."

"And you didn't follow her?"

"I don't want to live in California. It's not like we were engaged."

"Have you come close?" Not that it was any of my business.

"You're not one of those women who thinks a man who hasn't married by thirty has mommy issues, are you?"

"I'm not married, and I'm nearly there."

"True. Women have it worse. At least some people see me as a confirmed and happy bachelor."

"And you're not?"

"I'm all for marriage."

"So, did you come close?"

"Long time ago," he said.

At that point we were standing in a very dark room where a single woman stood with a candle to her face, crying in fright. Suddenly a dim light played on her attacker and we all screamed and ran.

"What happened?" I said after I'd peeled myself off Sam and took in a few calming breaths. That last one really got me.

"We were young."

"Was she an artist too?"

"Chef."

"Close," I said.

"How about you?"

296

"You know my type. I'm dating him."

Sam made a face that had condescension written all over it. "But were you ever close to marriage?"

"In college, yes. I was engaged. He was in medical school and when I told him I was going for my doctorate he..."

"He broke it off?"

"Worse. He laughed."

"You're kidding."

I shook my head. "He thought it was cute. He literally said it was cute. 'But what would you do with it, anyway? You're going to be a doctor's wife.' He expected me to be his social manager, I guess."

"Unbelievable."

"And he was so wonderful, other than the misogyny."

Sam chuckled.

"My mother was heartbroken," I said.

"Almost married to a doctor," he agreed. "And me, a lowly photographer. Is that why I'm not your type?"

"That's insulting, Mr. Preston."

He smiled and nudged me. "I didn't mean it."

While we held hands through the buried alive room, the witches brew room (people trying to crawl out of the cauldron), and a room with nothing but darkness and wind and a faint, childlike voice singing in a corner (very scary), we said nothing else. When it looked like we were stuck in a line for the exit, he turned to me and said, "So, your 'passionate behaviors theory' is why you've kissed me three times?"

"Twice. One of them is on you. You said so yourself."

"Okay, fine, you've kissed me twice, and took part willingly in a third, only because you can't stand me?"

"I can stand you. I'm just saying kissing you doesn't mean you're my type."

"That makes no sense at all. Come on." He put his arm around me, and we left the cold haunted building for the warm breeze of October. "You don't have to admit you like me. But just so you know, I'll kiss you anytime."

We saw the Divas with their men standing under a streetlight in the parking lot and headed their way.

"Why Mr. Preston," I said, laughing. "You're rather free with your lips."

He pulled me tighter and let his head bump against mine as we walked. "Just for you, Doc."

At that moment, I realized Eric was with the group and I stopped abruptly, my face growing hot with embarrassment.

"Oh, no," Sam said with a chuckle. "Caught in the act."

"Hush."

Part of me felt I'd done nothing wrong. I was just being chummy with the guy who'd gone through the haunted house with me. But I'd kissed him. Again! What was wrong with me? The guilt must have shown on my face and Eric didn't look happy. He took my arm and led me away from the group.

"We've been waiting for a while," he said. "What took you two so long?"

"I was...we were." I tried to think of a reason other than 'we stopped to make out.' "We were accosted by a group of–wait." I pulled away from him and looked down at myself. Nothing. "They sprayed something on people. Looks like I didn't get any on me." The thought of Sam's body pressing on mine, protecting me, filled me with a wonderful dread and my face flushed again. "Anyway, we got separated from the group."

"I thought we didn't like that guy."

"We don't. I don't." With a glance back at Sam and the Divas, I said, "I suppose there's nothing like being terrorized by a bunch of horror-addicted teenagers to make one set aside differences. At least for a while."

He looked at me with an odd, dare I say suspicious, look on his face. "Well, you're here now," he said. "Let's go."

"Where's your car?"

"I walked here." I detected an unspoken *duh* in his voice. "You didn't drive, did you?"

"Of course not. I just assumed you did." *Don't say it, Eric. Please don't say it.*

"You know what happens when you assume."

He said it. Sometimes he said the whole thing, about the ass and you and me. Most of the time, though, he liked to *assume* I knew the rest, which I found wildly amusing. But I didn't laugh that night. I trudged along beside him all the way back to the east end of Downtown Strawbridge and the Triple F festival, convincing myself that walking was a good thing. It cleared my head of cobwebs and kisses.

Chapter Forty-nine

The band on stage for Friday Fun Fest that month was a country group from Scottsmoor, up north a bit, called Git 'Er Dun. Eric and I had just got shaved ice from one of the street vendors–I was promised ice cream, but made no protest–when Karen showed up and dragged us down the street to the stage. I could tell Eric wasn't all that thrilled. He preferred jazz. At least, he always said he did. But I don't recall ever hearing him listening to it. As I stood on the outskirts of the dancing space where tons of people were doing their best line dance moves, I wondered if Eric liked music at all.

"You don't like country, do you?" I yelled into his ear.

He winced. "Not really."

"So, I guess you don't want to dance."

He looked at me as if I'd swallowed a bee. "Do you want to dance?" Like it was the most ridiculous idea he'd ever heard.

I shook my head. But I did want to dance. I'm not saying I'm the biggest country music fan, either. But it looked like everyone was having a lot of fun. Through the crowd, I caught sight of Sam Preston doing his best impression of Elvis. I grabbed Karen's arm, pointing. She laughed and just then he turned and caught us watching him. Karen waved.

"Cut it out," I told her and glanced at Eric. He didn't seem to notice.

The song ended, something about running home to Mama, and another one started up. My tongue was numb from the berry flavored ice, and I took Eric's empty cup along with my leftovers to the trash can nearby. The new song was a bit slower and had couples pairing off. When I got back to Eric's side, I watched in horror as Sam approached us, his eyes on mine.

"Good evening," he said and nodded at Karen.

I felt Eric's arm wrapping around me. I smiled as best I could, but it felt odd. I'd just kissed the man not an hour before and there I was with my sort of, not exclusive, Friday night boyfriend (Beau? Flame? Sweetheart? Why isn't there a better word for 'the guy I'm dating?').

"Shall we?" Sam asked Karen. They disappeared into the dancing crowd, and I watched, catching glimpses of them twirling around near the stage.

I was tapping my foot, bouncing a bit, I suppose, and finally Eric took my hand.

"Let's give it a try," he said.

I was so relieved and only then realized I'd been embarrassed. Eric and I were just standing there while all the other couples were dancing. It left me feeling... abandoned. There's quite a lot to be said for wanting to fit in. And I would always tell a client there's nothing wrong with that, as long as what you're wanting to do is harmless. Like dancing. Eric and I had no idea what we were doing. But that didn't matter. We moved. We wiggled. We attempted to mimic what was going on around us. After a few minutes, Karen and Sam bumped into me and, laughing, Karen twirled around and grabbed Eric. She carted him off to teach him how to two-step leaving me dancing with Sam Preston. Classic teen movie trick.

"I don't really know what I'm doing," Sam said with a laugh.

"Neither do I."

"Perfect."

He threw me away and spun me around and pulled

me back in and we dosey-doed backwards. If that's what dosey-doe means. Who knows? The music didn't seem to stop and before I knew it, I'd danced with Sam for three songs at least, before we were exhausted. He escorted me back to the spot where I'd been standing with Eric and, sure enough, there he was, looking perturbed.

"Thanks for the dance," Sam said. Then he looked at us both and said, "I guess I'll see you two tomorrow." And he was gone.

Before I could react to what Sam had said, Eric pulled me away from the street dance and when we were finally well enough away so that the music was only pounding in our ears from residual exposure, he asked if I was ready to head home.

"We practically just got here," I said.

"Okay."

So we walked through the crowds and shopped at the stalls. Sophie was in her book nook next to Reese's surf wear booth. We browsed a few of the craft tables. I was beginning to think Eric hadn't heard Sam mention tomorrow night. How could I have forgotten to tell him about Karen's party? Now it would look as if I didn't want him to go with me. Freud would have plenty to say about that.

"But it isn't true, Sigmund, I swear. I want Eric to go with me to the party."

"*Nein, Liebe*. You can keep telling yourself that but it *von't* make it true."

Finally, Eric said, "So what's going on tomorrow?"

"Oh," I said and stammered a bit. "Didn't I tell you?" That was a stupid thing to say. "Karen's having a get together. A showing of *The Wizard of Oz*. I've never seen it, have you?"

"When I was a kid."

"We don't have to dress up or anything. She said it'll be pretty crowded so there'll be floor sitting."

"Sounds like fun."

"Really? You won't mind sitting on the floor?"

"Do you not want me to go?"

"I didn't say that. I just didn't think it was your kind

of thing."

"So, you weren't going to invite me?"

"We don't usually do Saturday nights. Do you already have plans?"

He smiled at me. "As it happens, I'm free."

I was about to go on about how I intended to invite him earlier but forgot. Instead, I dragged him over to the Sweet Suite booth outside the bakery and bought two honey buns. "I haven't had one of these in ages," I said. Nothing like wad of dough and sugar to calm the mind.

We walked to my apartment, the distant sounds of the festival leaving us in an odd disconnected quiet. At my door, Eric kissed me briefly.

"I'd come in," he said. "But it's been a long day and I'm up early tomorrow. Fishing with Dad."

"It's great you spend so much time with him," I said, thinking, *I didn't ask you in.*

"You could join us."

My mouth fell open. *Say something, Pari.* "I...on the boat?"

"Too soon?"

"Yeah, bad memories. Vomiting and all that."

He grimaced. "Tomorrow night then?"

"We'll have to drive."

"We could bike it."

I must have looked terrified.

He laughed. "I'll pick you up at...?"

"Seven. Movie starts at eight."

We stood there for a moment, an awkward pause hanging between us. Finally he said, "See you then."

I nodded and kissed him, just a peck, and waited as his footsteps padded down the stairs outside my apartment. Our passionate kiss the week before now seemed like a mistake. But I couldn't blame Eric. He'd seen me in Sam's embrace and I'd neglected to invite him to Karen's party. Naturally he'd feel a bit peeved. Eric sometimes bugged me, and he certainly came across as condescending at times. But I liked his maturity. I liked that he tried to be kinder and more responsive as a boyfriend. Sam Preston, on the other hand, could be just as condescending, if not more so. And yet, every time I saw him I imagined kissing him and being wrapped up in his arms.

I got into my pajamas and dug one of the enormous, glazed doughnuts out of the bag–let's face it, that's what a honey bun is–and popped it into the microwave for a little warming up. And I thawed a bit with it, figuratively speaking. Eric simply wasn't usually a physically demonstrative guy. But clearly he was a passionate man and there was hope for a more intimate relationship between us. Having him at Karen's party wouldn't be so bad. He wanted to spend time with my friends; he'd said so before. Obviously, he enjoyed the double date with Sophie and Reese. But I had a hard time imagining him on the floor atop a puffy throw pillow, eating popcorn, and watching a children's movie. I had a feeling it wouldn't end well.

Chapter Fifty

Eric picked me up at seven the next night and drove us over to Karen's condominium beachside. She was up five floors and had a balcony overlooking the Atlantic. There were already about two dozen people there when we arrived and I led Eric around, my hand on his arm, introducing him or us, and then left him in a corner with an attorney from our office building while I helped Karen in the kitchen. Gold and red balloons hung from the ceiling all over the place. Trays of *Wizard of Oz* themed snacks were set about—cookies shaped and decorated like all the characters; cupcakes with red icing and red sparkles—and two stations for mixed drinks and sodas, one in the living room and one in her spacious den. In the kitchen, on the little round table, there sat tin man hats, lion mane hats, straw hats, witches' hats, and one huge clear plastic crown and wand.

"What on earth?" I said.

"That's Glenda's crown."

"There's a queen?"

"Oh, Pari," she said giving me a motherly pat on the head. Karen certainly knew how to throw a party.

"Everything looks fabulous," I told her. "I'm sorry I couldn't help."

"No worries. I had a great time planning it. And I've

decided, this is what we have to do."

"What do you mean?"

"Parties. We don't want to go out to bars. We want to host parties."

"My apartment is too small."

"But mine isn't. And we could rent halls if we wanted to. This is definitely the way to go."

I laughed and helped her carry out trays of cookies shaped like green blobs with witches' hats perched on top. I hadn't seen the film, but I knew there was a melting involved. Karen had three televisions set up. One huge flat-screen in the living room, hung on the wall–I found out later she purchased it just for the occasion–one in the den, and one in the guest bedroom where the was a comfy sofa and chairs. Once everyone had arrived, we all squeezed into the front room and she had us all quiet down. Hats were being passed through the group. Kaya and Sophie were there with Reese; Melissa and Vanessa were bundled together with Christopher and Sam Preston. I waved and mouthed hellos. I recognized most of the people from downtown. Noah from the flower shop and Octavia who sang all the time. Suri and Benjamin, the cool kids who worked at Namasté for Pat Willard, who was also there with Officer Palmer, our local protector of the peace and parking enforcer. Melanie from Brunch was there. This was, as it turned out, a Downtown Strawbridge event.

Karen waved a wand and said, "Come out, come out, wherever you are! May I have everyone's attention? Welcome to the land of Oz!" Applause broke out and I couldn't help but smile.

Eric had made his way to my side, looking uncomfortable.

"The crowd will spread out," I whispered, taking his hand.

"As most of you know," Karen continued. "We are gathered here this evening because we have a virgin in our midst." *Oh, no.* "Who here has never seen *The Wizard of Oz*?" *Oh, please, someone else raise a hand.* I dutifully put my hand in the air and looked around. "That's right," Karen said. "Our very own Pari Logan–"

"That's Dr. Logan," Sam Preston called out. *Very funny.*

"Dr. Logan," Karen said with a laugh, "has never seen–come on up here, Pari, you can't wheedle out of this–has never seen this iconic film. So, Pari, I dub thee..." She pulled the Glenda crown from out of nowhere and sat it on my head, "Ozzed."

Amid the clapping and shouting, I searched for Eric in the crowd for a commiserating glance but couldn't see him. How could he have disappeared so quickly? Maybe he was in the kitchen eating up the tin man egg rolls. That's where I wanted to be. A special seat was reserved for me in the middle of Karen's living room sofa and I was ceremoniously–seriously everyone hummed "Hail to the Chief"–placed in it.

"And now," Karen said with a sly smile. "Who else belongs on the couch of honor?" I had a very bad feeling about this. "Has anyone only seen some of it, but not all?"

I looked around nervously and saw one hand up in the air.

"Octavia," Karen said. "Come on down!"

"Somewhere," she sang as she plopped down beside me and rattled my shoulders with excitement. "Over the rainbow!"

"One more," Karen said. "Who has only seen it once."

Several hands shot into the air this time and one of them was Sam Preston's. "A choice," Karen said. "I think, as he's new around these parts–"

She wouldn't!

"–we should honor Mr. Preston, Downtown Strawbridge's own Ghost Whisperer."

I blushed deeply and scanned the room again for Eric as Sam eased himself onto the sofa next to me. This was a set up; I was sure of it. I was going to kill Karen as soon as I got the chance. Not literally, of course. I think.

Once everyone had found seats throughout the condo –on chairs, the sofa, or snuggled onto beanbags and pillows–the lights were dimmed, popcorn was popping in the kitchen, and before she turned on the film, Karen said, "Ok, people, we're gonna sing all the songs, but be quiet in between so Pari can hear the words. And no spoilers. Let *her* scream first."

"Scream?" I said. "Wait. This isn't a scary movie, is it?"

"Don't worry," Sam said. "I'll protect you."

"It's a kids' movie, right?"

He shrugged. "I saw it when I was four and had nightmares for weeks."

I could only hope he was joking. The film was scary, yes. But also hilarious. I was able to sing quite a bit of "Over the Rainbow," and I could sing parts of "Follow the Yellow Brick Road," but that was the totality of my *Wizard of Oz* soundtrack talent. Sam did less well, but Octavia sang loud enough for all three of us, even when she didn't know the words.

As the movie played, Karen called out trivia about the making of the film. For example, she said Shirley Temple was considered for the role of Dorothy.

"Who's Shirley Temple?" Benjamin called out.

"Oh, very funny," Karen said.

I wondered where Eric was and how he was handling all the noise. If there was one thing I knew about him, it was that he liked quiet during movies.

Just after Dorothy and the Scarecrow rescued the Tin Man and invited him along on their journey to the Wizard, Karen paused for intermission and the lights came up.

"How do you like it so far?" she asked the three of us on the sofa.

"It's adorable," I said.

"The music!" Octavia said. "I'm going to find that soundtrack. Whiz of a wiz of a something or other."

"How about you, Sam?" Karen said.

He looked at me and smiled. "Adorable is right."

After managing to get a chance in the bathroom, I wandered around the condo looking for Eric, but he was hiding well. I found myself out on the balcony with several others entranced by the moonlight on the Atlantic, listening to the ocean rushing onto the shore from the dark abyss.

"Can't find your boyfriend?" Sam was suddenly at my side. He handed me a glass.

"What's in it?"

"I think it's Sprite."

"Thanks."

"So, why did you wince?"

"I didn't wince."

"You did. When I asked about Eric. Things not going well?"

"Why would you say that?"

"Because you winced."

I rolled my eyes. "I just don't like the word 'boyfriend.' It sounds so juvenile."

"And you're very mature."

I knew he was only teasing, but I still felt the need to defend myself. "Karen agrees with me. About the word being juvenile, I mean."

"Well, what do you call him?"

"Eric."

He laughed.

"There's no better word, I'm telling you. Paramour? I don't think so. Lover? No way."

"Oh, so you too don't...haven't?"

My cheeks burned and I wanted to slap the glass of Sprite against my face. "That's not any of your business."

He panicked. "No, not at all. Sorry."

I managed a chuckle. "Anyway, there's no word that fits."

"Whatever you call him, I guess it wasn't cool for Karen to separate you two. You're on a date, after all."

"Yeah. But he knows most everyone here. Still, he's not the party type."

"How long have you been dating?"

"Not that long; but I've known him for years."

"So, it is exclusive?"

I started to protest but hadn't the energy. "I don't know."

"You don't know?"

"At what point in your relationships do you write out a contract?"

He grinned. "Two weeks."

I shook my head and breathed in. Typical, unserious, Sam Preston. "It doesn't matter. I'm dating him and I wouldn't see someone else without at least broaching the subject with him."

"So, you're waiting for a better opportunity."

"I didn't say that." I touched my right temple with a fingertip and gave it a quick massage. "Are you even interested, or are you just trying to aggravate me?"

"Maybe."

"Which one?"

Just then, Karen called us all back to our seats for the rest of the movie and I was forced to sit next to Sam Preston with that question hanging in the air.

"Well?" Karen said as the lights came up an hour later. "What did you think?"

Everyone was looking at me. Talk about wanting to fade away. "It was cute," I said. This brought out a few boos, but it was all in good fun. "No, I really liked it." And I did.

"What next?" Melissa said.

"We should do *The Princess Bride*," Vanessa said.

"*Some Like it Hot*," someone shouted.

"I'm way ahead of you all," Karen said. "For Christmas, we'll be watching *It's a Wonderful Life*. You've seen that one, haven't you, Pari?"

I grimaced. "I'm afraid not."

This was well received. I had the feeling I was a cause celeb and doomed to be outfitted and sat in front of a screen until I'd seen every great film known to those in Downtown Strawbridge. There are worse things. I finally found Eric once the party started breaking up. He looked tired and a bit irritated.

"I'm sorry I lost you," I told him. "I guess I was guest of honor."

He tried to smile.

"Did you have a good time at least?"

"I did," he said. "Actually, I took a walk on the beach."

"You left?"

At that moment, Sam Preston showed up at my side with Melissa and Vanessa, Karen on their heels. "Thanks for the movie, Karen," he was saying. "Count me in for the next one." Then he turned to Eric and me. "The beach is great at night." He winked at me. And then to Eric, he said, as if asking permission, "I just wanted to say goodnight to Glenda." He put a hand on my shoulder and smiled. "I'm glad I could stand in for your date while he was beachcombing. I guess I'll see you on Tuesday." And with a nod to Eric, he left, followed by Melissa and Vanessa who gave me knowing looks.

"What's on Tuesday, Karen?" I said, perturbed.

She opened her mouth, tilted her head, and shrugged with a sly smile. "Melissa has us booked on the Ghost Whisperer radio show."

"No."

She nodded. "Tuesday night. Starts at seven. Be there by six. I'll pick you up at five and we can do dinner."

"That's just great," I told Eric once we finally got into his car.

"Are you going to do it?"

"I have to."

"No, you don't."

"I promised."

"But this is way beyond being open minded, Pari. This is you actually participating in Preston's delusion."

"I wouldn't mind him so much if I didn't feel like he was always making fun of me."

"It's because of your profession. He's more comfortable with psychics than with rational people."

"Maybe." I didn't want there to be a real reason, I suppose. But if there were a reason, I didn't think that would be it. Sam Preston didn't seem to mind people not believing what he believed. He was confident, but not overzealous. "Maybe he does it because I'm not all that nice to him. I'm sorry you were left on your own tonight."

"You warned me."

"So I guess you're a "no' for the next one?"

"Not necessarily," he said as he pulled the car onto

A1A. "But probably."

That evening, he stayed for a while and we watched television, making out like teenagers. This time I didn't stop him and it wasn't until he rolled off the couch onto the floor with a thud that we both realized we weren't quite ready to commit to sleeping together. No words to that effect were spoken–it was just one of those things understood after your smooching session goes awry, ending in a possible concussion. It was only later, as I was lying in bed trying to get flying monkeys out of my head, that I realized on our way home from Karen's I'd acted as if Eric and I were a couple and would definitely still be dating at Christmas time. It felt presumptuous of me, but Eric didn't hesitate. I wasn't sure if that was a good thing, or a bad thing. Am I a good witch, or a bad witch? And with that, sleep came easily.

Chapter Fifty-one

S unday morning, I startled awake at seven with a terrible thought running through my head. I'd dreamt I was kissing Eric, but instead of Eric it was Rob Lowe. The *Parks and Recreation* Rob Lowe. And all I was thinking about was how attractive he was and how incredible it was to be kissing someone so beautiful. Suddenly Rob Lowe was gone, and I was kissing Chris Pratt. Not *Parks and Recreation* Chris Pratt but *Jurassic World* Chris Pratt. And instead of thinking how amazing it was to be kissing Chris Pratt, I was only thinking about how much I loved him and what a fabulous person he was.

This was all too Freudian for my liking. I struggled to remember how I'd felt while kissing Eric the night before. We were both aroused and longing for each other, but was I into Eric because he was so gorgeous? Or was I into Eric for himself? I couldn't remember and that's what brought me to jump out of bed and start pacing. And then I did the strangest thing. I marched across the landing outside my apartment and knocked on Sophie's door. She opened it, drowsy, still in her pajamas, same as me.

Squinting at me in the bright morning light, she said, "What's wrong?"

"I think I'd like a cat."

You'd have thought I'd surprised her with a sack of books. "I have the perfect one for you. She's young, about six months. But she's calm and introverted. Perfect for someone who works full time."

"Are you sure?" I said. "It won't harm her to be alone?"

"You could always get two."

And that's how I ended up with Pebbles, an orange tabby, and her sister, Midnight, description's in the name. I spent Sunday catifying my apartment and not thinking about kissing celebrities. Typical distraction technique. Once they were there and had been shown the sand box and their food and water station, I realized I'd been missing that connection you can only get with a cat. I'd had two cats growing up, and my mom expected me to always have one around. I was going to have to hear 'I told you so' when I called her later that day. But if I kept her occupied with cat tales, Mama wouldn't have time to question me about my dating life. I didn't want to even think about it.

Let's Review:

1. I had to admit I liked Sam Preston, as a *friend*, but don't tell anybody I said that.

2. I did like Eric. But I wanted to love him and, deep down, I knew he wasn't right for me.

3. I worked hard to see Sam's faults and ignore his good points, probably because I didn't want to go beyond friendship. I was obviously attracted to him. But he wasn't the type of guy I saw myself with.

4. Instead of working to resolve these issues–Should I break it off with Eric? Should I explore my attraction to Sam?–I took in two homeless felines.

5. There are days when I think I'm a terrible psychologist.

On Monday morning, my ten o'clock, Wilson James, said he heard that a group called the Downtown Divas would be guests on The Ghost Whisperer Show on WDTS. He Googled it and found nothing. Which is exactly what he should have found because the Downtown Divas aren't a real thing.

"So, I went to the WDTS website," he said, "and found out it was you and your friends. Do you sing or something?"

I said, "Not at all." But that was after I'd said, "What?" and scared him. Mr. James is sure that at any moment his whole world will be ripped apart and he'll find he's actually being watched and filmed for the entertainment of millions of people. It was *The Truman Show* that had done it, of course. After he'd watched it, he started to notice what he called clues to his being under surveillance.

"I can't for the life of me figure out why they'd want to watch me. But then, why would they have wanted to watch Truman?"

"*The Truman Show* is fictional," I'd told him. He'd gotten so much better this past year, but then I saw that look on his face when I'd cried out, "What are you talking about?" and had to do some very quick and strategic backtracking. After apologizing profusely and explaining I was not in any kind of singing group and there wasn't any group called the Downtown Divas, he began to relax again. "I only found out about it a couple of days ago." I said.

"You're not going to talk about me, are you?"

"No, no, of course not. My friends and I were challenged to go on the Ghost Whisperer tours, that's all. And one of the challenges is to do this radio show."

"Why?"

I squirmed. "One of my friends believes she saw a ghost and I'm embarrassed to say we made a bit of fun at her expense. So, she's asked us to have open minds and engage with this thing she very much enjoys. It's a bonding exercise for all of us. Very much like what you are trying to do with your group of friends. And how is that going?" Great save and diversion, if I do say so myself.

As soon as I got the chance, I called Sam Preston but he didn't answer so I left a crazed message about how dare he call us the Downtown Divas and allow my picture on his website. *Truce canceled!* Two more clients that day asked me about it. I had no idea The Ghost Whisperer Show and WDTS were so popular.

I turned to Eric for some comfort when he called me at lunch time, but he was hardly helpful. "You should have put a stop to it as soon as you found out. This isn't funny, you know. It's embarrassing."

"For you or for me?"

He paused. *Paused!* "For you, of course. I don't know how you've managed to allow yourself to get into this situation."

"I made a promise."

"That's no excuse for putting your professional reputation on the line."

You see? No help at all. I no longer felt bad for dream-kissing him while only thinking about how beautiful he was.

I called Karen and she encouraged me to see the bigger picture. "What's the harm? You've got the opportunity to bring balance to the situation. You, me, and Kaya—we're the skeptics. It's actually a good thing these guys are having us on the show."

"But they've booked us as the Downtown Divas. One of my clients asked me if we were a barbershop quartet and I found myself telling him there were six of us and he said, 'There are barbershop sextets,' and I said, 'That's a bit sexist, isn't it?' and he looked at me like I was crazy, which was completely warranted."

She laughed.

"You know what happens when I get muddled. Weird things fly out of my mouth. It's not funny."

"Yes, it is. It really is. You'll laugh about it later, I promise."

You know how, when you're being unreasonable, there's a little voice in the back of your head telling you to stop panicking, telling you everything is okay, and if you keep going, you're going to make a fool of yourself? Well, I killed that little voice. I took its tiny, annoying larynx and squeezed until it shut up. That's what I did. So,

I will admit I was already on a razor's edge when the Divas were crowded into the little broadcast booth at our local radio station. Five of us were cozied up on a small sofa, while Melissa got the chair of honor, as the organizer my professional demise. And all the Ghost Whisperers were there: Sam Preston, naturally, looking jovial and boyish in his typical jeans and tee; Christopher Reynolds, wearing a sport coat and slacks smiling at Vanessa as if they shared a secret; and Mary Ashford, the paranormal studies student who got to sit in a separate booth to answer the phone for the call-in portion of the show. Mary glared at me as if she was expecting me to do something awful. And I suppose I had rehearsed all sorts of terrible things I could say. But I knew it would do a disservice, not only to my clients but also to myself, to ridicule Sam Preston's work. I was happy the empathetic side of me won over my irrational lashing out. I should give some credit to Karen, who'd ended our phone conversation that afternoon with her oft repeated tease, "Psychologist, psychoanalyze thyself."

WDTS is located in a squat, bland building across the highway from the Indian River Lagoon, about a mile south of downtown with a huge tower sticking out its top. Not national radio huge, but huge for our little town. The show started with introductions all around. When Sam introduced us as the Downtown Divas, he looked at me as he said, "Now I have to apologize about that. We're not supposed to call them Divas."

"But that's what they call themselves," Christopher cut in.

"We're just a group of friends and business owners," Melissa said. "We're not actual divas."

"Not at all," Christopher said. "I can vouch for that."

"Well, whoever did the advertisement should be chastised," Sam said with a smirk.

"Agreed," I whispered. I was tucked between Karen and Kaya and they both turned to me with a "shh."

Melissa talked about her ghost experience and then ratted us all out about teasing her. But at least it explained to the world–well, Downtown Strawbridge–the truth

319

behind our weird challenge.

"Some of your friends are skeptics," Sam said.

"I'm afraid so," Melissa said. "Pari denies even the possibility of ghosts."

"Would you like to say anything about that, Pari?" Sam said looking at me.

"Not particularly."

"Aw, come on," Christopher said. "We're not afraid of skeptics."

"Aren't you one?" I said.

Sam piped up with an, "Oooh, told on you."

What was he? Twelve?

"I am skeptical," Christopher said. "And our listeners are aware of that. But it's good to allow other skeptics their say on our show."

"And you're a psychologist," Mary said, still shooting virtual daggers at me. "Could you speak to the issue from that viewpoint?"

"I'm not here as a psychologist."

"Do you believe in ghosts or not?"

"No, I don't."

"And you don't like what Sam is doing, do you?"

"Why would you ask me that?"

"Well," Sam said, "it's true, isn't it?"

"I've spoken against some things, yes. Like the sleepover at Executive Suites. I don't like our place of business being turned into a sideshow for your benefit."

"And speaking of the Executive Suites," Mary said. "Sam believes Downtown's most famous ghost, Aranthia, is in your office."

"There's no ghost in my office."

"Are you sure about that? Didn't Sam manage to charm his way in, Dr. Logan? Sam, why don't you tell us what you found in Dr. Logan's office?"

Sam's mouth was open and his head was moving, but no words were forthcoming.

"Come on, Sam," Mary said. "Don't be shy."

"I did feel a presence in her office."

"You hear that, ladies?" Mary said. "If you've got a ghost, Sam Preston is the man you want feeling his way into your haunted spaces."

"What is this?" I whispered to Karen. "Some kind of creepy ghost porn?"

Karen giggled and nudged me to shut up.

"Dr. Logan was kind enough to let me into her office for a short time," Sam was saying. "And I did sense Aranthia's presence."

"If Sam keeps up the famous Preston charm," Mary said, "maybe we'll all get a chance to meet Aranthia this weekend at our Overnight With Ghosts Event. If you'd like to join us for this and other Ghost Whisperer events, visit our website at—"

"Sam Preston didn't charm me into anything." I shouted, causing Karen to jump away from me on the couch.

"Is that so?" Mary said. "Then why have you been making out with him all over town?"

A stunned silence fell about the room. Even Sam sat paralyzed, his eyes wide as if he'd been hit with a basketball.

Chris said, "Uh-oh."

"I...what?" That's all I managed.

"That's what I've heard," Mary said.

"Three times," I said. "I kissed him three times. That's hardly making out all over town."

At that, Sam sputtered. "Mary, we've talked about this. Don't bring the personal stuff into the business."

"You've talked about it?" I said.

"And it was only twice." He looked at me, trying to keep the glee off his face. "You kissed me the first time. Then I kissed you. And back to you on that last one."

Mary, instead of glowing with triumph looked dejected. Other than seeing them leave together after the MacAuley Awley's interview, it didn't look like she and Sam were dating. But now I wondered what exactly was going on between them.

"Oh, we have a caller," Sam said, chuckling. "We weren't ready for that part of the program, but maybe we should just get to it. Hello, you're on The Ghost Whisperer Show on WDTS."

"You kissed Sam Preston?"

"Eric?" Of course, *why not?* "Eric, we're live on the radio."

"Three times?"

"Twice," I said.

"That's right," Sam said. "One of them is on me."

"I can't believe you've been complaining about him to me all this time but on the side you're having an affair with him."

"An *affair?* It was only kissing. It's not like I'm sleeping with him." Gasps and giggles erupted from the Divas. Thanks for not slapping your hands over my mouth guys. Thanks a lot.

"What's the difference?" Eric said.

Sam cleared his throat. "There's quite a big difference."

"You stay out of this," I said.

"I'm right in the middle of it."

"It's not like we're exclusive, Eric. I mean, we rarely speak to each other except for Friday night dates."

"Oh," Kaya said. "Saturday nights or it's not a real relationship."

"What is this obsession with Saturday nights?" Eric's disembodied voice filled the room.

I have to say, the last time I heard Eric so worked up it was over my having too many shoes.

"Saturday night is date night," Sophie said. "Everybody knows that."

"The Divas have spoken," Sam said.

"We literally *just* went out on a Saturday night," Eric said.

"Dude," Sam said. "You spent the whole night on the beach alone, while your girlfriend was at the party with me."

"It was a party," I said. "There was mingling...and beach walking."

"A party doesn't count as a Saturday date," Karen said.

"Eric, can we talk about this later?"

"I'm not sure I want to talk about it, Pari. I'll call you if I change my mind."

A loud clanking sound echoed in the little room and

I wasn't sure if it was real or a piped-in sound effect. Mary's face, a combination of dejection and triumph, held no clues. Again, an awkward silence fell over us like a damp cloud.

"Okay, then," Christopher said. "Where were we?"

I said, "Mr. Preston, did you or did you not try to charm your way into my office?"

Again, mouth open, eyes wide, no words.

"You want to know what I really think about your enterprise?" I said.

I heard Karen mutter, "Oh, boy, here we go."

"I think what you're doing with your ghost stories and séances and sleepovers is setting people up for heart-break, Mr. Preston. That's what I think. You try to convince them their loved ones are just beyond some spiritual wall and if they believe hard enough, they'll make contact. You keep people living in the past, in mourning, when they should be encouraged to make the most of their lives as the ones left behind. And you do it for your own selfish purpose."

More silence, until Christopher mumbled, "Is that your psychological opinion or do you speak from personal experience?"

All eyes were on me and I blushed with embarrassment and maybe a small bit of rage. "I don't have to be a psychologist to see the damage that can be done by hysteria, Mr. Reynolds. Now if you'll excuse me."

I got up and walked out.

Chapter Fifty-two

I was surprised to find Melissa had followed me out of the station and caught up with me at Karen's car. My plan was to lean on it pouting until the show was over. But at that point I was pacing, infuriated and embarrassed, along the sidewalk.

"Are you okay?" I wouldn't say Melissa was the most soothing person I'd ever met. She had something of a squeaky voice at times and a mad woman's joy in living. But now she sounded like a caregiver, tending to a frightened child. My heart melted.

"I'm so sorry," I said. "I've made a mess of your event."

"Oh, it'll be fine. Have you never listened to the show?" She watched me cross back and forth in front of her.

"No."

"Weird stuff like this happens all the time?"

"Really?"

She nodded. "A few weeks ago they had some people on claiming they'd been abducted by aliens. It was a riot. One lady stomped off much crazier than you did."

"You're just saying that to make me feel better."

"Honest, I'm not. It's no big deal."

"You don't understand," I said, picking up my stomping

speed. "I've just had a discussion about infidelity on the radio. I've been outed as a harlot."

"Harlot's a strong word. Floozy, maybe."

I couldn't help but laugh with her. I stopped my angry march and stood in front of her. "I'm so embarrassed."

"I know and I'm sorry. I didn't intend for this to happen. I wouldn't blame you if you didn't want to do any more challenges."

"What will people think? What will my clients think?"

She sighed, concern on her face, and looked around the dark parking lot for a moment before turning back to me. "That you're human? That you make mistakes like everyone else? It's not the end of the world when people find out we're not perfect."

"Everything's so messed up. I used to be a professional. I was a Bright Star. And now look at me. Outed as a serial kisser on the radio." I laughed again and began to find my center. "I know I'm being overly dramatic. But none of this was in my plans, you know?"

"I feel like it's all my fault."

"It's not, Melissa. Honestly. This is my doing."

Once she was assured I'd be fine, had no plans to jump into the lagoon, and would not return to the show, she left me in the parking lot where I did what any girl raised in a loving home would: I called my mother.

"What's wrong?" was the first thing out of her mouth.

"Mama," I cooed. "Can't I call you on a Tuesday?"

"We just spoke on Sunday. What's happened?"

I sighed.

"See?" she said. "I knew it. Are you hurt?"

"I'm fine. I was just wondering something. Would you say I'm a perfectionist?"

"Pari." Her mother voice had arrived. I knew she was sitting at the dining table, pouring herself some tea, ready to do some hard soothing. "You got your doctorate at twenty-six. You're a driven person. One has to be something of a perfectionist to achieve such goals. What do you think?"

"I might have gotten a bit lost recently, in striving...if not for perfection, for greatness."

"Nothing wrong with that."

"But I feel like I've lost my footing, Mama."

"Yes, that can be frightening."

"People are going to judge me."

"That's their problem, Pari. Your concern is how you get yourself out of the stumble."

"You're right, of course. I suppose I'm wondering if I am who I think I am, or who I want to be. Does that make sense?"

"You're still young. You have plenty of time to discover who you are. I'm not sure I know who I am yet. Not completely."

I smiled. "I think I've been hard on the people in my life lately, too. Expecting too much from them."

She sighed. "Do you remember Lance Armstrong?"

"What does he have to do with it?"

"You loved him. Had posters of him in your room. Your father was worried."

I laughed. "I remember."

"When the drug thing came out, you were devastated."

"I ripped up my posters and threw them in the trash."

"That's right. But you forgave him. You said to me, 'everybody makes mistakes.' But after that, I think you were harder on people. Especially yourself. I think that's why you wanted to become a psychologist, in the end."

"To make myself perfect?"

"No, Pari. No. Remember what the wise teacher once said, 'We teach best, what we most need to learn.' You have always been trying to teach yourself it's okay to not be perfect, even as you strive to be."

"Oh, Mama." I exhaled, and it was as if I'd not had a decent breath in decades. "Which Hindu teacher said that?"

She laughed, loud and joyfully. "Richard Bach. In that book *Illusions*. Remember him?"

"Never heard of him."

"Pari, first *The Wizard of Oz* and now Richard Bach. You've no cultural literacy to speak of. I'll send it to you. And the one about the seagull. You really should read that one."

"Okay, Mama. Thank you for helping."

"Call me anytime."

I felt much better. A warm breeze wafted off the lagoon. Cars buzzed past on the highway offering me snippets of music–country, metal, pop, and I'm pretty sure "Baby Shark." I tried not to think about my secrets being broadcast on local radio, told myself it didn't matter. I started to call Eric; I owed him an apology, but not for kissing Sam. The way I looked at it, Eric and I weren't exclusive, no matter how much I tried to waffle about it. So kissing Sam wasn't an awful betrayal. And how would I have told him about it? Oh, by the way, I kissed Sam Preston the other night. That would be silly. But Eric was right about one thing–he and I had dissed Sam a few times. And that made me a hypocrite.

When the Divas finally left the building about forty minutes later, they each hugged me in turn, apologizing for what had happened.

"Should we have left, too?" Karen asked.

Sophie said, "We couldn't decide if we should. In solidarity."

"I'm glad you stayed," I said. "One of us behaving like a child was enough."

"You weren't in the wrong," Kaya said. "It was like one of those sleazy talk shows where they try to get people to fight."

Vanessa nodded and said, "It was that Mary girl. I'm sure Chris and Sam didn't have anything to do with it."

"Well, they seemed to be enjoying it," I said.

Sophie said. "You should have heard the calls after you left."

"Were they about me and Sam?"

"Oh, no," Melissa said. "Wacky ghost stuff."

"Seriously," Kaya said. "Abductions, ghost attacks, ghost romances."

"Ghost pets," Karen said.

"Ghost pets?" I thought of Mrs. Nettlebaum and her inhabited cats.

Karen was unusually quiet as she drove me home and she followed me up to my apartment.

"Are you going to be okay?" She stood in my small

living room, worried.

"Why wouldn't I be?"

"You don't have to act like everything's okay all the time. Do you have chocolate in the apartment?"

I nodded.

"And you said you adopted some cats." She looked around.

"They're usually under the bed when I get home."

"That's not good."

"They come out eventually. They're not used to being mine yet."

Karen pursed her lips and glared at me. "I want to see them."

"You don't believe me?"

"It would be a really bizarre thing to lie about. But yes. Proof of cats or I'm not leaving."

"Look." I pointed to my bedroom door where little Pebbles was peering out at us. "Told you."

"Okay. I leave you in the warm embrace of chocolate and cats. The only real friends a girl can have at a time like this."

"A time like what? It's no big deal. Eric and I are done. Sam and I are done. I've embarrassed myself in front of all of Strawbridge, so my career might be done."

"Finally," she said. "The hysterics I was expecting. Should I stay? I feel like I should stay."

"No. We both have to work tomorrow."

She paused and chewed on her lower lip. "I'm sorry I tried to set you up with him. I had no idea he was just trying to get into your office."

Suddenly I laughed, frightening Pebbles back into the bedroom. "It is funny now I think about it."

"Still, what a jerk," she said with a sigh and a chuckle. "He probably hates cats."

"And no good man hates cats."

With another big comforting hug, she left, and a few minutes later, as if some spiritual connection or spy cam told him I was alone, Eric called. I curled up on the couch with my phone, ready for an uncomfortable conversation.

"I'm sorry," he said first thing.

"Me too."

"I don't usually act out like that."

"True enough."

There was a pause. An awkward, weird silence between us. And then he said, "I'm seeing someone else, too."

"On Saturday nights?"

"Yes."

"We're talking about a person, right? Not a fish or your parents."

He chuckled and a sad sort of relief fell over me.

"A girl," he said. "Woman. Person. Yeah. I should have told you."

"We didn't have an agreement. But I'm not seeing Sam Preston. We've just...kissed a few times."

"Why?"

Because I liked him. Because he was adorable, and funny, and easygoing, and never asked me about my shoes. "I don't know," I said.

"There must be something there. But he doesn't seem like your type at all."

"What would you say my type is?"

He thought for a few seconds. "I picture you with a guy who wears a suit and tie. Who looks like he gets a haircut regularly. A professional kind of guy. What do you think?"

"I think I've been trying too hard, Eric."

"At what?"

"At making myself fit into a particular box. Maybe I need to wiggle myself outside of it for a change."

"So, where does that leave us?"

"The other girl gets Saturday nights, so..."

"That doesn't mean anything."

Suddenly Pebbles and Midnight both leaped onto my lap.

"Oomph," I said.

"What happened?"

"I'm okay."

"What's that noise?"

"Purring."

"When did you get a cat?"

"I have two of them. Pebbles and Midnight. Pebbles is an orange tabby. She's the one purring the loudest. And Midnight is black with this tiny bit of white on her chest."

"I thought you didn't like cats."

"Why would you think that?"

"You said so. You said you'd never get a cat."

"I don't remember saying that. I just thought I worked too much to have a pet."

"Exactly." He sounded angry.

"Does it bother you?"

He paused. "A little."

"Do you not like cats?"

"Not particularly, no."

"I see." My own voice, telling Karen that no good man dislikes cats, echoed in my head.

"What does that mean?"

"Nothing, Eric. Nothing at all." *Except you don't like cats.*

"Cats kill birds. They disrupt the ecosystem. And they carry a parasite that controls your brain."

"Are you Googling right now?"

"Cats are aloof. Unfriendly."

"And yet there are two of them sitting on top of me right now trying to talk to you and licking the phone."

"That's disgusting."

"So, I take it you dislike dogs as well."

"I wouldn't own one."

In the purr-filled silence that followed, everything with Eric fell into place. He was definitely the one I thought I should like, the polished professional I thought I'd fall in love with, marry and settle down with, make a future with. But I was wrong. Dead wrong.

"Okay, then," I said finally. "I guess I'll see you around the Executive Suites."

He sighed. "Let's not end this badly. I'm sorry. I'm glad you got some cats. It can be hard living alone."

"And I'm glad you have a Saturday night girl, Eric. Really."

All in all, it wasn't that bad of a breakup considering Eric had turned out to be a psychotic* cat-hater.

Let's Review:

1. "It's not the end of the world when people find out we're not perfect."

2. "Remember what the wise teacher once said, 'We teach best, what we most need to learn.'"

3. "Psychologist, psychoanalyze thyself."

*Absolutely not my professional opinion.

Chapter Fifty-three

O h, honey," Ida Nettlebaum said as soon as the door was closed behind her the next morning. "Are you all right?" She took my hands gently in hers and gave them a squeeze. The concern on her face nearly brought me to tears.

"You were listening?"

"Of course." She dropped my hands, patted my arm, and took her usual seat in the comfy chair with the small table between us, her knees together, body tilted my way. "I've been listening for weeks now. But how are you feeling? Did you hear from your young man?"

I smiled. "I did."

"And, is it over?"

"It is." When her face fell, I said, "It was a mutual decision."

"Then you're okay? I'm so glad. But honestly, what's the big deal? So, you kissed the Ghost Whisperer a few times."

"Twice."

"Exactly. And he kissed you once, but who's counting? Although, if you were counting, he owes you one, don't you think? Anyway, I couldn't wait to get here today to say, you have nothing to be embarrassed about. Kissing's a lovely thing, don't you know? I used to kiss my cats all the time, before they became possessed. I feel odd kissing my brother. Not that I never kissed him—well, now I think about it I don't think I ever did. That's not abnormal, is it?"

"Do you think so?"

"No, I don't. I think it's fine. But now, about what you said to the Ghost Whisperer, just before you walked out." She paused, waiting for a response.

"How did you feel about that?"

"At first I was peeved, I admit. I'm not sure how it all works, but ghosts make sense to me. And as you know, I believe people stay with us after they've...expired, whether in spirit form or in possession of objects or animals. And I don't think it's caused me any harm. I'm only here because Lenny insisted, you remember."

"I'm sorry my words upset you."

"Oh, but that's the thing. After I talked it over with Arnold and Mother—I did the majority of the talking of course. I can understand their meows often enough, but to be honest, it's hard to say. Anyway, the thing is, and I'm certain Mother agreed, you do have a point. Not for me; I'm perfectly happy having Mother and Arnold and Aunt Rachel around. But as I said to them, not to be hurtful or anything, I still see them as cats. I talked to them before they were inhabited by my family after all. And I still feed them in bowls and won't allow them to scratch the furniture. Heavens, I have a stick with a feathered ball attached that we all still play with. No, you see? They're still cats. I'm not mourning my family anymore, at least not any more than a person would."

"But you said I have a point?"

"Oh, yes, yes. One can get too obsessed with their loved ones' afterlives. Why, I know a woman who refuses to donate her husband's clothes. It's been three years. I'm not criticizing. Well, maybe I am. I'm just saying, if she started telling me her husband's ghost was in the house and wanted her to keep them, well then I'd tell her to get herself right down here and see you, Dr. Logan. Because, well, that's nuts."

"I didn't mean to say it was abnormal, or even wrong,

to believe in ghosts."

"I know, I know. You said we have to continue living. And that's what I realized. I need to stop acting like Mother and Arnold and Aunt Rachel are possessing my cats. Because, well, they need to move on now. They have to live their afterlives, just as I have to live my now life."

I nodded. "How do you feel about this decision, Ida?"

"Oh, I feel marvelous. A bit sad, I suppose. But I told them they could stay as long as they needed to—I imagined you'd give them that advice—but as far as I was concerned, they were Whiskers, Fluffy, and Scuttlebutt."

"It's natural to be sad at saying goodbye again."

"Yes, yes. And I was ready to call Lenny and tell him I didn't need to see you anymore, when, wouldn't you know, my late husband Edgar showed up in the neighbor's dog."

"Oh, my. And how did you figure this out?"

"The barking. Taserface—that's his name. I think the young lady who owns him, er, cares for him, Sherry, said she named him after a character in a movie. It was such a long story I don't remember the details, and the dog does look like, well, a villain. Where was I? Oh, yes. Taserface rarely barked at me and when he did, it was something vicious. Now, all the sudden, he's happy to see me and his barks are more of an *awooool*. Adorable really. I think it's Edgar. Definitely Edgar. I almost hated to tell him his new name was Taserface. Almost."

"*Guardians of the Galaxy*," I told her. "The second one."

"Oh, the movie with the tree? Lenny wanted to watch that with me. A movie night, he called it."

"I think that's a wonderful idea, Mrs. Nettlebaum."

The Divas met up at my apartment that night for another sew-in. I got the distinct impression they'd all got together before hand and decided not to mention Sam Preston, kissing, or his charming himself into my office. For the first hour conversation was stilted and unnatural until we all finally found ourselves on the floor playing with Pebbles and Midnight.

"So, you're still doing the Halloween party obviously,"

Vanessa said. "What about this weekend?"

I looked at Melissa who was doing her best not to look back at me, instead playing with Midnight. "I'm still in," I said.

"We'll keep him away from you," Sophie said. "If you want."

"That won't be necessary. He's teaching my photography class, remember? I can't avoid him."

"Do you really think he was just trying to get into your office?" Kaya said. "He seemed to really like you."

"I don't know."

"You think you'll talk to him about it?" Karen said.

I shrugged. "If I were my own client, I'd encourage myself to talk to him about it. Just to get it all out there, so we can be civil to each other."

"Civil," Karen muttered. "How romantic."

I threw a catnip mouse at her. "You still have ideas about Sam and me, don't you?"

"I know what he did was wrong, and he acted like a jerk on the radio. But I do think he likes you."

"I got a call from the paper today," I said. "They want to do a story on me and the psychology behind mourning and belief in the afterlife. I imagine if Sam ever did like me, he won't after that."

"So, you're doing it?"

"I am. I've also been called by another radio show in Orlando, and the local PBS station."

"You're going to be the Anti-Ghost Whisperer," Kaya said.

"I'm not trying to be. I haven't said yes to those things, just the article."

"Maybe you don't give Sam enough credit, Pari," Vanessa said. "He'll be fine with some competition."

"I know what you're thinking," I told her. "But this isn't all out war or anything. It won't affect your relationship with Christopher. We can all still be friends."

The next afternoon, I had my third new client since the Gazette article. He'd called the day after it had been published and said he wanted to talk about his life but wouldn't give any details. Donovan Wetherby looked as if he'd stepped out of the Seventies with a silk shirt half unbuttoned, tight, bell-bottomed jeans, long wavy brown hair and a mustache the handles of which could be tied into a bow.

He sat leaning forward on the edge of the couch with a sigh, knees apart, elbows perched on them, fingers entwined and smiled at me. "So, you're the famous Dr. Logan."

"Am I famous?"

"I heard you on the radio the other night." He made a ticking noise with his tongue and winked at me.

"What brings you to see me today, Donovan?"

He dropped his hands to his thighs as he eased back into the cushion and gazed around the office. He looked at me again and with a grin, started talking. After Donovan left, I sat down in my usual chair, wrapped my arms around my shoulders and cried. I would be seeing Donovan Wetherby twice a week for a long time.

Abby called shortly after I'd emptied myself of the residual despair empathy forces upon us at times to let me know that Nelson Gardner, who'd left me for Isabella's Insights, had made an appointment for next Wednesday. None of the clients who'd found me because of the Gazette article had come to me for the sole purpose of trying to catch a glimpse of Aranthia, Lilian Vanderhoff's initial reasoning notwithstanding. Nelson had returned from his excursion with the spirit world. The Ghost Whisperer hadn't caused my life to spiral out of control. If anything, ghosts and psychics had brought the people of Downtown Strawbridge together. My reputation thus far was unsullied. I had nothing to charge Sam Preston with beyond being nice to me in hopes I'd let him hunt for his ghost.

Moreover, before I headed home that evening, I drove downtown for some chocolate and parked near Madaline's office–I'd rather walk a few storefronts down than risk not finding the ideal spot in front of ChocShop. I walked among the dinner and shopping crowds to the shop and picked out a half-dozen chocolate truffles and carried them back to my car in the little ChocShop lunch sack and just as I got there, Madaline called out to me.

"Fudge?"

I smiled. "You know me too well."

"I should hope so, Miss Bright Star."

I beamed and met her where she stood at the door of her office. I spied Cedric inside, hard at work at his computer. "But today I went for some truffles. Would you like one?"

"My figure says no," she slapped her hips, "but my psyche says, yes please."

I held out the bag for her and then took one for myself and together we enjoyed Lori Walker's chocolate expertise.

"She deserves those awards," I said. We both closed our eyes and let the creamy confection take us away.

"Speaking of awards."

My eyes popped open and I was suddenly alert.

"The APW's events committee finalized the banquet hall and the caterer for the awards ceremony. Only two months to go. You'll need to buy yourself something spectacular to wear."

"I will?"

"You didn't hear it from me, but yes. Of course, even if you're merely nominated, you'll want to look nice. But, and again, you didn't hear it from me, you're going to want to look amazing."

Now, I know what you're thinking: Madaline Richards was the town gossip, but she wasn't one to create rumors out of nothing. She was also chairperson of the Downtown Strawbridge Association of Professional Women's awards committee. Her committee took in the nominations, sent out the ballots, tallied the results, and– and I cannot stress this part enough–made certain the winner attended the awards ceremony dressed to perfection. As I drove the short distance to my apartment complex, all I could think of was Sam Preston. He'd come to town, upended my routine, brought on ghostly hysteria, was like a magnet for my lips and I to his, apparently, leading to a final break up between Eric and me, and yet, I'd come out unscathed. That didn't mean I wouldn't still have to face Downtown Strawbridge over being outed as a trollop on the local radio, of course. And I certainly wasn't eager to see him that night in photography class.

Nonetheless, I gathered my wits about me and slithered into the studio, ready to face him, but as it turns out, it was my classmates I should have prepared for. Sam was his usual self, jovial and helpful. Typical for him. Embarrassed on public radio? Laugh it off. Kissing a psychologist who's dating someone else? Just a lark. That psychologist calling you a danger to widows and orphans? What a joke! Yes, Sam Preston was unfazed. The rest of the class, however, smirked at the both of us as soon as I entered the room. I was immediately taken back to fifth grade–the taunting, teasing, shoving. But no, I reminded myself. These were adults, not children. And they'd get over it soon enough.

Our photos that week were supposed to be done using the manual setting, meaning we had to set the aperture, shutter speed, and ISO–don't even ask–ourselves. We only submitted one picture for the class this time and mine was, naturally, Pebbles and Midnight on my balcony, atop the round wrought iron table sniffing my newly potted money tree. The whole class cried, "Aw."

"Your best work so far," Sam said.

"Do you like cats?" I blurted out, instantly turning a lovely shade of pink.

"Who doesn't?" he said.

Exactly, I thought. Who doesn't?

I hadn't planned to wait after class to walk out with him. We'd made it a habit, but after all that had happened, I knew that would have to change. One of the other students approached him with a few questions, so there was no awkward moment in which I'd look unforgiving by leaving without him.

But as I got to my car, they both left the building as well, and Sam called out to me, approaching before I could open the door.

"I was going to call," he said. "But I think I should apologize in person. For the other night."

"When we were outed on the radio, you mean?"

He smiled. "Yeah. That wasn't cool, what Mary did."

"You're saying it wasn't planned?"

"No. Did you think it was?"

"You didn't seem to mind it? I recall you laughing quite a lot."

"But that didn't mean I planned it or wanted it to happen."

"But you found it funny."

He threw his hands into the air. "Obviously I handle tough situations with humor. I can't deal, so I laugh. Surely you can psychoanalyze that, Dr. Logan."

"No doubt."

"And It doesn't excuse you for basically call me a charlatan in response."

The anger of Tuesday night welled up inside me again. "Did you, or did you not, plan to charm me into submission over my office?"

"No. Yes. It's complicated." He stood there with guilt splattered all over his face.

"You did," I said and pulled my car door open. "I can't believe I doubted it for one second."

"Just at first," he said. "Honestly, Pari. Only in the beginning."

"Like that makes a difference."

"Doesn't it?"

I slammed my car door shut and then said, "No." Realizing I'd done it backwards, I pressed the button and waited for the window to glide down, then said, "No," again and watched Sam Preston try not to laugh. I waited until I was well away from The Art Center, the radio on loud, before screaming, "Arrgh!"

Chapter Fifty-four

MaryAshford has joined the chat.

MaryAshford: Just did the final with Trudy. We're all set. And the sleepover is pretty much done. Just need to get with their security guard for the final discussion on logistics.

LegitChris: Thanks. Are you two okay now?

SamPreston: We've come to terms, if that's what you mean.

MaryAshford: I got a little vindictive with the phones and I'm sorry.

LegitChris: A little?

SamPreston: It could have been worse, Chris. Much worse.

LegitChris: So...we're lucky?

SamPreston: Turns out before the show, one of her friends thought I was her dad, so that pretty much ended things on her side.

MaryAshford: That's not exactly how things went down, but sure, you look old enough to be my dad. So, what happened to Sam the Man?

LegitChris: He's gone professional all the sudden.

SamPreston: Maybe it's time you did, too.

MaryAshford: I approve. You two have probably had those names since the onset of computers.

LegitChris: We're not that old.

MaryAshford: Didn't they have cards with holes punched into them back in your day?

SamPreston: I have no idea what she's talking about.

MaryAshford: I still have to apologize to Dr. Logan.

SamPreston: She'll be at the conjuring.

LegitChris: Is she still speaking to you?

SamPreston: I doubt it. I tried to apologize.

MaryAshford: How does a person try to apologize? You either do it or you don't.

SamPreston: I think I have some psychological issues with humor.

MaryAshford: There's an understatement.

LegitChris: I can't tell if this is normal Mary/Sam banter or if you two still have some underlying hate going on.

MaryAshford: No hate. Anger, disappointment, frustration, degradation.

SamPreston: Okay, we get the point.

MaryAshford: I'm kidding. Seriously, we talked, we yelled, we're cool now.

SamPreston: There was no yelling, Chris. I promise.

LegitChris: I would hope not.

SamPreston: Let's move on to our current problem. We've had three emails telling us what we're doing is hurting people.

MaryAshford: Three's not bad.

SamPreston: Zero is better.

MaryAshford: I'm sighing dejectedly now. Can you hear it? Again, I'm sorry.

SamPreston: That part isn't your fault.

MaryAshford: I pissed her off.

SamPreston: I think she was glad to say all that stuff. That's how she really feels.

MaryAshford: I'm sensing humor isn't your only problem with apologizing.

LegitChris: You have to admit, it made for a great show.

MaryAshford: Which, I assume, is the reason I'm not fired.

LegitChris: You were never hired.

MaryAshford: Oh, yeah. This is a group project.

SamPreston: I'm sure we can dig up some stuff on you, Chris. Some old girlfriends we can bring on the show.

LegitChris: As fabulous as your public humiliation was, I think our listeners would get tired of that sort of show pretty quickly.

SamPreston: We should let them decide, then.

MaryAshford: I man the phones, so I think it's my call.

LegitChris: My god, Sam. She's been right all along.

SamPreston: About what?

LegitChris: She's the mature one. She's in charge.

MaryAshford: Obviously. I'll see you two at Trudy's tonight. Don't be drunk.

MaryAshford has left the chat.

SamPreston: I'm going to need a drink before the show.

LegitChris: Can't face her again?

SamPreston: I really screwed things up.

LegitChris: I'm sure it won't be the last time.

SamPreston: Hey, I changed my screen name. I'm a grown up now.

LegitChris: I'll see you at Tracks later. We can knock back a few and figure your life out.

SamPreston: Feels like it's too late for me. Save yourself.

LegitChris: I intend to.

Chapter Fifty-five

Sophie and I met up with Reese at his surf shop on Mangrove Road early Friday evening. The sun was low in the western sky and the heat of the day was just starting to give way. We walked to the corner of Mangrove and Strawbridge, where Trudy's Treasures was decorated for a ghostly gala, and immediately felt underdressed. As she had no yard to speak of in front of her store, Trudy had transformed the dirt-patched and weedy grounds on the west side and behind her building into a summer fairy land. Posts had been driven into the ground with twinkly lights strung between them. Cloth-covered tables perched on sturdy wooden platforms surrounded by white chairs held flower arrangements of magnolia, gardenia, hibiscus, and plumbago. Summer music wafted from the window of the attic room to her guests below. Across the tracks from Trudy's in the public lot, four food trucks pumped out delicious aromas. At least a hundred people, donned in party dresses and dinner jackets, mingled, chattering excitedly about the night's prospects. Would Aranthia show herself? Would we finally have undeniable proof?

"Mr. Cornell isn't going to like this," Sophie said with a frown.

"Trudy really knows how to throw a party," Melissa

said, joining us along with the other Divas. "I didn't get the memo on formal wear."

"I was thinking the same thing," I said.

Kaya, ever the voice of reason, and always looking fabulous in vintage, said, "It's only the mayor and city council, really."

"You can relax, Pari," Karen said with a wink. "Your professional reputation will survive jeans and a cute blouse."

I blushed and offered her a nudge.

"We've got a little while before the conjuring starts," Melissa said. "So, I guess we can enjoy ourselves." She pointed at me. "No leaving until after the main event."

"I'm not going anywhere besides the food court," I said.

"Hey, Divas," somebody in the crowd shouted. We all turned to see a group of downtown regulars lifting drinks in our direction and waving at us.

Kaya instinctively raised her hand and I pushed it down. "Don't encourage them," I said.

She grinned. "Don't you want to be famous?"

It was out of my control as Melissa declared that ignoring them would be rude and bad for business. So we all smiled and nodded to our fans.

"Come on, Karen," I said, now more eager than before to visit the food trucks.

We avoided the group of Diva admirers by making our way to the front of Trudy's store and then across the railroad tracks where Officer Palmer was minding traffic for hungry pedestrians. I'd already had dinner, unfortunately, but one truck was selling baklava, and I couldn't resist. Karen went for a bag of caramel corn.

"I'm going to be sticky," I said as we returned to the party.

"It's not as if you're trying to impress anyone...are you?"

"Of course not."

She smirked. "You know Sam Preston is here."

"Naturally. This is his gig."

"Still mad at him?"

"I'm mad at myself. Let's not talk about it right now."

Karen put an arm around my shoulders and brought me in for a hug. "Come on, bestie. Give us a sticky squeeze."

It seemed all of Downtown Strawbridge had gathered at Trudy's by the time we got back to the party. Mr. Cornell, Trudy's aggrieved rival, stood talking with Mr. Childers, Sophie's granddad. But Billy Cornell didn't seem perturbed; in fact, he looked delighted, which only made Karen and I suspicious. Was he planning sabotage? It took us twenty minutes to find Sophie and the rest of the Divas again and by then, the conjuring was getting underway so we didn't ask Sophie what she might know.

"Thank you all for joining us," Trudy called out. "Here's how this is going to work. Sam here, our local Ghost Whisperer, and his team of ghost hunters will be inside conjuring up Aranthia. And everyone will be walking through in an orderly fashion. The pathway is all laid out for you. You can walk through as many times as you like. But you'll see above you, from the second floor, in the window, there's a screen. Light her up, boys!" A rectangle lit up in the small window of her attic space and on it we could make out, just barely, the interior of her store. "For those outside, all the goings on can be viewed there."

"Reminds me of Bigfoot photos," I said.

"I'm going to have to agree with you on that one," Melissa said. "Unless Aranthia flies right at the camera, we won't see much. I want to be in the store when it happens."

"Too many people," Kaya said.

"It doesn't matter," I said. "This isn't really about ghost hunting or contacting Aranthia. It's about showing up Mr. Cornell."

"You're right about that," Sophie said. "And she's already done it, I'm afraid."

"What will he do in response?" Vanessa asked her.

"I don't want to think about it."

We all chuckled. I wondered how far Trudy would go to prove she had a ghost in her shop. I could see by the crowd that the whole of downtown was having a lot of fun and I hated to be the only anti-ghost curmudgeon. But it seems I'd cemented my place in skeptic-land. I'd have to wave my flag proudly.

"Hello, Divas," Sam Preston said as he stopped on his way into Trudy's shop.

"I thought you couldn't call us Divas," Karen said.

"It's better than 'ladies.'"

"Is it?" I said.

He ignored me. "Besides, it's out of my hands now. Everyone's doing it."

Christopher approached, adjusting his heavy backpack while carrying a tripod in one hand and a drink in the other. He bumped into Sam, sending him stumbling into me.

"Because you advertised us that way on your show," I said, pushing him off me.

"We apologized for that, Dr. Logan."

I rolled my eyes and frowned. "What's done is done."

"That's an admirable attitude," Sam said. "Come on. You–" He was obviously going to say Divas or ladies but stopped himself. "–guys can come inside with us. Guests of honor, and all that."

"Do we have to?" I said.

Melissa said, "Absolutely."

"Just another way to make amends." Sam bowed sarcastically.

I watched as the Divas followed him and Christopher to Trudy's front porch, not wanting to be singled out, but wanting to stick with my friends. Before I made a move to join them, Mary Ashford approached and stood in front of me, a mixture of disdain and resignation on her face.

"I owe you an apology," she said.

"You do?" I hadn't meant it to come out like that–incredulous and shocked.

"Sam told me you thought we did it on purpose. The show, I mean. Putting you on the spot like that. But it was just me."

"How long have you and Sam been dating?"

She was taken aback, and I admit it was abrupt. "We're not. We went out a few times."

"I gather it didn't end well."

Mary smiled timidly. "He didn't dump me so much as just let me go, if you know what I mean."

"And you weren't ready?"

"It wasn't that. It was more like...I didn't know it was over. Not that there was anything much to be over. But when you don't know it's over, you act a certain way and then feel embarrassed. It's really very confusing."

"When Sam Preston is involved, confusion is guaranteed."

"Exactly," she said with a laugh. "Anyway, I'm sorry. I can say it on the radio next week if you want."

"Please don't. I'd like it to just fade away."

"Thanks for understanding. You know, I think Sam likes you."

I started to protest.

"I don't see you two together myself."

I nearly laughed out loud. "Trust me, neither do I."

We walked together to Trudy's door where she disappeared inside, leaving me to enter with Karen who'd waited for me.

"What was that all about?" Karen said.

"She apologized for the radio thing. Why are we going in with the ghost hunting people?"

"I suspect Melissa set it up as part of the challenge," she said.

"Are we going to be on camera? I feel like I'm being pranked."

Trudy had cleaned out her store somewhat. A wide pathway at the front door zig-zagged its way to the back door. The west side of the store and the staircase were blocked off with yellow hazard tape and I suspected that was where she'd stashed her surplus antiques for the occasion.

"How do we know Aranthia will appear on this side of the store?" I muttered. "I get the feeling she prefers clutter."

The Divas had special seating in the front corner, east

of the door, while Sam and his team spread out around the cashwrap area. "Let's get started," Sam said.

Guests started moving through the store in one large wormy mass. The lights were dimmed for spooky effect, of course. The music had been turned off and instead Mary Ashford tinkled a little bell. How cute. I detected incense.

"Is incense a ghost hunting thing?" I whispered to Karen next to me.

"Maybe Aranthia is a hippie ghost," Kaya said.

The Divas stifled giggles as Christopher unzipped his backpack and pulled out some sort of specter measuring tool–a black box the size of a phone with tiny green and yellow lights on it, that started making a buzzing noise when he turned it on.

"How much did you pay for that?" Vanessa called to him.

He chuckled from across the room. "Shh. I'll tell you later."

"He doesn't mind when I tease him." Her eyes sparkled.

"New love," I said to Karen and grimaced.

"Shh," Sam said.

"It was Pari," Kaya said.

"Hush," I said.

"Do I have to stop this conjuring right now?" Mary Ashford said, and at that we all burst out laughing. The wormy line of people stopped and glared at us.

"Sorry, sorry," we Divas whispered and prepared to be amazed by the ghostly apparition of a despondent Aranthia wailing over her lost sea captain.

Conjuring a ghost is, if you ask me, a bit of a show. If you want to get results, you apparently have to chant a bit, prostrate yourself in the presence of said ghost, beg him or her to honor you with his or her presence, and basically empathize with the dearly, if not horrifically, departed. At least that's the way I saw what Sam was doing.

I don't know where the thunder and lightning came from, or the screaming, not until later. But I do know that when I saw a dimly lit lace dress moving in the opposite corner of the store, my first thought was to hide my face from the camera. One of the Divas grabbed me, and Karen shouted, "No!"

I looked up and Karen was laughing.

"Look," she yelled.

Then the lights went out. *Of course the lights went out.* More screaming. A stampede of sorts. Sounds of broken glass which led to more screaming and stampeding. Before I knew it, Sam Preston was cowering in the corner with us–I could see his face lit gently by a streetlight outside the front window.

"Why does it always end this way, Mr. Preston?" I said.

Trudy shouted, "It's Aranthia. She's here. She's speaking."

But nobody could hear anything through the chaos. I started laughing. Karen was *still* laughing. And soon enough, all the Divas were cracking up; Sam, too. We finally made our way outside only to hear more thunder rumbling in the darkening sky.

"Thunderstorm," I said to anyone near enough to hear me. "Not Aranthia."

"But I saw her," Mrs. Trentham from Across the Pond English shop said. "She was wearing a white dress."

"I saw a dress, too," someone else said.

The story spread quickly from those who'd seen something to those who hadn't but were now convinced they had. And those who weren't inside the store when it happened demanded a replay. Trudy was all too willing to indulge them with talk of another conjuring the next weekend. The last I saw of Mr. Cornell was his back as he walked down Strawbridge Avenue away from Trudy's Treasures with Mr. Childers at his side. And while it seemed unlikely that Aranthia's vaguely possible appearance was his doing, his step was light and joyous despite the coming rain.

"This bodes well for your sleepover," I told Sam when I found myself standing next to him as the crowd slowly dispersed.

He nodded. "We can use all the good publicity we can get after Tuesday night."

"I thought the show was a success."

"People are definitely talking about it. But we've been accused of exploiting the vulnerable. So, thanks for that."

"You asked for my opinion and I gave it to you. You must have known what I'd say."

"I guess I thought you'd be more diplomatic about it."

"Maybe I would have been if I hadn't been set up for a gotcha moment to entertain your fans."

He took in a breath, as if he were trying to muster some sympathy. "I said I'm sorry."

"My reputation was on the line."

"Nobody was trying to damage your distinguished reputation. And if they had, it wouldn't make it right for you to try to damage mine."

"Oh, so you think because I'm a psychologist I never lash out irrationally, is that it? I'm human, Mr. Preston. Just like everyone else."

"If you say so."

I turned abruptly and walked through the cluster of people who had witnessed our spat. I'm glad to say the Divas followed me, their mouths open, eyes wide. I stomped all the way down the street to Reese's shop and sat on the little ledge beneath the display window. The Divas gathered around me, concern on their faces.

"I'm just going to say this," I said. "If I had my druthers—"

"Druthers?" Vanessa said.

"What are druthers?" Melissa asked.

"Druthers," I said. "Didn't your grandmothers ever say 'druthers?'" Questioning looks all around. "My grandma Logan always said 'druthers.' It stands for 'I'd rather.'"

"Thanks for the lesson in dialect, grandma," Sophie said, smiling.

"So, if I had my druthers, I'd cancel on the sleepover." And before Melissa could put words to the look on her face, I continued. "But I promised. So I'll do it. But I'm going to keep an eye on Sam Preston. If he steps one foot into my office, I'm going to accept those interviews and guest spots and have my say about his little ghost hunting enterprise."

"Ooh," Kaya said. "I like battle ready Pari."

We all said our goodbyes and I left Sophie with Reese to walk home alone. I'd settled in my apartment with a glass of iced tea and was ready to curl up on the couch with the cats and find something to watch to distract myself from my anger, when Vanessa called.

"Pari, I'm so sorry," she said. "It just flew out of my mouth."

"What?" A dread fell over me and I set my glass down quickly, preparing for the worst.

"I met up with Chris tonight, after I left you all. We were talking about the argument. He was defending Sam and I was defending you and...it just fell out."

"What fell out?"

"I told him if Sam didn't lay off, you were going to go on television and tell everybody how harmful his ghost stuff was. I don't even know why I said it. I don't even agree with you—not about ghosts. Why would I say that?"

"It's natural to want to protect a friend, Vanessa. Even when you think she's wrong."

"Now Chris and I are on the outs and I'm sure he's going to tell Sam. I'm so sorry."

"It's not your fault. You should call him and apologize."

"I should?"

"Yes. Tell him you don't agree with me and you don't want this to come between you."

"But will you really do the interviews?"

"I don't know. Even if I do, it shouldn't keep you and Chris apart."

"Okay, but...Pari. Sam shouldn't have said that...about you not being human. I'm sure he didn't mean it."

"We just don't like each other. It's no big deal."

She didn't respond and I could almost hear her worry.

"This has nothing to do with us. Or the Divas. Or you and Christopher. Sam and I can be adults about it. Call him."

She promised she would. Everything just seemed so...out of hand. I tried a Let's Review, but all I came up with was that I felt angry and embarrassed and confused. Not a good combination for action. So, I resolved to relax and think it all over before doing anything out of the ordinary.

The Divas joined me the next morning for a sewing session. We finished our flapper dresses and hats, ordered pizza for lunch, and said not one word about Sam Preston or ghost hunting. Everything felt completely ordinary, except for the obvious phantom in the room and all the stops and starts in conversation in our attempts to avoid the subject. That evening, I packed up my jammies and a change of clothes and drove over to the Executive Suites building with Sophie to take part in a haunted sleepover. Not ordinary by any means.

Chapter Fifty-six

Imagine if you will, thirty-six quasi-adults, plus our intrepid ghost hunting team, all in their pajamas–from provocative silk and lace to giant quilted onesies–in various stages of drunkenness, creeping about the three floors of an office building in the dark, flashlights casting eerie shadows on the walls. That's right, most of the crowd was drunk, whether by design or poor planning, I couldn't say.

Sophie and I arrived at the Executive Suites building at ten o'clock. Hallway and lobby lights were on at that point. The lobby of each floor was set up with tables of snacks for our late-night activities: cupcakes, M&Ms, popcorn, and thank heavens, fresh fruit. Barrels of ice offered sodas, caf and decaf. But the big draw was the cash bar in the main floor lobby where most of the guests had gathered.

"So," I said after Karen, Sophie, and I had visited all three floors of goodies–I'd settled on a handful of M&Ms and a banana–and were back on the first floor. "The plan is to get us drunk and convince us we've seen a ghost. Is that it?"

"It's like a party," Melissa said peeling the paper lining from a cupcake–devil's food with ghostly white icing. "Except half the people are strangers."

"Sounds like all the parties I've been to," Kaya said.

"Let me have a look at everybody," Melissa said, forcing us to stand in a line.

Sophie and Kaya were in onesies, pastel and zebra, respectively. Karen and I both wore our seductive men's jammies, oversized cotton tops over drawstring pants, and were wrapped in thick terry robes. Vanessa wore a silky wrap over something very tiny, and Melissa was out of character in a granny gown.

"What?" she said when we all stared at her. "It's comfortable. I think. I usually sleep naked."

"Well, we appreciate you being clothed," I said with a wink.

The ghosting wasn't to start until midnight, giving everyone time to get soused. Guests were encouraged to roam the halls un-escorted until then. Limited tours of downtown would start at two o'clock, while those remaining would break up into teams and look for ghosts on every floor. The Divas stuck together, walking the corridors as I told them about the offices and the people who inhabited them during the day. We sat in my office for a while, letting Melissa and Vanessa try to commune with Aranthia. She didn't show. Then we went back downstairs and stood at the buffet table on the first floor as the haunting hour approached. The crowd had grown louder and rowdier, and I had the awful vision of a few drunkards trying to break into my office. I decided to say something to Christopher or Mary if I could find one of them. It was common knowledge by that point that Aranthia was supposedly haunting my office. Would it be too much to ask that one of them keep watch at the door? I scanned the people on the first floor and saw none of the Ghost Whisperer team.

"I'll be back in a bit," I told Karen and headed up the grand staircase. If nothing else, I could check on my office myself.

I jogged up the stairs and before I could open the door to the second-floor lobby, Sam Preston pushed it open and stood before me in a long, brown, terry robe with a wide belt. The legs of his pajama pants showed below it and grazed the tops of his slippers. I was ready to push past him, ready to roll my eyes at fate–which I assure you I don't believe in–always putting him in my path, but something made me stop. The door closed behind him and we stood in silence for a moment, looking at each other, the sound of his drunken party below us.

"I was hoping to get you alone," he said.

Something inside me fluttered and I shut it down. "Is that right?"

"I'm sorry about last night. I shouldn't have said those things."

A sudden thaw washed over me and I didn't have time to curse my politeness before I spoke. "It's partly my fault. Mary apologized. I was fine about the whole thing."

"Until you saw me." He chuckled.

"Whenever you're around, I get angry."

"I guess I have that effect on women."

"I don't want to be angry. But you're just so... irritating."

"I'm not trying to be." He smiled, his brows raised slightly. "Chris told me about your interview opportunities."

"I did get some offers, but what I said to the Divas...I was just mad at you. I might do them, but not for revenge."

"I understand. So...we're okay? Relatively speaking?"

I started to say yes, but I hesitated. And in some crazy, backward attempt to make sure he knew I wasn't interested in him, I said, "Look, we're clearly attracted to each other." I nearly gasped at my own words.

"And you don't want to be."

"Right." Maybe he did get my meaning.

"Because I'm not your–" Air quotes. "–type."

"Yes."

"And that's why you find me irritating. Because you like me."

"Maybe," I said. "In a strictly physical way."

"Am I supposed to be flattered by that?"

"I just mean..." A frustrated sigh escaped me. "I take my job very seriously, Sam. And I want to be with a guy who–"

"You don't think I take my job seriously?"

"Ghost whispering? Can you even call that a job?"

"I'm a photographer."

"And a ghost hisperer."

He shook his head and looked at me with pity. "You don't want a guy who takes his job seriously. You want a guy with a serious job."

I raised my shoulders with a resigned grimace. "Is that such a terrible thing to admit?"

"Yeah. It kind of makes you sound like a snob."

"I'm not a snob," I said. "I like professional men."

"Hello. I'm a *professional* photographer."

"I..." I was stuck.

"I get it. You want a guy who wears a suit every day and goes to an office. You have this ideal man in your head and you check him against any likely prospects to see if they measure up. Good luck with that."

"Well, sure it sounds ridiculous when you put it that way."

"It is ridiculous."

"I know what sort of man I want in my life and I don't think I have to apologize for it."

He sighed and I thought he was going to move on down the stairs, but he was looking at me, peering at me more like, and then a smile slowly lit him up and he laughed. "You are a snob," he said. "And a user."

"What?"

"I'm good enough for kissing and fooling around with, but not for a relationship."

"That's not—"

"No, no." He held up his hands in protest. "There are a lot of girls like you out there. I should have seen it earlier."

"You're being unfair."

"You're the one with the problem." He was smiling again and couldn't help but laugh, too.

"I'm sorry I kissed you, okay?" I said.

"You used me for my lips."

"I'm a cad. Sue me."

"I'm no psychologist, but it sounds to me like you're

letting your head get in the way of your heart."

"Let's put aside your assumption that you know what's in my heart..."

"Okay." He winked.

"You don't think following your head is the best course of action?"

"You *do*?"

"Absolutely. Reason trumps emotion."

"In science, sure. And mathematics. Probably zoology. But not in matters of love."

My mouth had fallen open slightly at the mention of the L-word when the lights went out and we were cast suddenly into darkness. I tensed, instinctively reaching out for him.

"It's okay," he said, taking my hand. "We're turning out the main lights for the tour."

Red emergency lights flickered on and Sam's face was sliced by shadow and color like a Picasso. I tried to imagine my face in the same fashion and smiled.

"Your guests are drunk," I said. "And now it's dark. I should check on my office."

"I was just there. Everybody's downstairs waiting for us to start." He moved closer to me.

I sighed in anticipation. "It's your turn," I said.

And he kissed me. Everything about him that aggravated me, every time he'd insulted me, everything I wanted to not like about him, was pent up in that kiss. Mathematics and zoology be damned, my heart would have its way. I pulled him backward, letting myself be pressed against the wall as his hands found their way inside my robe and against my very un-sexy cotton pajamas.

"We should go somewhere," he whispered.

I nodded. "But...the tour." We kissed again, hungrier this time. "My office," I murmured.

And as we started to inch toward the door to the second-floor lobby, still caught in our embrace, it opened and hit him, sending us both tumbling to the floor.

"Sorry, Mr. Preston," shouted a young man in a quilted onesie as he and his friends stepped clumsily over us and stomped down the stairs, leaving us lying on our backs, staring up at the ceiling and the emergency light. It flickered off and dim, half-lighting lit up the stairs in a muted but familiar yellow glow.

"I guess they got the nighttime lights figured out," Sam said climbing to his feet. He held out his hands to help me up. "We'll finish this later."

Disoriented, I followed him down the stairs where his guests had been spooked into silence despite an eager energy tingling throughout the crowd. There was enough light to see faces, but still enough darkness to cast shadows into the corners and down the halls.

"Why does it have to be dark?" someone asked.

"Shhh," a girl wearing pink slippers and curlers in her hair said. "We're sneaking up on them."

Sam chuckled. "We have reason to believe spirits feel more comfortable in the dark, which would explain why most sightings occur at night."

"Sure," I said. "That's why."

I was shushed as well, but Sam winked at me.

Karen nudged me. "I thought you two hated each other."

"We're grownups," I whispered. "We can disagree and still get along."

She looked at me, skeptical, and said, "Why is love so difficult?"

"Flashlights on," Sam commanded and waited while everyone enjoyed a few moments of flashlight play. "Let's get started."

He led us around each floor, quietly telling stories about all the ghosts supposedly seen in the building. A tourist in the late 1800s washed out to sea in a hurricane; a circus performer in the early 1900s eaten by alligators; a child who'd fallen from a tree on the grounds sometime in between.

"Why are all the ghosts from so long ago?" I said.

Sam was about to answer when a guy barely wearing a tattered robe over his boxers, drink in hand, sputtered, "Easy. When the newer ones die, the building's all filled up already. They have to go someplace else. Isn't that right?"

I had to give Sam credit for maintaining his composure. "We don't know for certain. But we have some stories of ghost sightings that speak to more recent times." He told us about an accountant who'd hung himself, which seemed plausible; a murdered grandmother with the overnight janitorial service, also possible; and a young woman who accidentally electrocuted herself with a curling iron over a sink full of water in a first-floor bathroom—we do have the best bathrooms in Downtown Strawbridge.

"And these deaths are verified?" I said.

All eyes, drunk and sober, on me.

"Not yet," Sam said. "We're cataloging all the stories and researching as best we can."

"Well, if it's not haunted," I said, "it's at least a death trap."

My office on the third floor was Sam's *pièce de résistance*. And because I'm a woman of my word, I unlocked the door as Sam told the story of Aranthia and her sea captain, then pushed it open and watched as one by one the drunkards and gawkers peered inside.

"Off limits, you say?" Boxer man said.

"Yep."

"Have you seen her?" A woman in a pink silk camisole and matching short shorts asked.

"Nope."

"But you said on the radio," the young man with Cami Short Shorts said to Sam, "you felt her presence in there."

"Dr. Logan was kind enough to let me have a whispering session and I did sense something. I'll need additional time in the building to learn more."

"Let us in." A woman wrapped in a thick purple robe pushed through the group. "We'll be quiet. Promise."

"It's not a matter of noise," I said.

"Then what is it?" Boxer man said.

"That's enough," Sam said. "If Aranthia wants to be seen, she can appear anywhere in the building."

And with that, he moved the group on.

By three o'clock everyone was settling down, but still staggering through the darkened halls. The last of the downtown tour groups had left with Christopher and the rest of us had been given two-way radios to alert Sam and Mary if a ghost was spotted. The Divas and I were in my office, having hoarded a bunch of third floor snacks. Karen brought DVDs to play on my computer. I turned the screen around to face the room and we were watching *The Exorcist* when we heard running feet in the hallway.

"Quick," Melissa said. "The radio."

We all fumbled about the room and she finally found one and clicked it on.

"No, second floor, sorry," someone was saying. "I'm confused. Hurry." Then screaming with an eerie singing in the background.

"It's happening!" Melissa said. "Let's go."

Tumbling out of my office, we followed Melissa to the elevator in the lobby.

"No way," Kaya said. "I'm not getting trapped in an elevator with a ghost on the loose."

"You think the stairs are safe?" Sophie whined.

"Oh, for Pete's sake, come on," I said and led them into the stairwell.

"They're screaming," Karen said. "What's happening?"

I started laughing. "It's a ghost; you scream."

So, naturally, we all screamed. Once on the second floor, we joined everyone else and ran round and round and back again. "It's here," a panic-stricken someone on the radio shouted. "Room 208." And once we got there, "Room 240!" And at room 240, "It sunk into the floor!"

The Divas collapsed on the grand curved staircase leading to the first floor, laughing and screaming while watching all the grownups go nuts.

"This is the best party ever," Kaya said. "Let's do it again."

Everything calmed down eventually and we hovered around the food spread in the first floor lobby, gabbing and eating and still catching our breaths. Mary Ashford was glowing, talking to Boxer man about what he saw and the Divas were deciding if they'd seen anything or not.

Curler girl had seen it, most definitely. "I don't know if it was Aranthia," she said. "But she was beautiful. And so sad. The way she just melted into the floor."

"Like the witch in *The Wizard of Oz*?" I said.

"Yes," she said, not caring at all that I was trying to make a joke.

It looked as if the party was going to be downstairs for a while, so I left the group to turn off the movie and lock up my office. I met a man on the stairs who told me to be careful. "The ghosts are definitely here," he said. I assured him I'd be fine. As I turned the corner on the third floor toward my office, I heard voices. The movie, I thought. But when I entered the room, there stood Sam Preston with Quilted Robe, Cami Short Shorts and her boyfriend.

"What are you doing in here?" I said. They all jumped as if I was wearing a white mask and carrying a machete. "Get out!"

"You don't understand," Sam was saying.

"Stop talking and leave."

"I'm trying to explain."

"I don't care. Just get out."

The others ran, but Sam stood at the door and let out an irritated sigh. "Fine," he said. "Forget it."

I slammed the door shut and stood in the middle of my office shaking with rage. The first chance he had, he got into my office and brought people with him. There was nothing for it but to take a few couch pillows and beat the crap out of the back wall. I *thwumped* and *thwumped* until I realized I was crying and let myself fall onto the couch.

"Pari?" Karen knocked at the door.

"Come in."

She tiptoed in, a look of fear on her face. "They said they saw Aranthia in here."

I wiped the tears from my face.

"Oh, honey, don't cry." She sat next to me, gathering me up in her arms.

"I'm not crying. It's the fury leaking out of me."

The rest of the Divas crept in and sat on the floor at my feet.

"He was really in here?" Melissa said.

I nodded. "I should have known."

"I'm so sorry," she said. "This is all my fault."

"No it's not. It's Sam Preston's fault and this crazy event. People are drunk, in their pajamas, running through the halls. It might as well be a frat party."

"Sam isn't drunk," Karen said.

"He swore he wouldn't let anyone in here," Kaya said.

"I can't believe he did that," I said.

"Let's leave," Sophie said.

"Yeah," Kaya joined in. "Let's go over to your place and finish the movie."

"And steal a bunch of cupcakes on the way out," Karen said.

"I'm in," Vanessa said.

And that's exactly what we did. Back at my apartment we finished *The Exorcist* and fell asleep on my living room floor watching *Ghost*. Best sleepover ever.

Chapter Fifty-seven

The Divas, groggy and disheveled, slurped coffee the next morning in my tiny living room and kitchen, trying to look put together enough to get themselves home. We agreed to meet up for an afternoon snack at Melissa's Café Flamingo to discuss the apocalypse of the previous night. As soon as they left, I found the cats under the bed and promised them I'd have no more rowdy sleepovers. They didn't look convinced but did come out for breakfast. As I sat at my little kitchen table, with nothing but the sound of cats purring and lapping up moist food to comfort me, I felt rage and disappointment wallowing up in my chest. I'd had a plan, a sound and reasonable plan. Climb the superstar business ladder in Downtown Strawbridge. Find success in my field, and yes, marry a guy like Eric Lawson–sharp, professional, and sensible. Live an idyllic, while still rationally objective, life. Then Sam Preston showed up and proved to me that one passionate kiss–okay, a series of increasingly passionate kisses–could throw it all out of whack. While I was grateful my practice hadn't suffered as I thought it would, I was disappointed in myself for believing in Sam Preston. Despite all evidence to the contrary, I actually thought he understood my concerns. And I thought he really liked me. Pebbles and Midnight sat at my feet looking up at me as if they knew I was troubled. "Call your mom," they seemed to say.

"I think I will," I told them. "Mama," I said as soon as she picked up her phone.

"What is it, Pari? What's happened?"

"Why must something have happened?"

"Your call isn't due until this evening."

"I can call back later, if you like."

"You're here now, we might as well talk. So, how's everything?"

I sighed. "Oh, Mama."

"I knew it. Something is wrong. Out with it."

"The sleepover thing was last night."

"And did you see a ghost?"

"Of course not. But...you remember I told you the Ghost Whisperer promised he wouldn't go into my office without my permission."

"And he did."

"Yes. I feel so stupid."

"Why should *you* feel stupid? He's the one who didn't keep his word to you."

"But I let my guard down. I'd started to think he wasn't..."

"Go on."

It was time to tell my mother the whole story. The intergluteal cleft incident. Sam's ridiculous charm and confidence. The feeling that he liked me and was waiting for me to decide about Eric. Only to find out he was just being nice to get into my office. How much I wanted to believe him when he said it only started out that way. The fight at Trudy's and the feeling I had on the stairs the night before that maybe he was right–maybe I have this stupid ideal in my head and I'm ignoring what's most important. And finally, the realization that I'd been had. He'd gotten exactly what he wanted and would have snuck everybody else in my office if he'd had the chance.

"I'd started to think he was being real with me, Mama. But it was all a lie."

"Just because he broke his promise doesn't mean he didn't like you. You would have known earlier if you were being conned."

"You'd think that, wouldn't you? But these last few weeks have been disorienting. I feel as if I've lost all concept of professionalism, rationalism, boundaries. I adopted cats, Mama. Two of them."

"Oh, you have lost it, haven't you?"

"What am I going to do?"

"You can't give them back now; you've made a commitment."

"Not about the cats." I smiled, grateful for Mama's levity. "About Sam."

"Oh, no. You don't want my opinion this time."

"Why would I call you after lunch if not for help?"

She sighed and I could hear her fingertips tapping on the table where she must be sitting, maybe glancing at herself in the mirror across the room. "I think you do nothing."

"Nothing?"

"That's right. You wait. He will come to you and apologize."

"Why would he do that?"

"Because for whatever reason, he broke a promise. In all you've told me, Pari, you describe a good man. Careless, perhaps. Easy where you are taut. Smooth where you are creased. But a kind and decent man who will come to you eventually and apologize. And then you will know what to do."

"I will?"

"Yes."

"And what if he doesn't apologize?"

"Then he is not the man you described to me, and therefore, good riddance."

As I was getting dressed to meet the Divas, I stood in my little closet trying on shoes. Pair after pair; sling backs, pumps, mules; two-inch and one-inch heels, flats. Nothing worked with the sleeveless, form-fitting floral dress I'd put on. I got on my hands and knees and dug through shoe boxes and when I came across the sparkly, sequined sneakers I'd worn a few weeks before when we were all concerned about Sophie climbing back into her bookish shell, I smiled. There's something about shiny, silly shoes that brightens up the landscape.

So, there I was, walking all the way from my apartment, westward on Strawbridge to Café Flamingo, in bedazzled sneakers, jeans, and my Captain America tee, hair pulled back loosely, an old blue silk purse swinging off my shoulder. It was a warm Sunday afternoon with storm clouds in the east. I looked around and smiled at the shoppers I passed. My mood was considerably lighter than the faces I found sitting outside the café watching me approach.

"You all look like you've just sat through a two-hour lecture on eggplant cultivation," I said as I took the last remaining chair around the two wrought iron tables. Each table had a pitcher of iced tea and a platter of heat-hardy snacks: carrots, celery, snap peas, and crackers. I poured myself some tea and sat back in my seat.

"Why do you look so happy?" Karen said. "Did something happen? Have you heard from Sam?"

"No. And I don't expect to."

"Are you and Eric back together then?" Kaya said.

"Why would you think that?"

"You walked here," Melissa said.

"And you're wearing your fancy sneakers," Sophie said.

"What does that have to do with Eric?"

They all stared at me.

Vanessa said, "We thought you only wore those shoes the first time because of him."

I looked down at my feet through the holes in the wrought-iron pattern. "Not exactly," I said. "But there might have been a little bit of him in my choices. I needed walking shoes today because fresh air and exercise helps the mood. And these particular sneakers cheer me up."

"I'm so sorry about all of this, Pari," Melissa said.

I shrugged. "It wasn't your fault."

"We can stop the challenge. It was really just a way for us to have fun. I didn't really expect to convince anyone."

"You're saying we're not open minded?" Karen said with a smile.

"I don't *think* that's what I'm saying." Then she laughed and a relief fell about us. "I know the challenge was supposed to go until Halloween, but I'd like to know now. Has anyone changed her mind?"

"I have," I said.

"Really?" Melissa nearly squealed.

"Yeah. I adopted two cats. And I finally ended things with Eric. Looking back on it, I think I knew from the start he and I weren't right for each other."

"But about the ghosts?"

I frowned at her. "Sorry, Pink Diva. I still don't believe in ghosts."

Let's Review:

1. I, Pari Logan, psychologist, determined to not be fooled again, do not believe in ghosts.

2. Melissa Stathem, restauranteur, still believes in ghosts.

3. Vanessa Torres, makes people beautiful, still only maybe believes in ghosts.

4. Sophie Childers, sells books, used and new, doesn't believe in ghosts.

5. Kaya Channing, store owner, still doesn't believe in ghosts and still thinks it would be nice if they existed.

6. And Karen Morgan, dealer in office supplies, does not believe in ghosts.

Nothing had changed.

"Well, we had fun anyway," Melissa said. Then she looked at me and added, "I mean, for the most part."

I did my best to smile and turned to Vanessa. "Is everything okay with you and Christopher?"

She nodded. "I told him why we left the sleepover and he understood. He said Sam's really sorry about it."

"He ought to be."

"He said it wasn't his fault."

"He was standing in the middle of my office with those people."

"They were already in there."

"Did he ask you to tell me this?"

Vanessa's face lit up. "No. I haven't spoken to him."

"Did Chris ask you to?"

"Enough with the third degree, Pari," Karen said.

"He didn't ask me to," Vanessa said. "I'm sorry I brought it up. From the sound of it, though, you're both acting like children."

"What's that supposed to mean?"

"You wouldn't listen." Vanessa was angry now, her voice raised, brow furrowed. I'd never seen her that way before. "He tried to explain what happened and you shut him down."

"There was nothing to explain, Vanessa. He was in my office talking to those people about Aranthia. Case closed."

"You're being too hard on him."

I fumed for a bit as tension floated about among all the Divas. This wasn't the way a Divas lunch was supposed to be. We were friends. We supported each other.

"I'm sorry," I said. "Let's drop it, okay? And I meant what I said before. This isn't going to affect our friendship, or the Divas. I mean, come on. It's not like he broke my heart or anything." There was silence all around as they each suddenly had other things to look at—their hands, the carrots, their glasses of tea. "I mean it," I said. A few nods and sips of tea. "You all think I'm overreacting."

"Maybe a little," Karen said.

"I just think," Sophie said, "if you like him—"

"I don't."

"—you shouldn't let something like that get in the way."

"We'll drop it now," Melissa said.

"Over and done," Karen said.

"Let's zip it, Divas," Kaya said and we all pretended to zip our lips, some of us more enthusiastically than others.

"Ooh, new Diva tradition," Sophie said. "The Zipping of the Lips."

That brought out a chuckle and the tension eased somewhat.

"So, what about the zombie walk and Halloween party?" Kaya said. "I'm still in."

370

"I'll understand if you don't want to do them," Melissa said to me.

"They're not Sam's events," I said. "And I've already paid for the party."

"So, you'll do it?"

"Sure, why not? I'm back on the market after all. Maybe I'll meet a nice zombie to keep me warm at night."

"Zombies are dead," Kaya said. "No warmth."

"Technically," Sophie said, "they're undead."

"Those slow zombies are probably cold," Melissa said. "But the fast ones could be warm blooded."

"Fast zombies?" Vanessa said.

"Yeah, like in that movie," Melissa said. "What was it called?"

"*Dawn of the Dead?*" Sophie said.

"*Zombieland?*" Kaya said.

"No, no," she said. "It was like *The Wizard of Oz.*"

"How could a zombie movie be like *The Wizard of Oz?*" Karen said.

Sophie laughed and said, "Why is a raven like a writing desk?"

We all looked at her.

"She's gone mad," Karen said.

"Sorry," Sophie said, still laughing. "Our conversations often remind me of the Mad Hatter's tea party."

"I've seen that movie," I said, "See? I'm cultured."

"The Disney cartoon or the one with Johnny Depp?" Kaya asked.

"Johnny Depp was in an *Alice in Wonderland* movie?" I said.

"But why?" Karen said.

"I suppose you'd have to ask Johnny Depp," I said.

"No. Why is a raven like a writing desk?"

"Who knows?" Sophie said.

"*World War Z,*" Melissa shouted. "That's the movie I was thinking of." She looked at all of us and as we'd all obviously forgotten, she added, "with the fast zombies."

"How is that like *The Wizard of Oz?*" I said.

She winced. "They both have a W and a Z in the title?"

"*The Wizard of Oz* has two Zs," Sophie said.

"And *World War Z* has two Ws. What's your point?"

It was nice to have the Divas back to normal.

Chapter Fifty-eight

MaryAshford has joined the chat.

MaryAshford: Hey guys. Okay, so I heard from security and they said no harm done. A few alcohol spills we have to pay to have cleaned. Other than that, we're good.

ChrisReynolds: It was fun, but I don't think we should do it again.

MaryAshford: You've gone professional, too, I see.

ChrisReynolds: Yeah, a lot more meetings online. I figured I should be a grownup now.

SamPreston: Just admit you're copying me so we can move on.

ChrisReynolds: You have one great idea and you think everyone's trying to copy it.

MaryAshford: Well, at least your screen names are grownups. I wouldn't mind doing it again, but no alcohol and we need a dress code.

SamPreston: I hate to admit it, but Dr. Logan was right about this one.

ChrisReynolds: Dr. Logan? So formal. Still mad at her?

SamPreston: Yes.

MaryAshford: I thought she was mad at you.

ChrisReynolds: He's mad too.

MaryAshford: What'd she do?

SamPreston: It's just like we thought at the beginning. She's...

MaryAshford: Don't say it.

SamPreston: I was going to say tough.

MaryAshford: I like you, Sam. You know I do. But you're kind of stupid.

SamPreston: Anyway, we couldn't control everybody. People were wandering the halls unsupervised.

MaryAshford: We could limit the number of guests.

SamPreston: I think we should just do it alone a few times to see if we get any ghost activity.

ChrisReynolds: But you still want to do the other events.

SamPreston: Maybe. I think so, yes.

MaryAshford: Don't let one crazy night change the whole game plan.

SamPreston: You're right. But let's forget about the sleepovers for now.

MaryAshford: Okay, I've got to call the carpet cleaners.

MaryAshford has left the chat.

ChrisReynolds: Maybe she's just hard around the edges.

SamPreston: What difference does it make?

ChrisReynolds: You two are like opposites.

SamPreston: How's that?

ChrisReynolds: You're soft on the outside but tough on the inside. And she's...

SamPreston: You don't know she's soft on the inside.

ChrisReynolds: I don't have direct experience with that, no. But you do.

SamPreston: Still. No difference.

ChrisReynolds: I hear opposites attract.

SamPreston: You sound like my mother.

ChrisReynolds: You're right. We've let Mary ruin us.

SamPreston: We need beer, bbq, and hot women or we'll die old men!

ChrisReynolds: Hot tub!

SamPreston: It may be too late.

ChrisReynolds: Too late for you, maybe. I'm going out to buy a pickup truck.

SamPreston: Don't forget the gun rack.

ChrisReynolds: ...

SamPreston: ...

ChrisReynolds: I think we should just let it happen.

SamPreston: I'll meet you at the store. We'll buy recliners and practice yelling "Get off my lawn!"

ChrisReynolds: Seriously, man. You have to keep trying. She's the one.

SamPreston: How could you possibly know that if I don't know it?

ChrisReynolds: Because I know you. And I think you do know it.

SamPreston: This bonding stuff is gross.

ChrisReynolds: Agreed. Let's not do it again.

Chapter Fifty-nine

The news about town was that the Zombie Walk on Saturday evening would end with a huge surprise. Everybody was talking about it, but no one knew what the surprise was or where the rumor started. I suspected Sam Preston had something to do with it. Leave it to the Ghost Whisperer to turn a zombie event into a ghost hunting enterprise.

My first client on Monday morning was Nelson Gardner, fresh from his foray into spiritualism with Isabella. He'd gone full bald, which I thought was an improvement over the struggle that had been going on atop his head for the year I'd been counseling him. And he'd put on a fair amount of weight, filling out his reed thin frame into something definable and pleasant. His frog green eyes sparkled with glee as he plopped himself onto the couch opposite me.

"I won't say I'm not going to see Isabella anymore," he began. "She's been a great help to me. But she told me I should come back to you."

"Did she?"

"Absolutely. She said she isn't in the counseling business. She said, and I quote–" Air quotes with his fingers. "'I dig up the bodies and Dr. Logan helps you mourn them.' So here I am again. Did you miss me?"

"Very much," I said. "Though, if the day comes that you feel you don't need me anymore, I'll celebrate."

"I get it," he said. "I really do."

"You seem happier."

He sucked in a deep breath and stretched his arms out in front of him, then ran his hands over his head. "I think I'm starting to understand what you were saying all along. About the good things. I'm not one hundred percent happy. And I know a person can't be one hundred percent happy, one hundred percent of the time, but you know what I mean."

Progress, I thought. And to think Isabella's Insights helped.

When Saturday finally rolled around, the Divas met up at Brunch for lunch and had to sit three outside and three inside, but we lucked out in having tables next to one another, if you don't count the wall and window barrier. Those of us outside—me, Karen, and Vanessa—shouted at Melissa, Sophie, and Kaya inside. And they in turn knocked on the window and made faces as often as possible.

After lunch, we all went to Crane Creek Apartments, where we finished up the final details on our Halloween costumes and then got to work zombifying one another. The zombie party would start at three with a slow, lurching parade from the west end, just beyond Café Flamingo, eastward to the train tracks. This would be followed by an awards ceremony: best costume, best face, best lurch, best undead girl, best undead guy, on and on. Then we'd have a street party with food trucks and music. This would be my first time attending as an actual zombie.

Vanessa did our hair. She put mine mostly up, in a messy fallen way, and pinned a faded, ragged blue velvet hat, with a dead flower stuck on it, on top of my head. Melissa went with her long blonde hair down and stringy with goop. Sophie spiked hers and tipped it in blood red, while Kaya piled hers up under a top hat. "I'm a dude today," she insisted.

I wore a dirty green floral house dress, falling below the knee, with a few well-placed holes in it, some old gray slippers, and a lone, pink sock, slipping down my leg. The others were similarly horrid, with Kaya in a dirty white button up, ragged vest with a shredded paisley tie, and ripped tuxedo pants.

We were the undead Divas.

We piled into two cars and parked behind Café Flamingo. From there, we joined up with other zombies under cloudy skies, the sun letting up on us a bit. Sunken eyes and cheeks. Faces deathly gray, some scabbed, others monstrously bloated. There were a few partiers who barely looked human, skin rotted beyond recognition. We all had trouble speaking, our mouths were so caked with makeup, giving us the chapped or decomposed look. Melissa assured us that by the time the food truck gorging started, we'd have loosened up all the gunk on our faces and would have no trouble eating.

We waited in line for an hour to register and get large numbers pinned to our backs. Finally, on a small gallows erected for the occasion, Isabella, her face zombified but still in her gauzy muumuu with her hair atop her head as usual, called out over a microphone, "Zombies! I hereby open the annual Downtown Strawbridge Zombie Walk. Please allow the judges among you as you lumber like the dead through town. And remember, by signing on the dotted line you agree not to eat the living until tomorrow."

The streets rang out with zombie grumbles.

"Last one to the train tracks wins slowest zombie," Isabella laughed.

An undead man approached her on the stage with an enormous black bird on his head.

"Are you ready?" Isabella said.

The zombies roared. Isabella held the mic up to the bird and it said "Caw!"

And we were off. I lumbered and lurched as best I could, but I have to tell you, being a zombie wasn't easy. There were certainly points at which several of us dropped the act to rest, but as soon as we spotted a judge –they all wore matching army green tees emblazoned with "Zombie Hunter" across their chests and backs–we fell back into undead-dom and moaned for brains.

We crossed the railroad tracks after what seemed like hours and headed to the Executive Suites parking lot, nearly collapsing from fatigue.

"We made it," Melissa said. "I'd smile but my feet hurt too much."

"I'd laugh," Karen said, "but my legs hurt."

"I'd jump up and down," Sophie said.

"But what?" Kaya said.

"That was all," Sophie said. "My brain can't come up with anything more."

Another stage in the parking lot of my office building had been set up for the awards ceremony and as we walked toward the crowd gathered there, two guys dressed in Ghostbusters jumpsuits approached. Christopher, with an old View-Master toy strapped backward onto his forehead, smiled through gory undead makeup and pulled Vanessa into a hug. Sam, zombified but still recognizable, camera hanging against his chest, looked at me for a moment, acted as if he was going to say something, then nodded a hello and continued past us.

"Cold," Karen said.

"As the undead," Melissa said.

I stood there, trembling. Not only had he not apologized, he'd basically snubbed me. *I should have said something*, I scolded myself. Maybe I was wrong to do it– Mama wouldn't approve–but I found myself chasing after him.

Chapter Sixty

S am," I called, and when he turned around I said, "Are
you mad at me?" But not in that sad pitiful way a
person might typically say such a thing. I'd said it in
that 'you're kidding me, right?' way. "*You're* mad at *me?*"

"Why shouldn't I be?" he said.

"If either of us should be mad it's *me*, at *you*."

"Why is that, Dr. Logan? Oh, that's right. Because a
few people were in your sacred office space. Well, roll out
the guillotine and heat up the tar."

"Everything's a joke to you, isn't it? You promised you
wouldn't let people in my office."

"I didn't let them in. They said the door was wide
open. And I told them to leave. We weren't in there five
seconds before you stormed in screaming at us like we'd
been doing drugs in the basement."

"What is that supposed to mean?"

"You know exactly what it means."

"I don't know why I ever thought you were nice."

"Maybe because I *am* nice."

"And I'm *not?*"

"No, you're not. You go around making demands of
everybody, expecting us to act like yours is the only
opinion that counts."

"I do not. You're the one who came here and turned

everybody's lives upside down with this nonsense."

"Everybody's? Or just yours?"

"Why don't you take your ridiculous ghost whispering fraud somewhere else."

"Oh, there it is."

"If you can liken me to your mother scolding you in the basement, Mr. Preston, I can liken you to a huckster."

"God, you're impossible."

"I'm impossible? You intentionally tried to charm your way into my office. I can't believe I fell for it."

"Well, you did."

It was the gasps from the crowd that made us both realize we were the center of attention, standing on the railroad tracks in the middle of Strawbridge Avenue, with Officer Palmer wincing, hoping we'd at least move out of train danger.

"I wish I'd never met you," I said.

"Works for me," he said. "As far as I'm concerned, we've never met, Dr. Logan. We don't know each other and never did."

And with that, he turned, pushed his way through the zombies and disappeared, leaving me standing in a sea of the undead with a look of shock and pain on my face, which was, as my picture in the Gazette the next day assured, the pose that won me Third Place in the Angry Zombie category. I took the stage to receive the award but refused when Sam and I both were awarded Best Zombie Argument. You know they created that one on the spot. Chris accepted for us. We won't be fighting over the ribbon.

Throughout the festival, Sam kept his distance. The rest of us ate, danced, lurched, and as the sun was deep in the Western sky, the band left the stage and Mayor Wilbury Hawn tapped on the microphone a few times and called for our attention–Zombie and food alike. Hawn was a slight man with a streak of hair greased across the top of his balding head and a squeaky voice. He was the kid whose face got shoved into his mashed potatoes at lunch in school. Tortured mercilessly until he got the highest score possible on the SATs and became a lawyer. And now there he was, adored and honored, presiding over the zombie apocalypse of Downtown Strawbridge. Dreams do come true.

"And now, for your entertainment," he squeaked. "And for the betterment of Downtown Strawbridge, we would like to right an age-old wrong. You are all about to witness the joining of two people too long kept apart. May I present, to officiate, Isabella Bolton of Isabella's Insights."

"What's going on?" I asked Melissa when I found her in the crowd with the other Divas.

"Don't ask *me*."

Isabella breezed onto the stage and thanked Mayor Hawn, then looked out to the sea of zombies and gawkers.

"Arthur, if you please," she said.

Arthur Merrimon, dressed as a punk zombie, who frequently deejayed events around town took his place behind his massive equipment and nodded to Isabella.

"You may begin," she said.

The opening bars of Mendelssohn's "Wedding March" echoed around us as a tall, rather distinguished zombie climbed the stage steps and stood to Isabella's left.

"Is that Mr. Cornell?" Sophie said.

"He's dressed as an old sea captain," Kaya said.

"A zombie sea captain," Vanessa said.

"What in heaven's name?" I said.

And as the music began its time-honored refrain, from the other side of the stage, walking sedately as any undead bride should, came Trudy Spencer decked out in a zombified wedding gown circa 1890 with its dropped waist and puffed sleeves. Torn and stained, their costumes cast the sedate affair with an eerie, gray pall.

"We are gathered here today," Isabella intoned with utmost decorum, "to join the captain and Aranthia in holy matrimony, uniting them forever more in the afterlife."

"Sure," I said. "Maybe next year we can do a pretend marriage counseling session."

"And the year after that," Kaya said, "divorce court."

Apparently, laughing at a wedding, even a zombie wedding, is frowned upon.

I slept fitfully that night. Every time one of the cats settled in by my side or on the pillow behind my head, I tossed about like a fish, sending her jumping and running. As much as I wanted to blame it on the excitement of the zombie invasion, all my dreams were taken up with Sam Preston. I was angry and felt foolish, but I did my best to convince myself that he was to blame.

"If anyone should be having trouble sleeping," I said to my open refrigerator at four in the morning. "It's Sam Preston." I ate strawberry jam out of the jar with a spoon and trudged back to bed. "Why do I even care?" I said to Pebbles, the orange tabby. She meowed. "I do *not* like him," I responded. "Why does everybody think I like Sam Preston? Anyway, it wouldn't matter now if I did."

I met up with the Divas at Brunch the next day where, once again, Sophie had saved a table for us outside. The October air was settling in, not too hot, but nothing like chilly. It was Sunday, and the whole of Downtown seemed hungover from the zombie shenanigans of the previous night.

"I missed a splotch of gray makeup on the back of my neck," Kaya said. "It was all over my pillowcase this morning."

"I wonder if Trudy and Mr. Cornell are going to be friends now," Vanessa said.

"Or better," I said.

"I doubt it," Sophie said. "Mr. Cornell said it was a lot of fun and he hoped people would stop taking sides. I think he only did it for the business."

"We'll see," Karen sang with glee.

"Why?" Melissa said. "Do you know something?"

Karen gave us a sly smile. "No. I just thought I saw love in their undead eyes during the ceremony."

"I told Mr. Cornell about your idea," Sophie said. "For next year. A marriage counseling session. He thought it was fabulous. Says it should be a musical."

"Well, there you go," Karen said. "An excuse for him

to spend more time with Trudy, practicing."

"I don't know," Kaya said. "If this was a sitcom, their getting together would be its death knell."

"I'm sure Downtown Strawbridge can find something else to obsess over," Melissa said.

"Speaking of obsessions," Vanessa said looking at me. "Have you spoken to Sam?"

"That's over," I said. "For good this time, I'm sorry to say."

"So you admit you liked him," Melissa said.

"I think it was more than like," Karen said.

"What are you talking about?"

"You said you were sorry about it."

"That's just a figure of speech."

"Freud would like a word," Sophie said.

When Thursday rolled around, I couldn't bring myself to go to my photography class. I changed my mind a dozen times and got all the way to my car before I gave up and decided an evening with the cats was better than an evening with Sam Preston. I knew he'd be civil, and that only made me want to skip the class even more.

"What do you think, Midnight?" I asked her as she snuggled on my lap while I flipped through channels on the television. "We focus on the career and stop worrying about Sam Preston?" She purred and flicked an ear. "You're right. He did behave terribly." I knew that over time my anger and resentment would fade and I'd be able to think about Sam's betrayal without wanting to *thwump* a pillow against the wall.

The next day, after my lunch break, Abby put through a call from a woman named Lulu Barnes. "She won't say exactly what she wants, but she claims it's important."

It took about three minutes of Lulu talking before I realized who she was: Cami Short Shorts girl from the sleepover.

"Hold up a moment," I said. "Go back to the office part. What were you saying?"

"We knew we weren't supposed to be in your office and we all—myself and Tom and Mrs. DeWickers. We just want to say we're sorry."

"I see. Please allow me to apologize as well. It was late. We were all tired and out of sorts. I shouldn't have yelled like that."

She giggled. "Tom and I did feel like we were back in Catholic school."

"Did, uh. Don't take this the wrong way but, have you talked to Sam Preston about this?"

"Sam who?"

"The Ghost Whisperer?"

"Oh, right. The guy in charge. No, but maybe we should apologize to him, too. When he joined us in the elevator, he looked like you'd slapped him or something. I guess we got him into trouble."

"Unless you forced him into my office, I wouldn't say–"

"That's pretty much what we did." More giggles. "Anyway, sorry it took so long for me to call. I went back and forth with it."

She went on for a few more minutes about her moral compass and how drunk she was that night. No one could be that good of an actress, right? As much as I wanted to believe Sam had orchestrated the whole thing, it now seemed unlikely. I deflated quite a bit. Or, in more colloquial terms, I slid ungracefully off my gargantuan horse and sat in the mud feeling dejected. The Divas were right. I'd made too much of it. It wouldn't be the first time in my life I'd overreacted.

Let's Review:
1. I drew a line.
2. Sam was dragged across it.
3. I yelled like a woman scorned.
4. He was rightfully angry with me.
5. And there we were.

I came to no conclusions. Even if I apologized to Sam, it felt as if I'd pushed things too far. But as I thought about it all day Friday, I realized there were some conclusions to be made, after all. Despite being able to understand other people, their needs and desires, and help them find their way, I'd been lost. I thought I had a plan and Sam Preston didn't fit within it. And yet, I kissed him. *Several times.* And I *liked* it. Even now, after all that had happened, I wanted to do it again. So there it was. One passionate kiss–another one!–on the stairs, and I was ready to reconsider an ideal I'd had for as long as I could remember. And to prove I'd become almost unrecognizable to myself, I'd walked from one end of downtown to the other in sequined sneakers.

I still had misgivings. I wasn't completely certain that, even if I wanted to listen to my heart a bit more than my head–at least where love was concerned–Sam Preston was the right kind of guy for me. So, I remained stuck, wondering what I should do. I supposed my mother was right. Best to do nothing, certainly nothing rash, until I knew what I really wanted.

Chapter Sixty-one

The Divas met up outside Tracks Saturday night, decked out in pastel flapper dresses, long chains of beads swishing down to our waists, brightly colored feathers in our headbands–even Kaya had a pink feather tucked into her black fedora–and entered the party as a team. Hundreds of people were there, in all manner of costumes, from the horrifying to the adorable. Every animal imaginable–Officer Palmer in a bear suit was voted most photographed, probably because he spent all evening sneaking up behind people with his hands, er paws, in attack position. All the typical Halloween creatures showed up for the festivities. Zombies, ghosts, witches, and Frankensteins were well represented. Novelties abounded and won most of the awards. Octavia Washington was dressed as a flower and stem. Noah Holland came as a pencil. Melanie from Brunch was a huge bowl of salad. Pat Willard of Namasté was a pile of poo. And Carolina Davies showed up as a star. Trudy and Mr. Cornell reprised their roles as Aranthia and the sea captain. And while there were a few other period pieces–Mr. and Mrs. Trentham of the all-things-English shop, Across the Pond, were decked out as George and Martha Washington–the Divas combined with Reese, Christopher, Sam, and their friends Richard and Michael won in the Best Historical category. We'd all expected Reese to show up as a 1920s gangster, but Vanessa had apparently spread the word to the others.

Sam and I barely exchanged a nod throughout the whole thing, but so much was going on, it was hard to let it be awkward. And there were plenty of other people to mingle with. Once the awards ceremony was over, the music started up and somehow the mob of ridiculousness danced. I climbed the stairs up to the roof for fresh air and quiet. I wasn't alone. About two dozen of us, some shedding their costumes, enjoyed the somewhat cool evening. One man had dressed as a television set and the enormous box with dials and knobs sat on the floor in a corner while he relaxed at a table for two. I stood at the south railing overlooking Downtown Strawbridge, letting the wind whip at my face.

"Excuse me," Sam Preston said.

I turned to find him, coat draped over one arm with thumb hooked in his gangster suspenders, holding a violet feather in his free hand.

"I believe you lost this."

"Oh," I said and took it from him. I felt the band around my head and tucked the feather back in, finding a bobby pin from my updo to hold it in place. "Thanks."

"I don't believe we've met," he said. "I'm Sam Preston."

I shook my head, imperceptibly, as if something had gone wrong. There was humor in his smile and his eyes were pleading. Suddenly, I understood. I offered him my hand and said, "Pari Logan. I'm in your photography class. I sit in the back so you probably never noticed me."

He took my hand and gave it a gentle squeeze. "But you weren't in class this week."

"That's right. Headache."

"Headaches happen. Your friend Vanessa and my friend Chris are dating."

"I'm aware."

"I thought it would be a good idea for us to get to know each other. You know, in case of a double date or something."

I did my best not to laugh. "All right. How do you suggest we proceed?"

"I tell you what." He leaned against the rail, facing me. "We'll each ask each other either-or questions. I'll start. Cats or dogs?"

I thought for a moment. "Both. And you?"

He nodded. "I'd say both as well, thought I might prefer dogs just a tiny bit. Your turn."

"Ice cream or pie?"

"Ah, a trick question. Both, when appropriate. But pie if not."

"Oh, dear," I said with a frown. "I'm afraid I will always go for ice cream over pie."

He *tsked* his tongue. "Strike one. How about, in the ice cream category...chocolate or vanilla?"

"Chocolate, definitely. Please don't say you like vanilla."

"Strawberry."

"No fair. Strawberry wasn't a choice."

"It should have been."

"Then I'd have said both."

"Me too," he said. "Don't tell anybody, but I get the Neapolitan containers and just eat the chocolate and strawberry."

"Me too!"

"I think that cancels out the earlier strike, don't you?"

"Agreed. What else?"

"How about we each tell the other something about ourselves that few other people know."

"You trust me with your secrets?" I said.

"Absolutely. But you go first."

We both laughed. I didn't have to think long. The one memory that had been in the back of my mind since Sam's entire ghost-hunting endeavor overtook Downtown Strawbridge needed to be said out loud, to somebody, *anybody*. Even to Sam.

"When I was in fifth grade, my family lived in a small rural town in the northern part of Florida. My father's an orthodontist, so I wouldn't say he was beloved by children. My mother and my brothers and sisters and me were the only Indian Americans in town, and while I don't want to paint anyone ill, I think it had something to do with the trouble. From the start we were viewed with suspicion. And for some reason, all the kids in school believed an alien water creature lived in the lake by the ballpark. The rumors had started long before we'd moved there, but after we arrived, the stories included this creature morphing into human form."

"Seriously?" Sam said.

I nodded and smiled. "So, my dad used to take his little fishing boat out to the lake and fish on the weekends. One day, early in the morning, very foggy, he saw some kids watching him. He was out of his boat and walking in the water to the shoreline when they ran away screaming. Next thing you know, my dad was an alien. And that meant my siblings and I were aliens, too."

"There's metaphor written all over this."

"Indeed. Anyway, one weekend I was invited to a big pool party. I wasn't a popular kid—"

"I find that hard to believe."

"Oh, but it's true. I hadn't had braces yet, for one thing. And so skinny. I was really excited to go. My mother even bought me a new swimsuit. But as it turned out, it was a set up—a way for them to throw me in the pool and watch me morph into a lake creature."

Sam took a step back and stared at me. "Well?"

"Well, what?"

"Did you?"

"Did I what?"

"You know." He nudged me—poked me more like, as if testing my muscles. "Did you turn into the monster?"

We laughed for a few seconds.

"It gets worse," I said. "I was hosed down walking home from school. Bottled water poured over my head at lunch time. It was a tough year."

"I'm sorry you went through that. I bet that's why you're such a great psychologist."

"You think I'm great?"

"I've seen the accolades on your office wall."

"Okay, your turn," I said.

He looked eastward, to the darkness of the lagoon and the edge of lights along the opposite shore. "Well, you know my brother died when I was young."

"I've heard," I said, trying to keep up the ruse.

"And you've heard that I saw his ghost and that he asked me to take care of my parents."

"Yes."

"Well," he paused and looked at me and I was afraid he would cry. "I failed."

"What do you mean?"

He shook his head. "They ended up divorcing six years later. I know the only reason they stayed together that long was for me. I feel like I owe Jimmy an apology. He was the best of us, I think. Looking back, I can see he was what held us all together."

We were quiet for a long time, while I sorted it all out.

"You think I'm nuts, don't you?" he said.

"Why would I think that?"

"About the ghost thing."

"Not really. You're not the only person in the world who believes in ghosts or a life after death. But I think you're confused."

"Confused, nuts, what's the difference?"

"Sam, your brother didn't ask you to take care of your parents. You did. That wasn't Jimmy. It was your vision of him."

"Maybe," he said.

"Do you really think your brother would have asked you to do such a thing?"

He looked at me then, curious at first, his brow furrowed. After a second or two, his eyes glazed a bit and he was turned inward, the lines of his forehead pulled taut. And suddenly he relaxed and saw me again. "No," he said. "Jimmy wouldn't have asked me to do that."

"You see? You were just a kid. You weren't responsible for your parents or their marriage."

"You're right. Of course you're right."

I smiled. "I have one question, though. What about the family plot at the cemetery? If your parents are divorced..."

"You have no idea," he said rolling his eyes. "Neither of them have remarried, but they still argue about not wanting to be buried together. I told them that's where they're going, and there's nothing they can do about it."

"I think you're going to be just fine, Mr. Preston."

"And I think you're one hell of a psychologist, Dr. Logan."

"Why thank you. I'm so glad we finally met."

"Me, too. Okay, back to our either-or thing."

"Whose turn is it?" I said. "Never mind, I've got one. Dating only your type, or throwing type out the window because it's meaningless."

"You know my answer to that one. Has yours changed since our last discussion on dating?"

"It has. But you can't really hold me to anything I said while being terrorized by teens."

"I suppose not. My turn. A serious one, this time."

"Sounds ominous. Go ahead. I can handle it."

"Love at first sight or love over time?"

I grimaced. "That is serious." I took in a breath, held it for a moment as if in a great deliberation within myself, and let it out. "Neither."

"What?"

"Neither. Love at first sight is impossible. You can't know a person just by looking at him. And love over time is nothing more than deep friendship. I suppose it can turn into a special, passionate love, but it's not for me."

"Oh," he said, obviously confused and a bit put out.

"No, I believe in love at first kiss."

"I've never heard of that."

"It's a well-known phenomenon. Kissing is how you know."

"I see how it is. So, I should kiss you now? Isn't it your turn?"

"But this wouldn't be our first kiss, Sam."

"You're saying all the way back at The Fort, when you stumbled and fell and gave me that drunken kiss...*that* was love?"

I smiled and put my arms around his neck. "I didn't know it at the time, but I'm going to have to say yes."

394

Epilogue

Two full weeks into November and Central Florida was finally not suffocatingly hot. Lows in the 70s, highs in the 80s. We could wear sweaters, finally. Thin sweaters, albeit, but sweaters by definition nonetheless. And only in the morning. But we were wearing them, *damn it.*

The Divas were in Florida heaven. It was Sunday and Sophie and I walked over to the Sweet Suite on our way to lunch to pick up the cake. It was Melissa's birthday and we ordered the richest chocolate cake the bakery had. The little bell on the door tinkled when we walked in and the Rollings twins, Kate and Barb, called out their boisterous hellos.

"It's ready," Barb said. Or Kate.

They weren't impossible to tell apart, but if you didn't see them regularly, you could lose your grip on who was who. While waiting at the register, I was surprised to see Twila Harper coming out from the kitchen area, beaming, carrying a large box.

"Dr. Logan," she said. "I did it myself."

She placed the cake box on the counter and opened it. Below the beautifully scripted Happy Birthday Melissa, there was a delicately painted pink flamingo.

"It's perfect," I said.

"I want to eat it now," Sophie said.

"This one's on her way to becoming a star baker," Barb or Kate said.

"She'll put us out of business when she opens her own shop," the other one said.

"Nah," Twila said. "I'll specialize in wedding cakes or catering. Or I'll open up shop far away."

"You could franchise," Sophie said to the twins.

"Now there's an idea."

"See you soon, Dr. Logan," Twila called out as we left. The girl was looking positively solid.

Sophie and I gathered Divas on our way to lunch: Vanessa from Glam It Up! across the street from the bakery; Karen, waiting outside Morgan's Office Supply, a pencil forgotten behind her left ear; and Kaya from her vintage clothing shop–she'd left her newest employee in charge and we had to drag her away as she called out instructions for every possible emergency. "I'll be at Café Flamingo! Number's on the register!"

As soon as we plopped down at our reserved tables out in front of the café, Melissa joined us and we presented her with the cake.

"Well, if I have to turn twenty-seven, I might as well do it with cake," she said. "Lots of cake."

"First one to thirty wins a huge party," Karen said.

"Who will that be?" Sophie said. "Not me, obviously."

"Me," I said. "Next May."

"It's a date," Karen said. "I can see it now. We'll do a champagne theme. Black and gold. Sunset on the beach."

"Sounds lovely," I said.

"Speaking of you being almost thirty," Melissa cooed. "How was the trip?"

I blushed. Sam and I had just flown back from Key West the night before. We'd spent two days touring Dry Tortugas National Park on a birding expedition. "What does that have to do with turning thirty?"

"Well, come on," Melissa said. "It's time you got married, isn't it?"

I laughed. "We've only been dating two weeks."

"And yet," Karen said, "you've already been on an overnight."

"Does that mean you've decided not to do the anti-ghost interviews?" Vanessa said.

"I'm not going to do them, but that's not the reason," I said.

"She's going to focus on writing a self-help book," Karen said.

"I've already taken the extra colon out of the title, so I'm on my way."

Karen nudged me. "We're all going to want to read it. But never mind that now. Tell us about the trip."

"It was amazing. We took a sea plane to the park each day and you wouldn't believe the sea life and birds. We have so many photos. I can't wait to have you all over for our presentation."

"Presentation?" Melissa said. "Sounds like school."

"We'll make it a party," Karen said.

"I'm more interested in the romance," Melissa said.

"Seconded," Vanessa said.

I gave in just a bit. "I have to admit, I can't imagine why I ever thought he wasn't right for me."

"It's because you're stubborn," Karen said.

"No comment," I said.

Suddenly they all put their elbows on the table and their chins in their hands—they'd obviously practiced. And Kaya said, "Come on, Pari. You're going to introduce him to your parents, aren't you?"

I smiled. "Absolutely."

"Told you," Karen said. "I'm betting she'll be married before her birthday."

Vanessa turned to Sophie. "Isabella said you and Reese would get married in December. Are we looking at a double wedding?"

Sophie and I smacked that idea down and tamped it. "Too soon," we said in unison.

"Speaking of Isabella," Melissa said. "I've been trying to figure out who my mystery man is."

"You mean the stalker?" I said.

"I'm determined to think of him as lovelorn, instead."

"You know practically everybody," Kaya said. "It could be anyone."

"Maybe it's Noah Holland," Karen said. "There's a character in his latest romance novel that sounds just like you." "But he owns a flower shop. If he liked me, wouldn't he be sending me flowers all the time?"

I said, "But he's a bit shy, isn't he?"

"He is," Sophie said.

"What about Benjamin?" Kaya said.

"The kid who works at Namasté?" Melissa said. "Too young."

"Isabella didn't say how old he was."

"I think we need a plan," Karen said. "The Pink Diva Man Hunter Plan."

"Works for me," Melissa said.

"Yes," I said. "It's Melissa's turn to be dragged about town on wild adventures."

Kaya said, "But we'll be looking for men, not ghosts. Much more fun."

"You should put an ad in the paper," Vanessa said. "Like that song about Piña Coladas."

"Those people were married," Sophie said.

"Oh, that's right. Still."

"But I don't like Piña Coladas," Melissa said.

"That's not the point."

"If you like booze and fruit smoothies," Kaya sang.

"And staying out until four," Sophie joined in.

Laughing, I turned to look eastward up Strawbridge Avenue and saw Sam and Reese headed our way. I turned to Vanessa. "What's going on with you and Christopher?"

She shrugged. "I'm keeping my options open."

"You guys remember when we got Sophie and Reese together, back in August?" Kaya said. "We were going to start the Downtown Divas Matchmaking Service."

"That seems like years ago, already," I said.

"Well, two down," Kaya said. "Four to go."

Let's Review:

1. Bad first impressions can cause a lot of trouble on the way to true love. But they sure do make for a great story to tell your grandkids.

2. Intergluteal cleft.

3. Hate him, don't hate him, hate him, don't—oh, wait, it's love!

4. *World War Z* and *The Wizard of Oz* have nothing in common beyond the Zs…and the Ws.

5. Most problems can be solved with good friends over lunch.

Books by Dianna Dann Narciso

Fiction by Dianna Dann
Camelia
Always Magnolia
Bury Me

Romantic Comedy by Dianna Dann
Bookish Meets Boy
Pari and the Ghost Whisperer

Fantasy by Dana Trantham
Children of Path: The Kell Stone Prophecy Book One
The Wretched: The Kell Stone Prophecy Book Two
Mark of the Faire: The Kell Stone Prophecy Book Three
The Kell Stone Prophecy: Complete Trilogy

Paranormal Humor by D.D. Charles
Zombie Revolution
JoJo's Ghost

Children's Fiction by Dana Trantham
Wayward Cat Finds a Home
Wayward Cat Saves the Day
Zombie Cats
Franken Lizard

For more, visit
waywardcatpublishing.com